For the Hegemony crews, it had to seem like the gates of hell had opened up in front of them. A superdreadnought fell out of line and staggered away, bleeding plasma from a dozen open wounds. The crews were already trying to escape – the sensors were picking up hundreds of lifepods blasting free of the doomed ship. Another superdreadnought, heavily damaged, was somehow still firing at the oncoming human ships. The remaining three were less damaged, their shields having held against most of the blast. They seemed stunned, even as the human cruisers fell on them like wolves on a flock of sheep.

The 2nd Cruiser Squadron swooped down on its target, one of the intact superdreadnoughts. It looked as if the enemy formation was falling apart, although it was impossible to be sure. The enemy flagship hadn't been badly damaged, which suggested that their commander was trying to adapt to a situation she would have considered impossible. Tobias barked orders and the 1st Cruiser Squadron reformed and headed towards the enemy flagship. Once she'd been taken out, it was possible that the enemy would surrender. Intact superdreadnoughts would teach Earth's engineers a great deal about the Hegemony's fleet – and rescuing survivors would look good in front of the other Galactics. It would...

"Admiral," Jackson said, "*Tirpitz*..."

Tobias looked – and swore. *Tirpitz* had one of the more aggressive commanders in the Federation Navy... and he'd taken her too close to the superdreadnought, which had lashed out hard enough to punch through the cruiser's shields and destroy one of her drive nacelles. Unable to adapt in time to change course, the cruiser spun out of control and slammed into the superdreadnought it had been targeting...

...And both ships vanished in a ball of fire.

HTN: HENUCFS601-PBCS-02409
ISBN-13: 978-1-941620-03-8
ISBN-10: 1-941620-03-5

Published in the United States of America.

First Strike

Christopher G. Nuttall

Also by Chris Nuttall:

The Empire's Corps
The Empire's Corps
No Worse Enemy
When the Bough Breaks
Semper Fi
The Outcast
To the Shores
Reality Check
Retreat Hell
The Thin Blue Line

Ark Royal
Ark Royal
The Nelson Touch
The Trafalgar Gambit

Royal Sorceress
The Royal Sorceress
The Great Game
Necropolis

Schooled in Magic
Schooled in Magic
Lessons in Etiquette
Study in Slaughter

Imperium Cicernus
On The Imperium's Secret Service
Death to the Imperium
Rebels and Patriots
Ure Infectus

Bookworm
Bookworm
The Very Ugly Duckling

Outside Context Problem
Outside Context Problem
Under Foot
The Slightest Hope of Victory

Democracy's Right
Democracy's Right
Democracy's Might

Martial Law
Patriotic Treason
Picking Up The Pieces

Standalone
Sufficiently Advanced
Technology
Guardian Glass
Invasion
The Invasion of 1950
The Fall of Night
A Learning Experience
Their Darkest Hour
A Life Less Ordinary
Barbarians at the Gates
Knight's Move
Storming Heaven
The Living Will Envy The Dead
Science and Sorcery
The Coward's Way of War
The Cross-Time Road Trip
The Black Knife
Alone

For Aisha,

The love of my life.

Prologue

It was a clear day over North America.

The President of the United States stared down at his country and felt despair. He'd felt little else since the first message had intruded its way into the United States Secure Communications Network, a network that hundreds of experts had claimed to be completely secure. The message had reached him and the leaders of the four other permanent members of the United Nations Security Council, inviting them to come to a remote location and meet with representatives from another world. He'd decided to go, even though the Secret Service had been horrified at the thought. The President of the United States would be going alone into the alien landing craft and flying to orbit.

He closed his eyes, trying to block out the sight. Earth was beautiful from orbit, a blue-green globe; if he stared, he fancied that he could make out the New Jersey coastline. And yet it seemed so vulnerable, a vulnerability that their host had demonstrated by his mere presence. The alien craft – one of their freighters, apparently – had remained undetected until its owner had chosen to make his presence known. It spoke volumes about humanity's vulnerability to an alien threat.

"My civilization is in decline," their host had said. He'd called himself Mentor, which suggested to the President – a keen science-fiction reader in his teens – that the aliens had spent literally *years* studying Earth. The thought of alien anthropologists watching humanity was horrifying – God alone knew what the aliens had made of humanity's inhumanity to its own kind – but if their host was to be believed, there were people out among the stars with less friendly motives. "The barbarians are at the gates. Your people do not have long to prepare."

The President, away from the network of analysts and briefers who prepared him for diplomatic meetings on

1

Earth, wasn't sure that he had followed the explanation. Their host, who looked rather like a humanoid cat, complete with fur, had apparently broken the rules of his own society by coming to Earth. He'd offered humanity technology that would solve many of Earth's problems, if they had time to put it into production. And if they didn't, he'd warned, Earth was in the way of at least one expanding civilization. The kindest outcome would be humanity being locked out of space forever. He didn't want to *think* about the other possibilities.

He looked over at his counterparts, the leaders of Britain, France, Russia and China. They shared the same stunned expression he knew dominated his own face. A week ago, they'd been confident that they knew their place in the world; now, the entire universe had turned upside down. There was a deadly threat out there and they had to prepare, but none of them really trusted the others, not when there was so much at stake. The nation that first put the alien technology to use would have an unbeatable advantage. For all of the idealism the President allowed himself in the privacy of his own thoughts, he knew that the idea of toppling the United States from the position of global superpower would be very attractive to his peers.

And as long as we're scrabbling like children who have been thrown a handful of dollars, he thought sourly, *the millionaires will draw their plans against us.*

He cleared his throat. "I think that we have to face facts," he said. But in truth he didn't know what the facts really were. Was their alien visitor telling the truth? There was no independent verification of everything he'd said. The President had looked into Roswell and other reported UFO contacts when he'd taken office, but the Air Force had assured him that the stories were nothing, but fabrications. Earth's first contact with alien life was standing right in front of him. "Our petty conflicts mean nothing in the face of what is bearing down on us."

There was no argument. A different issue, less momentous, would have caused bitter – if polite – scrabbling. "We have to make use of this gift," the President continued. Mentor had demanded nothing in return, but the President was too experienced a politician to take that at face value. "We have to prepare for more formal contact."

Years ago, he recalled from a history briefing he'd had before a diplomatic trip abroad, an American officer called Commodore Perry had forced the isolated state of Japan to open up and establish unequal treaties with the West. The British and other Europeans had done the same to China, but where the Japanese had managed to defend themselves and stave off Western aggression – and indulged some aggression of their own – the Chinese had never managed to adapt before they were overwhelmed. And the Native Americans had never stood a chance. The political and military disparity had simply been insurmountable.

"You have ten of your years at most," Mentor informed the small group. "By then, Earth will certainly be noticed by the expanding powers. If you cannot defend yourselves by then, you will be lost."

"Well," the President said, finally. "It's time to begin."

Chapter One

15 years later

"Ambassador," a voice said from behind her.

Ambassador Li Shan turned to see a Cat emerging from the shadows. She had to fight to keep the surprise off her face. The message summoning her had been urgent, specific – and unsigned. It had bidden her to come to a certain location on Center's immense flying city, using a channel that was only open to Ambassadors from the Galactics. She'd heard stories about how the Ambassadors to the Association's Commune used the system to strike secret deals that affected the fates of thousands of star systems, but she'd never been invited to take part. Why should she? Earth was a tiny planet and the human race only laid claim to eight systems – nine if one counted Terra Nova. The entire human race would vanish like a drop of water in milk if placed against the trillions of aliens that inhabited the galaxy. Earth was nothing to them.

The Cats – the founders of the Association - were roughly humanoid, with faces that reminded humans of felines from Earth, but they were covered in fur that changed colour to reflect their mood. No one knew much about their biology, but they'd made themselves immortal hundreds – perhaps thousands – of years ago. Since then, they'd had almost no children at all. And many of the other senior races were in the same boat. The previous Ambassador had joked that the boat was the *Titanic*. Shan found it hard to disagree with him.

"Your Excellency," Shan said. The Cats were the senior partners in the Association – everyone knew it, until the day came that the Association collapsed under its own weight. "I received your message."

Inwardly, she was thinking fast. It was rare for any Cat to talk directly to any of the younger races – Mentor had been a criminal by their laws, after all. Even the Cats who moderated in the Commune rarely interacted with anyone outside the colossal building that served as the Association's debating chamber and parliament. Shan had always assumed that, like the Emperors of Imperial China, they'd simply been too important to talk to mere barbarians from a minor world on the other side of the galaxy. Why should they have cared about Earth?

The Cat produced a datachip from his fur and passed it over to her. "Take this," he said. "It contains vital information. Warn your world."

Shan stared down at the chip. "Warn my world about what?"

The Cat started to turn and walk away. "About the oncoming storm," he said. "You may have a chance to save your world."

Shan watched him step into one of the side corridors and vanish, before she pocketed the chip and headed back to her office. It was rare – practically unprecedented – for the Cats to interfere directly in politics. Mentor had been an exception, but no-one knew what had happened to him. What did the Cats do to criminals anyway? In all her time on Center, Shan had never been able to find out the answer.

When she'd first arrived on Center, the capital of the Association, Shan had been awed by the view from the embassy. The Association had been exploring space and laying the groundwork for the quantum gate network since before humanity had learned to produce fire on demand and it showed. Hundreds of tall spindly buildings reached up towards the sky, testament to an alien aesthetic that turned creation into an act of joy, while thousands of starships glided through the skies overhead. The capital city floated on antigravity generators that cost more than twenty times Earth's combined GNP to maintain. It looked as if the Association was still powerful, still in the grip of the uncanny self-confidence that had led its founder race to the stars. Earth – poor primitive Earth, only aware of the existence of alien races for the last fifteen years – could not have hoped to match what the Association had built over the centuries.

And yet, the Association was dying. It seemed absurd – the Association's founder race had developed a form of biological immortality – but it was true. Theirs was a civilization in decline, burning up its resources and slowly becoming dependent on other races to maintain its infrastructure. The low birth-rate only contributed to the slow collapse into senility as the aging population, unable to die, lost interest in the universe around them. A society that could have rolled over Earth any time it chose was finding it harder and harder to care about the rest of the galaxy. They were already abandoning hundreds of colony worlds and migrating inwards towards Center. And the power vacuum they left behind was slowly being filled by other races, races more interested in seizing power for themselves than terminal navel-gazing. One day, the Association would look up and see those races landing on their homeworld, claiming their technology and their population. The Association was going to fall and fall hard.

Shan was Chinese, a veteran of diplomacy on Earth and Communist Party infighting in China in the chaos that had followed First Contact. Human sociologists had claimed that the Association bore some resemblance to Manchu China, back before the Communist Party had seized the reins of power, something that China had used to win the post of Ambassador for her. Personally, Shan wasn't so sure. Unlike the China of the Boxer Rebellion, the Association could have smashed all of its potential enemies within a few months, if they worked up the nerve to impose their will on the universe once again. The mighty dreadnoughts orbiting high overhead might have been hundreds of years old, but they were still formidable. But they didn't have the will to accept casualties any longer. They preferred to close their eyes and pretend that the universe no longer mattered to them.

But all the denial in the universe wouldn't change the fundamental truth. Throughout the thousands of worlds settled by the Association, hundreds of millions of guest workers supplied services that the Association could no longer be bothered to do for itself. Those workers, including humans, were raising families and claiming rights, even as

6

the Association became increasingly dependent upon them. The Association was slowly losing control over its infrastructure – and those who were aware that there was a problem, such as Mentor, were isolated. One day, they'd realise... but by then it would be too late.

It was hard to care about the Association – even the most benevolent Oligarch was utterly convinced of his own superiority over members of the younger races – but Shan knew that if the Association fell, humanity would be caught up in the chaos. There were a dozen races out there that would love to lay claim to Earth, if only to nip another potential competitor in the bud. The Hegemony – who had pushed humanity out of its first colony on an Earth-like world, Terra Nova – wanted humans firmly under their thumb. Humans were good at making otherwise inhospitable worlds habitable, creating new territory for the ruling Empress. And Earth's tiny sphere was blocking the Hegemony's line of advance towards the Rim. They had good reasons for wanting to suppress humanity before Earth became too powerful.

And maybe Earth's time had just run out.

* * *

Admiral Tobias Sampson, Chief of Naval Operations, was a tall, powerfully-built man with short brown hair and a reputation for not suffering fools gladly. His family had served in the United States Navy ever since there had *been* a United States Navy and there had never been any question of what Tobias would do with his life – until Mentor arrived and turned Earth upside down. Tobias, already marked down as a captain to watch, had transferred to the Federation Navy – humanity's combined space force – almost as soon as it was created. He'd risen to the top through a mixture of supreme competence and canny politicking, even though he still regretted never having had a chance to command a starship in action.

The Federation – Earth's semi-united world government – was a hodgepodge that puzzled the Galactics, who seemed to have assumed that humanity would gladly create a world government once it knew that there were other intelligent races in the universe. Humans being humans, unity didn't come that easily; the Federation, unlike the United Nations, was dominated by the nations that paid the bills. None of them were prepared to give up more than a little independence, leaving the Federation heavily dependent on consensus-building in order to function. If there hadn't been a consensus, particularly after Terra Nova, that the Federation had to be strong enough to stand up to the Galactics, Tobias wouldn't have given a rusty dollar for its chances.

But Terra Nova had rubbed humanity's collective face in its own inferiority. It had been the first Earth-like world to be settled by humanity – and, unlike the other colonies, it had been settled by colonists from all over the globe. Americans had rubbed shoulders with Iranians, Russians had lived next to Chinese… some of the sociologists had claimed that that was a recipe for disaster, but they'd never had the chance to find out. Five years after the planet had been settled, with over three hundred thousand humans living on the surface, the Hegemony – the Funks, as humans called them - had bullied the Association into ceding the planet to them. Terra Nova was now governed by a Hegemony Governor, ruling over a sizable human population. The reports of conditions on the surface – including some from Tobias' daughter and son-in-law – were not good.

He looked around the table, meeting the eyes of the thirteen most powerful men and women in the world. They'd come to Iceland secretly, ensuring that the media didn't catch wind of what was going on until the national governments could decide how to handle the new crisis. Critics claimed that the rest of the world was excluded, but Tobias found it hard to care. Not every nation actually wanted to pay for its own defence, yet they all thought they should have a vote on the Federation Council. Anyone could play, if they paid. The Federation Navy alone cost billions every year, as well as pretty much all of Earth's limited trade balance with the Galactics.

"The message from Ambassador Li makes our position quite clear," he said. The world leaders had already had time to digest the message. "The Hegemony has found a fig leaf to claim our territory for themselves. We expect that they will demand that we surrender peacefully to them – and if we refuse, they will bring their forces to bear against us and crush our resistance."

"My God," the French President said. "And there's no hope that the Association can be convinced to change its mind?"

"Li was not hopeful," Tobias said. "Unfortunately, there are limits to the ways we can influence the Association ourselves. The Oligarchs are richer than the combined human race, so we cannot bribe even one of them. And even if we did, committing the Association to war against the Hegemony would be hugely unpopular on Center. It would mean political suicide for those who proposed it."

"But they can't just give away our territory like that," the American President protested. "We own it; we developed it..."

"I think your Native Americans might have felt the same way," the Russian President pointed out. "They could never understand how white men signing papers on the other side of the sea meant that their territories could be taken away and their populations destroyed. The Association is convinced that it owns us and they have precedent on their side."

"Might makes right," the British Prime Minister said, in disgust.

"Historically, treaties and international law only work as long as someone is willing to uphold them by force," Tobias said grimly. "When they discovered Earth, we certainly didn't have the ability to dispute their ownership – we didn't even know that we *had* been discovered and claimed. The Hegemony will use the fig leaf they have to justify taking control of us. Our independence will come to an end."

He met the eyes of the American President, willing him to believe. "The best case is that they will leave us with limited autonomy on Earth, provided we kiss their behinds loudly and often," he added. "Humans have a reputation as hard workers, good soldiers and excellent technicians. They could certainly make use of us, but we'd never see the benefits of our own labour. The worst case...

"The worst case is that they wipe us out. Humanity will be exterminated from the universe. There may be some humans left alive in the Association's territory, but the Hegemony could presumably bring pressure to bear on the Association to expel them. The human race would come to an end."

"Jesus," the American President said. "They're that determined?"

"The Hegemony is dominated by a race that has a historical urge – almost a genetic compulsion – to reach out and take as much in the way of resources as it can," Tobias said, gently. "All of their other borders are occupied by powers that could put up more of a fight than ourselves – and a lost war would be a political disaster for the ruling Empress. So would holding what they have and refusing to expand any further. The only real target for expansion is us."

"I see," the Russian President said. "We will fight, of course."

"If we wait for them to attack us, we will lose," Tobias said, flatly. He felt his heart starting to race as they looked at him. There was a very real possibility that he was committing career suicide himself merely by bringing the proposal to their attention. Only five people knew about the plan; himself and four tactical analysts. "We have to strike first."

There was a long pause. "You just told us that we would lose a war," the French President said, coldly. "Why do you assume that we can win by starting one?"

Tobias tapped a key and a holographic star chart appeared above the table, the Nine Stars – Earth and its colonies – in the center. Terra Nova, occupied by enemy forces, was blinking orange, while the stars claimed by the Hegemony were blinking red. Space was a three-dimensional combat environment, something that confused many civilians who didn't understand why the Federation Navy couldn't guarantee safety.

"We have devoted much time and effort to setting up an intelligence network outside Earth," Tobias said. The Galactics had their own factions and some of them were willing to slip information to humanity. Humans settled on alien worlds also provided intelligence, although what they could provide was limited. "We know that the Hegemony maintains five Association-designed superdreadnoughts in orbit around Terra Nova, a sizable chunk of its entire battle-line. There are a handful of smaller ships, but the superdreadnoughts alone are – on paper – enough to safeguard the planet from all threats. Their confidence would be fully justified, under normal circumstances."

He smiled. "But we have new weapons and tactics to deploy," he added. "We can shatter that force before they have a chance to reinforce it – and liberate Terra Nova. At the same time, we will hit their base on Garston which provides support for their navy and capture the quantum gate in the system. That will impose massive delays on their response – and even when they do realise that they are at war, they will be unable to reinforce quickly. If they strip their entire border of mobile forces, one or all of their rivals will pounce on them. That would cost them the war – and even their independence."

The Japanese Prime Minister leaned forward. "My country has had its own experience with pre-emptive strikes," he said. "Not all of them ended well."

"There are no guarantees in war," Tobias admitted. "The sociologists claim that if we manage to bloody their nose and embarrass the Empress, her position will be seriously threatened and her clan will remove her before their dominance can be shattered and they have a civil war. In that case, there would be a long and bloody power struggle before a new leader emerges from the fighting, giving us time we can use to fortify the captured worlds and build new starships. But even if they don't fall into civil war, they would still have problems fighting us if they lost heavily in the opening rounds. They would never be able to bring their full strength against us.

11

"I have confidence that the Federation Navy can carry out this operation – can win this war – if we start it at a time and place of our own choosing," he concluded. "I have no confidence that we can stop them if they are allowed to reinforce and then advance on Earth unimpeded. We do not have time to build the starships we'd need to hold them off and no one else is likely to raise a finger to help us. The choice is not between fighting or not fighting, but when and where the war starts. They are not going to allow us to remain independent."

The debate surged backwards and forwards. Some of the world leaders were worried about deliberately triggering a war with one of the Galactics, even the Hegemony. War was always a gamble at the best of times – and few battle plans ever survived contact with the enemy. Secrecy would have to be maintained until the war began, something that would upset local governments and the media. In the end, the vote was very close.

"Admiral," the American President said, "you have permission to plan and execute the strike on Terra Nova. Don't fuck up."

"I will lead the fleet in person," Tobias said. "Operation Kryptonite will remain secret until we're ready to move. If the Galactics get one word of warning, we'll be screwed."

Chapter Two

Armstrong City had grown in the five years since Captain Joshua Wachter had last visited Luna. Like all human colonies, it was a mixture of human and alien technologies, with antigravity lifters running next to gas-powered tractors. The limited supply of Galactic technology meant that everything that could be done with human technology had to be done, despite claims that this would one day leave the workers operating the primitive technology hopelessly behind their fellows who had used the more advanced equipment. Joshua knew better. As long as there was a human race, there would be jobs for people who were willing to work on rocky worlds with little atmosphere. The long-term plan to terraform Luna would take centuries, at least, to come to fruition. Mars and Venus would be habitable sooner. One of Mentor's many gifts to the human race had been engineered microbes that started the long task of turning a barren world into a garden.

He strode through a series of endless corridors and finally reached the Naval HQ, positioned on the edge of Armstrong City. The Federation Navy had its own separate installations on Luna – the Federation Navy Academy had been established on the moon, away from nations and nationalist sentiments – but he would never have been invited to any of them. Half of the human race considered him little better than a traitor, while the rest considered him a hero. Anyone dealing with him would want to do so at arm's length. He'd actually considered declining when he received the message inviting him to return to Luna, before deciding to go. If the rumours he'd picked up were true, Earth would need all the help it could get, even from one of its most controversial sons.

The guards – three Federation Marines, carrying the latest in magnetic-accelerated rifles – checked his ID carefully, before detailing another set of Marines to escort him through the Naval HQ and into a small office. The last time he'd visited, he'd been extensively debriefed by both Federation Intelligence and the Office of Naval Intelligence, the civilian and military intelligence services studying the Galactics. This time, the officer who stepped through the other door was someone a great deal more senior. Admiral Tobias Sampson himself.

Joshua lifted an eyebrow as Sampson sat down and studied him. He saw a man who looked inhumanly young, thanks to the wonders of Galactic medical technology, with an unkempt mop of hair covering a thin body that could never stay still. Outside of the Association's founder race, there was no such thing as biological immortality, but nanites could do wonderful things for one's lifespan. The richer segment of the human race were prepared to pay almost anything to get their hands on such technology, technology that was almost free on any Galactic world. Joshua had made billions smuggling it to Earth and selling nanites to the highest bidder. If he'd incorporated his business on Earth, taxes would have gobbled up over half of his profits. The donations he sent back in alien currency were his way of contributing to Earth's desperate struggle to modernise itself before someone with more starships than humanity turned up and demanded surrender.

"I am not here," Sampson said, gruffly. "My appointment book says that I am meeting with two prospective commanding officers for new-build starships. I expect you to keep whatever you hear in this compartment to yourself, or there will be consequences."

Joshua smiled. Sampson was probably one of the officers who disapproved of him. Coming to Joshua for help had to rankle. "I understand," he said. "I think I have assisted you enough over the years to prove my trustworthiness."

"No such thing," Sampson growled. "Ideally, everyone connected with this would be in a secure environment for the next six months, where they wouldn't be able to talk to anyone not already authorized to discuss the matter. There are already too many people in on the secret and some of them have flapping lips."

Joshua shrugged. "You seem to have me at a disadvantage," he said. "Either tell me what you want from me or let me go back to my ship."

Sampson eyed him for a long moment. "You have contacts among the Galactics," he said. "Have you heard anything...interesting lately?"

"Rumours," Joshua said. He looked back at Sampson. "Rumours concerning Earth and the Hegemony. I take it that those rumours are true?"

"The Cats do love to chatter," Sampson sighed. "From what we've heard, the Association is on the verge of selling us out to the Hegemony. They'll come here, take our worlds and enslave the human race. We do not have much time to react."

He hesitated. "I assume you've heard nothing from Mentor...?"

"No," Joshua admitted. "Nothing. Not even a peep."

Mentor had been one of the few Association Oligarchs to realise that the Association was heading for disaster. His decision to take a small fleet to Earth and make humanity a present of advanced technology had been against most of the Association's strongest laws, even though they'd been broken many times in the past. After Earth had started expanding, Mentor had been summoned home to Center to face his peers. No one knew what had happened to him after his trial. The Association considered itself too civilised to apply the death penalty to an immortal being, but there were plenty of lesser punishments they could have used. Or maybe Mentor had simply decided to join his fellows in retreating from the universe.

It had also been Mentor who had started the young Joshua on his strange career. A group of human terrorists had tried to assassinate the alien, but Joshua had saved his life and – in return – Mentor had given him his own starship. The Oligarch was so rich that an entire starship, even one with its own gate generator, was pocket change to him. Joshua had ignored demands from the Federation Navy that he turn the starship over to them, instead setting out on an extended tour of the galaxy. Over the years, he had built up his own small trading empire, an empire that made him one of the richest men on Earth. And yet his entire fortune was still nothing more than pocket change to many Galactics. They tended to underestimate Joshua because he was poor by their standards.

Earth's technology didn't hold any attractions for the Galactics, at least not the races that had developed their own spacefaring technology before the Association had discovered them. The planet did, however, have many other resources they could trade, including artefacts and old movies. *Independence Day* had been surprisingly popular, although the Galactics who'd distributed it had branded the movie as a comedy. The sight of Galactics howling with laughter as giant flying saucers lowered themselves into Earth's atmosphere was not for the faint-hearted. Why didn't they simply bombard the planet from orbit if they wanted it so badly?

"The Hegemony intends to take Earth," Sampson said, flatly. "And as far as I can see, we're alone against the universe."

Joshua nodded. It tied in with his own experiences. Some races were friendlier than others, but as the Association's power dwindled, the more advanced races were starting to assert their own domination. The free trading network he'd used had been created by the Association and would probably die as the borders started to slip backwards towards Center. No-one would help Earth, save perhaps only races with little to offer.

"I see," he said, finally. "I notice that one of the colonist-carriers is gone...?"

"Classified," Sampson said, shortly. Joshua grinned. Mentor had brought Earth four colonist-carrier starships, massive ships capable of carrying a hundred thousand humanoids in stasis between worlds. One of them could transport a select group of humans – and a complete genetic template – beyond the Rim, hundreds of light-years away from the Hegemony. Humanity would live on even if Earth was destroyed.

"But we have only one option if we want to maintain our independence," Sampson continued, ignoring Joshua's grin. "We have to take the offensive and strike first."

Joshua stared at him. For a moment, he didn't believe his ears.

"You want to start a war?" he asked. "Are you *insane?*"

"I would prefer to fight now than fight when they have a chance to bring more of their power to bear against Earth," Sampson said. He ran through the strategic rationale. "In your opinion, as someone with more experience of the Galactics than most, do you think the plan is workable?"

Joshua paused, considering. "The Funks tend to bow down to those they consider their superiors," he said, finally. "If we gave them enough of a bloody nose, they'd probably give up on trying to take our space." He shrugged. "But it would have to be a *very* bloody nose to deter them from pressing on with the fight. Their Empress will be putting her own life at risk if she surrenders without their population being convinced of our superiority. Maybe less so if we start the war..."

He looked up. "Are we so advanced that we can attack them even without superior numbers? I've heard rumours..."

Sampson snorted. "Give us fifty years of uninterrupted development and we could roll over the Association any time we liked," he said, dryly. "The Galactics don't seem to have the same impulse we have to keep pushing the limits of technology. Most of them got their technology off the Association and never bothered to develop anything for themselves."

"But we don't have fifty years," Joshua said quietly. "Do we have enough to give them a bloody nose now?"

"I think so," Sampson admitted. "The technology we do have is enough to give them a handful of nasty surprises. But it won't be enough to give us crushing superiority. I'd prefer to keep all of the new technology under wraps until we could deploy it against the entire Hegemony and smash it before it has a hope of developing its own technology, but we won't have that time. After the first couple of battles... who knows?"

A holographic chart appeared over the table. Joshua studied it thoughtfully, his mind instinctively mapping out the trade routes his small fleet used, moving from quantum gate to quantum gate. The economics of the gate network ensured that stars with their own gate received more traffic than stars without gates, but the network grew thinner out towards the Rim. Earth and the rest of the Nine Stars hadn't received gates until they'd been constructed by human engineers. The Hegemony now owned Terra Nova's gate, forcing human technicians to maintain it. It was quite possible that the Hegemony wouldn't be able to maintain the entire network if it did absorb large chunks of the Association.

"We need to do something to keep the Hegemony off-balance," Sampson said, seriously. His gaze never left Joshua's face. "As you presumably know" – he smiled thinly – "the Hegemony actually has strong trading networks running through the more lawless regions of space here. They've settled some of their... *client* races on Tauscher, which is actually one of their more restless worlds. ONI estimates that the Hegemony actually needs to keep a major ground force on the planet just to keep the settlers under control."

"The other Galactics keep running in guns," Joshua commented. Tauscher sat in the middle of the trading lanes, giving the other Galactics a vested interest in supporting the settlers to keep the Hegemony busy. There were several pirate bases nearby, largely ignored by the Hegemony because some of their backers were *from* the Hegemony. "I've never actually been there."

"We need you to go there now," Sampson said. He tapped a switch and the display shifted, revealing a comparative fleet list. The Hegemony had more minor combatant units than the Federation Navy had *starships*. "They can't pull too many of their superdreadnoughts off the borders without risking war with someone bigger and tougher than us, but they can detach light units and send them our way. We need to give them a major threat in their rear."

Joshua chuckled. "With my trading fleet? You *do* realise that only a couple of my ships are armed and *none* of them are genuine warships?"

"We purchased a handful of ships from various sources over the years," Sampson said. The Association attempted to register starships, but the registry was hopelessly out of date and often lost track of starships after they'd moved onto the third or fourth pair of hands. Whatever else could be said about the Association, they built starships to last. Some of their ships were thousands of years old. "None of them have any obvious connection with Earth – originally, we intended to learn what we could from them and then press them into service as training vessels. Now... we have another use in mind for them."

"You want me to go play at being a pirate," Joshua said slowly. "And what happens when we run into a real warship?"

"We don't expect you to take and hold territory," Sampson said. "We merely want you to engage in commerce raiding and cause havoc, enough to force the Empress of the Hegemony to divert starships to hunt you down. If they start losing control of their borders, they're going to lose a great deal of face in front of the other powers. Their nature won't allow them to swallow the losses and concentrate on Earth."

"You hope," Joshua reminded him. "A plan where everything *has* to go right is a plan doomed to failure."

Sampson ran his hand through his hair. "I know," he said, his eyes meeting Joshua's. "It gets worse. We cannot afford to be linked to you – human mercenaries and pirates are one thing, but Earth itself... if the Galactics blame us for your attacks, our political position will be gravely weakened."

"They might join the war on the Hegemony's side," Joshua said. "Or put pressure on the Association to respond to the crisis."

"They might," Sampson said. "If you do this for us – and there are few others with the knowledge necessary to fit into the underside of Galactic society – you will be completely expendable. Should you be caught... well, you're already an outcast on much of Earth. We'll disown you and your crews. We'd much prefer it if you had alien crew members..."

"Or that we were never caught at all," Joshua said. "Do you want us all to take suicide pills with us?"

"Implanted vaporisers," Sampson said. "Ideally, there should be nothing left of you and your ships if they capture you. And there's another problem."

Joshua smiled. "*Another* problem?"

"I can't give you good officers from the Navy," Sampson said. "We only have a limited supply of trained personnel and we're going to need all of them for the coming war. I have taken the liberty of preparing a list of possible candidates for the operation, men who may be good at what they do, but have problems relating to discipline. Some of them would be better off in the brig than in space. Hell, some of them *are* in the brig. You can take as many of them as you want, but watch your back."

He passed over a datachip, which Joshua took and pocketed. "It's a shitty job," Sampson admitted. "If you get caught, the Galactics will be merciless and there will be no way that we can defend you. This could easily turn into a suicide mission. We can't even give you enough supplies to keep your ships operating for long."

"That won't be a problem," Joshua assured him. One advantage of the Association's technological gifts to the rest of the galaxy was that most spare parts were standardised. The Hegemony produced the same equipment as the other powers, even if they placed their own stamp on their starships. "I assume we're not getting much of a war chest as well?"

"We've got you some untraceable funds," Sampson said. "Anything after that…"

"Piracy had damn better pay for itself," Joshua agreed. He looked back at the Admiral for a long moment. "Can we actually win this war?"

"Maybe," Sampson said. "I…have reason to believe that the Hegemony is increasing its efforts to penetrate our security. They believe in divide and conquer – it's quite possible that they have been trying to make contact with one or more nations on Earth and offering them a deal that allows them to maintain their independence, as long as they help the Hegemony against Earth. We *think* that we have their networks under control, but we don't know for sure. I had to take the plan directly to the world leaders and if a single word gets out ahead of time..."

Joshua nodded. He hadn't seen the strategic reports from the planners, but it didn't take a genius to realise that Earth's forces were very limited. Any reinforcement of the stars near humanity could be disastrous – but then, the Hegemony didn't seem to take humanity seriously. Why should they when they'd bullied Terra Nova out of humanity's clutches so easily?

He knew how the human race felt about the Funks; hell, he *shared* their attitude to the biggest bullies in the local sector. But it struck him that he was being asked to risk everything he'd built on a plan that might or might not work. He could leave and no one would be surprised, not after he'd been the subject of so many angry political broadcasts. Those politicians wouldn't hesitate to throw him to the wolves if they thought they could get away with it.

And yet he knew that Sampson was right. There *was* no one else...and besides, the thought of poking the Funks in their bright red eyes was attractive. They deserved a sharp lesson in how they treated other races.

"I understand," he said, finally. He'd do it, after taking a few steps to ensure that his people wouldn't suffer if he messed up. "No one will hear a peep from me until the shit hits the fan. How long do I have to prepare?"

"Two to three months," Sampson said. "We're going to be making preparations for the offensive over the next two months, before actually kicking off the attack. You have that long to get into position and prepare to start raiding."

"Two months," Joshua said. "It'll take upwards of a month to even *get* there, assuming we can't risk going near the shipping lanes. Even in quantum space, that's one hell of a trip. It certainly won't be long enough to make local connections."

"Which will at least minimise the risks of betrayal," Sampson said. "I don't know if we dare risk waiting any longer than three months before launching the offensive. If they start reinforcing their battle-line anyway, our operation becomes much less workable."

"Which would be disastrous," Joshua agreed. "I'll do my best to expedite my departure."

Sampson stood up and held out his hand. "Good luck, Captain," he said. "We're counting on you."

Joshua shook his hand firmly. "Just make sure that there's still an Earth for me to come back to," he said. "I do want to return home one day. There's nowhere in the galaxy quite like Earth."

Chapter Three

Adrienne Lawson had one rule. No-one, bar no-one, was to call her after she returned home until the following day. She'd spent the last week in Saudi Arabia reporting on the provisional government's attempts to hold the country together after the House of Saud had fallen due to the collapse in oil prices and sheer barbarity had thoroughly discredited the Islamic fundamentalists who'd seized power in the confusion. News services, even the increasingly online newspapers that pulled reports from all over the globe, still needed trained reporters and Adrienne considered herself one of the best. She liked to think that she was more famous than the President.

The sound of her cell phone brought her back to wakefulness in a hurry. She cursed under her breath as she sat up in bed and glanced around at the clock. It was morning and they *knew* not to call her on a morning following a trip overseas. Only her fellow reporters had that particular number, the only phone she kept on at all times. It was a policy she promised herself she'd rethink whenever she had a moment.

She reached for the phone, checked the caller ID to make sure that it really was important, and answered the call.

"This had better be important. I need to get back to sleep."

"This is very important," a droll male voice said. She would have recognised Owen Ward's voice anywhere. Her immediate superior had a remarkable gift for getting the best out of his reporters, even though he hadn't reported himself since before First Contact. "The Federation Navy just put in a request for embedded reporters."

Adrienne smiled, even as she rubbed her tired face. *Request* was a little too much, at least in her view; the military believed that it had no obligation to bring reporters along into the front lines, or at least as close as they could without putting lives in serious danger. Adrienne had reported from Prince Sultan Air Base, currently held by a multinational force intent on securing the oil wells and ensuring that there were no further oil shocks. Oil might be less important with fusion power, but it was still important for many requirements and Arabia held one of the world's largest sources.

"And they asked for me," Adrienne said. It wasn't a question. Reporters who put soldiers in danger or reported lies tended not to be invited back, no matter how important they considered themselves to be. Adrienne considered that she'd done a good job, striking a balance between being inquisitive and respecting military security. "What's so important that it couldn't wait until the afternoon?"

Ward coughed. "Apparently the Federation Navy is planning a major exercise, involving almost the entire fleet," he said. "From what little I was told, they're going to be rehearsing the plans for defending Earth against the Galactics. You'll be told more when you reach the Naval HQ. If you want to go, of course…"

Adrienne snorted. "If they asked for me," she said dryly, "should I refuse them?"

"We could always send Alicia in your place." Ward said. "Market Research says that she's very popular among young males – and the military is largely composed of young males."

"Of course she is," Adrienne said. "Every time she looks like she's losing viewers, she takes a deep breath and pushes out her rack."

"You said it, not me," Ward said. He chuckled. "But Market Research thinks that she has what it takes to interview people in the military. If you don't go, I'm afraid that she's going to go in your place. That wouldn't be very patriotic, would it?"

"I suppose not," Adrienne said. "But then, Alicia is a bimbo who never had an original thought in her life. All of her viewers pray for another wardrobe malfunction…"

"No doubt," Ward agreed. He returned to business. "You're expected at Naval HQ tomorrow, so take the shuttle from New York Spaceport to Armstrong City this afternoon.

The Navy will assign someone to meet you and escort you into lockdown..."

"But..."

"No buts," Ward said. "It was quietly, but firmly made clear to me that every reporter on this mad junket was going into lockdown, with no communications in or out until the military sees fit to lift the lockdown. You breathe one word without permission and your next boyfriend will be a horny prison guard. The rules haven't changed just because you're going into space."

Adrienne nodded, reluctantly. She *had* been on an extra-solar voyage, something that most of the population of Earth couldn't claim, but the colony established on Edo had been on a drab rocky world circling a dying star. The Japanese were shipping thousands of settlers to Edo every month, intent on turning it into a second home for their people. Rumour had it that large bribes had secured Federation support for their scheme. Adrienne had investigated, but hadn't been able to turn up anything beyond the fact that Edo enjoyed a population density in its domes that few other cultures would likely have been able to tolerate.

"Besides, it's not as if you have anyone on Earth waiting for you," Ward added. "Your father died a long time ago and your mother disowned you."

"Enough," Adrienne snapped. "I'll be on my way this afternoon. Have Jenny book the tickets for me and I'll pick them up at the spaceport."

"Good luck," Ward said. "Don't forget that I will be expecting regular reports from you as soon as the lockdown is dropped. And don't forget to get their agreement to regular reports in writing."

Adrienne sighed. "I won't forget," she assured him. "See you in a few months."

She put down the phone and looked into the mirror. The blonde girl with long hair and tired eyes seemed a stranger. She had a lifestyle many would envy, with a chance to travel the world and even fly through interstellar space to another world, but she was tired. Perhaps the lockdown wouldn't be such a bad thing. Maybe there'd be a chance to relax.

25

Reporters tended to get star treatment unless they embedded in frontline units.

Shaking her head, Adrienne returned to bed after setting her alarm. The spaceport wasn't that far from her apartment, after all. There'd be enough time to catch forty winks and then take a taxi to the spaceport. Ward could hardly complain if she slept in a little after she'd agreed to go straight out again on assignment, could he?

* * *

Topsham was a pleasant little country town in Devon, England, on the east side of the River Esk. Sergeant Conrad McDonald had fallen in love with it the first time his Royal Marine platoon had driven through the area to attend a wedding in nearby Torquay, and it had been an easy choice to decide to have his own honeymoon there. Transfer to the Federation Marines – who had been crafted along the same lines as the Royal Marines – meant that he couldn't leave the country without special permission, if only because the Federation Marines were kept permanently ready to go into action within 48 hours.

He looked over at his wife of three days and smiled at her. The wedding had been a brief service in a nearby church, followed by a dinner at a countryside lodge in an area of natural beauty. Conrad had been posted to Clarke and seen video of Terra Nova, but the English countryside was still the most beautiful place in the world to him. Some of the old Bootnecks, the ones who had fought in Afghanistan, claimed that that shithole of a country was remarkably beautiful, but Conrad wasn't inclined to agree. Having someone taking pot-shots at him from a distance or placing IEDs along his path wasn't his idea of a pleasant day out with his wife. Afghanistan was now even more of a shithole than ever, particularly since the NATO forces had been pulled out with indecent haste after First Contact.

"Fancy a beer?"

"I could do with one," Cindy agreed. She was the daughter of an older Royal Marine, now retired and tending a pub in Portsmouth. Her father had threatened all sorts of

26

things, just to see if his prospective son in law could be deterred, before cheerfully standing beside Cindy to give her away at the altar. "Just don't drink too much or you'll be paralytic in bed tonight."

"Nag, nag, nag," Conrad said. He leaned close to kiss her, and then reach down to her chest, stroking her breasts gently. They were getting into heavy petting when his bleeper went off. "Oh shit!"

"Ignore it," Cindy said. "There isn't time..."

Conrad shook his head, not without regret. All of the Bootnecks – the slang for Royal Marine had transferred into the Federation Marines – knew better than to ignore their bleepers. No one became a Federation Marine without a perfect service record in their national militaries, if not Special Forces experience in combat. Conrad had taken part in operations in Jeddah five years ago, working with American and French soldiers. It had been enough to get him into the qualification course for the Federation Marines, but sheer determination had taken him the rest of the way. Even hardened SAS blades and Paras had been known to blanch when confronted with the Federation Marine training course.

He picked up the bleeper – he was supposed to wear it on his wrist, where it also served as a watch – and scowled at the tiny screen. REPORT ASAP, it ordered, nothing else. At least they hadn't used any of the code words that warned of imminent invasion or emergency services under MACA rules. The rules were clear enough; he should take a train from Topsham to the Federation Navy base at RAF Waddington, where transport would be laid on to get the Bootnecks to Luna. Being late would result in anything from a bollocking by his CO to being marked down for dereliction of duty. It might be an exercise – hell, it was *probably* an exercise – but they had to treat it as if it were real.

"I have to go," he said, reaching for his socks. They'd rolled under the bed in all the excitement. "Listen... you can enjoy the rest of the..."

"Don't be silly," Cindy said. She was the daughter of a Royal Marine, after all, and knew what happened when duty and personal life conflicted. "Do you think I can stay here while worrying about you? I'll speak to the owner and get them to take something off the bill before I get back to Portsmouth. Dad will want some help when everyone comes off exercise."

Conrad nodded, reluctantly. He'd never understood why some Bootnecks found it hard to come back to base after visiting their wives and families, until now. "Just remember not to flirt with anyone," he teased. "You're my wife now."

"I have that big poster of you up on the wall to keep them quiet," Cindy agreed. "Don't you worry about me. Just get back home safely and I'll see you when I see you. Email me when you have a moment, all right?"

"All right," Conrad said. He leaned forward to kiss her. "I'd better get over to the station now."

"I'll come with you," Cindy said. "I can kiss you on the platform until the train gets here."

* * *

Archimedes Penal Colony held ten thousand human criminals, around nine thousand of them serial killers, mass murderers, paedophiles and terrorists. No civilian was sent to the Penal Colony unless they had been sentenced to life imprisonment, without hope of having their sentences cut short. Volunteer convicts performed dangerous tasks on the Luna surface, in exchange for better food and drink, but none of them would ever be allowed to escape. There were no spacesuits or pressurized vehicles in the colony to provide safety from the airless vacuum outside. A convict who opened one of the airlocks would merely be committing suicide.

The remaining prisoners were military personnel who had committed offenses severe enough to justify incarceration, although most of them weren't sentenced to life imprisonment and were kept separate from the general population. Their crimes tended to range from minor, but persistent misbehaviour to more serious offences, ones that merited more punishment than receiving a Bad Conduct

28

Discharge. The Federation Navy had largely copied the Uniform Code of Military Justice from the United States, although there were some minor additions from other countries.

From above, there was little to see as the flitter dropped down towards the mounds of lunar rock that had been piled over the dome to provide some protection from solar radiation. Joshua had spent the time reviewing the files Admiral Sampson had given him, looking for military prisoners who might be interested in serving with the small squadron under his command. He had never had any formal military training, but he did have experience with selecting and recruiting crew for his ships. Some of the personnel were beyond redemption, others were clearly unsuited to the mission, but the remainder... most of them might be usable. Their files agreed that they had potential; they'd just never made use of it, or they'd abused it. The Supply Officer who'd gamed the system to ensure that his ship received the latest updates before anyone else was particularly interesting. Someone with that sort of background would be very useful. Another had been finally put in the brig for repeated racial statements directed against the Funks, the Hegemony's master race. Joshua couldn't understand why he'd been punished when such sentiments were widespread until he looked at the specifics. The spacer had made them in front of the Galactic news networks.

The Prison Warden's android met him as he entered the airlock. For safety – and to make taking hostages impossible – all of the warders interacted with the prisoners through remote-controlled androids, each one almost impossible to destroy with nothing more than hand-powered tools. Joshua looked up at the towering android, shaped in an exaggerated parody of humanity, and shook his head. The androids would have little difficulty restoring order if the prisoners decided to riot – or, perhaps, they'd let the prisoners kill a few of their fellows before intervening. No one cared what happened to the prisoners in this complex. The civilians had been permanently removed from society and sent here to die.

"I have had the prisoners you requested gathered," the warden said. Even the android's voice was inhuman, completely atonal. "They are waiting for you in the visitor's room. I must warn you that if they attempt to take you prisoner, we will have no option, but to flood the room with capture gas."

"Understood," Joshua said. He wouldn't allow the prisoners to intimidate him. They were humans, after all, not aliens shaped like humanoid crocodiles with smiles to match. "Take me to the compartment."

The android bobbed its head and walked backwards without changing posture. It could move in almost any direction, twisting in ways no human could match. Perhaps there were AIs behind the androids rather than humans, although rumour suggested that most of the operators were actually cripples. Remote operations was a field that even a paralysed man could enter.

Joshua smiled as the prisoners looked up when he entered. Some of them had clearly maintained military appearance while in custody, others had let themselves go, growing their beards and hair until it fell around their waists. Only one of them was female, a butch woman who had been charged with striking her commanding officer and refused to either apologise or accept guilt. Nearly all of the civilian prisoners were male. Female prisoners found themselves in a very unpleasant kind of hell.

"My name is Joshua Wachter – yes, *that* Joshua Wachter," he said, by way of introduction. "I'll keep this brief. I require a number of experienced crewmen to carry out a very sensitive mission – a dirty dozen or two. Your superiors have agreed that those of you who volunteer for this mission and come back alive will have their sentences commuted. Those who wish to remain in the military will have their records wiped; I can offer jobs to those who want to serve in space or you can return to Earth without any further time in jail."

He smiled thinly. "I should warn you that the odds of survival are low and we may all be killed," he added. "I don't have any tolerance for military formality, but I'll space anyone who imperils the ships or the mission. No drinking or drugs will be permitted" – he gave a hard look to a weasel-faced man who had been charged with smuggling cannabis onto a military base – "and bad behaviour will result in the culprit being thrown in the brig and then returned to this hellhole. Any questions?"

It was the butch woman who spoke first. "What's in it for us?"

Joshua pretended to consider. "Well, you'll be out of here for a start," he said. "And then there's the extra pay and the chance to live a normal life afterwards. I can even throw in a shitload of money if you want. Those who survive will be set up for life."

"I don't know," the weasel-faced man said. "I hated military discipline when I joined."

"So why did you join?" another man snapped. He'd been thrown in the brig for rioting on base. "Sir, I accept. What do we do to join?"

"You have two hours to decide," Joshua said. "If you want to join the team, call the warden and inform him. You'll be shipped to a base and transferred to the squadron within two days. If not...well, thank you for considering it."

He nodded to them and strode away, leaving them alone to think while he returned to his flitter. Organising a small squadron was tricky. He'd never had to outfit warships before, let alone ensure that there was nothing onboard that had come directly from Earth. But then, the crew DNA alone would prove that they'd been human. The Admiral might be disappointed if *anything* survived a ship's destruction.

But the Admiral had been right. There was no other choice.

Chapter Four

"Where the hell did you get these clunkers?"

Joshua chuckled. *Clunkers* was an apt description for six starships that had been constructed over seven hundred years ago and traded from planet to planet until they had finally been purchased by the human race. The hulls were the only parts of the ships still original, but much of the interiors were still decades old. They'd been updated over the years by successive owners. The Association had long since lost track of what had happened to them, or of their current capabilities. Hundreds of other starships had fallen into unsafe hands over the centuries.

The Association's drive fields allowed it to design starships to fit their sense of aesthetics, without needing to worry about visible drives. Each of the starships was a flattened oval shape, bristling with weapons and sensor blisters. Like most starships designed by the Cats, they wouldn't require any reconfiguration to be used by other humanoid races – and the interiors would be standardised. Up close, he could make out scorch marks on the hulls, the legacy of years spent serving less savoury owners. Piracy was epidemic along the Rim and even in some of the inner sectors as the Association lost interest in patrolling the space lanes.

It didn't surprise Joshua to know that the Federation had established some links with the pirates. There was an entire network of planets and settled asteroids out beyond the Rim, worlds colonized by races intent on escaping the Association and the brushfire wars between states that wanted to take its place as the premier galactic power. Joshua had even heard rumours that thousands of humans had headed out to the Rim themselves, particularly after Terra Nova.

He smiled as the shuttle drew alongside the light cruiser and mated airlocks, before there was a faint hiss as pressure equalised and allowed his small crew to board their ships.

The clunkers had been hidden along the edge of the solar system, well away from any prying eyes, and the flight from Earth had taken hours. There was little point in establishing a quantum gate so far from Earth, even if its presence wouldn't have been a flag to hostile powers that something was afoot at the edge of Earth's system. But then, the Association and the other Galactics tended not to think about the vast reaches of space between stars, not when they could skip through quantum space and reach their destinations far quicker than sublight traffic through normal space. The hidden colonies along the Rim used that trait to their advantage. Even with the most advanced sensor technology in existence, it was incredibly difficult to spot a hidden base unless it was radiating betraying emissions. A smart crew could remain hidden even at very close range.

The dry air of the clunker caught at his throat as soon as he stepped through the airlock and boarded the ship. Earth hadn't had much time to work on the ships before committing them to the raiding party, but the engineers had had time to scrub the air processors and fumigate the ships. The Association was plagued with infestations of small rodent and insect-like creatures that had hitched away on starships and been accidentally transplanted to a new world, the results of careless policies back at the start of their expansion era. These days, starships were regularly vented by their crews every few months. It didn't seem to help very much. Terra Nova had reported infestations of cockroaches before the Hegemony had bullied humanity into giving up the colony world.

"No stink," Lieutenant Karla Richardson said. She'd punched her commanding officer – she claimed it was for incompetence. The court-martial board hadn't been impressed, even though she'd had a good record and a promising career. "That's a surprise."

Joshua nodded. He'd had enough experience with starships that had passed from owner to owner before winding up in his hands to know that some ships weren't properly cared for by their crews. It was insane not to take good care of the only thing protecting them from vacuum, but some crews just didn't seem to take it seriously. The

Association had assisted hundreds of races to climb to the stars, often without teaching them the basics of how their technology worked. Many of those races were utterly dependent upon the Association for spare parts and even basic maintenance, just as Third World countries had bought weapons and supplies from the West on Earth. Joshua had never been able to discover if it had been deliberate malice or carelessness – but then, the Cats had never been a particularly malicious race. It was more likely that they'd assumed that their clients would either learn how to maintain their ships or remain dependent upon the Association.

"The crews did some work on her before handing her over to us," Joshua said. He wondered, briefly, what would happen to the engineering crews, before remembering that the Federation Navy needed all the trained technicians it could get. They'd probably be sent to Titan Base or somewhere else isolated until the war began. He would have preferred to take them with his small squadron, but Admiral Sampson would never have agreed to let them go. "We need to check the command systems first, and then go over the entire ship in cynical detail."

The Association's founders had better eyesight than humanity, eyes that could see into the parts of the spectrum that were invisible to humans. Their command and control systems had been designed to be replaced if necessary by equipment more suited to other races; indeed, judging from the command nodes on the bridge, someone already had replaced them. Joshua powered up the first console and input the command codes, accessing the ship's processor and ordering it to start the power-up sequence. There was a long pause and then the main lighting came on, revealing the bridge in all of its glory. Unlike the freighters Joshua knew and loved, there was a command chair in the center of the bridge for the commanding officer, one designed for a humanoid form. He could have sat on it comfortably.

"Nice," Karla commented. She ran her hand over one of the other consoles, bringing up a status display. The ship's fusion reactor was powering up, flash-waking the rest of its systems. Passive sensors activated, revealing the other five starships floating nearby, but little else. There was very little commercial activity along the edge of the solar system, apart from a handful of comet miners angling comets into the inner system and aiming them at Venus or Mars. The water-ice within the comets would help the terraforming projects. "It's almost as good as new."

Joshua shrugged. "Bring over the rest of the crew," he ordered. "We need to check this ship completely before we even consider leaving the solar system."

The Association had once had a mania for registering and certifying starships and their standards were still used throughout the galaxy. Every ship was supposed to pass basic checks before being allowed to leave the shipyard, and be regularly retested just to make sure that the crews weren't allowing their ships to sink into disrepair, but many commercial ships evaded the checks or falsified their results. Independent owner-captains lived on the margins and had no choice but to cut costs wherever possible, even though it risked running afoul of the law. Besides, they also knew exactly where they *could* cut corners. And it was their lives at risk if the life support failed while they were in quantum space.

Once the crew had boarded the starships, Joshua started to work through the entire set of checklists provided by the Association. Like so much else, the checklists were standardised and easy – if tedious – to follow. Five hours passed slowly as each system was checked and rechecked, a handful of components were marked down for replacement, and then supplies were drawn from the nearby stockpile to replace broken equipment. One of the ships had had a busted air processor that might well have killed the crew, if they'd failed to realise the danger in time to save themselves from the effects of oxygen deprivation. The supposedly infallible atmosphere monitoring systems had failed. Another had had the targeting system for its main phase cannon removed before they had been passed on to humanity. Joshua rolled his eyes when he heard the news. Someone probably intended to pass on the targeting system to pirates, confident that no one would be able to trace it back to the source.

Finally, the Clunker Fleet was ready to depart. Two smaller freighters would accompany them into quantum space, carrying what few supplies could be borrowed from Earth and some trade goods. It was a general rule of space trading that items gained value the further they were from their point of origin. Alcohol affected several other races like it did humans and vodka, scotch and rum had become surprisingly popular among the Galactics. Joshua had used wines to make money in the past, when he'd been buying other starships and trying to break into markets that were jealously guarded by commercial cartels. Even cheap wine on Earth could earn thousands of credits if sold to the right people.

"So," Karla said, finally. "What are we going to call the ships?"

Joshua had thought about that on the shuttle. The Association's ship naming conventions were incomprehensible to human minds, governed by a logic that didn't quite seem to make sense. Most of the other races had their own naming conventions, with the Hegemony taking the prize for producing the most pretentious names for their ships. But the ship had been renamed so many times that no trace remained of her original name and her previous owners had been careful to remove all traces of their own use before letting her out of their hands.

"This one will be *Blackbeard*," he said, finally. He would have preferred to use names that suggested that the ships were being operated by the Hegemony's more powerful neighbours, but they might have taken offense and – if they found out the truth – joined the war against Earth. "The other ship commanders can pick their own names – as long as they're ones we can write down."

Karla chuckled. One tradition the Federation Navy had borrowed from the Association was allowing small craft crewmen to name their own ships. Some were sentimental, some were amusing... and some no one dared write down. Every so often, senior officers would consider revising that policy, particularly after the media picked up on a particularly embarrassing nickname and gleefully posted it all over Earth and the Nine Stars. No one would forget the *Horny Goat* in a hurry.

"Not that we're going to be announcing our names to our victims," he added, after a moment. "Even flying the Jolly Roger would point them to Earth."

"Unless someone nonhuman learned it from our culture," Karla pointed out. The Galactics *loved* many of Earth's old movies. Even the Funks of the Hegemony consumed westerns and blockbuster action movies, no matter how trite or overplayed. "I'm pretty sure there are a few pirate movies out there too."

"It can't be helped," Joshua said. There was nothing they could do if an alien pirate ship started pretending to be human. Instead, he picked up one of the datapads and checked the final results from the other teams. "We're going to leave tomorrow, ideally. The supplies should be ready for us by then. Do you want to record a message for your family?"

Karla shook her head. "I ran away to join the Navy because of my family," she said. "They wanted me to work at their little mom and pop store, if you can imagine that. I would have died in that little town where the only fun was trying to get to second base with your cousin, and then marrying some inbred moron and having ten kids with him."

"You might not be coming back," Joshua warned her. "Are you sure...?"

"They will be much happier without a message from me," Karla said, firmly. "And don't you dare offer them my money if I die. They don't deserve it."

* * *

"We received an update from Captain Hastings," Commander Sooraya Qadir said. "*Cunningham* and *Halsey* have both completed their drive refurbishments and are ready for deployment. The 2nd Cruiser Squadron is now at full strength."

"Good," Tobias said. Sooraya was an oddity in the Federation Navy, a mustang officer who didn't come from one of the G13 nations. But then, given that she'd found the strength to escape Afghanistan and join Earth's defence force, she deserved a chance to show what she could do. Starship command was unlikely, but a gunboat was a definite possibility. "I assume that the other squadrons have completed their own checks?"

"Yes, sir," Sooraya assured him. "The IG teams will be on their way to the squadrons in another day, unless you wish to bring the inspection schedule forward."

Tobias shook his head. The Federation Navy had been obsessive about readiness long before he'd become Chief of Naval Operations. Earth couldn't afford to copy the sloppy maintenance habits of the lesser Galactics, even with the reliable and interchangeable Association technology. The entire fleet – two hundred starships in all – had to be ready for immediate action if the Hegemony decided to move up their timetable and annexe Earth without bothering with a surrender demand. A commanding officer who allowed his ship to become unfit for service would be relieved and never allowed to command again, no matter what political or national patrons he had.

"No need," he said, finally. He glanced down at the datapad in his hand. "Did Colonel Williams get back to us about ammunition stockpiles?"

"Not as yet, sir," Sooraya said. "I believe that his staff are still chasing up the suppliers and attempting to ensure a speedy delivery."

"I should hope so," Tobias grunted. Earth had never performed a full-scale deep-space exercise before and all sorts of tiny problems were coming to light. It would have provided the Federation Navy with all sorts of useful data on how well its procedures worked in real life, if the exercise had been real. But instead they were going to war. The young men and women under his command didn't even realise that they would be seeing action within a month. He had faith in them, but so much was a dangerous unknown. How well would Earth's surprises perform in a real battle? "Inform the IG that I will be joining the inspection party for one of the cruisers. I'll pick the ship tomorrow morning."

"Yes, sir," Sooraya said.

Tobias smiled. "Thank you," he said. "Dismissed."

He watched her leave the compartment, the door sliding closed behind her, and then looked back down at the datapad. Hundreds of readiness reports scrolled up in front of him, each one from a single starship. The Federation Navy had worked hard to cut paperwork back to an absolute minimum, but even so there was just so much to review and remember. He was going to lead the fleet into battle in a month, and then...? They'd find out how good their training and equipment actually was when compared to the Galactics.

One of the reports caught his eye and he smiled. The small group of reporters who had been embedded in the Navy were complaining about the food – and the lockdown. That wasn't too surprising; every reporter he'd ever met had been a prima donna, convinced that their shit didn't stink. The ones he'd met before First Contact had demanded good food, better accommodations and complete access to everything, which they'd shared with the enemy. At least the Federation Navy could take a harder line. A reporter who broke the lockdown without permission would be thrown into the brig and transferred to the penal colony on the moon. Given what was at stake, it was unlikely that anyone would complain.

The next report was a contingency plan for calling up national military forces to reinforce the Federation Marines. For political reasons, the Federation Marines had been limited to ten thousand men, a force that could deliver one hell of a punch, but not occupy an entire planet or pose a threat to Earth's independent nations. Tobias had always thought it a silly thing for the politicians to worry themselves about – the Federation Navy would have had a mutiny on its hands if it had tried to bully any of the major nations – yet there had been no choice. Reinforcements would be provided by national military units, if necessary. They couldn't be called up until the war began, for fear it might tip off the Hegemony that something was being planned. God alone knew if the Federation's counter-intelligence operations had worked as well as they hoped.

Shaking his head, he stood up and looked over at the display on the far wall. His office was buried deep under the lunar rock, but like most Luna residents he'd chosen to display an image from the outside world in his private compartment. Earth hung in the sky over the moon, shining blue-green against the darkness of space. Tobias had visited a dozen worlds, including some inhabited by races that would have found Earth unpleasant for one reason or another, but Earth was special. It was the cradle of the human race, the source of mankind. The thought of Earth being dominated by the Hegemony was intolerable. It must not be allowed to happen.

It won't be allowed to happen, he promised himself, firmly. The plan he and his staff had devised would give the Hegemony enough of a bloody nose to make them break off and leave Earth alone for a few decades. And in that time, humanity would become far more advanced than they could hope to match. If some of the programs bore fruit, the Hegemony wouldn't stand a chance.

Picking up the datapad, he returned to his notes. There was too much to do in the time before they went to war.

Chapter Five

"I'm afraid that it's worse than we thought," Conrad said into the camera of a tiny recording booth. It was soundproofed, but not - quite - enough to drown the bustling sound of his activating Marine unit outside. "There's a full-scale exercise under way and we're being deployed out into deep space. They're going to be transporting us to the assault carrier in an hour or so - probably longer. Hurry up and wait is still a part of military life."

He hesitated. "The boss hasn't given us any details - I don't think he knows much more than he's told us - but he has warned that we're going to be away for several weeks, at least. Lots of bitching in the barracks, but no one is paying attention. We did volunteer for this shit, after all. I love you and I will return to you as soon as I can. Pray for me, OK?"

Conrad touched a key and the message stopped recording. He played it back, wondering if he sounded too mawkish, before deciding that it definitely came from the heart. Cindy would understand, he told himself firmly; her father, too, had been forced to put his duty ahead of his heart while he'd been in the service too. The thought that she might find someone else while he was gone... if he hadn't been sure of her, he wouldn't have asked her to marry him.

He sent the message, uploading it into the base's communications network. In lockdown, every message would be reviewed by senior staff before being transmitted to the recipient, ensuring that he couldn't say anything that might breach security. He still remembered the Marine who had been given an icy dressing down by his CO for recording himself masturbating for his girlfriend. The poor bastards' mates still called him by the nickname 'Wanker'.

The last few days had been a hassle, ever since the platoon had arrived in the forward base on Luna.

Everything had had to be checked, from armored combat suits to assault rifles, personal equipment and survival gear. The senior staff were insistent that everything had to be perfect, even though it was only an exercise. Some of the younger Marines had wondered out loud why they were being such assholes over each and every little detail. It was their job, Conrad had pointed out at the time, but part of him wondered if something was going on that the brass hadn't bothered to tell them about. Perhaps the Hegemony had decided to move in on Clarke or one of the other colonies and the Federation planned, this time, to resist.

He took one last glance at the photograph of Cindy he'd hidden in his uniform and strode out of the room, leaving it vacant for the next Marine. The corridors were jam-packed with Marines carrying supplies and equipment from the storage dumps to their barracks. Sergeants were bellowing orders, trying to keep the entire brigade moving towards its eventual destination. There was order to the chaos, even though a civilian would have seen nothing more than a group of muscular men carrying junk around the base. Conrad evaded a pair of Marines carrying a heavy plasma cannon and walked into the barracks used by his unit, 3 Company, 2 Battalion. The younger Bootnecks were frantically preparing for the deployment while the older and more experienced men were taking it all in their stride. Some of them had finished preparing their bags and were taking the opportunity to catch up on their sleep. Conrad cleared his throat loudly and they snapped awake.

"We are to board the shuttle to the assault carrier at 1300 precisely," Conrad informed his men. The Federation Marines were less formal than most military services, but discipline didn't suffer. Every Marine had been in a highly-trained unit before trying out for the Federation Marines. "The time is now" – he made a show of checking his watch – "1223. We will leave this room at 1240 and march down to the shuttle. Any questions?"

Jimmy, the joker of the platoon, stuck up a hand. "What is the price of sliced ham, per portion?"

"More than you can afford if you keep earning demerits," Conrad said, dryly. "Any *relevant* questions?"

There were none. Instead, the Marines hastily finished packing and pulled on their rucksacks, each man checking his partner's bag and uniform for missing items. The procedure had been drummed into their heads since the first day on Mars, where the Federation Marines practiced serving in a hostile environment. Space could kill someone far easier than the Hegemony's soldiers – and all it took was a moment of carelessness. Too many people from Earth got to the asteroids, or even the moon, and then found that they had qualified for a posthumous Darwin Award. Even experienced Marines could be caught out.

"Follow me," Conrad ordered, when his watch reached 1240. He would have chewed out any Marine who wasn't ready in time, but they were all ready. "Jimmy – bring up the rear."

The platoon followed him outside, linking up with the rest of the company and marching down towards the shuttles. They'd done it before, thousands of times, but this felt different even to the rawest Marine. If the brass had intended to make them exercise perfectly, as if they were already at war, they'd succeeded. The shuttles, black-painted boxy shapes that looked like something out of a low-budget science-fiction movie, were waiting for them. Their pilots weren't exactly Marines, but they'd trained alongside the Bootnecks for years, clocking up hours in their craft. And they were on the front lines themselves, which won them some respect. They were hardly REMFs.

"Take your seats, if you please," Conrad ordered sardonically, counting his men into the shuttle. Each shuttle would lift forty men to the assault carrier, and then transport them down to the surface of Clarke or wherever they'd be carrying out the live-fire parts of the exercise. "Don't wait up. We've got work to do."

There was a crackle from the intercom. "Welcome to Marine Flight 001," a mock-falsetto voice said. "Take your seats and long-legged stewardesses will be along shortly to buckle you in."

The younger Marines chuckled at the joke. Conrad and the older sweats rolled their eyes. The joke hadn't been new when the pilots had started cracking it, even if it did help to dispel the tension in the air. Live-fire exercises were deadly serious and Marines had been known to be badly injured, or killed, in the crossfire. No precautions could guarantee perfect safety – and besides, none of them had signed up because they wanted a safe life. There was very little safety for any human in the universe, but they could have stayed on Earth and been as safe as the planet itself.

There was a long pause, and then the shuttle hummed to life around them. The gravity field seemed to fluctuate as the craft lifted itself off the landing pad and rose up above the Luna surface, heading for the mighty assault carrier. Each of the three carriers humanity had built were huge, the largest and most complex starships humanity had yet constructed. It was daunting to realise that the Galactics had built much larger ships – and that one of their superdreadnoughts could vaporise the assault carriers if they got into weapons range.

He pushed that thought aside and concentrated on composing his mind. Once they reached the carrier, they'd have to get into their compartments and get ready for operations – and then they would be preparing during the trip through quantum space. No rest for the wicked – or Federation Marines.

* * *

The Federation had endured a long political debate over naming conventions for its starships, one that had almost threatened to bring the entire edifice crashing down. Adrienne Lawson had heard that some countries had demanded that their names be selected, even though they'd made little contribution to the cost of the ships. Eventually, the Federation Navy had decided to name its assault carriers after famous generals – and selected the first three names from history. *Wellington, Napoleon* and *Zhukov* had been political compromises, ones that still aroused debate on the internet. The Emperor Napoleon had, in the end, lost the wars named after him.

Adrienne watched, fascinated, as the assault carrier slowly came into view. It – she – was a colossal boxy design, with launch bays hanging down from her superstructure. She was studded with sensor blisters, or perhaps they were weapons systems. The Federation Navy had been coy about precisely what weapons outfitted its ships, hoping to prevent the Galactics from hearing about any unpleasant surprises that might be waiting for them. One single assault carrier alone looked capable of dealing with any opponent. And yet the briefers had warned that they could never be included in the line of battle. They couldn't stand up to heavily-armed warships.

"She's an amazing piece of work," her minder said. Lieutenant Barbara – "call me Barbie" – Greenhorn had been assigned to Adrienne shortly after she'd arrived at Armstrong City and had been escorted to Naval HQ. Barbie looked blonde, so blonde it was easy to believe that she was dumb, and yet the Navy would hardly have assigned an idiot to chaperone a reporter. Adrienne had to keep reminding herself that Barbie was almost certainly nowhere near as dumb as she looked. "Do you know how long she is?"

Adrienne shook her head. It was difficult for her to tell sizes in space. "Over two kilometres long," Barbie informed her, with an air of someone imparting a valuable piece of knowledge. "Each of them can carry an entire reinforced Marine brigade – that's over four thousand troops – and land them on any planet the Navy desired within minutes. At crash-launch, they can put over two hundred shuttles into space..."

She grinned at Adrienne, who smiled back. "Everything has to work like clockwork on one of those machines," Barbie added. "We have to be careful not to get in the way."

Wellington grew until Adrienne could see nothing, but the darkened ship's hull. The shuttle altered course slightly and headed down towards one of the launch tubes, leading right into the hangar bay. There was a brief fizz of energy around the shuttle as it passed through the force field keeping the atmosphere inside the bay, before settling down on the deck. Outside, Adrienne could see hundreds of men in brightly-coloured uniforms moving pallets of supplies and weapons around the bay. It was a massive compartment, but tiny compared to the entire ship. The briefing she'd read – carefully edited to ensure that no useful details leaked to the enemy – had said that each assault carrier had no less than eight hangar bays.

She stepped out of the shuttle and tasted the ship's air, scented with engine oil and the familiar smell of a starship crammed with living breathing humans. It was almost like walking on one of the aircraft carriers supporting operations in the Middle East, carriers that would be blown out of the water in seconds if someone hostile took the high orbitals away from the human race. They'd never be built again in human shipyards, something she was inclined to regret. They had been amazing ships.

"Stay inside the marked walkways," Barbie said, pointing to the yellow lines on the deck. "No one is supposed to go outside the walkways without permission from the crew chief – even an Admiral would have to ask permission before entering. It's a safety precaution to prevent accidents."

"Of course," Adrienne murmured. "Do you have many accidents?"

"Something always goes wrong when we prepare ships for departure in a hurry," Barbie admitted. "It's a good idea to take as many precautions as possible, particularly when live weapons are being moved from deck to deck." She nodded towards one of the small groups of crewmen, who were pushing a pallet across the deck. "Hellfire missiles, designed for launch to suppress enemy air-space defences. Also can be fired at enemy aircraft, but they're not ideal for such missions."

Adrienne looked up at her. "Why can't you build missiles that can accomplish anything you wanted?"

Barbie smiled, launching into what was clearly a pre-prepared lecture. "Each specific task requires the missile to be different for optimum results," she said. "There are limits to how far we can reprogram them for different operations. A missile configured for deployment against a starship would be massive overkill if deployed on a planetary surface. Even the warheads are different depending on the missile type."

She led the way out of the hangar bay and up through a network of corridors, crammed with crewmen working desperately on tasks Adrienne couldn't understand. "I should remind you," Barbie added, "that anywhere outside your quarters is restricted unless you have me with you. The crew doesn't have time to nursemaid you around the ship. I also need to review any recordings you take before they are transmitted back to Earth."

So I can't talk to anyone who would give me an unofficial line, Adrienne thought, without rancour. She'd expected as much. It would take some time to build up her own network of informants, people who would talk to her even without a minder. The trick would be in figuring out what was true and what was crap put forward by someone who resented not being promoted.

"You can have some time to freshen up and then there's a video briefing with Brigadier Jones, the CO of 1 Federation Marine Brigade," Barbie continued, after a moment. "I understand that you have already met the Brigadier...?"

"Only a brief meeting while I was on Luna," Adrienne confirmed. "He congratulated me on my reports from Saudi and said that he hoped I'd do as well here. But what are we going to do?"

"Exercise, of course," Barbie said. She grinned, again. Several crewmen took more than casual notice of her chest, despite her uniform. "This is the most complex exercise the Federation Navy has ever carried out. It is *important* that the Galactics understand that humanity isn't a small power, barely capable of hanging onto its own homeworld, but a formidable race capable of making its will felt in the sector. Your reports will help shape their impressions of our power."

"I see," Adrienne said. It seemed like a great deal of effort for a very small return, but the Federation Navy presumably knew what it was doing. Another passing crewman checked her out, and then had the grace to blush when she looked back at him. "Aren't there many women on this ship?"

"The Marines are all men," Barbie said. "The Federation Navy gives women equal opportunities, but there is no guarantee that there will be equal outcomes. Men outnumber the women twelve to one." She shrugged. "Not everyone in the Navy comes from a culture that accepts women as equals in the military. A Russian Captain was relieved of duty and discharged for harassing one of his female subordinates, which was one of the nastier incidents.

"And there *are* strict rules on fraternising between the sexes while the ship is away from home," she added. "You're forbidden to sleep with anyone in your chain of command, or someone senior or junior to yourself. The Navy generally ignores sex between equals, but the commanders come down like a hammer on anyone who violates the regulations. For an officer, it can ruin their career; for a crewman, it can mean discharge or time in the brig."

They stopped outside a cabin door. "These are your quarters for the next few months," Barbie said, changing the subject. "Like I said, stay inside when you're not with me. In the unlikely event of the Captain requiring my services in another position, I'll see to it that someone brings you food from the mess."

"I feel like a prisoner already," Adrienne commented.

"I'll tell you the same thing that officers have been telling their grumblers for years," Barbie said, more seriously. "You volunteered for this. If you didn't want to be under harsh discipline and work like a mad bastard for the next five years, you shouldn't have joined the military. Or embedded yourself in the military, for that matter."

"I suppose," Adrienne said. She stepped into the cabin. "And thanks for showing me around."

"You're welcome," Barbie said. "I live to serve."

* * *

Joshua looked down at the control panel and then tapped a key, activating the quantum gate generator. It came to life quickly, ready to hurl the starship into quantum space. Each of the Clunkers had a surprisingly modern quantum drive, but perhaps that should have been expected when the ships had been refurbished so often. Besides, it would be harder to operate if they had to wait ten minutes between opening gates and slipping into quantum space. Civilian drives left their ships unable to return to quantum space until the drive had repowered, leaving them vulnerable to pirates and hostile powers.

"Drive online," he said. He'd decided to pilot the ship himself, at least for the first voyage. The ship might have been reliable – the Association built to last – but he needed to get a feel for how she operated. Some ships could perform amazing manoeuvres and others had problems making even a tiny course change. "All other ships confirm ready?"

"Everyone says they're ready," Karla informed him. He'd had to switch around some of the crews until he found combinations that actually worked, in terms of interpersonal chemistries and styles. He hadn't told them exactly what they would be doing, but enough had leaked out to give them a good idea. The more greedy of them were already speculating on how wealthy some carefully-targeted piracy could make them – if, of course, they lived long enough to spend it. "Captain?"

Joshua triggered the quantum drive. Space seemed to blur in front of *Blackbeard*, shimmering into the eerie lights of quantum space. The higher-energy dimension – at least according to the scientists who'd studied what little the Association had told them about quantum space – allowed starships to move at speeds that, in normal space, were many times that of the speed of light. And with their own drives, the Clunker Fleet wouldn't even need its own quantum gates. They could operate completely independently.

"Well," he said, finally. "Only a month to go until we reach our operations area. And then the fun really begins."

Chapter Six

It was time.

Admiral Tobias Sampson stood on the bridge of *Nimitz* and watched as the First Strike Fleet prepared to enter quantum space. Fifteen cruisers, each one more technologically advanced than anything the Hegemony had ever seen, escorted by fifty destroyers, three assault carriers and a small fleet of freighters with military-grade drives. Apart from a handful of officers, no one on the fleet knew where they were really going – or what they were going to do – but they'd responded splendidly. The fleet was ready for war.

He closed his eyes for a long moment, recalling the final meeting between him and the Federation Council. There had been no reason for hope, no reason to believe that the Association would stand up to the Hegemony, no matter what Ambassador Li did on Center. Federation Intelligence had even reported that the Hegemony's Queens were already dividing up human space between them, ensuring that their clan maintained sole grasp of humanity and the worlds it had developed. There would be war. Two weeks from the moment they entered quantum space, they would reach Terra Nova and start the war.

The thought was chilling. He'd *seen* war; humanity's petty fighting on its own planet and a handful of brief brushfires between the Galactics. Many of the fine men and women under his command would die, their bodies vaporised as fusion plants blew, preventing them from being laid to rest on their homeworld. It was even possible that one of the destroyed ships would be *Nimitz*, that he himself would never return home. Civilian leaders often talked about war as if it was the easy option, but the cost was always high. Tobias had steeled himself to start and fight a war more desperate than any in humanity's history, yet now part of him wanted to quail. A lost war would be utterly disastrous for the human race. It might mean the end of humanity itself.

But there was no choice. Fight now or fight later, under worse conditions.

He looked over at Captain Kevin Rupert, CO of the teardrop-shaped starship. "Take us into quantum space," he ordered quietly. Once they were in quantum space, he'd issue the order for the commanding officers to open the sealed orders from the Federation Council, authorising the attack. "It's time to start moving."

Earth vanished from the display, replaced by the flickering lights of quantum space. Tobias felt another pang, knowing that they were leaving Earth critically exposed to the Galactics if they chose this moment to invade. There were two more cruiser squadrons in the solar system, but both of them were still working up after being released from the shipyards. They couldn't have put up more than a brief fight if the Hegemony launched a sneak attack of its own. The sociologists claimed that that was unthinkable – they wouldn't bother when they were about to get the territory legally – but Tobias was less sure. Respect for the Association's law had been falling sharply long before Mentor had arrived at Earth and brought the human race into space.

Navigating through quantum space was a tricky task. Other races might have figured out how to enter quantum space, but it was the Association that had devised the network of quantum gates and navigation beacons, opening up vast swathes of space for exploration and colonisation. Outside the Association, beyond the Rim, navigation was much harder. Starships had to return to normal space frequently just to check their positions. Even the most advanced quantum drive in existence would have problems jumping in and out of quantum space so often. Operation Bolthole's ship had the most capable navigation computers mankind had been able to devise and yet they'd still have problems finding a safe world to colonize.

"Open your sealed orders, Captain," he ordered quietly. "And then join me for the all-ships conference at 1450."

"Yes, sir," Rupert said, quietly.

The Association Navy had developed traditions over the thirty thousand years the Cats had spent in space that had proved incredibly difficult to dislodge. One of those traditions was a form of consensual decision-making that would have been intolerable to any human commander. Captains of individual starships would participate in democratic debates about their objectives and how they'd achieve them, finally voting to endorse or reject a particular operational plan. Humanity hadn't been able to build ships large enough to hold all of the fleet's commanding officers, which meant that meetings had to be virtual. It did ensure that discussion remained focused on the objectives at hand. Tobias was determined that while Captains would have ultimate authority over their own ships, the Federation Navy's Admirals would set overall policy – without allowing junior officers to vote on it. No effective military force could function democratically.

One by one, the Captains and Brigadiers commanding his ships and Marine units signed into the secure conference system. In theory, it was impossible to intercept transmissions in quantum space except at very close range; in practice, no one knew for sure. The tachyon bursts the navigation beacons used were detectable at long range. Tobias had ordered that all transmissions were to be heavily encrypted, just in case. Paranoia was a survival trait if they really were out to get you.

"Gentlemen," he said, by way of greeting. "I assume that you have read your orders?"

He smiled at the faces looking back at him. Some looked shocked, as if they'd really expected nothing more than an exercise, or that humanity wouldn't set out to *start* a war. Others looked delighted, seeing it as a chance to avenge the humiliation of Terra Nova and liberate a large human population from the claws of the Hegemony. Several of them had probably checked and rechecked the orders, confirming that they came directly from the Federation

Council. The worst nightmare of a thousand states was a rogue officer starting a war.

"In two weeks, we will arrive at Terra Nova," Tobias said. The operations plan hadn't been loaded into the fleet's datanet, not yet. "A tanker with HE3 from Jupiter will be visiting the planet shortly before we arrive. The crew will use military-grade sensors to pinpoint the locations of the Hegemony's starships and then meet us in quantum space, allowing us to target our exit with pinpoint precision. We will engage the enemy as soon as we leave quantum space.

"Our objective is the complete destruction of that Hegemony force and the liberation of Terra Nova," he continued. "Once the fleet has cleared orbital space of enemy ships, the Marines will be landed to liberate the planet and round up the Hegemony population. Their client races will be permitted to remain under human rule, if they wish, but the Funks themselves will be removed from the planet. However" – his gaze swept around the holographic faces – "I want to make it clear that there are to be no atrocities. The population is to be rounded up with the minimum necessary force consistent with the safety of our troops. We do not need something the Hegemony can use as a propaganda tool against us.

"Assault Force Two will concentrate on the Hegemony base at Garston. As that base doesn't have any major combatants, the overall objective will be to either capture or destroy the orbital installations, preventing them from being used against us. Depending on the outcome at Terra Nova, we may move cruisers forward to Garston and then strike deeper into the Hegemony's space. Garston itself is useless to us; we won't bother invading and occupying the world once we've smashed their military bases from orbit."

"I figure that we could use a whole new habitable world," Captain Zeke drawled.

"It has a population of nearly ten million intelligent beings, mainly Funks," Brigadier Jones pointed out. "Do you propose to evict them all, or merely keep them as slaves? Or maybe we should push them all into death camps and commit genocide?"

"They took one of our worlds," Zeke said, sharply. "Why shouldn't we...?"

"Because we are a small power and we don't want to either force the Hegemony to rally around their Empress and do what it takes to defeat us, or for other powers to start viewing us as a danger and join the war against us," Tobias said. "Garston will be immaterial to the war once we've taken out the base and occupied the cloudscoop and we will not waste manpower occupying it."

He looked over at Jones's face. "National units on Earth will be called up as soon as they receive a burst transmission reporting our success," he continued. "They will relieve the Marines for further duties, allowing us to head further into Hegemony space if necessary and land on their military colonies."

There was a long pause. "Are there any points that need to be raised before I transmit the operations plan to you?"

"I must say that I find the idea of starting a war to be distasteful," Captain Garibaldi said. "Even if we're not about to bite off more than we can chew, we... we don't start wars."

"The war started the moment they bullied us into giving up Terra Nova," Zeke said, flatly. "All we've had since then is an uneasy truce, one that could have been terminated at any point they desired. How long will it be before they stop extorting HE3 from us and start demanding political control instead?"

"Not long," Tobias said. "You'll find the background brief included in the operational plan, but the short version of the story is that they're pretty much on the verge of claiming political control over Earth. War is coming whatever we do – we strike now or we risk being crushed by superior force."

"I understand that many of you have doubts," he added. "Those doubts will also exist on Earth when the population realises that the war is underway. This is a gamble, one that might backfire and cost us everything we've worked for over the past fifteen years, ever since we realised that the greater universe was not going to ignore us. But I have faith that each and every one of you will do their utmost to ensure that we win this war. We will claw out our place in galactic society and prove to the predators out there that we are not to be trifled with."

He stood up. "I'll be making a general broadcast to the fleet this evening," he concluded. "Until then, study the operational plans and consider possible alternatives. We will reconvene tomorrow."

One by one, the holographic faces blinked out of existence, leaving Tobias alone with his thoughts – and his worries.

There was one thing he hadn't told them. They all had orders to destroy the sealed orders once they'd confirmed them to their subordinates. What they didn't know was that the official orders would make it look as if Tobias had launched the attack on his own, without permission from higher authority. If the war went badly wrong, Tobias would be blamed, perhaps giving Earth some protection.

It wasn't much, but it was all he had.

And his own death was a small price for humanity remaining alive.

* * *

It seemed to be a rule that larger ships, with much more internal volume than their smaller cousins, had less room for junior officers, crewmen and Marines. Even *Wellington*, over two kilometres long, crammed thousands of Marines into tightly-confined spaces. Some of the crew had even been forced to sleep on the hangar deck because additional technicians had been taken onboard before they'd left Earth. To Conrad, it all added up to trouble. There was little need to bring civilian techs onboard unless there was a truly desperate requirement for trained manpower.

Regulations stated that each Marine had to spend at least two hours per day exercising in the ship's gym and running laps through internal passageways. Like the rest of the ship, it was crammed with Marines, most performing press-ups on the deck or using muscle-building machines to give themselves a proper workout. Conrad was exchanging places with two other sergeants, allowing him to get in his own workout. No Federation Marine sergeant – or officer – could afford to skip his exercises, particularly in front of the men. Few would trust a sergeant who didn't lead by example, even if he was supposed to be supervising them at the time.

He looked up as nine chimes rang through the ship's intercom, calling them to attention. Throughout the gym, Marines stopped exercising and stood up, listening carefully.

"This is Admiral Sampson," a voice said. Conrad had met the Admiral once, back when he'd been stationed at Luna as part of the Naval HQ protection detachment. The Admiral sounded older than he remembered, picking his words carefully. "Ever since First Contact, ever since learning that the galaxy is filled with predators, we have known that we would one day have to fight for our freedom. What happened at Terra Nova taught us that nothing, but force would convince the Galactics to leave us in peace. Our time has run out. The Hegemony intends to claim our worlds and enslave the human race."

Conrad felt, more than heard, the rumble that passed through the massive compartment. Some of the Marines had relatives on Terra Nova, under the Hegemony's jackboot. Others knew people who had family on the planet, or had watched in horror the reports filed by independent journalists who had been allowed to visit the occupied corridor. None of them would have tolerated the occupation any longer than strictly necessary.

"There is only one option," Sampson continued. "We must strike first, taking the offensive while we have the chance. Our target is Terra Nova, the world we claimed and settled before we were bullied into surrendering our people to alien oppression. We will liberate Terra Nova and teach the Hegemony that human slaves don't come cheap.

"It will be a hard war. I can offer no guarantees of victory, or even survival. But there comes a time when you have to stand up and fight, or submit to permanent slavery. Our fight – and our deaths – will buy every human a chance to breathe free. Earth expects that every man and woman on these ships will do their duty. I expect no less."

Conrad joined in the cheering that followed, privately congratulating himself on deducing that they were heading off to more than just another exercise. Marines were shouting and slapping hands, before gently being urged back to their workouts. The thought of going into war drove them forwards. There would never be a chance to rehearse the operation, not before they landed on Terra Nova. What little intelligence he'd seen suggested that the Hegemony had a major military base on the planet, protected by a force field that ensured that it couldn't simply be smashed from orbit. The Marines would have to take the planet by landing on the ground and crushing the Hegemony troops.

"Back to work, guys," he said. They'd have to review the intelligence on the Hegemony's ground soldiers and their weapon later on. Well-briefed soldiers tended to last longer than those kept ignorant by their superiors. "We're going to war."

* * *

Adrienne sat in her cabin, unable to believe what she'd just heard. They were going to war? The fleet was going to assault a world held by the Hegemony, a galactic power that far outmatched the human race? They were all going to die... she found herself shaking helplessly, sweat beading on her brow. She'd been into danger before, but it had been under controlled conditions, escorted by soldiers who knew how to protect her if necessary. Now... she was on a starship she knew to be fragile when compared to the massed energy batteries of Association-designed capital ships. And she was expected to follow the Marines down to Terra Nova, assuming they managed to land without being slaughtered.

She stood up, trying to control the shaking that threatened to overwhelm her. Logically, the military wouldn't have set out to start a war unless it was certain it could win, but cold logic provided no reassurance. And to think that she'd accepted the chance to embed without realising that something more important than simple exercises, no matter how radical, was underway. Maybe she should have asked more questions, or maybe she wouldn't have learned anything more until the war actually began. No one, even the Association, could transmit from quantum space to normal space. There would be no way for anyone to blow the secret until it was too late.

And there was no escape. Even if she protested, the fleet would still go to Terra Nova and launch its assault. And then she would have to explain to Ward why she hadn't filed any reports from the front line. It would certainly cost her the chance to win another prize, even if he didn't fire her on the spot. No one would trust her to carry out a sensitive assignment again.

She sat back down again and stared into the mirror, seeing her own face reflected back at her. She'd been in danger before, she reminded herself firmly, and she'd survived and reported back from the front lines. The danger wouldn't be any less if she hid in her cabin, or made a fuss and ended up in the brig. She would do her job to the best of her ability and survive the experience. After recording from Terra Nova itself, just after the liberation, there would be another prize for her. Assuming she survived the experience and the planet was actually liberated, of course.

By the time Barbie arrived to escort her on her first tour of the mammoth starship, she was ready to interview the entire crew for their reactions. None of them seemed in doubt about the likely outcome of the war. They were confident that humanity would win.

Adrienne could only hope that they were right.

Chapter Seven

Terra Nova had everything a spacefaring society could want, except a gas giant that could be mined for fuel. The Association had surveyed it while humanity was still mastering basic metalworking and deemed the system largely useless, not even bothering to plant a small colony on Terra Nova's surface. They hadn't even established a quantum gate in the system; the gate that served Terra Nova had been built by the Federation, the third quantum gate produced by human engineers. Gates were, by long convention, open to all, but the galactic powers that felt confident in their strength charged access fees. The Hegemony, with a major battle fleet in the system, were quite willing to tax human shipping heading to Terra Nova.

Pelican lumbered though the quantum gate and emerged into the Terra Nova system. Like most commercial shipping, the massive HE3 tanker possessed no quantum drive of her own and was completely dependent upon the quantum gates for FTL travel. Producing commercial ships was surprisingly cheap once someone had built the ship yards; after all, they really needed little more than life support and hull volume. *Pelican* looked crude, like a set of oil drums bolted together, but Captain William Zeller loved her. She was his ticket to see the universe.

Earth had established a cloudscoop over Jupiter shortly after Mentor had contacted the human race, providing vast quantities of HE3 to power the switch to fusion power and fuel Earth's growing fleet of starships. The Hegemony had demanded that Earth continue to supply Terra Nova with HE3, even though Earth no longer controlled the planet and there were gas giants nearer to the system than Sol. The Federation had made nothing more than a muted protest, after ONI pointed out that sending the freighters into the system would allow them to take a careful look at the Hegemony's fleet dispositions. One day, Earth would have the firepower to teach the Hegemony a lesson. Good intelligence would be needed on that day. *Pelican's* sensor suite was military-grade, far more sophisticated than any commercial ship would need for its routine activities. William would have expected the Hegemony to insist on searching his ship and demanding explanations for the advanced sensors, but they'd never bothered. He was unable to tell if that was arrogance or simple carelessness. What could tiny Earth's puny fleet do against five superdreadnoughts and their support ships?

"I'm picking up a challenge now," his pilot said. No separate disciplines on *Pelican*, even if she was a Federation Navy ship in all, but name. The crew officially worked for the Jupiter Consortium; unofficially, they were Federation Intelligence and ONI. "They're demanding that we pay our access fees or get back into quantum space."

"Charming," William said. A quick glance at the sensor take showed that the Hegemony's fleet was already coming into view, surrounding Orbit Station. Humans had built the station, back when Terra Nova had first been colonised, only to lose it to the Hegemony. These days, a tiny human staff maintained the station for their masters. They were one of the best sources of intelligence that humanity had. "Ship them some credits and request an orbital slot."

He waited patiently for the reply. The Association's currency was still in widespread use across the galaxy. Some of the younger races had their own currencies as well, but the Association credit was interchangeable throughout the entire known galaxy. Some economists had predicted that that would change rapidly once the Association collapsed completely, perhaps reducing interstellar economics to barter unless a successor power with the same clout as the Association arose rapidly. William hadn't bothered to try to follow their arguments. It was enough that Earth's small stockpile of credits was still good.

"They're telling us to dock at the fuel dump and start the transfer," the pilot said, after a moment. "Should I take us in?"

"The alternative is hanging around here," William pointed out, dryly. "Take us in."

Terra Nova grew rapidly on the viewscreen as they approached the planet. Like Earth, Terra Nova was a blue-green world, although there were only two main continents. No one was quite sure why some worlds evolved intelligent life and others didn't produce anything more interesting than versions of sheep and wolves; Terra Nova had produced few creatures larger than lizards or rodents. Crops and animals brought by humans from Earth had swiftly spread across the first continent, competing with the local fauna. Unlike Clarke, which was dominated by savage plant and animal life, Terra Nova's local wildlife hadn't been able to cope. Humanity had effectively terraformed the planet far quicker than either Mars or Venus.

The Hegemony battle squadron was orbiting the planet, sensors and weapons stepped down to prevent wear and tear. Each of the five superdreadnoughts possessed enough firepower to blast a planet into atoms, or dominate the skies so thoroughly that resistance would be impossible. They were hulking brutes, their hulls designed so that all who saw them would know just what they'd been designed to do. There was little of the elegance the Association had built into its explorer or cruise starships, none of the fancifulness that they worked into pleasure craft that didn't have to obey Newton's laws. The ships were intimidating, even from a distance. All of Earth had seen footage of similar ships in action, in the brushfire wars that had started to appear along the edge of Association space. Everyone *knew* that they were the most powerful and capable warships in existence. Nothing could stand up to them.

He tore his gaze away from the sensor feed as the tanker approached the fuel dump, a separate station in orbit around Terra Nova. It too was human technology, allowing vast quantities of HE3 to be stored well away from the planet's surface – and the civilians who had colonised the new world. The planners hadn't realised that having the fuel dump would make it far easier for a hostile force to dominate the planet – or perhaps they had, intending that *they* would be the hostile force. William had heard a hundred conspiracy theories about what the Federation intended to do with Terra Nova in the long term. Doling out fuel to power the colony's fusion reactors was such an easy way to control the planet that he'd be surprised if it had never occurred to the planners.

The tanker shuddered gently as she made contact with the platform and started to transfer the fuel. William left the automated systems to get on with it while he reviewed more of the sensor take from the system – and the planet below. The Hegemony military base, established right on top of Gagarin City, seemed to have grown larger in the months since he'd last surveyed the planet. They kept the human population under strict control, forbidding any further expansion, although many humans had managed to slip out of the city and into the undeveloped regions of the planet. Some reports suggested that there was even a small insurgency underway on Terra Nova. It couldn't come close to evicting the Hegemony from humanity's planet.

There were no new orbital fortifications beyond a small network of orbital weapons platforms. The Association, which had produced much of the Galactic military doctrine, had believed that starships were a better investment than orbital fortresses, pointing out that starships were mobile and could be moved from one system to another. Some of the most important worlds had heavy fixed defences – the Hegemony homeworld was supposed to be heavily fortified – but most colony worlds were barely defended. The OWPs could stand off a pirate ship, yet a small squadron could blast its way through them in minutes. Privately, William suspected that the Association needed to rethink its doctrine. It had been so long since the Cats had fought a proper war that they'd lost the habit of continually questioning and rewriting their contingency plans. If human military forces had lost that habit in a few years of peace, and had to redevelop it in a hurry when war appeared out of nowhere, how much harder would it be for a race that hadn't fought for thousands of years?

But maybe it wasn't entirely a bad thing, from humanity's point of view. Most of the Galactics had learned from the Association, concentrating on starships instead of orbital defences. There would be flaws in their doctrine, weaknesses that could be exploited by a human naval force with the willingness to fight back against the Hegemony and the other galactic bullies. They'd learn, of course – some of them had probably been learning in the brushfire wars – but could they learn as fast as humanity?

The Association claimed that most races shared the same basic level of intelligence. Some races had traits that bent them towards one kind of thinking or another, or lacked the emotions that drove humanity, yet there were no races that thought significantly *faster* than anyone else. The cultural stasis that had gripped most of the galaxy came from the Association, from its stagnation and slow decline, not from anything intrinsic to the Galactics. As the established order continued to disintegrate, war would break out again and again until a new order was established, one dominated by a race that had managed to adapt quicker to the change in the galactic balance of power. It was hard to imagine the Funks having such imagination, yet they'd come to terms with the existence of other forms of intelligent life quicker than humanity. And they'd been in the Iron Age when they'd been contacted by the Association.

He glanced up as the console bleeped, warning him of a flight of shuttles heading towards the tanker. They flashed past at full speed, lighting the ship up with their weapons systems as they made their approach before vanishing into the darkness of space. Such crude intimidation was typical of the Hegemony, an unsubtle reminder of their power. But then, *Pelican* was not only unarmed – she was defenceless. A single burst from a phase cannon would cut right through her hull and destroy the ship.

The tanker shivered again as the final drop of HE3 was extracted into the fuel dump, which disconnected itself rapidly from *Pelican*. There was no point in asking for shore leave on Terra Nova, even if his orders hadn't specified that he was to return to quantum space as soon as possible. The Hegemony mostly refused to grant permission, and even when they did Gagarin City was a depressing place these days. William was old enough to remember the hope felt by the colonists that they would build a new world, a new melting pot that would take the best from humanity's disparate cultures and create something newer and stronger

63

than Earth. Their dreams had come to an end the moment the Hegemony had bullied Earth into surrendering the planet. He looked down at the blue-green globe and shivered, despite himself. The humans on the planet below were living in bondage, slaves to an alien race. They would never be anything other than a client race, if they were allowed to live at all.

"Take us back to the gate," he ordered quietly.

His orders had stated that he was to attempt to determine if the Hegemony had placed any watching starships in the outer system, if possible. Humanity had established a small asteroid mining station before the Hegemony had taken over, but the Funks had shown no interest in either forcing the miners to work for them or shipping in their own labour to take their place. It was so much easier to bully Earth out of raw materials – and efficient, if they weren't actually paying for it themselves. A handful of commercial drive fields could be detected near a couple of the mining asteroids, but nothing else. It didn't really mean anything and only a politician would think otherwise. Space was vast and a starship that stepped its drives down to the bare minimum – or cloaked – would be almost impossible to detect with passive sensors. The entire Hegemony Navy could be hiding there and they'd never know about it.

The viewscreen shifted as *Pelican* continued to lumber towards the gate. To human eyes, the gate didn't look very impressive. It seemed to be nothing more than a ring of metal over twenty kilometres in diameter. To advanced sensors, it was far more complex, existing simultaneously in normal space and quantum space. William didn't pretend to know how they worked. Few did, outside the research laboratories – and the Association itself. The Cats were normally obsessive record keepers, with a mania for paperwork that made even the worst of humanity's bureaucrats look like a piker, but they were curiously silent on how they first discovered how to open a permanent gateway into quantum space. Some of humanity's historical researchers, mining the records of a society thousands of years older than humanity, speculated that the breakthrough had happened by accident. Others, the more controversial researchers, claimed that someone *else* had given the Cats the technology. William privately believed the former. Apart from rumours, there was no proof that there was any spacefaring race older than the Cats – and they had built the Association.

"Transmit our ID and request that they open the gate," he ordered. The Funks would probably hit them with another service charge, just to rub their superiority into the puny humans one more time. Or maybe they'd just be glad to see the human ship leaving the system. A starship, even a freighter, could make one hell of a mess if it deliberately rammed the planet. "Pay them if necessary."

"Another fifty credits," the pilot reported. He shook his head. "They do make a good thing of it, don't they?"

"Bastards," William agreed. Ahead of them, a shimmer of light appeared inside the gate ring, a chink in the normal universe leading directly to quantum space. As always, it fascinated and repelled him in equal measure. There was something profoundly *unnatural* about quantum space. It wasn't a realm for humanity, or any other race. "Take us out of here, and then set course for the RV point."

They'd been given very specific orders before they'd undocked from Jupiter Station. *Pelican* and her crew was to depart the normal shipping line to Earth once they'd cleared the ring and head instead to a point roughly a light-year from Terra Nova. Quantum space didn't quite map onto normal space perfectly, one of the reasons why early explorers had tended to get lost and never return home. The navigation beacons were all that made interstellar commerce possible. Once they reached the RV point, they were to wait. The orders puzzled him because they made little sense. Maybe the higher-ups knew what they were doing, but he wouldn't have put money on it.

He took the helm himself, allowing the pilot a chance to get a cup of coffee and a snack before returning to duty. Quantum space could shift from placid to dangerous very quickly, forcing any starship travelling within the dimension to be ready to change course at any moment. Even the merest energy storm could wipe out an entire unwary fleet. He'd been a young cadet when Earth had heard that seventeen starships built by an alien race had been caught up in a storm and vaporised. If even the Galactics couldn't master quantum space, what hope did humanity have of taming the alternate dimension?

It was rare to see another starship in quantum space away from the shipping lanes. Indeed, even on the shipping lanes commercial ships rarely saw other starships unless it was a deliberate interception. Pirates had been known to hover around the gates and engage unwary freighters, forcing them to surrender and looting their holds before casting them loose to be destroyed by quantum space's energy storms. Some pirates were true sadists, torturing their victims before killing them; others took hostages and extracted ransoms from their relatives before returning them alive, if they bothered to keep their word.

He blinked in surprise as a handful of starships appeared on the display. They were *human* starships, small teardrop-shaped cruisers and bulky assault carriers, waiting for his ship. He stared, unable to quite believe his eyes, until he realised that they had to be planning a war. Or perhaps the war had already started and no one had bothered to inform him...no, that couldn't be right. The Hegemony would never have let him close to Terra Nova if they'd been at war with the human race. Maybe it was just the fleet exercise the media had been waffling about for the last month before he'd left Jupiter. But so close to Terra Nova...?

There was a brief pause as ID codes were exchanged and verified, and then the data dump began. William felt the first flash of excitement – and fear – as he realised what it meant. There was only one reason to want an up-to-date survey of any system; the fleet in front of him planned to *attack* Terra Nova – and the Hegemony starships in orbit around the human colony. It would be suicide... or would it? There was no shortage of rumours about human technological advances, even if the Galactics pooh-poohed the suggestion that a race as young as humanity could possibly have anything to teach them. The Association had stagnated, unable to develop further – or had the Cats simply lost interest in basic research? They were the richest and most powerful culture the galaxy had ever seen. What more did they need?

A face – Admiral Sampson – appeared on the display. "Good work," he said gruffly. "I'm going to have to ask you to remain with the support ships now."

"I understand," William said. They'd be paranoid about someone warning the Hegemony before it was too late. It was insulting, but he understood. And there really wasn't any other choice. "Good luck, sir. Give the bastards hell."

Chapter Eight

The humans who first set eyes on the Mer'fuk had immediately thought of them as lizards or snakes, even though their evolutionary path was very similar to humanity's. Unlike Earth, their homeworld had been dry and resources were scarce, forcing the early Mer'fuk to compete savagely for resources. Their successful leaders were the ones who claimed and held the most territory, using it as the basis of their power and forcing lesser Mer'fuk to submit and serve them in exchange for food and water. It was a trend that drove them onwards even after the Association had given them spaceflight and the First Empress had united their world under her iron heel.

Lady Dalsha reclined on her command stool and studied the males working busily below her, feeling her gaze on the back of their necks. Males couldn't be trusted to do anything other than fight or breed – trying to get them to consider the long-term effects of their actions was impossible – and they would slack off, or start picking fights with each other, if she and her fellow females left them to their own devices. It was the females who had built and led the clans, who had masterminded the wars that had seized vast territories for exploitation and – finally – led them out into space. If males ruled the world – as they did with some of the lesser races – they would probably have destroyed themselves by now, either through a civil war or attacking one of the stronger races in the galaxy. The Association might be decadent, with no fire left in its blood, but it still had numbers. They could have crushed the Hegemony if they'd been willing to accept bloodshed.

The thought made her smile. Males were expendable – with four males for every female, the Mer'fuk could afford to lose a few million in a war without seriously threatening the existence of the race. It would have been acceptable if the war had brought vast new territories, or destroyed a formidable enemy; it might even have been considered cheap! She couldn't really comprehend why the Association seemed unwilling to bring the other Galactics to heel – they *had* to know that the lesser races were climbing towards the point where they would be able to fight the Association openly and win – but there was no need to push the issue. A few hundred more standard years and the Hegemony would be all-powerful, the new ruler of the galaxy. And *they* would not be so foolish as to allow the lesser races so much latitude. They could do as they were told or they would perish and vanish from the universe.

She looked up towards the holographic image of Terra Nova – such a strange name for a planet, but the human settlers had had the right to name it – and smiled again. The Empress, hallowed be her name, had forced the humans to surrender their colony on pain of war and total destruction. Once the Association had finally, cravenly, surrendered the rest of humanity to the Hegemony, the soft-skinned race would be taught their true place in the universe. Their clever little people would serve the master race or die, begging for mercy that would never come. There was no room in the universe for those who didn't have the will to do what needed to be done to safeguard their interests. The strong would survive; the weak would become slaves – or perish.

But humans were a strange species. Human culture was infecting the galaxy, even the Hegemony itself. Males *loved* many human entertainments, even though their plots were awful and their special effects laughable. The Empress had banned it, of course, but males defied the females whenever they thought they could get away with it – if they bothered to reason it out that far. Humans had the strange notion that the sexes should be equal and that the population should participate in the decision-making process. It was a seductive concept to the more thoughtful males – and even to females so lowly as to be only a bare step above the males. Of course they wanted a democracy! The concept of the strongest being the supreme ruler, the concept that had driven the Hegemony to the stars, was under threat from an assault they were ill-prepared to counter. It wouldn't be long before the Empress forced the final showdown and

69

crushed the upstart human race. She would prove to the universe – and her own people – that human ideas were nothing compared to the united power of the Hegemony.

A male stepped towards her, bowing in submission. "Great Lady," he said, "the soft-skins on the planet below have sent yet another petition for your attention."

Lady Dalsha fluttered her crest in disdain. Even crushed, even beaten, humans were irritating. Why did they expect that pestering her would get her to give them what they wanted? Let them come up with something she wanted, or a way to threaten her, and *then* she would listen. Nothing would be allowed to detract from their role as a client race. They weren't useful as fighters either. Some of the human mercenaries who had taken service with the Galactics had impressed the Empress's advisors enough that they'd insisted on landing a larger garrison than normal, but the colonists hadn't put up an impressive resistance. Even when she'd ordered their religious buildings smashed they hadn't fought back. They were weak.

"Ignore it," she ordered, bluntly. The foolish male should have known not to bother her, but males weren't known for reasoned understanding of orders. Too strong a rebuke and he'd probably keep *everything* from her, including something she needed to know. "Do not even bother to send a reply…"

An alarm hooted through the compartment, causing the males to hiss in alarm. "Report," Lady Dalsha ordered, her tone calm and composed. Dominating males was easy as long as one refused to be flustered. "What is happening?"

"Multiple quantum gates, opening right on top of us," the sensor officer reported. He was unusually clever for a male, and much less aggressive. It was a shame that he couldn't be used for breeding stock, but the Hegemony needed aggressive males much more than it needed ones who could count to nine without taking off their boots. "They're far too close to the planet!"

Lady Dalsha, for a very brief second, experienced absolute disbelief. The Association was alarmingly cautious about risks that any lesser race would have taken in their stride. They never established a quantum gate in planetary orbit and warned of the dangers of opening a gateway too close to a planet's gravity well. The Hegemony had risked coming in closer, but the unknown intruders were coming in closer still, alarmingly close to her fleet. Had one of the other Galactics decided to destroy her force before it could be reinforced from the main fleet?

"Battle stations," she hissed. They'd kept their drives and weapons powered down – after all, who would dare attack them *here*? It might have been a mistake, even though doctrine was inflexible. "Raise shields. Prepare to engage the enemy."

* * *

Tobias let out a breath he hadn't realised he'd been holding when *Nimitz* slipped back into normal space. Humanity's scientists had claimed to prove that one *could* emerge from quantum space far closer to a gravity well than the Association believed possible, but no one had known for sure until they'd actually done it. Fifteen cruisers and their supporting destroyers had appeared from nowhere, heading right towards an unwary enemy fleet. The sensor take from active sensors – there was no point in trying to hide when the entire system would have detected their arrival – showed that the Hegemony ships were right where Captain Zeller's report had indicated. They certainly weren't ready for a fight.

"Enemy is bringing up active sensors," the sensor officer reported. The fleet was already launching recon drones towards the enemy, giving their crews additional sensor platforms to parse out the Hegemony's defences. "I'm picking up energy signatures from their weapons and targeting systems. They're flash-waking their defences."

Tobias nodded. That wasn't unexpected. Even with their power plants stepped down, starships maintained at least one shield generator ready to shield the hull at all times, another gift from the Association. Space wasn't empty and even a tiny piece of junk could damage an unprotected hull. But how quickly could they bring their ships to full alert? ONI hadn't been able to give him anything other than informed guesses, ranging from five minutes to an hour. It depended on just how carefully the Hegemony maintained their ships.

No military force could remain on alert forever, whatever the politicians and armchair generals might think. Tobias knew that standing guard for day after day could induce a lethargy into the system, no matter what senior officers said or did. It was why sentries were regularly rotated on and off guard positions. The Hegemony had *known* that humanity didn't dare attack them. Was it too much to hope that they'd allowed their ships to slip into disrepair, their crews into idleness? They didn't dare assume the best.

"General signal to all ships," he ordered. "They are to open fire with phase cannon as soon as we enter range."

The distance between the two fleets closed with staggering speed. Humanity might not have been able to build superdreadnoughts – at least not yet – but the *Admiral*-class cruisers compensated by being faster than any other ship in space, as well as packing enough advanced weapons to make them a match for anyone else's battlecruisers. It would take the Hegemony months, at least, to duplicate the weapons, assuming they figured out the basic principles or paid someone else to do it. But most of them were nothing more than variants on technology the Galactics had possessed longer than humanity had had fire. They'd probably deduce what humanity had done as soon as they saw the weapons in action.

Signals flashed between the ships, designating targets. The Hegemony kept its ships on a tight leash, with one flagship and little room for independent action on the part of subordinate commanders. They hadn't realised – at least not yet – that the sheer volume of signals from the flagship made it easy to identify. And once it was taken out – crippled or destroyed – it would be impossible for them to re-establish their command network. None of the junior commanders would have the authority to take command.

"Entering range," Commander Jackson said, quietly. "Phase cannon online… and firing."

Phase cannon were relatively simple weapons, designed by the Association and copied by all of the Galactics. They fired a phased beam of immensely destructive energy towards their targets, burning through iron or steel as if they were made of paper. Humanity had improved the weapons considerably, both enhancing their power and adding a second refinement. The simulations claimed that the second refinement would be a total surprise to the Galactics, but there was no way to know until now. Tobias leaned forward as the fleet opened fire, bright red beams of light lancing towards their targets.

Brilliant spheres appeared around the superdreadnoughts as the phase cannon hit the shields, which started to deflect the energy away from the ships. Normally, shields would have to be battered down before the cannon could start cutting into the hull, giving the Galactics time to respond to the attack. Now… the phase cannon started rotating their modulation, hunting for the frequency that would allow them to penetrate the shields instantly. The Galactics had to leave one frequency open or they wouldn't be able to return fire. As he watched, several of the beams lanced *through* the shields and dug into enemy hulls. The fleet's electronic servants, acting quicker than any human mind could follow, swiftly updated the other phase cannon, switching them to the correct frequency. Superdreadnoughts staggered as the powerful beams started to burn through their hulls. The hulls were tough, made from a synthetic compound developed by the Association, but not tough enough to stand up to phase cannon for long.

"Enemy is returning fire," Commander Jackson reported. The Hegemony ships had started to fire back frantically, many of their shots going wild. Their targeting systems were having problems with so many of their sensor blisters – exposed on their hulls – wiped out by human weapons. "They're trying to lock onto us."

"Evasive action," Captain Rupert ordered. Phase cannon were light-speed weapons. There would be no telling that they were under attack until the blast struck them. *Nimitz* and her sisters had far more powerful shields than anything else their size, but they didn't have the strength to stand up to a battering match at close range. "Continue firing."

The fleet passed *through* the Hegemony formation, still firing, and spun around to reengage the enemy. Lumbering superdreadnoughts couldn't hope to match their speed and manoeuvrability. Sensors reported that all of the superdreadnoughts had been damaged, but none of their more important systems – their drives, power plants and command stations – had been destroyed. They were buried deep within the hull, heavily protected. Taking them out would be harder than merely scarring their hulls. Smaller Hegemony ships were taking up position around the superdreadnoughts, trying to shield their tougher consorts. They might even succeed if they were allowed time to prepare for the next attack run.

"Lock antimatter torpedoes on target," he ordered. "Fire at will."

Nimitz shuddered as she unleashed a spread of antimatter torpedoes towards the enemy ships, each one powerful enough to wreck a planetary ecosystem if they detonated on the surface. The Association had devised a cheap method of producing antimatter centuries ago, but they'd always been reluctant to make full use of the incredibly dangerous substance. A single glitch in an antimatter containment pod and there would be a colossal explosion. Indeed, the Association Navy had forbidden their ships to carry antimatter warheads in peacetime, fearing the consequences of a single malfunction. The Hegemony – and humanity – had no such qualms. Antimatter was so powerful that it had to be used in war.

Humanity had modified the standard torpedo casings with better drives and devised a way to compress more antimatter into a warhead. The Hegemony was about to find out that humanity's torpedoes were far more destructive than anything the Association had ever built – and faster too, harder to intercept. But the Federation Navy hadn't had it all its own way. The cruisers couldn't carry more than a hundred torpedoes apiece – and when they expended their entire load, there would be no more until they could rearm. Each of the superdreadnoughts carried more torpedoes than Tobias's entire squadron.

"Hegemony attempting to target the torpedoes," Commander Jackson said. "Their point defence is having problems locking onto the weapons."

Tobias smiled as the first torpedoes struck home. Unlike the phase cannon, torpedoes couldn't slip through defence shields as if they weren't there, but they were so powerful that it hardly mattered. Even fratricide wasn't a problem when each detonation only added more force to the explosion. The blasts were so powerful that they blinded some of the recon drones the squadron had launched the moment it emerged from quantum space. For the Hegemony crews, it had to seem like the gates of Hell had opened up in front of them.

A superdreadnought fell out of line and staggered away, bleeding plasma from a dozen open wounds. The crews were already trying to escape – the sensors were picking up hundreds of lifepods blasting free of the doomed ship – even though the Hegemony expected their crews to fight to the death. It was a mystery why they'd even bothered to install lifepods in the first place. Another superdreadnought, heavily damaged, was somehow still firing at the oncoming human ships. The remaining three were less damaged, their shields having held against most of the blast. They seemed stunned, even as the human cruisers fell on them like wolves on a flock of sheep.

They'd learned from the last pass, Tobias realised as the two fleets came together once again. Their weapons fire was more targeted, moving rapidly from target to target, their computers trying to predict the random jinks used by human ships to evade incoming fire. *Nimitz* shuddered again as a phase cannon burst struck her forward shields, only to be repelled and evaded as the helmsman threw her into a tight turn. Her weapons were still firing, raking into her target's hull whenever the phase cannon matched the enemy's shield modulation. Someone on the other side had a brain, Tobias realised. He – more likely she – had been smart enough to start rotating their shields as soon as the first bursts of human fire slipped through their shields and into their hulls. It hampered their ability to return fire –

they'd have to keep altering their weapons to match the shield frequencies – but it might keep them alive.

The 2nd Cruiser Squadron swooped down on its target, one of the intact superdreadnoughts. It looked as if the enemy formation was falling apart, although it was impossible to be sure. The enemy flagship hadn't been badly damaged, which suggested that their commander was trying to adapt to a situation she would have considered impossible. Tobias barked orders and the 1st Cruiser Squadron reformed and headed towards the enemy flagship. Once she'd been taken out, it was possible that the enemy would surrender. Intact superdreadnoughts would teach Earth's engineers a great deal about the Hegemony's fleet – and rescuing survivors would look good in front of the other Galactics. It would...

"Admiral," Jackson said, "*Tirpitz*..."

Tobias looked – and swore. *Tirpitz* had one of the more aggressive commanders in the Federation Navy... and he'd taken her too close to the superdreadnought, which had lashed out hard enough to punch through the cruiser's shields and destroy one of her drive nacelles. Unable to adapt in time to change course, the cruiser spun out of control and slammed into the superdreadnought it had been targeting...

...And both ships vanished in a ball of fire.

Chapter Nine

Lady Dalsha had been trained to remain calm in all circumstances. No-one was permitted to command a starship, let alone an entire squadron, unless they were both loyal to the Empress and capable of remaining calm even in the worst of circumstances. But the disaster unfolding in front of her was utterly outside her experience. No one had seen an Association-designed superdreadnought destroyed in hundreds of years. Even the worst of the brushfire wars had never cost anyone a superdreadnought. Everyone *knew* that the ships were invincible.

Except for the intruders, who were attacking her ships. Tactical analysts claimed that they were human-built vessels, even though that was obviously impossible. *Humans* couldn't have built such ships and yet surrendered Terra Nova without a fight. It was vaguely possible that someone else might have assisted the humans, but why? Impeding the Hegemony's expansion would have delighted a dozen other races, yet it would have meant war, if their hand had been discovered. And even if they had, why would they have given new weapons to humanity instead of arming their own ships?

The impossible ships closed in again, firing a second spread of torpedoes. Point defence fire reached out to target them, the gunners suddenly having become very motivated. A normal torpedo spread posed little threat to a superdreadnought, but each of those torpedoes was a deadly threat. She couldn't understand how the unknowns had managed to compress so much antimatter into such small torpedoes, yet in the end the how and why hardly mattered. All that mattered was defeating the enemy or extracting her command before it was completely wiped out. Terra Nova and the garrison on its surface would have to fend for itself.

And there was so much disruption in normal space from the antimatter blasts that she couldn't even contact the Hegemony and warn them of the new threat.

"Bring up the main drives," she ordered. They'd have to run – and while no Hegemony fleet had ever run from an opponent before, no fleet had ever faced such a lopsided battle. Those cruisers were so small that losing one had to be only a tiny portion of the enemy fleet, while each lost superdreadnought cost the Hegemony dearly. Even the Association, back when it had been building superdreadnoughts, had never been able to build one in less than a year. It took the Hegemony more like two years to complete a superdreadnought. "Take us to minimum safe distance from the planet and open a gateway into quantum space."

Ripper's very hull seemed to scream in protest as two torpedoes struck her shields, burning out two of her shield generators. There were a dozen shield generators built within the hull – the Association believed firmly in multiple redundancy – but they were all burning out. No one had envisaged weapons that rotated their frequencies until they found the one that would allow them to go right through the shields, therefore no one had bothered to design shield generators that could switch frequency instantly. Making the change placed extra wear and tear on generators that were prone to burning out if overloaded.

One superdreadnought gone, another a powerless wreck, unable even to self-destruct. The Empress would not be pleased. The males on the ships would be forbidden breeding privileges and dumped on an isolated world without any females, one where their natural impulses would lead them to fight until they killed each other off completely. She... the Empress would not be merciful, if only to make it clear that failure would not be tolerated. There were worse fates than death and the clan that had ruled the Hegemony since First Contact knew all of them. She silently prayed to the gods her people no longer believed in that they could escape. The unknowns seemed to have them at their mercy.

They closed in, dancing around her fleet in random patterns that her tactical computers couldn't follow or predict. They'd learned from the destruction of their comrade, making sure not to expose themselves for too long, twisting and turning to take the blasts that did hit them on unexposed parts of their shields. Association-designed shields were omnidirectional, creating a bubble that surrounded the entire ship. The intruders had shields that seemed to rotate, sharing the burden among several different shield generators. They could lose part of their shields without losing them all.

Her ship shuddered again, and again. So close, the intruders didn't seem inclined to use torpedoes – or perhaps they'd fired them all already. Her first command had been a destroyer that had barely carried ten torpedoes. But their phase cannon were digging deeper and deeper into the hulls of their targets, hunting for the vital systems that kept the ships going. For the first time, she grasped the essential weakness in simply copying Association-designed starships. All of her ships – and those belonging to most of the Galactics – had the same configuration as the Association had specified, thousands of years ago. Anyone who learned how to destroy one superdreadnought could destroy all of them.

She showed her teeth in a gesture of defiance. Whoever they were, whatever they were really doing by attacking her fleet, the Hegemony had thousands of starships at its command. The Empress would lead her people to a war that would only end when they bombarded the enemy homeworld into debris, exterminating their entire race. They would...

The lights flickered as one of the enemy beams sliced through a power distribution node. There was no hope of concealing from the enemy just how badly they'd harmed her ship, not now. Anyone with passive sensors – let alone active systems – would be able to monitor her ship's power signature fluctuating wildly as power was diverted to drive nodes and weapons systems, even from life support. Her crew could live for hours before exhausting all the oxygen in the hull.

And then the enemy started launching torpedoes again. And for the first time, she knew despair.

* * *

The Hegemony had boasted, when they'd bullied Earth out of Terra Nova, that they never surrendered territory they'd claimed. It was practically ingrained into their very genes. The concept of sharing what they had, of distributing wealth and resources evenly, was alien to them. It wasn't too surprising, given how hard they'd had to struggle to survive on their homeworld, but it made them dangerous. They were more unpleasant neighbours than Nazi Germany or the Soviet Union.

But now they were starting to retreat. The three superdreadnoughts that were still capable of moving under their own power were inching away from Terra Nova, their drive fields flickering in and out of existence as they fought to keep their drives operational. Their remaining escorts were forming a line and attempting to bar the human ships from reaching their larger consorts, an act that would have won them some respect if the Hegemony had been more inclined to be friendly to its weaker neighbours. Instead, they were merely a problem that had to be removed.

Two of his own destroyers had moved closer to the drifting hulk, allowing Marines to fly out of their airlocks and board the derelict ship. It was a risk – there was no reason why the Funks couldn't turn off the containment chambers in their warheads and vaporise the remains along with the boarding party – but taking the hulk intact would be worth it. Even damaged, it would give the human race valuable intelligence.

"Engage the smaller ships with torpedoes," he ordered, as the fleet closed in on the enemy line. They were opening fire before the human ships had entered range, hoping to score a lucky hit. He didn't intend to give them the chance. Some of his ships had lost parts of their shields, leaving their hulls vulnerable if the enemy put a shot through the gaps in their defences. And his cruisers couldn't stand up to a heavy bombardment on their unshielded hulls. "Blow them out of our way."

The enemy destroyers attempted to evade as the spread of torpedoes roared towards their ships. Standard doctrine called for the torpedoes to concentrate on a single target; instead, his torpedoes spread out, each one going after a different ship. The enemy had to find it more than a little intimidating, particularly if they'd realised just how powerful his warheads actually were. There was a good chance that a single hit would be enough to cripple or destroy the smaller ships.

He smiled as antimatter warheads started exploding. Some had been picked off before they hit their targets, but others had struck home... and destroyers vanished in flashes of brilliant white light. Several others were badly damaged, limping out of formation or coming apart at the seams. They hadn't been designed to do more than support the wall of battle, even before humanity had started rewriting the rule book. Two ships turned and fled, racing past the superdreadnoughts and trying to make it to clear space. Tobias ordered two cruisers to leave formation and try to run the enemy destroyers down before they could escape. Accurate data on what human weapons had done would make it much easier for the Hegemony to duplicate humanity's inventions. Knowing that something was possible was half the battle.

"Take us in," he ordered. The superdreadnoughts were still firing, but their drives were crippled. They'd never make it to clear space in time to escape. "You may fire as soon as we enter range."

Nimitz's phase cannon opened fire, digging into the enemy hulls. Tobias gripped his chair as the cruiser slipped closer, feeling a cold exaltation as humanity gave the galactic bully a bloody nose, proving that the Hegemony was far from invincible. They'd won the first battle through luck, skill and better weapons and the next battles would be harder, but the human race would find its confidence soaring once the reports reached Earth. No one would ever be able to refuse to take humanity seriously in the future.

One of the enemy superdreadnoughts staggered out of formation as her shields failed, just before an antimatter torpedo struck her hull. For a moment, she still seemed to be struggling for life before the blast tore through her structure and vaporised the entire ship. Both of the enemy ships were now radiating flagship-style emissions, a cunning ruse that might have worked earlier, before his fleet had managed to identify the flagship. The antimatter dischargers hadn't been anything like powerful enough for his ships to lose track of the enemy flagship, even though her commander had managed to keep her intact despite Tobias' best efforts.

And then there were two, he thought. His formation closed in on its targets. *It won't be long now.*

* * *

The sound that groaned through *Ripper's* hull spelt the death-knell of the entire ship. Centuries ago, the Association had produced hull and structural metal that held up even in extreme circumstances, but it was not completely indestructible. The chain of explosions that had rippled through one of the lesser weapon bays had compromised the entire starship's integrity. Internal structural fields that were supposed to reinforce the raw material were failing one by one. Another shudder ran through the mighty ship as her drives finally died, trapping her in the Terra Nova system. It was even possible that the planet's gravity would pull them in and slam them into the surface. A belated revenge... except the intruders would simply vaporise the hulk if they didn't deem it worth salvage.

Lady Dalsha saw the males starting to panic and knew that she'd lost control over the situation. They'd start fighting and tear the rest of the ship apart, if the enemy left them alive that long. The handful of other females on the ship wouldn't be able to regain control until it was far too late. Males had problems comprehending that someone was stronger than they, particularly when it came to fighting. It was females who provided the long-term thinking... and there was no longer any future for any of them. The males would understand that on a level that no female could match. And then they would destroy themselves in fighting.

She flipped up a hidden panel in her command stool and tapped in two codes known only to her and her superiors. The first would activate the sleepy gas that would force the males into hibernation, a gas she'd been warned could only be used in the event of mutiny. Some females didn't have the knack for commanding large numbers of males, or were unable to maintain the balance between reward and punishment that kept the males in line. The second would do something that she would once have considered inconceivable. It would shut down her ship's weapons and broadcast surrender, *her* surrender. The Hegemony had never surrendered before...

...But there was always a first time.

This won't be the end, she thought, as she waited for a response – or an antimatter torpedo that would vaporise what remained of her command. The males were still twitching where they'd fallen to the gas. It didn't affect females unless there was a much heavier concentration in the air, for reasons tied to their biology. Females were studier than males. *Whatever happens to me, the Empress won't let this pass.*

The communications screen lit up and she found herself staring at a human face. She wanted to scream, to rend and tear at the air with her claws, but instead she kept herself under tight control. Humans would understand Galactic Three, one of the artificial languages the Association had devised for its client races. The Empress had talked of the days when the One Tongue would be spoken across the galaxy, but those days had yet to come. How had the humans grown so mighty? Had some of their entertainments been based on reality after all? Or had someone more advanced than the Association helped them?

Or was the Association more interested in galactic politics than everyone believed? They were an old race, the oldest spacefaring society known to exist. Had they shared all of their technology, or had they kept a few surprises back for the day when the younger races tried to take their remaining worlds? There was no way to know, but the Empress would find out.

"Great Lady," the human said, in passable Galactic Three. Her – no, *his* – tone was faintly shaded with an emotion she didn't recognise, but suspected was scorn. "You wish to surrender?"

No, she thought.

"Yes," she said. The Hegemony would need her observations of the battle so the Empress could plan their counter-offensive. Whoever had given the humans such technology wouldn't have very much of it, or they would have struck the homeworld directly. It crossed her mind that they *had* struck the homeworld and pushed it aside. "I offer you my ship and my submission."

It was an old ritual, one that had never been extended outside the race. But it was the only one she had. And if the humans refused to accept it...

...The Empress would never know what had happened in the system.

* * *

Tobias studied the alien face, wishing he knew how to read her properly. Even the Association had had problems creating automatic translators that allowed different aliens races to understand one another, let alone follow body language from a thousand different worlds and races. A human shaking his head was saying no; an alien headshake could mean anything from 'I hate you' to 'I want to have sex with you' – if it meant anything at all. There were races so cold, so emotionless, that they were difficult for humanity to accept and understand.

And the Funk wanted to surrender. Part of him wanted to press the offensive, to wipe her and her fleet out of existence, to avenge Earth's humiliation in blood. But he'd told his subordinates that he wanted no atrocities. How could he demand that if he ordered an atrocity himself? And it *would* be an atrocity. There was no sound tactical reason for slaughtering a crew that wanted to surrender.

They could take prisoners and interrogate them. A Great Lady would know enough to please even ONI.

"My Marines will be boarding your vessel," he said, finally. "If there is any resistance, you and your ship will be vaporised. Do not attempt to destroy computer records or kill members of your crew. Do you understand me?"

The alien bowed her head, her crest hanging low. Humanity had studied its most likely opponent for long enough to know that that was *supposed* to be a sign of surrender, the acceptance of someone else's incontestable superiority. And yet...it could be an act, one good enough to fool humans who were only outside observers. Aliens were alien, not humans in funny costumes. They always had to bear that in mind.

"I understand," the alien said.

"And you will order the planetary garrison to surrender," Tobias added.

The alien looked up, unblinking eyes meeting his. "I have no authority over the garrison," she said. There was no way to know, but Tobias suspected that she was telling the truth. The Funks didn't believe in united commands, particularly commands that would-be usurpers could use to try to overthrow the Empress. "They will not surrender on my command."

"I see," Tobias said. The Marines were already on their way. "Do not attempt to impede my forces taking control of your ship."

He cut the communications link and looked up at Commander Jackson. "Have the positions of planetary defence sites been plotted?"

"Yes, sir," Jackson said. "Most of the outlying ones are well away from human populations, but a handful are near major settlements – including the main garrison."

Tobias nodded. At least the Funks probably wouldn't think of taking hostages as human shields, at least not at first. They showed such a frightening lack of concern about their own civilians that they had problems grasping the fact that humans cared. How long would it be before realising that they could deter orbital bombardment by packing their bases with human children?

But they won't have the chance, he told himself. *This is the sole major human population under their rule. And we're going to take it from them.*

"Then give the order," he said. "Deploy the landing force!"

Chapter Ten

Conrad *always* got nervous before a drop – he'd read *Starship Troopers* in school and the book had left a permanent impression, long before humanity had learned how to produce armored combat suits in real life. The assault shuttles were heading right towards Terra Nova, each of them carrying two platoons of armored Marines, their lives dependent upon the skill of the pilots. No one was entirely sure how well defended Terra Nova was; Galactic doctrine called for only placing small forces on a planet's surface, but the Hegemony had needed to keep the population under control. The intelligence services hadn't been able to get anyone into their bases.

"Entering atmosphere," the pilot's voice crackled in his ears. "Prepare for drop."

He tensed, despite himself. By the time they qualified, Marines had spent hundreds of hours learning how to operate the combat suits, but it would be the first time they jumped into combat on an alien world. There were some things that no amount of training could prepare one for, no matter how detailed the simulations. Even live fire was different when the enemy genuinely intended to kill their targets. A single burst from a plasma cannon intended to shoot down shuttles or aircraft would vaporise the suit and kill him before he even knew what had hit him.

The display in front of him updated rapidly, a dozen screens monitoring the progress of the assault, the status of his Marines and intelligence amassed by the drones and starships in orbit around Terra Nova. Multitasking was difficult – more would-be Marines flunked out through failing to learn to handle their suits than anything else – but he'd learned how to take what information he needed and ignore the rest. Some officers believed that Marines should only have access to some of the data and have the rest doled out by their superiors, yet exercises had shown that sometimes caused problems on the ground. So did the superiors looking down from orbit and trying to dictate orders to the Bootnecks on the ground, bypassing the Marine officers trying to run the show. Conrad suspected that senior officers would one day manage to secure more control for themselves, hopefully long after the human race had secured its place in the universe. Less adaptable tactics would turn the war into a war of attrition, one the human race couldn't hope to win.

He felt the shuttle shiver around him as it dived into the atmosphere. They were coming in over the ocean, heading towards Gagarin City. The garrison squatting beside the city was a vast brooding superstructure, protected by a force field and the presence of human settlements around it. Updated reports warned that the Funks were launching drones towards the shuttles, hoping to down some of them before they began to spew out armored Marines. The starships picked them off from orbit, clearing the path to the city. A timer appeared in front of his display, counting down the seconds. Ten, nine, eight...

There was a jerk as his suit was picked up and tossed out of the shuttle, falling down towards the ground. Captain Smythton led the way, followed by Conrad and the rest of his men. Warning lights flashed up on his display as the Funks turned their attention to the Marines, trying to pick them off before they reached the ground. The combat datanet activated automatically, bringing ECM and other countermeasures online. Several Marines fired back towards their tormentors, using their targeting systems to pick off the small plasma cannon normally deployed against armored vehicles. Others curled up and waited for the antigravity system to cut their fall, a second before they hit the ground.

Gagarin City had been built on one side of a river, a site that had reminded him of early London when he'd first seen the maps during the planning sessions. The original prefabricated buildings had been rapidly replaced with brick and wooden buildings constructed from materials found on the planet itself, while hundreds of small villages and farms had been established upriver and fishing boats had set out on the vast ocean. Some of the alien fish were inedible, others were considered a delicacy – or they had been, until the Hegemony took the planet. The cynical part of Conrad's mind wondered if some of the higher-ups were more irritated over losing their expensive food than losing the planet itself.

The Funks had built their garrison on the other side of the river, a security measure that had seemed perfect when they'd landed and established their control over the high orbitals. There *was* a small insurgency underway, after all, and they knew better than to trust any human, even the turncoats who had gone to work for them. But now it would work against them, for there should be no humans in their garrison to be caught in the crossfire. Or so the planners had hoped. The Funks might just think of taking hostages if they were given long enough to consider.

He hit the ground and instantly crouched down, watching for possible threats – and targets. The Funks would have deployed their own troops to counter the landing as soon as they realised the threat, and they'd cleared away much of the foliage around their garrison to give their people clear fields of fire. They'd also built a small town for their own people, including a number of servants from their client races. Intelligence claimed that the Funks hadn't actually brought a large civilian population of their own, although Conrad knew better than to take that for granted. The spooks had been known to be wrong before.

A small detachment of enemy troopers appeared out of nowhere, firing towards the Marines. Conrad was in motion almost before he realised what had happened, jumping towards cover and firing back towards the enemy. Tanks – including the Challengers he'd worked with on Salisbury Plain – were heavily armored, but also alarmingly easy to see – and kill. Combat suits were far smaller and presented more difficult targets, as well as carrying weapons that would have made the tankers green with envy. A single Galactic-grade plasma cannon or HVM would tear through a Challenger like a knife through paper.

The Funks had their own suits, of course, and they moved forwards with a grim determination that any human would envy. They combined the fanatical fearlessness of terrorists and insurgents with workable doctrine and an understanding of their own weapons, making them far more dangerous enemies than anyone else the Marines had fought since they'd been founded. Funk males were supposed to be more aggressive than any other intelligent race, even human males competing for female attention. They certainly lived up to their reputation.

A plasma bolt scorched through the air, alarmingly close to his position. Someone had tracked him, then. He fired back as he crouched low and moved to another position, while three other Marines took advantage of the enemy's preoccupation with Conrad to take up forward positions and pour fire on the enemy. A brief note flashed up in front of him, informing the Marines that plasma weapons fire had set the alien town on fire, before he dismissed it. There was no time to worry about the alien settlement when he was fighting for his life.

He saw a Funk pop out of cover and run forwards, seeking a better place to fire on the human invaders. Conrad snapped off a shot before he had quite realised what he was doing, striking the alien suit in the center of its torso. The blast punched right through the armor and crisped the alien inside, killing him instantly. Conrad wondered if the suit would try to continue the fight on its own – some human-designed suits could do so – but instead it just hit the ground and lay still. The Funks clearly agreed with the Cats that making AI *too* intelligent was asking for trouble.

Inch by inch, the Marines pressed forward towards the alien base. The force field shimmering overhead protected it from the starships, but it didn't touch the ground. Some of the briefers had explained that force fields would attempt to cut through the earth and completely shield the base, tearing through underground piping and installations in the process. All that really mattered to the Marines was that they could slip through the gap and take out the force field generator themselves, exposing the base to orbital fire. The Funks could surrender or the garrison would be taken out from orbit.

The outer shell of the base itself was made from hull metal, contemptuously repelling plasma shots from the Marines as they confronted the trenches and emplaced weapons the Funks had constructed to bleed an attacker white. They'd clearly had some reason to be paranoid about the locals, even though it looked as if they'd overdone it. Conrad stayed low – the automated weapons would snap off a shot at any Marine who exposed himself before biological minds could see and react – and pressed forward, leading four Marines behind him. A thought activated the grenade launcher and he fired a spread of grenades into an alien trench, before nipping forward and diving into the space cleared by the explosions. One Funk was clearly badly wounded, if not dying; the other seemed to be stunned, but alive. Grenades just weren't as effective on armored troopers as they were on unprotected men.

He lifted an arm to shield himself as the Funk threw himself forward and crashed right into Conrad. The blank metal of his facemask seemed to mock the humans as blows rained down with armored strength, shaking the entire suit. An unsuited human would have been smashed to pulp with just one blow. They were too close to risk using his plasma cannon and so he fought back, matching the alien blow for blow. Neither one of them could gain an advantage, even with their augmented suits. He found himself wishing that he could see the alien face, to look into the red eyes that had haunted humanity's nightmares since they'd realised that not all of the Galactics were friendly. The thought drove him on as he kicked the alien in the chest, knocking him backwards and down the trench. A burst of plasma fire from one of the Marines cut the alien down before he could get back up and return to the fight.

"Follow me," Conrad barked. The updating display showed the Marines closing in on the base itself, pinpoint plasma fire picking off the automated guns that were trying to wipe out the Marines before they got too close. In some ways, the aliens had reinvented the art of building castles or forts – but humanity had learned that there was no such thing as a perfect fortification. Lords from the Dark Ages had been able to defy their kings, until the kings and their armies had started to use gunpowder and cannon to bring rebellious lords to heel. The Funks had barely started to work iron before they'd been introduced to the greater galaxy. But that didn't stop them being dangerous.

An automated weapon turned rapidly towards him, spewing out white-hot bursts of light. Conrad wasn't sure what it was tracking, or if it was tracking at all, but he took it out before it could start firing on him. The plasma containment field lost cohesion and exploded, scorching the garrison's walls without actually doing any serious damage. They'd had good reason to be confident that their base was safe from anything the insurgents could do. One by one, the defences were eliminated, but the Marines had to get inside the base. And the Funks knew it too.

Some Marines launched a diversionary attack on the main doors as Conrad led an assault right up the side of the garrison, scrambling up the walls. A set of armored Funks met them as they reached the top of the brooding dome, only to be picked off by the snipers that had moved into position now that the automated weapons had been destroyed. Marine snipers could shoot an insect out of the air at five kilometres; even half-camouflaged, the Funks were easy targets. If they had snipers of their own, no one had ever encountered them and lived to tell the tale.

He fired a set of grenades into the hangar doors before the Funks could finish closing them. The explosions blasted through the air, destroying a set of helicopter-like aircraft and igniting stored ammunition, but the garrison barely shook. They'd separated the hangar from the rest of the base with another layer of hull metal, a precaution that would have seemed excessive if it hadn't paid off so well. Just because the Funks had been primitive when the Association had first encountered them didn't mean that they were stupid.

The Marines pressed into the hangar themselves, rushing through the burning debris and down towards the armored door. Two Marines fixed HE charges to the weak points while the remainder covered them, watching for any armored Funks that had survived the explosion. Conrad spied a suit and put a plasma burst through it before he realised that the Funk had been killed already. Another Marine found an alien so badly wounded that there was no hope of survival, even with Galactic medical care. He was put out of his misery as the Marines fell back and detonated the explosions. The armored door blasted inwards, clearing the way into the base. Armored Funks inched forward, firing as they came. They had to know as well as the humans that if they lost the force field, the fight would be over.

Conrad lunged forward as Marines fired grenades and small HVMs towards their targets. Explosions blasted through the garrison, tearing through the weaker interior and destabilising the entire structure. The Funks seemed determined to fight for every inch of ground, refusing to fall back even when it would have made sense. Conrad suspected that they were rushing defenders to the breach, fighting a delaying action while the remainder of their armored troopers set up defences further inside the complex. Unlike most of their technology, the garrison hadn't been copied from the Association. No human had ever been allowed inside the complex and then permitted to depart. What few reports they'd had from Terra Nova stated that prisoners who entered the garrison never came out again.

A warning light flashed up in his eyes as Captain Smythton died. It was a risk officers took, sharing combat with their men, but it was still a shock. Smythton had been a good man, even though – like all officers – he'd started out as a green lieutenant with a great deal of theory and very little experience. But he'd learned quickly. There would be time to mourn later, he told himself, as the Marines pressed onwards. The enemy didn't give them any time to relax, but kept throwing in their own attacks while they rigged booby traps further along the corridors. Another Marine died when he stumbled over a plasma charge some crafty Funk had pulled from an overheated cannon and rigged with a simple detonator. Two other Marines, their suits badly damaged, had to withdraw from combat. Their protests were still echoing in his ears even when they'd managed to return to the shuttles on the ground.

Another explosion tore through the complex, burning through walls and floors. The entire interior might collapse at any moment, he realised as the Marines activated their antigravity systems and flew over the holes. He saw a set of what had to be alien offices below them, empty of their occupants. The planners had believed that the Funks would order all non-combat personnel into bunkers under the garrison when it came under attack, but it was just possible that every one of the Funks was a combat soldier first. Conrad was silently relieved that the planners had been right. Killing Funks who were trying to fight was in the line of duty, but he didn't want to kill enemy civilians. Besides, intelligence could interrogate them and learn more about their opponents.

The enemy attacks became even more frantic as the Marines closed in on the force field generator. It was easy to detect now as it struggled to compensate for the bursts of human fire that brushed against the field, even though the incoming fire was nowhere near powerful enough to overload the system. Conrad picked off two of the final defenders, and then ordered several Marines to fire grenades into the generator room. There was no point in trying to turn the system off when they could just destroy it. The explosion ripped through the base and started the collapse; Conrad had to jump and scramble for safety as the remaining floors started to crash inwards. But the force field was gone. The Marines fell back to safety, ignoring the remaining defenders. They could surrender or the fleet would reduce the garrison to rubble from orbit. Marine datanets updated, rapidly redefining fire teams, platoons and combat leaders. Seventy-four Marines had perished in the assault; thirty-two were wounded, some badly enough to require immediate treatment. Their suits would do what they could, but anything that burned through the suit was certainly capable of inflicting horrific damage, if it didn't kill them outright. The odds were not good.

There was a long pause as the Marines fell back from the garrison while the fleet demanded that the enemy surrender, and then the Funks threw down their arms. Conrad wasn't too surprised. They would have known that the fight was hopeless as soon as they lost their force field. If they'd defended it better, there might have been a long siege – or worse. The Marines might have had to carry a tactical nuke inside the garrison and set it off, maybe more than once.

"Take them as prisoners," he ordered his men. "And watch your backs. They may not all have given up."

Chapter Eleven

"We picked up the message," Captain Walsh said. "We are good to go."

Commander Markus Wilhelm nodded as *Formidable* slipped back into quantum space. Transmitting a tachyon-burst signal across hundreds of light years took a vast amount of power, but receiving one was a simple matter. The message *Formidable* had picked up would seem harmless to any Galactic listening posts, even though it was the instruction to head to Garston and commence the attack. There would be no warning until it was far too late.

He glanced over at his co-pilot – and wife – Carola, who smiled back at him. Gunboat crews had the shortest life-expectancy in the Federation Navy – a single direct hit from a Galactic weapon would blow the gunboat to atoms – and most of the normal regulations were relaxed for them. No one else really understood the stresses of piloting a gunboat, particularly when the crews were kept isolated from the rest of the Navy. The Galactics could not be allowed to know about the gunboats until they'd been deployed in action. It wouldn't be long before they came up with countermeasures to minimise their effectiveness, assuming that they were effective. No one had actually tested the theory outside simulations, until now.

Formidable didn't look very formidable, not from the outside. She was a simple bulk freighter, a design that Earth had copied and put into mass production, undercutting several Galactic consortiums in the process. The civilian versions of the design had no quantum drive and were completely dependent upon the quantum gates to move from star to star, like most commercial shipping. Inside, she was the first gunboat carrier in existence, transporting her parasite ships from world to world. The best of it, according to the briefing, was that when the Hegemony realised that seemingly-innocent freighters were carrying gunboats, they'd have to stop and search *every* freighter before they entered orbit. It would not please the other races when their traders were delayed by Hegemony security patrols.

The timer started to count down as *Formidable* made her slow way towards the quantum gate. It was possible for patrols to be flown through the areas of quantum space that corresponded to inhabited star systems, but rare for anyone to try it outside a quantum gate, where shipping was bottlenecked. An entire fleet could approach a star system and remain undetected until they emerged into normal space. Some of the tactics used by the raiders included lurking in quantum space near a gate until a likely target came along, and then moving in to capture the ship. Markus ran a hand over his console, checking and rechecking *Knife's* systems. When the time came, the shit was really going to hit the fan.

"Here we go," Carola said. The quantum gate opened up around *Formidable*, allowing her back into the inky darkness of normal space. Stars glowed in the distance, watching as the puny races lived and died like mayflies while they burned on. Some of the Galactics actually worshipped the stars, believing them to be gods. Others had no time for the entire concept of religion and regarded it as absurd. "Don't forget to give the bastards hell."

Garston sat on the nexus of no less than five trade routes, giving the Hegemony a chance to extract user fees from thousands of starships. The system's gas giant had no less than four cloudscoops operating, drawing up HE3 for starships and fusion reactors, while there were hundreds of asteroid mining operations drawing raw materials for the industrial nodes orbiting the planet itself. Garston had been settled for over a thousand years, first by the Association and later several other races, before it had been ceded to the Hegemony. The sheer scale of activity in the system was impressive. Earth had worked desperately to build up its industry, but Garston had far more productive capability than Earth. The Hegemony's iron grip on the planet hadn't changed that, even though they weren't fond of free enterprise.

But then they have to worry about Galactic opinion, Markus thought, as *Formidable* inched towards the planet.

Wallowing like a fully-loaded freighter might offend the captain's dignity, but it was part of the act. *They can't crack down on most of the races here without pissing off Galactics with the ability to make the Hegemony pay.*

He watched as Garston Base slowly came into view. By treaty, the Hegemony was the only power allowed to station armed forces in the system, which simplified the problem facing the gunboats considerably. Anything that shot back at them was Hegemony and could be destroyed without compunction. Accidentally killing other races, on the other hand, could result in a diplomatic disaster. The point had been hammered into their heads time and time again. Earth did not need more enemies.

Garston Base was a massive ring, positioned neatly at one of the Lagrange Points between Garston and one of its moons. Long struts expanded out into space, providing docking ports for military starships. The design was thousands of years old, produced by the Association during its first expansion into space. Markus couldn't understand why the Association – or one of the other Galactics – hadn't attempted to improve the design, but the briefers had said that the Cats stuck with what worked. And even though they were in decline, they still set the standard for the rest of the galaxy. Humans, on the other hand, looked constantly for ways to improve what they had. How long would it be before humanity raced ahead of the rest of the Galactics?

"We're picking up a Hegemony battlecruiser near the station," Captain Walsh said, "and a pair of destroyers on mobile patrol. Kill the battlecruiser first."

"Yes, boss," Markus muttered. The battlecruiser was a surprise, although they'd been warned that ship schedules couldn't be completely relied upon. Chances were that her arrival had surprised Garston Base as much as it had surprised the Federation Navy. "All systems online?"

"Of course," Carola said. "We're ready to launch."

Humanity had dreamed of starfighters – fighter jets in space – long before obtaining the technology to reach the stars. In practice, the idea had proven impractical, even for the Association. Building a starfighter was easy, but designing a compensator that could fit into such a small craft was impossible, at least so far. Torpedoes pulled such high speeds because they didn't have frail pilots to be squashed by their acceleration. The gunboats were a compromise design, light attack craft that could harass enemy starships... and give them a very nasty surprise. There was another concept that the Galactics had deemed impractical, until human ingenuity had made it work.

"They're challenging us," Captain Walsh said. Ideally, *Formidable* would have inched closer to Garston Base before starting the attack, but they'd known that it wasn't likely to happen. The Hegemony bullied human ships frequently, along with ships from other races too weak to make a fuss. *Formidable* had transmitted an official manifest as soon as she had cleared the quantum gate, one carefully crafted to avoid attracting officious customs officers, in the hopes it would prevent an inspection until it was too late. "Gunboats... launch!"

The hangar bay opened wide, tractor fields pushing the gunboats out into space. Sensor readings would be a little confused, making it harder for the Funks to react. It was quite possible that they'd think that *Formidable* had suffered a terrible accident and was coming apart at the seams. They'd probably launch a rescue shuttle and charge humanity through the nose for the service. Markus smiled as he activated the gunboat's drives. They were about to get a very nasty surprise.

"All Grumbles form up on me," he ordered, as the gunboats raced away from *Formidable*. The Funks would see them coming; they'd know that they were under attack. "Our target is the big brute. Eagles; concentrate on the station. Ivans; cover our backs from those destroyers. Good hunting."

The Hegemony battlecruiser – her IFF transmitter identified her as something that translated loosely as *Manifest Destiny* – slowly came to life as the gunboats zoomed closer, bringing their weapons systems online. Her crew had probably been enjoying a little intercourse and intoxication on the planet, assuming that the Hegemony males were allowed to do either, but almost all space navies ensured that enough crew to operate and fight the ship remained onboard at all times. The battlecruiser might run, or she might fight; they'd certainly be a little contemptuous of the tiny gunboats. No one else had devised either the craft or a doctrine to use their advantages against enemy starships.

"Attention, all shipping," the recorded message in Galactic Three stated. *Formidable* was pulsing the message right across the Garston System. "A state of war exists between Earth and the Hegemony. All civilian ships are advised to identify themselves to us and remain clear of military operations. Our attacks will only be directed against Hegemony starships; I say again, our attacks will only be directed against Hegemony starships. Remain clear of military operations for your own safety."

Markus silently prayed that the Galactics would listen as the battlecruiser started to spit deadly fire toward the gunboats. The crews instantly abandoned their first formation and fell into the second, a chaotic pattern that shifted rapidly. It looked as if the force's commander had lost control and his pilots were panicking, but it was a carefully-planned operation. The rapid and unpredictable motions made it extremely difficult for targeting sensors to track them and open fire. Some of Earth's little improvements to the ECM systems developed by the Galactics would made targeting the gunboats even harder.

"Concentrate on the drive section," he ordered, as the gunboats slipped into weapons range. They were so close to the battlecruiser that they could see it through the cockpits with the naked eye. "We don't want her getting away..."

A gunboat vanished in a puff of light as the Hegemony gunners scored a direct hit. Markus had known that there would be losses – pilots he had known and had trained beside for years – but it was still hard to accept. He wanted to stick his hand down on the firing key and blast away at the enemy ship until it bled. Instead, he forced himself to concentrate as the gunboats pulled out of their dive, skimming along the edge of the battlecruiser's shields. One gunboat pilot misjudged the turn and slammed right into the shield. The Funks would find it a little reassuring, for a few more seconds. It would be clear that the gunboats weren't carrying antimatter.

"All right," he ordered. "Fire at will."

"Hey," one of the other pilots said. "Which one of them is Will?"

Markus snorted as implosion bolts rained down on the enemy drive section. Implosion bolts, for reasons no one outside the engineering departments understood, went right through shields as if they weren't there. They seemed the perfect weapon, but the Galactics – who had devised the technology – had never made good use of it. Even for the Association, it was impossible to devise a way of projecting the bolt more than several hundred meters before it just came apart. Any starship armed with an implosion bolt weapon would have to close to suicidal range before opening fire, during which time their opponents would have shot the shit out of them. They simply weren't a very practical weapon...

...Unless they were mounted on small craft, ones considered expendable by the senior officers who had devised the concept and put it into production. Earth could trade a handful of gunboats for a Funk battlecruiser and come out ahead, a trade that couldn't be made with starships. The gunboats did have some limitations – they couldn't carry quantum drives and their life support was very limited, even with extension packs – but none of the pilots worried about such details. It was enough that they could fight... and give humanity's tormentors a bloody nose they'd never forget.

The battlecruiser seemed to jerk in shock as deadly blasts tore through her drive section. Her gunners kept firing, even as she tried to twist away from the tiny attackers. Markus grinned as the gunboats followed, still pouring fire down on the enemy ship. The gunboats, like most small craft, were far more manoeuvrable than any starship. And they could accelerate far faster than their target. The ship's only real hope was to jump out into quantum space, but it was already too late. They'd lost their quantum drive within seconds.

They'll be ready for us next time, Markus thought. Reprogramming their tactical computers would be simple, once they knew what they were facing. Garston's military presence wouldn't survive the attack, but most of the commercial starships would make recordings of the battle, hoping to sell them to interstellar news networks. The secret would be out the moment one of them sold their recording to the Funks. *And then it will be far harder.*

He twisted the gunboat through a complicated evasive pattern as the battlecruiser lashed out at its enemies, a lion being stung to death by tiny wasps. Two more gunboats were picked off, but it made no difference. A direct hit on one of their fusion plants took out most of their power, leaving the ship drifting in space. Lifepods were launched as the crew desperately tried to escape, far fewer than there should have been. Perhaps the lifepods had been ripped apart by the attack, or perhaps the Funk crewmen thought that the gunboats would simply pick them off one by one. Markus wouldn't have done it even if he'd been ordered to slaughter the helpless escapees. It would have been an atrocity.

An explosion blew the rear section of the battlecruiser to pieces, leaving the remains cart-wheeling across space. Weapons fire fell away and finally stopped altogether. The ship no longer posed any threat and so Markus led the Grumbles away from their target. Once the gunboats had left the system, the commercial ships could pick up the lifepods and save the crews. Behind them, Ivan Squadron had destroyed one of the Funk destroyers while the other had fled into quantum space. That wasn't too surprising. Retreat had been the only logical course, even though the Funks weren't known for running from the battlefield. But they weren't as bad as the spider-like race on the other side of the galaxy, which regarded themselves as completely expendable, just like any other form of military technology. Even the Association had had problems communicating with them.

Garston Base was fighting back savagely. Unlike a starship, which had to devote large parts of its internal space to drives, orbital bases could cram extra weapons and shield generators into their hulls. The time they'd taken to destroy the battlecruiser had given the station's crew a chance to adapt to the gunboats. Eagle Squadron had damaged the base, but seven of the gunboats had been blasted into space dust – including the one flown by the squadron commander. What little coordination still existed among the pilots wasn't enough to cripple the station.

"Ivans and Grumbles, target the station," Markus ordered sharply. The shortage of real experience had thrown up another nasty problem, one they should have expected. There was no reason why the Funks couldn't pick off the squadron leaders. "Eagles; pull back and reform."

The station grew rapidly in front of him as they closed in. It was larger than any superdreadnought, large enough to allow starships to dock *inside* the base's hull, where they could be powered down and repaired. And it lacked a place that could be destroyed and set off a chain reaction that would destroy the base, unless they burned right through to the fusion plants. Doing that would require burning through the entire station. The gunboats swept out, targeting the station's point defence and picking the guns off, one by one. Several gunboats died before even realising that they were under attack. Someone on the other side had already managed to reprogram their tactical computers.

Good thing we're going to kill her, Markus thought, as he picked off another point defence weapon. With clear space, the gunboats were taking up positions and pouring fire directly into the station itself. Explosions billowed out in the darkness of space, none of them powerful enough to tear the station apart until one blast shattered the struts holding the ring together. Slowly, magnificently, the entire station began to disintegrate. Something exploded deep inside and kicked a mountain of debris out into the system. Markus allowed himself a moment of silence to appreciate what they'd done, and then barked an order to his gunboat crews. They turned and fled the dying station before it shattered completely. A few hundred lifepod beacons appeared on their displays, screaming for help. The commercial ships would have to rescue them.

Formidable was already heading back towards the quantum gate when the gunboats formed up around her. She *could* slip into quantum space herself, but that would have revealed that she carried a quantum drive. Letting the Galactics think that she needed a gate to enter and leave quantum space might come in handy as the war raged on. None of the other ships tried to stop them leaving the system, leaving the Hegemony's military reputation in tatters. A report would be transmitted to Earth as soon as they reached a safe distance.

The eerie lights of quantum space surrounded them as they passed through the gate. Gunboats *could* enter quantum space if a starship or a fixed installation opened a gate for them, allowing them to return to their carrier once they were safely away from the battle. And if they were lucky, the Galactics would assume that the opposite was true. Nowhere would be safe from gunboat attacks.

"Good work, everyone," he said. "Time to return to the barn – and debriefing."

He ignored the groans from his crewmates. They needed to analyze the battle carefully and work out what they'd done wrong – and right. Learning from success was harder than learning from defeat, but there was no choice. The next time the gunboats faced a Hegemony fleet, the Hegemony would know what to expect.

And then they would *really* test the gunboats to the limit.

But then, these are the problems of victory, he reminded himself. *Just think how they must be feeling.*

Chapter Twelve

The streets of Center's floating city looked normal, even though the universe had just turned upside down. Hundreds of thousands of people, from a hundred different races, thronged the streets, coming together in an association supervised by *the* Association. The Cats had dreamed of a universe where every race worked together for the common good, but the way they'd gone about it had been largely counterproductive. And now they were losing interest in maintaining the edifice they'd created.

Ambassador Li Shan walked through the streets, badly shaken. She'd known, of course, that both Federation Intelligence and ONI operated out of the human embassy on Center. It was still the heart of the explored galaxy, still a place where humans could learn about the Galactics and dig through records that stretched back over thousands of years. But to be told that there was a set of intelligence operators that she'd never known about, until one of them had been ordered to reveal himself, was shocking – and the discovery that Earth was embarking on a war was terrifying. No one had told her, not until the first strikes had already been launched. Logic told her that they couldn't have sent a message until the war actually began, for fear of interception and decryption, but it was hard not to resent their decision.

Four men from the embassy walked behind her, all trained and experienced Federation Marines. The Cats didn't permit others to carry weapons on their world – it was meant to be a place of harmony – but the Marines had a few surprises up their sleeves. It was quite possible that the Funks would attempt to assassinate Earth's Ambassador, once they realised that the war had begun. They'd probably have to disown the assassin and pay reparations – after all, they wouldn't want the Association to wake up until it was too late – but it would pay off handsomely. Earth wouldn't be able to get another accredited Ambassador out to Center for years and her deputy wouldn't be accepted by the Galactics. Just another convention that the Galactics couldn't be bothered to change.

The streets looked busy, with market sellers trying to sell their wares, but it was easy to see what was missing. There were no Cats within the crowd, and indeed few of them within the city itself. The terminal ennui that was wearing away at their determination to tame the universe and bend it to their will was slowly killing them, even though no Cat had died naturally for thousands of years. No one was entirely sure just how many were still inclined to take an interest in galactic affairs or were even *alive*, out of a population that once numbered in the hundreds of trillions. There was no demographic data available on their population these days. Shan was inclined to believe that some Cats realised the danger and were doing their best to hide their weakness from the rest of the galaxy, but there was no way to know for sure. Even her sources on Center couldn't find out everything.

She tensed as she saw a pair of Funks heading across the street. Neither of them seemed aware that they were at war with the human race, but it wouldn't be long before the news reached Center. Some of the hypothetical war plans she'd seen had suggested blowing up the relay stations, before the diplomats had seen the plans and vetoed them. The relay stations were linked to the quantum gates and *nothing* would be more likely to bring the entire galaxy down on Earth's head. Destroying a gate was regarded as the ultimate crime, because it threatened the very foundations of civilization. Even mass-producing and deploying subversion nanites was less dangerous.

Like all races, the Hegemony maintained its own embassy on Center. It had been built in the style they'd used before they'd been contacted by the Association, a weird building that reminded her of a cross between a castle and a tent. Their homeworld had had few permanent cities, not unlike Earth in the years before humans had moved from hunter-gatherers to farmers. Indeed, the Funk culture – such as it was – had disdained the city-folk before they'd gained access to advanced technology. Maybe they would have evolved away from the demands of their homeworld if they'd been allowed to develop naturally. But the Association had never given them that chance.

And yet they'd adapted to the existence of more powerful races better than humanity...

By custom, any Ambassador could call upon another Ambassador at any time, without warning. The Association's traditions for a declaration of war were rather less detailed, if only because the brushfire wars were really nothing more than minor skirmishes. When the Cats had been strong and determined, they'd been able to keep younger races from fighting each other. Now... even without humanity starting a war with the Hegemony, no one expected the uneasy peace to last more than a few decades. Scrabbling over the division of the Association's space had already begun.

She stepped up in front of the forcefield and held up the pendant that certified that she was an accredited Ambassador, appointed by Earth and accepted by the Association Commune. The guard – an unarmored Funk, with no visible weapons – looked at it, make a motion that reminded her of a shrug, and pushed a button. Oddly, she realised as the forcefield flickered out of existence, the guard was female. It was rare to see Funk women in menial jobs, unless they were being punished. Of course, keeping one's temper was essential on Center and a Funk male might have started a fight by now. Maybe it was a more important position than she'd realised.

The Funk's voice was almost atonal, save for a hissing sound that seemed to underlie her Galactic Three. "The Ambassador is eating," she said. Galactic Three wasn't a particularly polite language, reducing messages to their bare essentials. The guard didn't mean to be rude. Probably. "She will see you after she has dined."

Shan smiled and pushed forward. "The Ambassador will see me now," she said. She took a breath, puffing out her chest. The Funks didn't take males seriously, but if they recognised that she was female... of course, all humans looked alike to them, just as many humans had difficulties telling the difference between different Funks. "This matter is too important to be left to wait."

There was one thing about the Funks that reminded her of her old tutor's comment about the Russians. They saw the universe in terms of superiors and inferiors. Convince them that you were superior and they would genuflect and obey; fail to convince them and they would happily take advantage of you. But it was often harder than it sounded. The guard would have had her orders from a known superior and might not break them for another, particularly a human.

The Funk bowed her head, slowly. "I will escort you to the Ambassador," she said. "Your guards may wait outside."

"Of course," Shan said, coolly. The thought of not having her bodyguards was terrifying, but she knew better than to let them see it. Besides, four guards might not be able to get her out safely if the Funks went against thousands of years of tradition and murdered an Ambassador in their own Embassy. That would seriously annoy all of their neighbours. "Lead the way."

The guard scurried ahead of her as Shan strode into the Embassy as if she owned the place, passing through a security scanner that informed her hosts that she carried nothing more dangerous than a datapad, a single datachip and a secure terminal. Not that that would reassure them. There might be a general consensus that murdering Ambassadors was not civilised, but there was no law against spying – and plenty of ways to carry surveillance tools into a secure building. She could be carrying a handful of nanotech bugs with her, or something even smaller. But they had to see her. She was Earth's Ambassador.

She'd never visited the Funk Embassy before and part of her was curious. The interior of the building smelt faintly of rotting meat, reminding her that the Funks liked to eat their meals raw. Rumour had it that they dined on alien flesh in a perverse form of cannibalism, although she doubted that that was true. Humanity had been quite prepared to believe the worst of them after they'd taken Terra Nova and stories of them devouring human children had spread widely.

Who knew? Maybe they would convince one of the other Galactics to intervene.

In the dim light, she could make out the plain stone walls, decorated by remarkably fine carved letters. Like humanity, the Funks had kept their own languages after learning the various Galactic tongues, but they'd never had a written language until they'd adapted one from the Association. Reading it was tricky; some words were comprehensible, probably taken straight from Galactic Three, others were new to her. The Association would have been wiser to note what the Funks had done and realise that absorbing and dominating was part of their nature. But the Cats had probably just seen it as another primitive race copying technology from their betters.

A handful of other Funks glanced at her as they passed her in the corridor. Most were female, but a couple of males hissed at her when they saw her. They'd probably smelled her first – their noses were sharper than human noses – and recognised that she was alien. Her escort eyed the males until they were gone, almost as if she'd expected them to lose control and attack Shan. It would have been disastrous if they had, even if Shan survived without serious injury. The Hegemony's reputation would have taken a terrible blow.

The Funk Ambassador was seated at a table that had been hastily cleared of raw animal flesh and the jugs of strong wine the Funks brewed and sold to the rest of the galaxy. Meeting her in the dining hall was a subtle insult, which she pretended to ignore. She *had* demanded an immediate meeting, after all, and could hardly complain when they pretended to take her at her word. The Ambassador was older than the average Funk, almost certainly – although it was hard to tell – a close relative of the Empress. Nepotism was how the Funks operated, which had the added bonus that anyone without family loyalty wouldn't be able to rise to a senior position they could use to mount a coup. The pendent around her neck glowed as it recognised the presence of Shan's pendant. No-one else would be able to wear it until they received accreditation in their own right.

"Great Lady," Shan said, with a slight bow. Galactic protocol could be very complex at times, with hundreds of different races adding their own spin on events. "I thank you for agreeing to meet with me."

"I thank you for visiting," Great Lady Vanla said. It was always difficult to read emotions behind alien words, but Shan was sure that she was lying through her sharp teeth. The Great Lady hadn't missed any opportunities to remind humanity of its lowly place in the galaxy, or to intimidate or bribe potential allies into staying away from Earth. "I am sure that your urgent request represents an urgent matter."

Shan took a breath. "Over the past ten years, ever since our races first encountered each other, your race has pushed us hard," she said. Part of her had wanted to simply deliver the declaration of war and get out, but her terminal was recording the entire meeting. It would be necessary to show it to the other Galactics when humanity started looking for allies... assuming that the war went as planned. She couldn't remember if any war had ever gone according to plan, but she doubted one had. "You have demanded concession after concession from us, impeded our efforts to move into the wider galaxy and taken a whole population of humans captive. Now you are attempting to claim our worlds, to end our independence. We can no longer tolerate your dishonourable interference in our affairs."

The Great Lady cocked her head slightly, a Funk smile. "The world you call Terra Nova was transferred to us legally, from the race that originally claimed it," she said, with some clear amusement. "The fact that a number of... squatters landed on the world, without permission from the owners, is of no consequence to us. We were happy to invite them to join the Hegemony, with the same rights and duties as any other client race."

And those rights were very thin on the ground, Shan knew. The Association's founders had patronised the younger races for years, but they hadn't acted out of malice. But the Funks believed themselves superior to everyone who couldn't stand up for themselves. Humans would never be anything more than second-class citizens under their rule, denied even the hope of freedom.

The hell of it was that they *did* have a point, under Galactic law. Terra Nova *had* been claimed by the Association, although the Cats had never raised any objection to humans settling on the planet – or, for that matter, the countless other worlds in similar positions. But the Cats had never given up the settlement rights to humanity, and when the Association had convinced them to sign the rights over to the Hegemony, it had all been perfectly legal. It just hadn't been particularly *ethical*. Who would have thought that, among all the races humanity would encounter, there would be hundreds of fanatical lawyers?

But human visions of the universe outside Earth's atmosphere had always been limited. Aliens had been depicted as unified cultures, either benevolent federations who would give humanity the keys to the stars or implacably hostile empires that would destroy humanity if humanity didn't destroy them first. But *real* aliens were people, even the ones so alien that holding a conversation was almost impossible. And in the snake pit the Association had accidentally created, the rules were more important than any concept of ethics, particularly human ethics. Might made right and the Hegemony simply had a bigger stick than Earth.

"And our homeworld?" Shan asked, meeting the bright red eyes. How could anyone escape realising that the Funks were *predators* first and foremost? Just because they were matriarchal rather than patriarchal didn't make them any less determined to cling onto their own culture than any number of human tribes on Earth. "What claim do you have on Earth?"

"The Association claimed your world as well," the Great Lady said. "Why should we not seek settlement rights from them?"

Several arguments rose in Shan's mind, but she pushed them down. The Great Lady would either laugh at them, or regard them as proof of human weakness. And maybe she'd be right.

"You have been attempting to prepare us for the kill," Shan said, coldly. It had been clear ever since Terra Nova

111

had been awarded to the Hegemony. They were gradually weakening and isolating Earth, before moving in to take the human race for slaves. It was a slow process, but what did the Funks have to fear from Earth? "We can no longer allow you to weaken us into insignificance."

She produced a standard datachip from her pocket and dropped it on the table. "While we enter this course of action reluctantly, regrettably" – a piece of fluff for the Galactics who would hear the recording, later – "we see no other choice, but to push you back as hard as we can. Earth is formally declaring war on the Hegemony. We will drive you out of our territory, liberate Terra Nova and prove that while you may have the law on your side, we have the determination."

For the first time, she saw the Great Lady surprised. Her jaw hung open, revealing teeth sharp enough to rend and tear at human flesh. Male Funks were supposed to be as strong as humans, perhaps stronger, but there was little data on how strong their females were, just speculation. The thought that the inferior would turn on the superior was outside their comprehension. Sun Tzu had known better, all those years ago. And yet she was closer in time to Master Sun than she was to the founders of the Association.

"You are insane," the Great Lady managed, finally. "The entire combined tonnage of Earth's puny fleet is nothing compared to a single task force of our navy. You will be obliterated. Your worlds will become ours without the necessity of convincing the Association to give us settlement rights. You..."

"Will not go down quietly," Shan said. If nothing else, at least they would be taking action. "We will not let you take us down without a fight."

She bowed again, walked backwards to the door, and smiled. Her escort hadn't heard the discussion and merely escorted her out of the building, rather than trying to do anything to impede her departure. Shan allowed herself another smile as she stepped out into the bright sunlight and left the Embassy behind her. She couldn't escape the feeling that she'd barely escaped with her life.

"Back home," she said, shortly. Earth's embassy was two kilometres away, on the outskirts of the floating city. Tradition demanded that everyone walk from place to place, except in life-threatening emergencies. "We have work to do."

And they did, she reflected as they began the long walk. She had to get humanity's side of the story out into the galactic news networks and begin using all of her contacts to start pressuring the other Galactics to support Earth. Galactic reporters would probably want to start setting out for the war zone, hoping to watch one fleet beating the other. The brushfire wars had been one thing, but an outright war launched by a minor power against a major power was something different. Once they got over their shock, the Hegemony would be doing the same. Convincing the other Galactics to support Earth might be just as important as actually winning battles in space and liberating Terra Nova.

Now, all they needed was some victories to convince the Galactics that humanity wasn't about to be crushed. And that wouldn't be easy.

Chapter Thirteen

Fires were still burning throughout Gagarin City and the Funk settlement beyond as the shuttle swooped down towards Heinlein Spaceport. Most of the Funks had surrendered, but a handful of males – crazed with battle lust – had carried on the fight, forcing the Marines to hunt them down and take them out one by one. The human population had savagely turned on their former masters as soon as they realised that liberation was at hand, slaughtering dozens of Funks before the Marines could take them into custody. They'd also assaulted members of the Funk client races, creating potential problems for the future. Humanity needed allies among the enemy's slaves.

Heinlein Spaceport had expanded during the years the Funks had ruled Terra Nova, apparently one of the few installations to have seen any growth during their rule. They'd added prefabricated hangars, runways and a series of guard posts that prevented humans from entering or leaving the spaceport except under controlled conditions. It reminded Tobias of the bases the various militaries had established in what remained of the Middle East, the zones where the population could move in seconds from friendly compliance to fanatic hostility. No one could be permitted to enter without supervision, for fear of suicide bombers or terrorist gunmen. The precautions created additional enemies for the troops, something that was regrettable, but unavoidable. No doubt the Funks had had the same problem.

The shuttle touched down and the hatch opened, revealing a pair of Marines serving as an honour guard. Protocol demanded that the Admiral be escorted by a platoon, at least, but there was a shortage of Marines who could be spared for close protection duties. The city was on the verge of collapse and the Marines were all that were holding it together, replacing the police force the aliens had created. One lesson humanity had learned in its long history was that both liberation and occupation forces needed to impose order right from the start. Freedom, democracy and human rights could come later. And the colonists had been through hell for the past five years. Tobias couldn't blame them for wanting a little payback.

He exchanged salutes with the Marines as another flight of shuttles roared overhead. The spaceport was the only place on the planet that could take an influx of troops from orbit quickly, even if it was alarmingly close to the main city. Brigadier Jones and his command staff had already established their headquarters in the spaceport, although if Tobias knew the Brigadier he was commanding operations from within his armored suit, far closer to the action than Tobias would have preferred. Marines were a law unto themselves; their commanding officers served on the front lines, taking insane risks to win and keep the respect of their men. Tobias allowed his escort to lead him towards the largest of the spaceport buildings, once the processing center for new immigrants to Terra Nova. His daughter and her husband would have gone through the center before being allocated their land, a place where they could start building a new life together. Now, the building had fallen into disrepair. The Funks hadn't wanted more human immigrants and they'd been reluctant even to allow visitors.

Colonel Lafarge looked up from where he'd been studying a map when Tobias entered. He inclined his head in greeting, but didn't salute. Saluting senior officers in a combat zone marked them out for enemy snipers. Some of the Funks were still trying to hurt the liberators before they were wiped out. The map was paper, rather than one of the electronic plotting displays Tobias was used to using, but the Marines didn't seem to have any problems with using it to represent the city. They'd marked the location of patrols on the map with pencils.

"Admiral," Lafarge said. His accent was French, even though – like all Federation Marines – he spoke English perfectly, along with Galactic Three. "The city is largely under our control."

"Good," Tobias said, shortly. Lafarge had drawn the short straw, no doubt, and had to remain at the spaceport while his CO and the other colonels were on the front lines. It worked for the Marines, even though it wouldn't have worked for the Federation Navy. "And the Funks?"

"We've taken over several large buildings and turned them into makeshift prisons," Lafarge informed him. "The Funks are being searched, processed and then guarded by a pair of companies. I've had to issue orders for no locals to be allowed to enter the camps after one of their more unwilling collaborators killed a prisoner."

"Good thinking," Tobias said, ruefully. He'd intended to be gentle in victory – it would have made for good publicity among the Galactics – but the locals really did have other ideas. "How secure is the city itself?"

"Most of it is fairly secure, but some parts have been consumed by riots before we could get troops in there to deal with them," Lafarge said. "And there are still a handful of Funks out there, looking for trouble. We'll bring it to them when they show themselves."

"Riots," Tobias said, quietly. The Funks had steadily created an underclass of humans, one that had fallen into criminal activity as the only way to stay alive. Of course they were rioting, now that the iron hand of Funk control had been removed. Terra Nova would take decades to recover from the trauma of alien control, assuming that humanity won the war. "And how much of the local government has survived?"

"The original Governor has not been found," Lafarge said, "but a number of collaborators were killed when we stormed the garrison. And..."

He hesitated. "And we found proof that some of them had been indulged by the Funks as a reward for their collaboration," he added. "They were permitted to rape, torture and murder as the whim struck them. Two of them were found with preteen children in their quarters..."

Tobias blanched. "Take them all into custody," he ordered, flatly. He wanted to unleash the Marines without a trial, to punish the collaborators as they deserved, but they had to make it clear that they were punishing the guilty. And what of those who had had no choice, apart from collaboration? Could they really blame someone if the

Funks had put a gun to his child's head and demanded his services, or else? "Make sure that enough evidence is recorded to use against them when we hold trials."

"Yes, sir," Lafarge said.

"I need to go to the city," Tobias said. It was selfish of him, but he wanted to see what the Funks had done with his own eyes. The reporters were already being shipped down from the assault carriers, ready to beam their reports back to Earth. They'd known that conditions on Terra Nova were bad, but they hadn't realised just how bad they'd become. "I'll need to meet with the Brigadier personally."

* * *

Conrad kept a wary eye out for Funks – or angry civilians – as the small platoon advanced down the street. He would have preferred a more subtle approach than a patrol that stood out for miles, but their orders had been clear. The Marines were to make a show of strength to convince the Funks that further resistance was futile, and warn the civilians that the colony was now under martial law. Some of them had been very ungrateful and started to riot as soon as the Funks were gone. Others were starting to kill collaborators, or to hunt down anyone who had helped the Funks, even against their will.

The sound of sobbing caught his attention as they turned the corner. He stepped forward, motioning for two Marines to follow him while the others remained behind, covering them. A young woman – hardly more than twenty years old – lay on the pavement, crying. Two other women stood over her, one hacking away at the crying girl's hair while the other held her down. Their victim looked pitiful, awakening Conrad's protective instincts. He lifted his rifle and pointed it directly at the hairdresser.

"Let her go, now," he ordered. Civilians were strange; sometimes they obeyed orders and sometimes they wanted to debate them, as if they didn't feel the need for discipline. But then, he'd been a tearaway before the Royal Marines had knocked some sense into his head. The distance

117

between him and the youths lashing out at their former tormentors was less than he would have preferred. "Now!"

He clicked the safety off and had the satisfaction of seeing the first woman stumble backwards. The hairdresser, made of stronger stuff, glared at him. Up close, he could see bruises on her face, inflicted by someone who had intended to hurt her without causing permanent damage. He'd seen them before, on women in places occupied by Western military forces. Their husbands liked to compensate for perceived insults to their masculinity by knocking their women around. They were brave enough to hit their wives, but not brave enough to confront the armed Marines.

"This... *bitch* used to sleep with Howell," the hairdresser said. Conrad winced, inside. The Marine network had already informed him that Howell had been one of the worst collaborators, a failed - by his own mismanagement - farmer before the Funk arrival. He'd been unemployed up until the moment he'd realised that he could sell his services to the Funks. "She used to entertain the lizards. Why should we not punish her?"

Conrad doubted the last charge; interracial sex was rare, almost non-existent. There were no actual laws against it, but as most intelligent races didn't really feel attraction for other races the Association didn't need to bother. The Hegemony males wouldn't find human females attractive, if they even recognised the difference between male or female humans. It was more likely that the hairdresser was exaggerating. Conrad certainly hoped she was exaggerating.

"Because all collaborators will be tried and, if found guilty, will be punished," Conrad said, firmly. He understood how they felt, but another thing learned from human history was that revenge was a road that had no ending. The losers would seek their own revenge as soon as they felt strong enough to take it. "She will be tried, along with the others. Let her go."

"And then she will walk," the hairdresser said, angrily. "Someone like her will flutter her eyelashes at the judge and jury and convince them that she was an unwitting dupe! A fancy lawyer will get her off on a technicality. She used to name people suspected of being part of the resistance and Howell's police picked them up and beat them until they confessed. I..."

Conrad pointed his rifle right at her heart and her voice trailed off. Regulations concerning the care of prisoners, whatever their crimes, were clear. The Marines were to prevent anyone harming the prisoners, particularly the ones who might have useful information for intelligence teams. Conrad doubted that the crying girl would have anything in her mind that ONI could use, but regulations were clear. Besides, rough justice offended his sense of order.

"Release her now or I will shoot you," he said, flatly. Behind him, the two Marines took off their own safety catches. "Step away from her."

The hairdresser looked into his eyes, and then reluctantly let the girl go. "You don't understand what we've been through," she said, finally. "You should help us."

"We did," Conrad said. "Now please go home. We'll take her to the camp."

He shook his head as the two women walked away. It was going to be a long day.

* * *

Gagarin City had once been a prosperous, if rough, city. Tobias had seen pictures sent home by Judy and he'd admired the neat little houses and the brick buildings that were steadily replacing the prefabricated structures produced on Earth. The Old West must have looked similar, back before civilization had crawled over North America, with small towns islands of human settlement in the wilds. Some of the colonists had been wealthy enough to afford to buy and operate a groundcar, but most of them had used bicycles or horses to get around the city – or outside. Terra Nova lacked any animals that could be domesticated to take the place of the horse.

Now, parts of the city were in ruins and the rest looked decayed. Many once-prosperous buildings were falling apart through lack of maintenance. The city's water and electricity infrastructure had been taken by the Funks, who often cut the supplies just to remind the humans who was in charge. Several buildings housed homeless families who'd had nowhere else to go. Some colonists had managed to turn a profit in the years of occupation, but they were the exception. The majority were poorer now than they'd been before the Funks arrived.

He'd done his best to read through all the reports, but they didn't prepare him for the reality - and there were sights he never wanted to see. Terra Nova had suffered a food shortage in the second year of occupation, a combination of a bad harvest and the demands placed by the Funks on the food supplies. They'd attempted to solve the problem by rounding up hundreds of unemployed humans and shipping them out to work on the farms, only to discover that the results were nothing short of disastrous. The people they'd chosen as farmers had *never* been farmers and most of them had been too ignorant to know how to start. Vast stretches of farmland had been ruined before the Funks realised that they'd made a mistake and gave up.

There was worse. People had been forced to turn to crime to survive. The Funks didn't seem to care about what humans did to each other, which allowed criminal syndicates to survive – hell, some of them had clearly allied with the Funks. Hundreds of women had been forced into prostitution, serving the few humans able to afford their services. A loaf of bread, a slice of meat, an egg or two… that was all it took to buy a prostitute for the night.

He winced as the groundcar turned a corner and he saw the man hanging from the lamppost, very definitely dead. Someone had hacked away at his body just to make sure and blood was pooling under his swinging corpse. A collaborator, no doubt, or perhaps someone murdered to pay off an old grudge in the confusion. Even the Federation Marines couldn't be everywhere at once. Small patrols moved through the streets, constantly broadcasting warnings for people to remain in their homes. In the distance, he could hear brief crackles of gunfire as the Marines stumbled across lurking Funks. They still hadn't completely surrendered.

The park had once been Gagarin City's pride and joy. A group of settlers had brought flowers and trees from Earth and planted them in the heart of the city, in front of the town hall. It had been beautiful before the Funks had destroyed it, burning the entire garden to the ground. Now, fencing had hastily been erected around the blackened soil and used to construct a POW camp. Inside, several hundred Funks sat listlessly, their bodies inhumanly still. They never wasted a movement, Tobias knew; it was a point of pride with them that they never wasted anything. Their homeworld had never encouraged conspicuous consumption.

Outside, a handful of Marines held their weapons at the ready, guarding the POWs. At least the Funks could be fed on human rations, making it easier to feed the prisoners. They could eat a far wider range of food than humanity, another legacy from their homeworld. Some races could only eat foodstuffs from their homeworld, or grew sick if they didn't eat precisely the right food every day. Feeding them would have been a great deal harder even with Association-level technology. No one had yet managed to produce something out of nothing.

The Town Hall had been patterned after the White House, although it was far smaller. There had been a minor scandal when it had first been designed, as critics had pointed out that the Governor only really wanted a spectacular mansion for himself. The Governor had been replaced at the end of the year, but the Town Hall had been completed just in time for the Funks to take over the planet. They'd installed the worst of the collaborators in the Town Hall and used them to administer the planet. A human would have used the building for himself. Tobias couldn't tell if the Funks didn't like the Town Hall, or if choosing to place their Governor in their garrison had been a security decision. Or perhaps it made perfect sense from their point of view. The supreme commander should have the securest possible accommodation, if only to intimidate possible opponents.

Inside, a handful of Marine intelligence specialists were moving from room to room, removing papers and computer

121

processors from the Town Hall. The spooks would work their way through them and extract any useful intelligence, although Tobias doubted that they would turn up anything interesting. Whatever else could be said about the Funks, their operational security was very good. They didn't tell their people anything unless their superiors believed that they needed to know.

"Admiral," Jones said. The Brigadier had ditched his armor as soon as the main body of fighting came to an end, like most of his men. "Welcome to Terra Nova."

Tobias smiled. They'd won the battle, even if the war would go on. The Hegemony would probably know that it was at war by now. He'd sweated bullets over the timing of the declaration of war – it might have come too early or too late – but it hardly mattered. The report from *Formidable* had confirmed that the Hegemony base hit by the gunboats had passed on a warning before it was destroyed.

"Thank you, Brigadier," he said. "It's great to be here."

Jones smiled. "We found someone in the basement you're going to want to meet," he said, and tapped his wristcom. "Send her in, please."

The door opened... and Tobias stared, all decorum forgotten. It had been years since he'd seen Judy, and she'd aged from the girl she'd been as a child, but he recognised her at once. He swept her up into his arms and hugged her tightly, kissing her forehead. His daughter was alive and well!

"I knew you'd come," Judy whispered. Tobias felt hot tears pricking at his eyes. "I waited for you and you came!"

"I came," Tobias said. It was suddenly very hard to speak. "I came for you."

Chapter Fourteen

"Apart from *Tirpitz*, which was completely destroyed, all of our cruisers suffered only minimal damage," Commander Sooraya Qadir reported. It was a day after the Battle of Terra Nova. "Captain Tallyman estimates that repairs to *Woodward*, the most badly damaged of our cruisers, will take no more than three days now that the Fleet Train has entered orbit. We could advance against the next target once repairs are completed.

"However, five destroyers were lost," she added. "Two of them hadn't been refitted with the reinforced variable shield generators that gave the rest of the fleet additional protection, but all five of the lost ships were picked off by the superdreadnoughts as they closed in on their attack runs. They just don't have the defences to stand in the wall of battle."

"We knew that when we went in," Tobias said, flatly. He would have loved to visit Judy's farm – the Funks had arrested her after discovering that she was involved in the resistance – but there was no time. The news about the war was already out and spreading. "And the Marines?"

"One hundred and nineteen died in the assault on the garrison," Sooraya informed him. "The largest single loss was the destruction of a shuttle before the Marines had finished bailing out, taking out fifteen Marines and the shuttle crew. Thirty-seven have also been injured severely enough to merit a return home to where they can receive proper medical care. They're currently in stasis in the Fleet Train."

Tobias nodded, sourly. Every one of the Galactics with ambitions to replace the Cats as the dominant race in the galaxy maintained a Fleet Train, a fleet of supply and transport starships that supplied their navies as they advanced away from their homeworlds. Humanity, on the other hand, hadn't had the time or resources to do more than improvise a fleet train from commercial freighters and a couple of mothballed deep-space survey ships purchased from the Association. Given time, he had no doubt that the Federation Navy would build a proper supply fleet of its own, but they would have to make do with what they had for the moment.

"The Hegemony lost two superdreadnoughts outright, a third wrecked beyond hope of repair and two more that surrendered," Sooraya added. "By any standards, it was the most one-sided victory in recent galactic history. We took over nine *thousand* prisoners from the superdreadnoughts alone and the spooks are already cooing over what they've managed to extract from their computers. We..."

Tobias held up a hand. In one sense, she was right; it *had* been a one-sided victory. But losing *Tirpitz* inflicted more proportional damage to the Federation Navy than the loss of five superdreadnoughts to the Hegemony. The balance of power, at least on paper, favoured the Hegemony, something the other Galactics would consider when they started thinking about who to support. So far, there had been little reaction from anyone else apart from a bland statement condemning the violence from the Association Commune. No one knew how the Hegemony would react to the defeat they'd suffered.

"Those are minor priorities, right now," he said. Earth had no superdreadnoughts, but while he was tempted to repair one of the captured ships and add it to his fleet, he knew that it would be worse than useless. Superdreadnoughts were ponderous brutes while his cruisers were light, fast and armed with superior weapons. There was no way to justify the cost in resources it would take to repair the captured ships. They'd be better spent on the new construction in Earth's orbital yards. "The priority is to advance on Garston."

The planners, those few who had known about Kryptonite, had been divided on the question of mounting further assaults. Some had pointed out that Earth had no claim – legal or moral – to Garston and that taking the planet would give the Hegemony a chance to score a major propaganda coup. Others had insisted that only hitting the Hegemony again and again would convince the Empress to back off, and that delaying the advance would give the Funks a chance to reinforce the threatened sectors. Tobias had clung to the middle ground until the decision actually had to be made. His fleet had won one battle and it was largely intact. They could advance before reinforcements were dispatched from the Hegemony.

And there really wasn't any other choice.

But there was a problem. The Hegemony was small compared to the Association, but it still held upwards of five hundred stars and trillions of Funks. There was little hope that humanity would be able to overrun and occupy it all, even if that didn't provoke intervention from the other Galactics. They would have to come to peace terms eventually, or the Hegemony would eventually grind them down and push humanity all the way back to Earth. Pressing the offensive might guarantee that the Hegemony couldn't discuss peace… and one of his private nightmares was his fleet advancing further and further, until it was cut off from Earth and trapped.

"Contact the commanders," he said, finally. "Inform them that I wish to depart no less than one week from today."

It would require superhuman effort to prepare the fleet in time, but it had to be done. Remaining static at Terra Nova, as the Hegemony might have done, was merely asking for defeat. They had to remain on the offensive…or risk losing the war.

"And then have the Marines send up the enemy commander," he added. "I want to have a word with her."

The psychologists swore blind that the Funks would recognise and understand their own ancient conventions. Sending a captured leader back to his – her – side was a gesture of contempt, a gesture that suggested that the enemy leader was of no value to either side. But he wasn't so sure. Anyone who had seen human weapons in action would at least *know* what was possible, even if she didn't know how. They could be giving the Funks a free gift, an intelligence bonanza, simply by sending her home.

He shrugged. The alien wouldn't be released until the next battle. By then, some of humanity's surprises would be known to the Galactics. And the others wouldn't have been shown to the Funks until they were deployed into combat.

And, again, there really was no other choice.

* * *

How *had* the humans become so advanced?

The question tormented her, overriding even her concern for her own safety. Lady Dalsha knew what would have happened to any important prisoners taken by the Hegemony; they'd be brain-sucked and whatever was left of them afterwards would be dumped into the nearest star. Most of the prisoners the humans had taken were nothing more than ordinary males, ones never trusted with any secrets, but she knew how much she knew. The armored humans who had taken her into custody would probably not hesitate to do whatever it took to dig information out of her mind.

But even that might be a preferable fate to what would happen to her if she returned home. The hunt for a scapegoat was the Empress' favourite choice of sport, if only to maintain her own position. After all, being ultimately responsible for the most disastrous defeat in the Hegemony's history would weaken her position... and then the rest of the aristocracy would start sharpening their knives. The Empress would put the blame on the officer who'd been in command - Lady Dalsha – and then have her brain-wiped and thrown to the males. There was no worse punishment in the Hegemony.

The humans had treated her reasonably well. They'd given her edible food – not always guaranteed when dealing with aliens – and enough water to keep her alive. The air was cooler and wetter than she preferred, but the human ships were so small that setting up a comfortable atmosphere in the brig would probably be impossible. Besides, the part of her that remembered the times when her ancestors had searched frantically for water knew that she should be grateful. Not all worlds were as harsh as the one that had given birth to her race.

She looked up as two humans entered the brig and stopped in front of the forcefield holding her inside. They both wore armor, concealing their repulsive human features. It was impossible to tell if they were male or female; with humans, anything was possible. They believed in the equality of the sexes. It was an absurd concept to her, but humans were an alien race. Surprises had to be expected.

The forcefield vanished with a crackling sound. "You will come with us," one of the humans said. "Do not attempt to resist."

Lady Dalsha rose to her feet with as much dignity as she could muster and allowed the humans to lead her out of the cell. The interior of their starship was painted an uncomfortable shade of white, with data terminals and consoles everywhere. It was so unlike one of the Association-built ships that the sheer alien nature of the humans was brought home to her. No Hegemony-built ship would have scattered data terminals around for the crew. They might have found something that was not suited for junior eyes.

She wanted to ask questions, but she had a feeling that the humans would refuse to answer her – assuming that they knew the answers. The Hegemony kept its juniors ignorant; many Galactic societies did the same, leaving the seniors in power to keep the system running. Instead, she kept silent and watched, hoping to see something that would unlock the secrets behind the alien ships. She saw nothing, but humans. If they'd obtained technology from another race, their unknown benefactors had not chosen to serve on their vessels. Perhaps they didn't want to be seen by the Hegemony, or perhaps the humans had stolen the technology from someone else. It seemed impossible that any race could advance so far, so quickly. Even the Cats had taken thousands of years to work out a gateway into quantum space.

The guards halted outside a sealed hatch, which opened a second later. Lady Dalsha stepped into the room and stopped, looking around her in surprise. The human commanders were given smaller living spaces than Hegemony males on superdreadnoughts, something that puzzled her. How could the superior be superior if there weren't clear marks of her – his – status? The human seated behind the desk rose up and nodded to her escort, speaking to them in one on the human tongues. There *were* translation programs that could handle human languages, but she had none. They'd taken everything before they'd brought her onboard.

"Welcome onboard the *Nimitz*," the human said. The human naming conventions for their starships puzzled her. Why name starships after their ancestors when there were so many ideals in the universe? "I am Admiral Tobias Sampson, commanding officer of this fleet."

Lady Dalsha felt her claws itch under her scales. She wanted to lunge forward and tear into the human, but she knew that his guards would stop her instantly with their suit-augmented strength. The results would be painful, and humiliating, at the very least.

"I am Lady Dalsha," she said, finally. "You have attacked my ships without provocation."

The human snorted. "I think we both know that there was ample justification," he said. "The important detail is that we won and took you and your surviving crewmen prisoner."

"So you did," Lady Dalsha agreed. The Association had tried to enforce certain rules when it came to dealing with prisoners, but she was uneasily aware that those rules were often flouted. "I should remind you that the Empress will not look kindly upon any mistreatment of my crewmen and myself."

The human smiled, barely showing his teeth. "Do you think that she would love us any better if we didn't mistreat you?"

Lady Dalsha waved one hand in the air, absently. "I am your prisoner," she said. "Why have you brought me here?"

"I wish you to take a message back to the Hegemony," the human said. "It is possible that your Empress will continue to fight the war, even after we have established our superiority in weapons systems. I want you to tell her that she can have peace, instead of getting her fleet slaughtered when it tries to counterattack. We don't really want anything apart from Terra Nova – and it's back in our hands. There can be peace."

Lady Dalsha stared at him. The human had to be insane – or ignorant. There was no way that the Empress would accept the loss of Terra Nova, not without trying to recover it. If human superiority wasn't clearly demonstrated – and it hadn't been – the Empress couldn't surrender Terra Nova without looking weak. The war would continue until the human race was crushed. Their new weapons, wherever they had come from, wouldn't be enough to even the odds. She'd seen enough to have a good idea how to counter their tricks.

But the Empress wouldn't know everything. She hadn't been able to get a signal out before the humans had forced her to surrender; everything she knew about the human tactics and technology would be useless, unless she managed to take the information back home. And if the humans were prepared to let her go...

"I will certainly take your message to the Empress," she said, slowly. "But you have attacked us savagely, striking from the shadows. We will not take that lightly."

"We didn't take Terra Nova lightly either," the human said. "We will provide transport for you from here to Garston." He smiled, as if there was a joke in his words she couldn't understand. "I'm afraid the military base there has suffered an... accident... but you should be able to find a civilian ship willing to take you the rest of the way home. Or you could pass on the message through the communications network. I dare say that one of the other Galactics in the system will agree to let you use their transmitter."

"Thank you," Lady Dalsha said. Perhaps she could win back a little honour through her report, and her thoughts on how to combat the human technology. Maybe the Empress would even spare her life. "I will do as you wish."

* * *

129

The President of the United States stared into the camera, putting every ounce of his experience into maintaining the solemn, grave and yet optimistic expression that the situation demanded. It wasn't easy. People said that the President was the most powerful man in the world, and there was a certain amount of truth in that saying, but he was hardly the most powerful man in the galaxy. The Empress of the Hegemony wielded more power than anyone on Earth could match, commanding fleets that could turn Earth's surface into radioactive ash if she willed it to be done. Earth had never quite recovered from discovering that humanity wasn't alone in the universe. There were times when the President felt that humanity was sinking towards self-inflicted destruction even without the Hegemony.

But then, humanity was really nothing more than a microstate to the Galactics. That realisation had stunned millions of humans. They weren't just unimportant, but insignificant, barely worthy of consideration. Fifteen years of effort had gone into changing that, into building humanity up into a minor galactic power, and yet the culture shock had never quite gone away. Earth had slipped into a siege mentality and a growing paranoia about the universe outside. Americans were stockpiling guns and building bomb shelters, shelters that would provide little protection if the planet was blown apart by antimatter torpedoes. And yet any politician who tried to get in the way was crushed. The panic was too strong to be easily controlled.

"My fellow Americans," he said. They'd cleared a slot for him on *every* television, radio and internet channel in America. Galactic-level computers had changed the internet beyond recognition, making it the most powerful medium for sharing ideas in history. They were far harder to censor or block than anything produced by mere humans. "I come to you with grave news. The long-expected war between humanity and the Hegemony has finally broken out."

His advisors had debated endlessly over the question of admitting that human ships had fired the first shots in the war. The President could understand their feelings;

Americans liked wars to be honest and open, even though wars had never been either. Pearl Harbour and 9/11 had both been sneak attacks perpetrated against America and both had galvanised the country. But then, so had the loss of Terra Nova. A good third of the planet's population was American.

"Human ships have liberated Terra Nova from alien rule," he continued. "The first battle was a stunning success. Humans have shown the Galactics that we cannot be taken lightly."

He paused. "But wars are not won by one victory alone. This will be a long hard struggle, a war that will define the future of both Earth and the Hegemony. I ask you all to pray for the success of the gallant Federation Navy, fighting to defend Earth, and for the American soldiers who will soon be joining the Federation Marines on alien planets. And I ask you to pray that we will emerge victorious from this war, secure in our place in the universe and confident that we will not be bullied and eventually enslaved by an alien race. God bless America."

The camera clicked off and the President relaxed, wiping his brow. God alone knew what would happen when the Hegemony responded to the attack, but he was sure that it would be bad – and if humanity wasn't ready, the devastation could be immense. He felt powerless to affect events, even though he was the President of the United States of America. No one truly realised just how much power the Federation Navy had, not until it had gone to war. The divided command structure gave the CNO remarkable latitude to fight the war as he saw fit.

At least we have a good man in charge, he told himself, and hoped that he was right.

He stepped into the briefing room and looked down at his public relations staff, the men and women who monitored public opinion and tried to urge him to surf the shifting tides through to win the next election. Half of them were already tapping away at laptops, reading internet forums and trying to put together a consensus on how the public was reacting to the news. The President was less impressed. The internet was a shifting maze of attitudes that seemed exaggerated through anonymity. No doubt there were already trolls sneering at his message online.

"The first results are already in," the youngest member of the group said. "People are scared, but also confident. They want victory and they believe that we can win it."

"Of course," the President said dryly. It would be days before they had a *real* picture of how the country was feeling. "So do we."

Chapter Fifteen

"They used to take children away to the garrison," Beverly Troy said. She was around forty years old, according to the colonist database Adrienne had downloaded before leaving *Wellington*, but she looked at least sixty. Many of the other colonists who had lived through five years of hell looked just as bad, if not worse. Some of them had fallen ill and died because they didn't have the right diet. "We all knew what they were doing with them, but we told ourselves that we didn't, that the kids were just visiting... oh God!"

She started to sob, noisily. "My little Eric went into the garrison," she said, between sobs. "He was only seven years old when they took him and... and I prayed that he'd be fine, that he'd be untouched, but he was such a pretty boy. They'd love him! Where is he? Was he alive or dead or did you put him out of his misery... I need to know!"

Adrienne shook her head tiredly as the woman kept sobbing. The Funks had been brutal, stamping down hard on any bursts of independences from their human captives, but they hadn't been outrageously cruel, at least not by their own standards. But the human collaborators, the ones who had served the Funks willingly, had indulged themselves in activities unthinkable to a sane mind. They'd preyed on men, women and – worst of all – children, to the point where the Funk troops were almost popular. No one had been able to tell if the Funks had allowed it on purpose or if it had been a simple oversight, but it hardly mattered. No wonder the colonists wanted to tear the collaborators limb from limb.

Three days after the battle, the fires were finally out and workers were starting to repair some of the damaged buildings. Others were beyond repair and would have to be demolished and replaced by new construction. The colonists had set to work with a will, although the Navy hadn't tried to hide the fact that the Funks might slip back in and occupy Terra Nova for the second time. Barbie had been vague on precisely how many Federation Navy ships had been damaged or destroyed in the battle, but Adrienne didn't need precise figures to know that the combined navy was weaker than the Hegemony. That had been one insight that wouldn't be going into her reports. The Funks would no doubt listen to human broadcasts with as much interest as humans listened to theirs and it wouldn't do to give them any idea of loss rates.

Down the street, most of the Funk prisoners were being marched out of the city, towards a POW camp that had been established several miles from human settlements. Adrienne found it hard to understand why the military would want to keep the aliens alive – instead of allowing the locals to throw rocks at them endlessly – but she supposed that they had their reasons. Some of the reporters had suggested leaving the prisoners in the city as human shields – *alien* shields, technically – before being shouted down by the others. There was not a shred of evidence to suggest that the Funks cared one whit about the safety of their own civilians. The battle they'd fought against the Marines had showed a frightening lack of concern for their own lives, let alone human lives. And besides, it would look very bad to the other Galactics.

She walked closer, studying them with genuine interest. Earth had played host to thousands of aliens over the last fifteen years – the Federation had worked hard to attract aliens with technical skills humans needed – but a surprisingly few number of humans had seen an alien in person. Adrienne had never seen a Funk before, even though they were humanity's main tormentors. They didn't look very intimidating now, with Marine guns trained on their backs. If they'd had tails, they would have been dragging them through the dirt. They'd been defeated and it showed.

A handful of locals were watching from the other side of the street. Two of them looked old enough to remember the days before First Contact; the other three were young children, barely older than the colony itself. A few more years and Howell and his gang of sadists might have come

134

calling to take the children away to their den. Adrienne ambled over towards them and held up her press card. The reporters had been wandering the city ever since it had been declared safe, collecting interviews from the colonists. Everyone seemed to have a story to tell.

But not all of them would talk. Some were fearful that the Funks would come back, although they'd have to start rebuilding the collaborator force from scratch. Others were frightened that their peers would deem their own little compromises collaboration; deprived of their main target, the mobs were turning on anyone who had been forced to work with the Funks. There was even another POW camp nearby for rioters who refused to listen to reason, forcing the Marines to arrest them. And then there were people who just wanted to put the whole nightmare behind them as quickly as possible.

"They took my brother away one day," the woman said. She looked down at the ground, sadly. "Howell's men said that he was tied into the resistance, that he'd been responsible for planting bombs in the city. I never knew if that was true, but I never saw him again. They killed him..."

Her husband took her hand, looking up reproachfully at the reporter who had intruded into their private grief. Adrienne understood; there might never be any answers for those who had lost friends and relatives to the Funks and their collaborators. Howell's men had destroyed their records when the Marines landed, while the Funks hadn't bothered to keep any proper records of humans they'd executed during the occupation. Most of the bodies had been destroyed, or buried somewhere without a marker. Local rumour said that the Funks had eaten the bodies, but Adrienne hoped that that was just a sick joke. Humans had always made up horrifying tales about their enemies to justify their hatred.

"I wish I could find out," Adrienne said. Reporters had a great deal of access, more than most people realised. But she couldn't find records that weren't there. "I could ask..."

"If you would," the woman said, but it was clear that she didn't expect anything to work. Adrienne couldn't blame her. "His name was Cameron Williams, but everyone called him Buck. It used to be a joke before the end of the world. He used to love bucking the rules..."

Adrienne looked at the children, and then turned and walked away, leaving them to their grief. They'd been traumatized by the occupation, as had every other human on the planet – and Earth itself would be shocked when the full truth was released. She'd already had two brief messages from Ward, one congratulating her on a piece that had been released just after the President's speech to the nation and the other ordering her to attach herself to Admiral Sampson and send stories and feature articles. Unfortunately, Admiral Sampson's aide had merely promised to pass on the request and had never got back to her. The military knew the importance of cooperating with the press, but the Admiral was likely to be very busy. There was a war on, after all.

The faces of the woman and her children kept flickering through her imagination later that afternoon, when she was allowed into the detention center run by the Marines. Unlike the POW camp for Funks, the detention center for collaborators kept them separated from each other by wire, preventing some of the suspected collaborators from murdering others. At least one person had claimed to be a collaborator, according to rumour, so he'd have a chance at murdering the bastard who had raped and killed his sister. He would have succeeded if it hadn't been for a meddling Marine.

A small investigation team had been charged with gathering evidence to use against the collaborators, confirming and quantifying their guilt. Those who had collaborated willingly, or engaged in atrocities, would face the hangman once they had been tried, or dispatched to Luna Penal Colony. The others, the ones who had been forced into collaborating, would be tried more leniently than the willing collaborators. But that probably wouldn't satisfy their enemies on Terra Nova.

"It's something of a legal gray area," the Marine Legal Officer explained, in the small office he'd taken from a Funk. It was a vaguely disconcerting place, close enough to what a human would find comfortable for the oddities to stand out. "You see, the Federation Charter strongly restricts where the Federation has jurisdiction – no one in the national governments wanted to create a world government that would eventually be able to dictate to them, not unlike the US Federal government dictating to the states. A typical compromise and one that probably would have bitten us on the ass sooner or later, even without the Funks. The Federation does have jurisdiction over Terra Nova, but there is no provision for overseeing criminal trials, let alone trials for treason and collaboration. It's not even certain if we could legally *charge* them with anything."

"But that's insane," Adrienne protested. "Surely there are rules..."

"There are, but precisely where those rules interact is the question," the Legal Officer said. "When I was a jarhead, I was bound by the Uniform Code of Military Justice – I volunteered, so there was no question about the UCMJ applying to me. When I requested transfer to the Federation Marines, I moved to the Federation Code, which was partly based on the UCMJ anyway. But in both cases I volunteered to accept entering that particular sphere.

"But treason against Earth isn't on the statue books," he added. "No national government wanted the Federation deciding what constituted treason. Who knew what would happen if that particular can of worms was torn open? Not them, that's for sure. Now, Terra Nova had – has - a limited criminal code dreamed up by the idealists who spearheaded the colonisation project, but it doesn't include treason and collaboration. No one considered the possibility when they started settling the planet."

He grinned. "Confused, yet?"

Adrienne nodded. "Yes," she said, bluntly. "We went to war without knowing what we were going to do to collaborators."

"That always happens, every time something changes," the Legal Officer assured her. "I think that, technically, our best choice would be to charge them under national laws against treason – they're still citizens of their home nations, even if they live here. Luckily, none of the children are old enough to be put on trial – they'd have to be tried under Terra Nova's law and that..."

"Doesn't cover it," Adrienne said, impatiently. "So...what is going to happen to them?"

"The spooks are currently picking through the prisoners' brains," the Legal Officer said. "Those who cooperate will have it entered in their records – perhaps they will be offered life imprisonment instead of execution. The others...will be charged once we figure out which body of law we can charge them under and put on trial. Whatever else happens, the victims will demand justice.

"One possible thought is convening courts here, with Admiral Sampson as the judge," he added. "If you squint at the regulations in the right way, it would be just about legal and quicker than anything else. But I don't think that national governments are going to go for it – it would set a dangerous precedent. An alternative is convening a trial here with a local jury, at least for the ones who have committed crimes that *can* be charged under the local legal code. Getting an unbiased jury, on the other hand, might be a little tricky."

"I don't envy you," Adrienne said. "Should I write articles complaining about the lack of anything to bring the bastards to justice?"

"Hard cases make bad law," the Legal Officer quoted. "And so does political pressure to get laws passed quickly without considering the consequences. They tend to make a lot of money for lawyers."

"You *are* a lawyer," Adrienne said.

"I rest my case," the Legal Officer countered, with a grin that Adrienne would have found charming under other circumstances. "But..."

He looked up. "Hey, do you want to *see* them?"

Adrienne nodded, allowing him to turn on a monitor screen. "I'm not entirely sure why the Funks built this place," he admitted. "It was largely abandoned by the time we landed and the locals say that no one was taken here for at least six months. But it not only keeps several hundred prisoners in confinement, it allows us to watch them constantly. That one there" – he switched the screen to display a single prisoner – "is Howell. The evidence we collected just on the first day will be enough to justify his execution under local law, even if he is never charged with treason. We won't even need the kids we found in his quarters to testify against him."

He shrugged. "And why did he do it?

"Apparently, if you believe him, he never got a break," he added, sardonically. "I can see why he might feel that way, right up until the moment I realise that he never even *tried* to succeed. He thought that success came automatically; he never realised that he had to learn and work and work damn hard. Maybe he was always twisted, maybe he was slowly twisted by bitterness... I don't know or care. He lost his right to freedom and life when he started molesting kids and tormenting their parents. Damn the bastard to hell."

"He doesn't look very impressive," Adrienne said, after a moment.

"They never do," the Legal Officer said. "I did some *pro bono* work during downtime between tours; one of the cases I handled was a group of Klansmen who'd been caught red-handed in the process of burning down a black church. None of them looked impressive; some were fat, some were disabled... one had a missing chin. The great champions of the white race were among its least healthy members.

"We saw the same in the sandbox," he added. "The nutcases who'd throw themselves on our guns were often the worst of the population. They could only thrive in chaos – not that any of them really did, of course. The ones who slap women for showing some skin are the poorly-educated men who have little hope of rising out of poverty, never realising that it is themselves that keep them back. And the whole bloody cycle goes on for year after year."

He shook his head. "If nothing else, we can do one thing," he concluded. "We can take those bastards out of the gene pool."

* * *

"The Federation Council extends its congratulations on your victory, Admiral," Admiral Sun Ji Gouming said. The Chinese admiral had become the Deputy CNO through political compromise, but he was a fighter and Tobias trusted him implicitly. If the US had ever had to fight China over Taiwan, he sometimes wondered what would have happened if Admiral Sun had been commanding the PLAN. "National populations have experienced mixed reactions, but the news of Terra Nova gave public moral one hell of a boost. We may see fear later on, once the delight wears off..."

He shrugged. China was less sensitive to what its civilians thought than America. "The Council has also accepted your proposal to push on and complete the reduction of Garston before the Hegemony can reinforce the world. If you detach the gunboats for raiding missions, you should be able to add to the enemy's confusion. I'm afraid that neither of our two intelligence services have been able to report much on what the Hegemony is doing – reports are always at least several days out of date before they reach us. From what we do know, the Hegemony has no intention of throwing in the towel just yet. Their Ambassador has been projecting high confidence to the Commune – she hasn't even attempted to rally support, as far as we can tell. But it's early days yet.

"Complicating matters is the presence of a Hegemony heavy cruiser and a light cruiser in the Heavenly Gate System," he continued. "ONI fucked up – we didn't know about their existence until the Canary Ambassador quietly passed the information to Ambassador Li. We're not sure what the Canaries will do; technically, any Galactic neutral should intern the ships until the end of the war, but the Hegemony will probably start pressuring them to be a little more accommodating soon if they're not already doing so. I don't think the Funks are particularly welcome guests..."

Tobias snorted. The Canaries had populated their solar system by the time the Association stumbled across them, meeting the Cats from a stronger position. But unlike the feline explorers, the Canaries had a religious taboo against leaving their system and very few had ever journeyed more

140

than a light-year from their star. They were tough, with an understanding of their technology that the Hegemony lacked, but not strong enough to stop the Hegemony invading their system if the Funks were prepared to soak up the losses. Tobias could easily believe that the Canaries wanted the Hegemony ships gone, or destroyed, yet they couldn't do it openly.

"The Council wants your thoughts on the matter soonest, before you head off to Garston," Admiral Sun concluded. "Just remember to keep reading Sun Tzu and apply it to the war - you won't go wrong."

He laughed, just before the recorded message came to an end. Tobias replayed it, listening carefully, and then read through the attached documents. The Canaries had always been friendly to the human race, but then they'd been friendly to everyone who visited their system. And they had no ambitions to become a major galactic power.

Picking up his terminal, he began to issue orders. He had an operation to plan.

Chapter Sixteen

"I think we have a contact," Karla said. "It's definitely a Hegemony convoy."

Joshua smiled, coldly. The Hegemony didn't control this sector of space very well, although not even the Association possessed a fleet large enough to patrol quantum space. With so many raiders on the loose, it was no surprise that the Hegemony preferred to use convoys rather than sending ships out on their own. The chances of any given ship being detected and intercepted were low, but losing even one ship could be irritating. Besides, even though the Hegemony was rich and powerful, replacing a lost ship was expensive.

"Good," he said. They'd been waiting for five days for a suitable target. Two other ships had passed near their position, but they'd both belonged to other powers. Attacking them wouldn't have harmed the Hegemony and possibly expanded the war. "How many ships?"

Karla frowned down at her console. Sensor readings were untrustworthy in quantum space, even at relatively close range. The convoy might be little more than a mirage, or it might be a fleet of warships heading to the front. Even with the best equipment money could buy, they still needed to slip closer to their targets before they could be sure they weren't flying into a trap.

"At least five ships," she said, after a moment. She'd developed a knack for reading sensors in quantum space, better than anyone else Joshua had met. It was still dangerous to take anything for granted. "Four of them are freighters, judging from their mass; the fifth is a destroyer, or possibly a light cruiser. It keeps altering position so I can't get a solid look at their emissions."

"Alert the other ships," he ordered. "Prepare to attack."

The borders between major galactic powers were infested with pirates, rebels and independent settlers, but very few of them would have dared to attack a warship. It would have been unprofitable even if they'd won the fight. The

Hegemony's decision to send along only a single escort hadn't been a bad one, assuming that they would be facing common pirates or raiders. What pirate would dare to pick a fight with a warship, even if he outmassed his target?

But Joshua had brought along *six* warships to his first operation, each one more powerful than the Hegemony escort ship. They'd destroy the ship and capture or destroy its charges – and when the Hegemony worked out what had happened, they'd know that they needed to send additional starships to escort their convoys, drawing reinforcements away from the war front. Joshua had spent the time between Earth and their current base researching the enemy's economy and their operations along the borderlands, concluding that many of the lesser clans within the Hegemony were heavily involved in trade with the Hegemony's neighbours. They would put pressure on the Empress to react strongly to the pirates, even if there *was* a war on. Some of them couldn't afford more than a few losses before they collapsed.

He tapped his console and *Blackbeard* slipped forward, heading towards her target. The other ships hung back, watching as the Hegemony destroyer finally realised that they were there and turned to face the oncoming ship. Energy weapons and shields weren't always reliable in quantum space either – few militaries would have chosen to fight a battle there if it could be avoided – which meant that they would be throwing torpedoes at each other. Joshua smiled darkly as the ship's ECM – ironically, bought from the Hegemony – went to work, creating ghostly sensor reflections around his ship. If they were *really* lucky, the Hegemony clans might start blaming each other for the raiders. It wouldn't be the first time one clan had started attacking another to clear the way for their own expansion.

"Enemy vessel is locking on," Karla said. "They're countering our ECM."

"Open fire," Joshua said, quietly. That shouldn't have been a surprise; if the Hegemony had built the ECM systems, they would have at least some idea of how to counter them. "Take the bastard out."

143

Blackbeard shuddered as she unleashed a full spread of antimatter torpedoes. Their target did the same, but some of her torpedoes rushed after the sensor illusions rather than *Blackbeard* herself. Joshua took a moment to note that torpedo sensors seemed to be less capable of penetrating ECM than the sensors mounted on enemy starships, before the first set of torpedoes impacted on the enemy ship. Four direct hits knocked down her shields; the fifth struck her naked hull. The crew never stood a chance. Their ship vaporised in a blinding flash of light, agitating the unstable folds of hyperspace around her.

One torpedo struck *Blackbeard*, shaking the light cruiser without inflicting any major damage. Joshua allowed himself a brief moment of relief, before triggering the message he'd recorded earlier, ordering the four freighters to surrender or die. Regular pirates saw no profit in destroying freighters either, but he didn't particularly care if they surrendered or had to be destroyed. Either way, the Hegemony would take a loss. He waited as the recording played out – he'd altered his voice so that he sounded like a Funk female – and smiled as the ships signalled their surrender. Their clans might ransom them, after all, if they were taken prisoner rather than being forced to walk out of the airlock. Or there might be a chance to escape when they reached the pirate base.

"Send in the troops," he ordered, as his small fleet took up positions around the freighters. "Remind Kang that I want the crews alive, if possible. No need to kill them when they can be interrogated."

"Of course," Karla said, dryly. "And Kang is so good at leaving people alive."

Joshua shrugged. Ideally, the crew would never realise that their captors were human. They'd purchased armored combat suits designed for several different races, ones that revealed little of their precise proportions, but it was difficult to be certain of anything when the suits still had to be humanoid. Kang had been booted out of the Federation Marines for excessive violence, which had amused the hell out of Joshua when he'd first heard it. He'd thought that was how people got *in*.

144

"Prisoners can be interrogated," he said, sternly. It would be too dangerous to try to ransom them back to their clans, although they *could* be sold on to others who might try to ransom them. Galactic law forbade the slave trade, but it was coming back along the borderlands. "And who knows what they might have to tell us?"

* * *

"Quite a valuable cargo," Kang said, an hour later. The freighter crews had been searched and then locked in their own holds while the boarders took control of their ships. "High-tech tools, several industrial modules and a ton of colony equipment. Their manifests record their destination as Hegemony-III, which suggests that they were working directly for one of the major clans."

Joshua nodded, thoughtfully. Hegemony-III was a major shipbuilding center, only a dozen light years from the dry world that had given birth to the Funks. Humanity's research had suggested that the Funks had problems duplicating some of the more fiddly Association technology, but the items they'd captured was the first real proof anyone had found. Their raid would have caused problems for the Hegemony even if they'd had to blow the ships and withdraw without ever knowing what they'd destroyed.

But if he recalled correctly, Hegemony-III was owned and operated by a clan that had ambitions to replace the Empress with one of their own. Given enough time, they might just have succeeded... particularly if they'd managed to put together a small fleet of their own. They'd *have* to suspect that one of their rivals had organised the intercept, even if they'd thought that their security was airtight. And their paranoia would do the rest.

"Good," he said, finally. Much of the cargo would be easy to sell onwards, pulling in thousands of credits to finance their private war. The fences would demand a share in the proceeds, of course, but it would still be worthwhile. He wanted to sell off the cargo and return to operations as soon as possible. "Did we find anyone interesting among the crew?"

"Most of them are low-status males," Kang said. "Even the females are lowly. None of them even tried to fight."

"Freighter crews," Karla said. "Sheep, the lot of them."

Joshua snorted. He'd spent long enough trading with the Galactics to know that the Hegemony freighter crews were among the worst in the galaxy. It wasn't entirely their fault; the Hegemony treated warship crews like kings, while freighter crews were regarded as the worst of the worst. Their commanders were females who had been political failures, too insignificant to be taken seriously by their queens, or offered the choice between serving as a freighter commander or jail. The quality of personnel rarely rose above mediocre.

It wasn't the only problem either. Where he'd been careful to give his freighter commanders a wide degree of latitude in how they commanded their ships, the Hegemony gave their commanders almost none. They were expected to follow orders and nothing else, even when it was obvious that their orders had been written by someone with no real appreciation of the situation, hundreds of light years away. Their maintenance was poor, leaving them to push their equipment until it finally failed; it didn't take much imagination to realise that their fleet train was likely to have all kinds of problems as they finally started to respond to the war. Or so Joshua hoped. Admiral Sampson had been confident, but Joshua knew too much about the crushing power of the Hegemony Navy to feel sanguine about the war's outcome.

But there's another reason for us, he thought, inwardly. *If Earth loses the war, if most of humanity is exterminated, at least we can seek revenge.*

"We'll drop them off on one of the isolated worlds," he said, shaking his head. The clans probably wouldn't pay ransom for any of their crews, even though their cargo had been important to their clan's long-term plans. They could have sold the crews into slavery, but he had his limits. Maybe the crews could find work on one of the other rogue ships. It wouldn't be the first time freighter crews had turned pirate – and given what they had been carrying, it might be a safer career choice than going home to report to their queens. "Leave the boarders on the ships – we'll take them directly to Shadow and offload their cargo there."

"Got you," Kang said. He was a big man, a descendent of Korean immigrants to the United States. His record had suggested a man who was a perfect soldier, except for outright racism against the Galactics – and the Funks in particular. But it was hard to blame him when his sister had been killed during the occupation of Terra Nova. "And if they give us trouble?"

Joshua didn't hesitate. "Kill them."

* * *

The Shadow system had been dismissed as worthless hundreds of years before humanity had even dreamed that the lights in the sky were just like the sun. It had been a red giant in the final stages of expansion before collapsing back in on itself – and, to humans and even the Galactics, appeared unchanged over the years since it had been surveyed by the Association. There were Galactics, Joshua knew, who worshipped the stars themselves, believing them to be gods. It was easy to understand why when a dying system lived longer than some intelligent races. Only the Cats, with their immortality, could really watch over the millennia as the star slowly died.

Maybe that explained a great deal about them, he thought, as *Blackbeard* and her freighters coasted in towards the pirate base. Few races lived longer than a hundred years naturally, even with the very best of medical care; to the Cats, humanity and the Funks had to look like swarming insects, living and dying so rapidly as to be almost unnoticeable. And compared to what the Cats had done, the younger races had created almost nothing. No wonder they didn't seem to realise that the races they'd helped rise to the stars might one day pose a deadly threat to their existence.

Shadow itself was a mass of asteroids, the remains of a Pluto-sized planet that had shattered aeons ago. It had been inhabited for hundreds of years, first by refugees from the Association and then by pirates, smugglers and black

147

marketers. Any of the Galactics – even Earth – could have taken the asteroid out, but it was simply too useful as a place to meet away from the eyes of law and order. Even the Hegemony had been known to send envoys to the asteroid, establishing links with races that might be able to trade them technology for raw materials or military support. Joshua had once heard that more diplomacy took place on Shadow than on Center. It was easy to believe when one considered just how many starships routinely visited the system.

There was no formal procedure for docking at Shadow. The docks were operated by several private companies – formed by pirates who had retired from piracy to spend their ill-gotten gains, according to ONI – who charged a small fee in exchange for docking rights and access to the small tanks of HE3. Shadow possessed no gas giant and so all of the fuel had to be brought in from another system, smuggled in from one of the major galactic powers. Joshua had worked as a freighter commander long enough to understand just how tightly the galactic economy was bound in to HE3. Earth had had a similar dependence on oil, before First Contact, but the difference was that gas giants were so plentiful and readily-accessible as to be politically meaningless.

Leaving most of the crew onboard to guard the ships, Joshua took Karla and boarded the asteroid, wearing encounter suits that should have concealed their origins. Like most multiracial structures, it looked larger than necessary to the human eye, a giant's house simplified almost to the point of insult. No experienced spacer would complain, even if most races found the asteroid slightly disconcerting. Few races would have problems visiting or even living within the asteroid, and those that did could hire representatives or send remote-controlled machines in their place.

Each of the asteroid's giant chambers held a place for visiting crewmen to get drunk and spend their booty. Joshua rolled his eyes when he saw the virtual brothel, boasting about sexual programs from all over the galaxy, with a long line of clients awaiting their turn in the booths.

148

It was cleaner than regular brothels, and they didn't have problems supplying precisely what the client wanted, but it still struck him as silly. There were people who became addicted to VR simulations and never wanted to leave and return to the mundane world. On Shadow, there were no precautions to prevent a customer from remaining so long in VR that they lost their mind.

"Look," Karla said. "Funks!"

Joshua followed her gaze and saw a pair of Funk females heading away from them. Both of them wore dark tunics rather than the golden scales that represented the Funk aristocracy, nor were they escorted by small armies of males, showing off their power to their fellows. They were either political refugees or travelling incognito. It would be interesting to find out what they were doing on Shadow, but one of the few rules the asteroid's operators did enforce was privacy. The Funks would be left alone as long as they didn't threaten other patrons.

"Ignore them," he said, as they reached a particular booth. The entrance was blocked by a solid hull-metal door, forcing him to press his hand against the scanner to inform the occupant that they were waiting. There was a long pause, just before the door slid open, revealing a darkened chamber illuminated by a faint light shimmering in the distance. He stepped inside, followed by Karla, and the door hissed closed behind them. "I have come."

Water moved in the distance, revealing a sheet of transparent metal holding in the liquid and keeping them from drowning. The alien – no one could pronounce what they called themselves – lived in a giant fish tank, breathing water as naturally as humans breathed air. It – Joshua didn't want to even *think* about the details of their sex lives – reassembled a giant crab, complete with sharp claws and unpleasant-looking tentacles. The Association had given them the stars, but their limitations meant that they rarely participated in galactic politics. He had no idea why one of them had come literally thousands of light years to live on Shadow, but there was no better fence in the galaxy. Perhaps its race had started to spread themselves across the galaxy, hoping to ensure their long-term survival. Most races did the same when they realised how easily they could be exterminated if they remained on one single planet, orbiting a single star.

"I have reviewed your message," the alien said. The voice was completely atonal, betraying not a hint of emotion – if they felt emotion. No one knew for sure. "You have obtained valuable goods."

There was a pause. Joshua waited. The water-born aliens had their own sense of time, regarding most of the land-dwellers as hasty mayflies. He'd once asked around and discovered that this particular crab was over two hundred years old, unless another of its kind had replaced it when the first one had died. No one cared enough to ask.

"I am prepared to deal for them," the alien said, finally. Unlike most of its kind, it liked bargaining. Maybe that was why it had travelled so far to find a place it was happy. Joshua wouldn't have wanted to be separated from the entire human race, but the crabs took a different view. "My first offer is twenty thousand credits, in cash or kind."

Joshua smiled and got down to haggling.

Chapter Seventeen

"The scouts have returned, Admiral," Commander Sooraya Qadir reported. "The only new Hegemony ships are a trio of light cruisers. They're running an eccentric patrol pattern around the planet."

Tobias frowned. The Galactics had had thousands of years to dream up tactics for their militaries, but the pattern the Hegemony ships were following made little sense, unless they were hunting for cloaked ships. But any cloaked ship with passive sensors could have carried out its work far away enough from the planet to remain safe, no matter how determinedly the Funks searched. Unless...

He smiled as it suddenly clicked in his mind. "They think that our quantum drives are much more precise than their own," he said. "We came out of quantum space right on top of the fleet defending Terra Nova. Maybe they think we did it deliberately."

"We did," Sooraya reminded him.

"Yes, but we could only do that because their fleet was in a fixed position," Tobias said. "We knew exactly where it was when we jumped in, but if they haven't realised that we surveyed the system first..."

He tapped his console. "It's either an attempt to prevent us hitting them before they see us coming, or a first attempt at building an anti-gunboat doctrine," he added. "Either way, it won't save them from us. Alert the fleet. We jump into the system in five minutes; endpoint" – he tapped a position on the display – "here."

Sooraya started speaking into her headset, leaving Tobias alone with his thoughts. Deploying the gunboats had been a risk, giving the Funks – and the rest of the Galactics – a look at them before they could be deployed in overwhelming force. But there had been little choice. By the time there were enough gunboats to tear apart the entire Hegemony Navy, Earth would have been occupied for years. If they'd had more ships, or enough time to develop weapons far superior to anything the Hegemony possessed...

And if wishes were horses, beggars would ride, he firmly reminded himself. *You knew the risks when you devised the operational plan. It's a little late to complain now.*

"All ships report ready, Captain," Sooraya reported. The gunboats had had to use the quantum gate, which might have been why the Hegemony had towed a number of OWPs to the gate and positioned them to block *Formidable* if she returned to the system, but his cruisers weren't so limited. "Quantum drives are online and ready to take us out into normal space."

Tobias took one final look at the last images recorded by the scouts. Most of the vast numbers of freighters observed by the gunboats had departed, but a number remained; ONI reported that some of them had been ordered to observe the battle and report back to their owners. It was difficult to trace public opinion among the Galactics, particularly among the races that had less open governments than humanity, but their military forces would be very alarmed by the Battle of Terra Nova. Five invincible superdreadnoughts had been destroyed or captured by a handful of mere cruisers. And with the superdreadnought the yardstick - the *former* yardstick - for measuring galactic power...

"Take us out," he ordered, quietly. He'd already issued orders to his crews, reminding them to make damn certain they were shooting at the Hegemony before opening fire. There were too many neutral ships in the system for his peace of mind, even if most of them were in orbit around the planet, keeping their distance from the Hegemony ships. "We'll aim right at the quantum gate and engage the OWPs as soon as they come into range."

He smiled at the thought. Charging transit fees was considered bad form among the Galactics, but placing actual defences near the quantum gate was almost taboo. There was too great a chance of the automated defences accidentally engaging friendly or neutral ships before they realised their mistake, if only because a hostile ship could engage the defences before the defences decided that they were allowed to open fire. Most planetary systems placed their quantum gates well away from anywhere that needed to be defended, giving their militaries time to react if the shit hit the fan. The Hegemony was *not* going to make itself popular by putting hair-trigger defences in the midst of a vital system.

The display altered rapidly as the fleet slid back into normal space. Irritatingly, they'd emerged some distance from the Hegemony starships, which gave the enemy some time to react to the new threat. Tobias wouldn't have been too surprised if the Hegemony cruisers simply opened up gates of their own and jumped out; even without the advanced weapons, his ships overmatched their squadron. Instead, they seemed to be playing a cagey game, watching and stalking his ships outside weapons range.

"At least they won't be trying to support the orbital weapons platforms," he said. The recorded message was already going out over the system, warning the Galactics that they were in the midst of a war zone – and that humanity intended to take the planet. Tobias had already planned the occupation, ensuring that the Galactic shipping lines would still be able to use the planet – and reducing transit fees by more than half. "The fleet will advance to clear the gate."

Galactic OWPs weren't that heavily armed, individually. Each of them mounted antimatter torpedo launchers and phase cannon, but they were almost defenceless compared to orbital fortresses and superdreadnoughts. Few Galactics would consider striking an inhabited planet deliberately – it would have alienated the entire galaxy – leaving the platforms more intended to deal with pirates and rogue starships rather than attacking fleets. Other Hegemony worlds were more heavily defended, but Garston had always been something of an oddity. Besides, the gunboats had already obliterated the system's main defence.

"Enemy platforms opening fire," Sooraya reported. "They are combining their fire against *Perry* and *Jellicoe*. Their commanders are deploying countermeasures now…"

"The remainder of the squadron is to move to cover them," Tobias ordered. Concentrating fire against his ships was a smart move, another reminder that the Hegemony's commanders weren't stupid. Unlike a standard ship, his ships could lose one aspect of their shields without losing them all, but the enemy could shoot through the holes and burn into their hulls. "All ships are to continue firing."

Jellicoe flipped over and evaded a spread of antimatter torpedoes, which flamed out before they could lock onto a second target. Moments later, the torpedoes detonated as their confinement chambers lost power, seconds before their launcher was obliterated by a phase cannon burst from *Cunningham*. The remaining OWPs started to fire wildly as their command and control systems broke down, before they were swiftly wiped out by the human ships. Tobias smiled in relief as the fleet spun around and headed away from the quantum gate. No ships lost; only one mildly damaged.

"The Hegemony ships are starting to draw away from us," Sooraya reported. "They must be redlining their engines just to pull that kind of speed."

"Looks that way," Tobias agreed. Human engineers were sure there was a way to reduce the time necessary for a superdreadnought-massed ship to reach cruising speed, but so far none of their experiments had produced anything workable. Ironically, without heavy ships of their own in the system, the Hegemony would be able to pull a faster rate of acceleration than their enemies. "Are they just trying to make a good show for their superiors...or are they stalling?"

"Stalling?" Sooraya asked. "What for?"

"I don't want to wait around and find out," Tobias said. Without a gunboat element of their own, the First Strike Fleet would only be able to overrun the Hegemony ships after a long chase – assuming, of course, that the Hegemony cruisers didn't jump into quantum space and escape after forcing Tobias to waste time chasing them down. Chasing them was pointless at best and, if they were trying to lure Tobias into a trap, deadly. "Order the fleet to reverse course and take us back to the planet. I want Marines ready to deploy to the orbital installations and the surface if necessary."

Intelligence had sworn blind that the five superdreadnoughts at Terra Nova had been the only heavy combat element available to the Hegemony for a hundred light years – but they'd missed the ships at Heavenly Gate and they might well have missed others. Tobias knew better than to take anything Intelligence said for granted, no matter how closely it agreed with what he wanted to see. It was quite possible that something nastier than a trio of light cruisers was waiting in quantum space or even normal space for their chance to take his ships by surprise. Or perhaps they were just stalling before they had to return home. The Hegemony wouldn't be kind to anyone who returned reporting defeat, no matter how badly outmatched they'd been.

Or maybe they're gathering intelligence, he thought sourly. The distance between the two squadrons was widening now that the human ships had reversed course. Absently, he wondered if the Hegemony ships would dance closer now that they could do so safely. He considered using the new ECM drones and cloaking devices to ambush the enemy ships if they risked coming closer, but it wasn't worth it for three minor cruisers. Giving the other Galactics warning of what the Federation had developed over the last fifteen years would give them a chance to pass the information on to the Hegemony. Even with a bloody nose, the Hegemony was still intimidating – and really, all they'd need was a considerable bribe. A few million credits would be a small price to pay for accurate sensor data.

"A number of freighters are spinning up their drives," Sooraya reported, flatly. "Some of them are signalling and requesting permission to leave through the gate; several others have started to head out into the outer system."

Tobias shrugged. There might be nowhere for the freighters to go without a quantum drive, but their commanders would probably be glad merely to get away from the fighting. Freighters had no business in the line of battle, even the few but increasing number that carried weapons to deter pirates. In theory, the ships were supposed to remain in orbit until his Marines had had a chance to intercept them, but few freighter commanders would want to take the risk of having their ships confiscated. Besides, it wasn't as if they could do any harm.

"Let them go," he ordered. "The gate is unlocked?"

"Not yet," Sooraya said. "The Marines would have to board the station and capture the control system."

"Detail a Marine unit to capture the station intact," Tobias ordered. "Broadcast a general message to the fleeing freighters; inform them that they have permission to leave and that we will unlock the quantum gate as soon as it is in our hands."

"Yes, sir," Sooraya said. "The Marines are on their way now."

Garston had been settled for hundreds of years. Even though it was a minor system even to the Hegemony, the system had hundreds of mining and processing nodes scattered throughout the asteroid belt, with dozens of industrial production satellites orbiting the planet itself. The Funks weren't the only power to have invested in the system, even though they owned it formally; they couldn't afford to simply destroy other investments without risking serious repercussions. Earth would make use of the Funk industry if it were captured intact – the supply base on the moon had already been targeted by a couple of Marine companies – but the remaining industry would have to be rented, or left alone. Besides, even if Earth lowered the fees and taxes, the system would be a nice source of Galactic currency for Earth's war effort.

The Hegemony cruisers continued to hold position, watching from well outside weapons range. Tobias kept glancing at the three red icons, unsure what – if anything – they had in mind. Intelligence had already noted tachyon-burst transmissions from the massive arrays in orbit around Garston, no doubt sending updates to the Hegemony's Empress. By now, it was certain that she knew what had happened, even by the most pessimistic modal of galactic communications. And then the Hegemony would start plotting its counterstroke.

"The Marines report that they have secured the weapons dump," Sooraya said. "They haven't been able to draw more than a handful of files from their computers yet, but what they have found suggests that the Funks pulled the antimatter torpedo launchers and weapons from the dump and transported them out-system. The antimatter generators have been destroyed."

"Smart thinking," Tobias noted. The Hegemony could have destroyed the entire dump, but instead they'd chosen to pull out the most important weapons and abandon the rest. Maybe it was a trap... but the Marines would have known to search the base carefully. Even so... "Tell the Marines to check again for unpleasant surprises and then find us a manifest. If there's anything we can use, I want to use it."

The Hegemony could trade space for time indefinitely. Tobias knew that Earth couldn't afford the same luxury. The further the fleet advanced into Hegemony space, the harder it would be to keep maintaining and operating the fleet's systems, even if the Hegemony didn't start slipping raiders in behind their lines to take out the fleet train. If they could capture and use Hegemony supplies, advancing further would be easier, at least until they ran into something so hard they had to stop. The Hegemony had to know that too. A human commander, left to his own devices, might accept the loss of unimportant systems, knowing that they could be recovered once the counteroffensive began. But his political masters might have different ideas.

And any show of weakness from the Empress would encourage the lesser clans to start thinking about overthrowing her...

"Admiral," Sooraya said, "the Marines have secured most of the orbital stations. There was no resistance, even from the males. They're ready to start unlocking the quantum gate now."

"Tell them to proceed," Tobias said, grimly. He would have preferred the enemy to attack, even if they had brought two superdreadnought squadrons to the party. Instead, the enemy seemed to be waiting. But waiting for what? If intelligence was right, there was nothing to wait for...

The hour passed slowly until the quantum gate was finally unlocked and opened to traffic. He watched a long line of freighters slowly making their way out of the system, some of them no doubt carrying important Funks who had paid heavily for passage away from the human ships. Some of the transmissions they'd intercepted from the planet below spoke of civil unrest, even of frantic males turning on females. The Funks were far from the only inhabitants of the system. Some of their client races would turn on their masters as soon as they realised that there was a chance at freedom. Or maybe the Funks would start lashing out at the others as soon as they realised they were about to lose their grip on the planet.

"Admiral," Sooraya said, sharply, "two of the Funk starships just jumped out. The third apparently cloaked and vanished. We can't track it at this range."

Tobias frowned, although in truth he'd expected it for some time. Leaving a picket in the system to watch the human ships was sound tactical doctrine, one of the aspects of Galactic thought that humanity agreed with wholeheartedly. The Hegemony ship would probably be able to evade capture or destruction as long as she was careful, transmitting burst messages back to her high command. No doubt the other ships would serve as pickets elsewhere, heading back towards their next major system.

"Understood," he said. "Remind all ships to be on their guard. We have to assume that the Funks will attempt to attack our ships if they feel that they have an advantage."

He hesitated, and then keyed his console, opening up a link to Brigadier Jones. "I want to try to prevent the rioting from destroying too many lives and properties," he said, shortly. "Can your Marines go down there and protect the population?"

"We can protect some of the larger cities, but not easily," Jones said, after a moment. "We don't have the manpower to cover the entire planet and... Admiral, there *will* be civilian casualties. Stunners designed to work on humans won't work so well on other races."

Tobias winced. The Marines had never been intended to serve as a peacekeeping force; rather, they'd been designed to serve as the tip of Earth's spear. Once national forces moved into in place, they'd have some reinforcements, but the latest from Earth warned that the national populations were reacting strongly against deploying such units away from their homelands. Everyone wanted Earth defended first.

And a single... *incident...* could provide the Funks with a political windfall. They'd already picked up transmissions from Galactic reporters, who'd suddenly found themselves watching the greatest story for the last thousand years. Trying to save the planet's population could be disastrous; not trying to save the planet's population could be worse. At least they could try...

"Prepare your men for deployment," he finally ordered. Half of the Marines had been scattered out over the orbital platforms. They'd have to be recalled once they transferred the prisoners to a harmless freighter. Even the Funks wouldn't try to argue with a man in powered combat armor. "And warn them to be careful."

It was an unnecessary order and he knew it. The Hegemony had been keen to keep its clients and outside visitors disarmed, but it didn't take more than a little ingenuity to come up with makeshift weapons. Funk troops stationed on the planet itself might be going a little crazy if they felt they'd been abandoned by the Empress and her navy. He could be sending the outnumbered Marines into a death trap.

But there was little choice.

"And send some of the reporters down with them," he added. "We might at least try to get good press out of the incident."

Chapter Eighteen

The Hegemony's cities were strange to human eyes, even though they had been constructed from modern materials. They reassembled giant anthills constructed from mud, joined by roads that looked out of place compared to the buildings. Behind them, on the outskirts of the city, were buildings that had clearly been built to a different set of aesthetics. Towering spires rose up to greet the sunlight, outlined by pillars of smoke rising up towards the sky. The live feed from the advance drones left no room for doubt; the remainder of the population was rising up against the Funks.

Conrad winced as the shuttles screamed down towards the center of the city. It had an unpronounceable name – hiss, squeak, hiss, as far as he could tell – and so the Marines had nicknamed it the Mud Palace, but there was no mistaking its role. Nor was there any mistaking the crowds laying siege to the building and threatening to break inside and lynch the remaining Funks. The aristocrats who had ruled the planet for so long had fled, but the junior bureaucrats had remained. And if they didn't save them from their own victims...

Some of the Marines had wondered out loud why they were bothering to risk their lives saving Funks. Conrad had reprimanded them, pointing out that even if some Funks were evil little shits, the remainder of the species was hardly indictable for their crimes. Besides, there was the question of perception. If humanity acted to save its enemies, it should make for some good press among the Galactics. Maybe the Funks would see humanity as an honourable enemy, rather than a race they could pick on whenever they felt evil. Privately, Conrad doubted it, but it wasn't his choice. The Admiral had made his orders quite clear.

"Prepare for drop," he ordered. Coming in so close to the city was a deadly risk – all it would take was a single HVM and the shuttle and its Marines would be scattered in

160

pieces over several miles – but there had been no other choice. Intelligence had provided maps of the city, yet getting from the outskirts to the Mud Palace would have taken too long even if no one put any obstacles in their way. The drone feed showed barricades being constructed by rebels within the city itself, while large columns of farmers and settlers from the countryside were advancing towards the home of their tormentors. "On my mark..."

He'd found himself effectively promoted in the wake of the battle on Terra Nova, as a result of so many officers being killed in the fighting. Typically, the actual rank and increased pay *hadn't* caught up with him, although it wasn't as if he had anything to spend it on while serving with the fleet. There had been little time for shore leave on Terra Nova, but they had managed a few hours in the city before departing – and no one had expected them to pay for anything. Some of the younger Marines had enjoyed themselves so thoroughly that Conrad had had to chew them out for straggling back to the spaceport late. If they'd had to leave ahead of time, he'd warned them, they would have been left behind and declared AWOL.

"Now," he ordered. The shunt caught him and propelled him through the hatch, falling down towards the planet below. His datanet came active as the remainder of his unit spilled out behind him, already falling into formation. The alien city was far larger to his naked eyes than it had seemed on the drone feed, a fairly common problem. Military maps were very detailed, but they were never quite the same as the terrain. He'd seen plenty of senior officers throwing fits because the map said that their subordinates should be advancing far quicker than they actually were, if only because the map hadn't mentioned that the terrain was covered in mud.

The antigravity field slowed his fall as the Marines fell around the Mud Palace. It was surrounded by a great teeming mass of intelligent life, some humanoid and others so alien that it was surprising to see them in person. One was nothing more than a mass of tentacles mated to a shell and a pair of large, almost cartoonish eyes. He'd seen one of those aliens before, but it took him a moment to remember

161

that it had been in a post-First Contact remake of *Star Trek*. The movie had bombed, if he recalled correctly. Spock looked much less impressive when compared to *genuine* aliens.

He touched down and raised his rifle, ready for anything. The last report they'd had from the ground was that the Hegemony soldiers had been ordered to return to barracks, but not all of them had obeyed orders. They were supposed to be utterly faithful to their queens, the females who ran their lives, yet when passions ran high the females tended to lose control of their men. His lips twitched into a smile as they advanced towards the gates, despite the danger. The Funks were closer to human than they would have liked to admit.

The gateway was barred by a glittering force field, sparking and crackling as the mass of aliens pressed against it. Some of them would have been injured as the pressure on the field slowly increased, but that didn't seem to stop them. Judging from the brief reports flickering across the datanet, any Funk outside their own districts would be lucky to live through the day without being murdered by the rest of the population. Indeed, two of the Funk districts appeared to be having their own civil war. The lesser clans would have been outraged at how quickly the planet had been lost, along with their vast investments. It wouldn't be long before their outrage manifested in plots against the Empress.

A set of Funks were watching the crowd nervously, barely heeding the Marines sidling up behind them. Conrad couldn't blame them for being worried; they carried no weapons, as ordered by the human occupation authority, and the crowd would certainly tear them limb from limb if they got their hands on them. He'd never been on the ground during a riot, but some of the older Royal Marines had been in Iraq or Afghanistan and their stories had been horrific. Some of their comrades had died because of restrictive ROE that prohibited firing back even when there was a clear and present threat to their lives. At least Conrad's orders were a little looser.

One of the Funks turned to look at the Marines. She seemed almost glad to see them, which had to be a first. They'd been warned, time and time again, that human body language didn't always match the Galactics, but Conrad was sure of it. Her hissing voice, according to his suit's analysis program, was definitely relieved. Someone else would be taking responsibility for the safety of the Mud Palace.

"Go inside," Conrad ordered. The second detachment of Marines was already inside, securing the building and its people. They'd probably lost their chance to capture the Mud Palace's files before the Funks destroyed them, but intelligence's computer experts would take a look at them and see what they could pull out of the systems. Some of the Funks probably had computer skills to match any human hacker, yet they might not have been allowed to rig the systems to completely wipe everything. Or so ONI had suggested. "We'll provide protection from the crowd."

Beyond the walls, he could see flames rising up in the distance. The rebels had torched a number of buildings, including one with a title that translated as Human Resources. It took Conrad a moment to realise that it was the Funk's version of a labour exchange, a place where unemployed Funks – or aliens – were ordered to work on specific projects, no matter how unsuited they were to the job. On Terra Nova, the Funks had tried to push humans into working as slaves – here, it proved that they did the same to every race under their control. No doubt someone could get some good propaganda out of that, once the city had quietened down a little. Maybe the Galactics would be outraged at how the Funks had treated other life forms.

The forcefield started to glow brighter, a sure sign that it was on the verge of collapse. Conrad barked orders and the Marines advanced, weapons at the ready. A quick check through the combat database revealed that there were no less than nineteen different races represented in the crowd, ranging from aliens so fragile that a stun burst would kill them to aliens tough enough to be able to tear apart an unarmored human. Conrad cursed under his breath as the Funk guards fled back towards the building, knowing that there would definitely be casualties. None of the crowd seemed to be carrying anything more dangerous than neural whips – designed by the Funks for use on reluctant slaves – which meant that the Marines themselves were probably in no danger. The real problem would be avoiding mass slaughter if the crowd pushed over them.

He checked the datanet as the forcefield started to fail. Other Marine units had landed in the city, securing defence posts and military buildings, but there were none close enough to aid him if the shit hit the fan. The shuttles were broadcasting warnings over the planetary communications network, urging everyone to remain in their homes and stay off the streets, but as far as he could tell no one was actually listening. Officially, the city had upwards of five million residents and they all seemed to be gathered outside the gates. The Hegemony would probably have started using their version of sleepy gas and to hell with the consequences, but humanity didn't have that option. Too many civilians would die.

"The forcefield is going," one of the Marines said. Conrad barely knew him; he'd been transferred over from another company to make up the shortfall. The Federation Marines hadn't been designed for rapid expansion and there were almost no reserves, something that would have to be rectified in the future. Sergeants were often asked to put forward their view on what had worked – and what hadn't – in post-combat reviews and he was already planning a scathing attack on the political leaders who had forbidden the Marines more than ten thousand soldiers at any one time. "Here they come..."

The forcefield gave one final crackle and failed. There was a roar of triumph from the crowd as it lunged forward, smashing through the gate as through it were built of paper. Conrad cursed again and started to broadcast the recorded message, even though he knew it would be useless. Even if the people at the front of the crowd had thought better of it and wanted to break free, the ones behind them would keep pressing them onwards. The training they'd had for mob situations had been limited, but the instructors had warned them that many injuries occurred when someone fell to the ground and was trampled under the crowd's feet before they could get back up. Some of the aliens in the mob were child-sized, small enough that their larger fellows might knock them down without even noticing. Conrad shivered as the mob closed in. People were about to die.

"Link arms," he ordered. The Marines braced themselves, taking up positions that would allow them to halt the mob without – he hoped – using their augmented strength. He caught a glimpse of an alien mouth, green and disgusting, before the aliens slammed into the Marines. The pressure was great enough to push the line back before they could compensate, pushing back as gently as they could. Conrad forced himself to watch as the aliens pressed against his suit, a multitude of different hands tearing away at the metal. They couldn't get in, he kept reminding himself, but it was no reassurance. It was impossible to escape a sense of claustrophobia as hands clawed at his suit.

"Disengage your close interface," one of the Marines suggested. Conrad nodded in agreement. The interface with the suit allowed the Marines to wear their armor as if it were part of them, but it worked *too* well for mob situations. Even the most focused Marine found it hard to escape the conviction that the crowd was tearing at his unprotected skin. It would be dangerous to go into combat without it, but they could reengage at any moment. "They can't get to you without it."

He was wrong, Conrad suspected. The crowd, balked at the gate, was trying to scramble over the wall. It was covered in wire and sharp metal prongs that would tear away at unprotected flesh, but so was the fence around Marine bases and *that* didn't stop Marines sneaking out for a night on the town. The crowd pressure would force them onwards unless they were stopped, yet how could they stop them without resorting to live weapons? Two of the shuttles made passes over the crowd at terrifyingly low height, but most of the crowd wasn't discouraged. Anyone at the rear who wanted to break free and go home could have done it by now. The remainder wanted revenge on the Funks – and God help the humans who were trying to save them.

"We're going to lose this unless we use live weapons," he said, into the datanet. He glanced backwards, at the Mud Palace. God alone knew how many Funks lived there. "I think we need to start flying their targets out of the mob's reach."

An explosion, billowing up in the distance, underlined his words. "And I suggest that you hurry," he added. Parts of the wall were starting to crumble. Once they fell, the Marines would have no choice, but to disengage and retreat back to the Mud Palace, if they could without hurting the crowd. A Marine who'd been knocked down would have to wait until the crowd dispersed before he could escape. "We don't have much time left."

The crowd howled in rage as the first shuttle came in and hovered above the roof of the Mud Palace, using tractor beams to pick up the Funks and a handful of their collaborators. Conrad checked the datanet, which reported that there were over two hundred Funks in the Mud Palace, including some children. Humans brought their children with them on assignment too, although he was surprised that the Funks had brought male children away from their clans. Perhaps the Funks on the planet had ambitions to form a clan of their own. What little he'd heard about the clan system suggested that it was possible, but the other clans wouldn't be too happy about it.

His suit shook as the first rock crashed down on his helmet. The crowd was pushing harder, throwing rocks and bottles towards the Marines. One bottle was filled with petrol and set on fire, exploding just behind the Marine line. It wasn't enough to break through armor that could stand off bullets and even missiles, but it was dangerous to the crowd. Conrad detailed a pair of Marines to stamp out the fire, even though it would suggest that they were intimidated by the flames. The irony didn't escape him; they were working to protect a crowd that was trying to kill them. If they hadn't been wearing armor, they would have had to resort to live weapons by now.

"We need some fucking riot foam," a Marine with a German accent said. "Something that will get them away from us before it's too late."

"Half of the bastards are allergic to riot foam," Lieutenant Piebald said, over the datanet. "We might as well spray them with nerve gas. And there are some races that think that nerve gas is a great afternoon tipple."

"We have shuttles picking up water from the lake," a senior Marine injected. "They'll drench the crowds, maybe give them some incentive to disperse."

Another shuttle took off from the Mud Palace as the walls finally collapsed. "Too late," Conrad said, grimly. "All Marines... back, now!"

Augmented legs threw him back towards the Palace. He was sickeningly aware of what had happened to the aliens pressing against him, but there had been no other choice. The mob howled in victory and lunged forwards, charging right at the fragmented Marine line. Conrad snapped a second set of orders and the Marines leapt upwards, landing on the side of the Mud Palace and scrambling up towards the roof. The datanet claimed that all of the Funks had finally been evacuated, removed before the mob could get its hands on them. Conrad hoped that they were right as the shuttles came back for the Marines. At least most of the other buildings they'd needed to secure were safe. The rest of the rioting would have to be left to burn itself out, unless dropping water was enough to disperse the crowd.

The tractor beam caught him and whisked him up towards the shuttle, just as the mob broke out onto the roof. Another Marine was less lucky and was shoved over the edge by the mob, his antigravity systems saving him before he hit the ground. Some of the crowd were pushed over by their own people, falling down the side of the building and hitting the ground before anyone could save them. The remainder were busy looting the Mud Palace, looking for the vast taxes the Funks had collected from those unfortunate enough to live on their world.

"Well," he said, as he was finally pulled into the shuttle, "that could have gone better."

"Maybe," his captain agreed, "but at least we got the Funks out."

Conrad shrugged. Marines were taught to be aggressive and a retreat, no matter how necessary, didn't sit well with

167

him. But orders were orders. And besides, they would have accomplished nothing if they'd remained at the palace. And it should definitely get them some good press.

Chapter Nineteen

"Blimey," Lieutenant Piers said. "Just look at all the industry in this system."

Markus nodded in agreement as the first squadron of gunboats spread out from *Formidable*. Heavenly Gate had been home to a spacefaring race decades before the birth of Jesus Christ and every world in the system was inhabited. Massive cloudscoops orbited the gas giants, while worlds that had once been like Mars or Venus had been terraformed into something more habitable. They'd even started a long-term project to convert a gas giant into a second sun, although the report had suggested that the Canaries were having problems devising a way to do it without causing problems for the rest of the system. Even the Association had thought better of trying to create new suns.

But it might have made sense for the Canaries. They were an avian race, unique in that they could still fly after evolving into intelligence, giving them their own slant on the universe. Much of their theology was not shared with infidels, even the Cats, but from what they had allowed the rest of the galaxy to find out was that they couldn't leave the light from their star, which was called – roughly translated – the Light of God. They'd been the second race to make a theoretical breakthrough into quantum space, but unlike the Cats they'd never set out to colonise the rest of the galaxy. Maybe it was better for humanity that they hadn't wanted to spread their wings some, because they would certainly have discovered Earth long before the Association had made contact – and who knew how they would have reacted to the human race?

Instead, they'd settled their solar system and thoroughly developed their limited real estate. Massive orbital fortresses defended their planets, backed up by a fleet of starships that were none the less dangerous for lacking quantum drives. Indeed, where Association-designed starships had to include space for FTL drives, the Canaries had used that space to carry extra weapons and shield generators. Heavenly Gate could probably be taken by the Hegemony – or another power who wanted it badly enough – but the cost would be staggeringly high. One estimate from ONI had suggested that upwards of three-fourths of the Hegemony Navy would be required to take the system. And the Canaries themselves would fight like mad demons to repel any offensive into the Light of God. No one even remotely rational would try to take the system. They'd have to exterminate most of the population to win, destroying the infrastructure that made the system so valuable in the process.

Which raises the obvious question, Markus thought, as the small force powered towards the fifth world in the system. Place of Meetings was another multiracial planet, although the Canaries were solidly in control. They didn't understand how other races could leave their own Lights of God, but they were happy to welcome anyone who came in peace. *What the hell are we doing here?*

The briefing had made that clear. There were two Hegemony capital ships in the system, visiting Place of Meetings for an unknown reason. Intelligence had put forward several possible theories, from wanting to trade with the Canaries to trying to intimidate them into supporting Hegemony proposals in the Commune, but it didn't really matter. All that mattered was intercepting those ships before they could leave Heavenly Gate and throw themselves into human shipping lanes. A single heavy cruiser in the right place could have a disproportionate impact on the war.

"Grumbles, remain on alert," he ordered. There hadn't been any time to get replacement gunboats and crews, which meant that they were still short several craft. "They might try something, but do *not* fire on anything unless it belongs to the Funks."

Galactic law didn't have much to say about interstellar warfare – the Cats, who had established most of it, had tried to avoid even *thinking* about war – but there were some protocols agreed by most of the Galactics. Neutral races had certain obligations if they wanted to remain neutral, including not assisting either combatant in any way. The Canaries, at least in theory, should have no choice, but to either expel the Hegemony ships or intern them and their crews. But in practice...? No-one was quite sure which way they would jump.

Captain Walsh was already broadcasting to the Galactics. The Canaries were in charge of their system – no one doubted that – but there were other starships in orbit around Place of Meetings, including some from the other major Galactic powers. Markus suspected that the intelligence officer had deliberately understated the diplomatic nightmare that could result if they fucked up, perhaps by firing on the wrong ship. The Canaries had no real alliances with any of the other Galactic powers, but just about everyone thought well of them. And if they decided to refuse to cooperate, all hell could break loose.

The minutes ticked away as the Canaries debated what to do. There was a small community of humans on Place of Meetings, including a handful who apparently worked for ONI as well as for the network of human traders who visited the system. Each terse update made Markus more concerned, particularly when the Hegemony commander started urging the other Galactics to escort his ships out of the system if they refused to restrain the imprudent humans. But few of the Galactics were willing to intervene openly on the Hegemony's side, not when the Hegemony was known to be extremely aggressive and expansionist. Most of them would view a bloody nose for the Hegemony as a good thing.

Eagle and Ivan Squadrons remained on the carrier, waiting for the order to launch. They'd scramble well before the Funks could reach a safe distance from the planet to open a quantum gate – and they had orders to follow the Funks into quantum space if possible. In their place, Markus suspected that he would go right for *Formidable*, trusting to his ship's armor to protect them long enough to take out the only way home for the gunboats. If that happened, the gunboats would have no choice, but to surrender to the Canaries and accept internment.

The datanet crackled. "All right," Captain Walsh said, "the Canaries have insisted that the Hegemony ships either disembark their crews or leave their system. I think that they're preparing to leave now. Stand by."

Markus frowned. He hadn't expected the Hegemony ships to surrender, but would they be escorted by the other Galactics? If so...

The datanet updated again. Both of the Hegemony ships, docked at a station that was over a thousand years old, were slowly powering up their drives and preparing to make a run for open space. A handful of cruisers belonging to the Canaries were advancing towards the station, ready to intervene if fighting spread into orbit. They had to be more worried than they wanted to admit, but Markus would worry about starships unleashing antimatter torpedoes in orbit too. And then there was the risk that the Hegemony would assume that the Canaries had deliberately warned the human race that the ships were there and take revenge at some future date. Raiding the system would be fairly easy, if not exactly risk-free.

Captain Walsh spoke again. "Ivan Squadron, launch to support Grumble," he ordered. "Eagle Squadron will remain in reserve."

"Oh, they're going to hate that," Carola commented. Markus chuckled. Fighter jet pilots had been hot dogs ever since fighters had been invented, an attitude that had transferred into the gunboat pilots. "Unless someone else decides to intervene..."

Both of the Hegemony ships had disconnected from the station and were moving past the other Galactic starships, blinking their running lights in salute. Markus caught himself tapping on the console in irritation as they waited, wondering just what the Funks were doing. Delaying their destruction as long as possible, or... hoping that the gunboat life support would run out before the Canaries started enforcing their orders with force. Gunboats were a new concept for the Galactics, but they didn't need their blueprints to calculate a rough estimate for how long their life support could endure.

A display appeared in front of them and he studied it thoughtfully. Most starships with a heavy cruiser mass needed to be some distance from the planet before they opened a gateway into quantum space. The Association's safety regulations were overcautious – humanity hadn't been the first the first race to realise that it was possible to shave a few ten-thousand kilometres off the safety line without risking serious consequences – but the Funks would still need to leave the protective cover of the Canary forts before they could escape, even if they attempted to leave at the minimum safe distance from Place of Meetings. There would be at least seven minutes between the forts and a safe distance, allowing the gunboats their chance to intercept the enemy ships. Captain Walsh was already broadcasting an offer to accept surrender, but if the Funks had been unwilling to be interned, they weren't likely to surrender.

"Here we go," he said, as the Grumbles formed up on his position. Both of the Hegemony ships were advancing past the forts, a pair of ugly blunt instruments studded with sensors and weapons blisters. The Association had termed a particular class of superdreadnoughts the *Blunt Instrument*-class, showing a wry sense of humour that was surprisingly human. Markus doubted that the Funks got the joke. "All Grumbles, your target is the heavy cruiser; Ivans, concentrate on the light cruiser."

"These buggers have point defence," Carola added, a moment later. The Association had designed the light cruiser to provide additional protection for superdreadnoughts, replacing torpedo launchers with additional phase cannon and particle beam generators. Markus suspected that similar ships would be pressed into the anti-gunboat role until the Hegemony produced a dedicated design or constructed gunboats of its own. Estimates of how long that would take ranged from a year to never. "Watch yourself."

"Go," Markus ordered.

The gunboats slipped forward, instantly accelerating to near-maximum speed. The distance between the two forces closed rapidly, pushing the Hegemony ships into opening fire as soon as the gunboats came into range. It was unlikely that they'd actually score any hits at such a range, but it forced the gunboats to break formation and evade long before they'd planned to slip into attack formation. Someone had studied the records from their first operation and drawn sensible conclusions, Markus noted sourly. By now, the entire galaxy would be aware of the war – and of some of the new weapons humanity had deployed. And not all of them were as poor as the Hegemony at developing their own technology.

"They're firing as soon as they get a lock," Carola observed, as the gunboats corkscrewed through space. "Not standard practice, but clever given what they're facing. One hit and we're screwed..."

A spread of white antimatter torpedoes launched from the heavy cruiser. Markus evaded desperately, seconds before the first torpedo exploded between two of his gunboats, wiping them both from existence. *That* hadn't been anticipated, an oversight that would cost his squadron dear. But what sort of madman would consider using antiship torpedoes against gunboats? Someone on the other side was clever, or desperate. The expense of replacing the torpedoes would be worthwhile if they managed to get out of the system intact.

"Closing into attack range," he grunted. The enemy was shifting fire now, attempting to force the gunboats to separate and fly individual attack runs. It was a clever tactic too, he noted absently, although it wouldn't be as useful as they expected. The human weapons designers had improved upon the original implosion bolt to the point where even a single hit would do some damage. "Fire at will."

The gunboats engaged, launching a spread of implosion bolts towards their targets while evading the increasingly desperate fire from the heavy cruiser. One of the gunboats was hit, either through luck or skill, but the remainder kept firing, pouring implosion bolts into the ship's hull. No significant damage was done to the drives, but several of the weapons blisters were disabled, limiting the cruiser's ability to hurt the gunboats as they swooped around and came back in for a second run.

Information flickering between the gunboats noted which enemy weapons had been taken out and how it could be used to reduce the losses on the next attack run. The Hegemony ship was twisting, trying to allow the rest of its weapons to engage the gunboats, but there was no way it could move fast enough to bring its weapons to bear. Ivan Squadron had disabled the light cruiser, which kept firing with a fanatical determination even though the crew had to know that they weren't going to leave the system alive. Markus could have respected their courage under other circumstances, but right now they were just in the way.

Another spread of antimatter torpedoes were launched, but this time the gunboats were ready and accelerated away before they could explode. The heavy cruiser staggered as implosion bolts cut deeply into her hull, yet somehow she kept going. Her comrade wasn't so lucky; less heavily-armored, she exploded when implosion bolts cut through into her drive rooms and her fusion plants blew. One of the Ivans was caught in the explosion; the others swooped around and fell upon the heavy cruiser.

"Shit," Carola said.

Markus yanked the gunboat around as emergency icons flared up on the display. The Funks were still far from the minimum safe distance, but they were trying to open a quantum gate! They had to be insane – but then, they knew they were doomed if they remained in the system. The odds of dying when they opened the gate were higher than the odds of surviving the battle. Markus led the Grumbles towards the ship's drive section, but it was too late. Space tore open and the quantum gate manifested, spilling out gravity waves that bounced the gunboats as if they were floating on a sea. He saw the gate with his naked eyes and knew instantly that something was badly wrong. Gates were normally spinning discs of light, shimmering into existence in front of the starships. This one was a spitting funnel of energy, ethereal tentacles reaching out for the heavy cruiser. Markus could almost have sworn that it was a living creature, just before the Funks started moving towards the vortex. They *had* to be insane. Nothing could enter that vortex and make it safely into quantum space.

Sheets of energy were flashing through space, just waiting for them.

He couldn't take his eyes off the sight, part of him praying that the Funks would succeed in entering quantum space. All differences were forgotten. For a moment, it looked as though they would succeed, but then the energy feedback grew too powerful. Brilliant lightning seemed to flare along the hull of the heavy cruiser, just before her hull split open and she vanished in an eye-tearing ball of light. The entire universe seemed to hang in the balance... and then the distorted gate vanished, as if it had never been. His sensors couldn't even detect a trace of debris from the heavy cruiser.

"All ships," he said. His voice was weak and he had to swallow hard before continuing. "All ships, return to the barn. It's time to go home."

Behind them, a handful of Canary ships watched carefully as the gunboats retreated. They'd probably take what had happened to the Funks as proof that their religion was the one true faith. He couldn't understand how anyone could refuse to leave their solar system, if only because one day their star would die. The Canaries would have to choose between changing their religion or dying when their worlds were swallowed by an expanding red giant. But that was millions of years in the future. Perhaps they would discover how to keep their star burning long before then.

Formidable was already heading towards the quantum gate when the gunboats docked, their crews glad to be alive. Nine gunboats had been lost; there would be a number of empty bunks in Pilot Country tonight. They'd have to scratch one of the squadrons unless reinforcements were rushed forward from Earth. He doubted they could do that again unless they got some extra support. The Hegemony had already made progress towards tactics that would allow them to confront the gunboats on more even terms.

* * *

That night, they performed a brief service for the dead gunboat pilots before heading to their bunks. There was little space for private cabins on *Formidable*, although even if that space had existed the military was unlikely to have used it for crew comfort when a few more missiles could have been carried instead.

One thing had arrived before they left the system; the mail. Markus had plenty of family back on Earth and most of them had written to him, although typically most of the messages were several days late when they arrived. The military censored letters going from the crew to their families, but – in theory – the civilians shouldn't need to be censored. They didn't know anything more than Earth's news services had been telling them – and *that* was heavily controlled.

He skimmed through the message from his sister as Carola read her own messages. Earth seemed to have taken the news about the war in stride, although there had been some panic and massed peace demonstrations in major world capitals. Markus rolled his eyes as his sister recounted how a number of her girlfriends had been in the middle of a protest in Stockholm and ended up spending the night in jail. Some of the girls were hot, but their combined brainpower had been drained away by a school that seemed to specialise in turning brains into mush. Quite what they thought the Hegemony would do if it ruled Earth was beyond him. Terra Nova's experience offered some clues.

"Idiots," he muttered dryly as he prepared for bed. "Stupid idiots."

Chapter Twenty

"We condemn in the strongest possible terms the human intrusion into the Light of God," the Canary intoned. "It has long been our determination to remain aloof from the power struggles among those who have not embraced their own Lights of God..."

Ambassador Li Shan allowed herself a tired smile as the Canary – an atheist, apparently – kept speaking. She'd been nervous as soon as she'd realised that the Commune was due to call an emergency session on the issue of the Human-Hegemony War, if only because the Funks were calling in debts from the last few hundred years, but the Canary didn't seem inclined to offer more than a token protest. It wasn't too surprising – he'd been the one to tip her off about the two ships in the first place – and yet she'd been all-too-aware of the sheer level of diplomatic arm-twisting from the Hegemony. The Canaries were better able than most to resist that sort of pressure, but they literally had all their eggs in one basket. Who knew what sort of pressure the Hegemony could bring to bear against them?

The Association had envisaged the Commune as a form of United Nations, a forum where different races could meet and discuss their issues openly, without needing to resort to violence. But few of the major powers were prepared to allow the Commune to dictate to them, while every race had veto power to derail anything they didn't like. The result had been inevitable from the start; the Commune was nothing more than a talking shop. But that didn't stop hundreds of races from using the chamber to cut deals of their own.

Shan had hoped that pressure to stop the war would grow slowly until the Hegemony was prevented from retaliating against Earth. She had no idea how long Earth's tech advantage would last against the Hegemony's overwhelming force; ideally, Earth would be able to keep the Hegemony off-balance until the other Galactics intervened to stop the fighting. But it didn't seem too likely that any outsiders would become directly involved. The motives were different for each race – and some were incomprehensible – yet the results were the same. No one would attempt to stop the war.

The Canary finished speaking and sat down, while the Ambassador from the Kockoo stood up. Several of the other Ambassadors looked irritated, not even bothering to try to hide it. The Kockoo were an old race, old enough to be on a par with the Cats – or they would have been, if they'd developed spaceflight before the Cats discovered their system. Their sense of entitlement was larger than an entire fleet of superdreadnoughts, as was their tendency to filibuster until they got what they wanted out of any political dealing. They were widely disliked, which didn't seem to bother them. Shan's few meetings with their Ambassador had suggested that they were simply too arrogant to care.

"While we deplore the act of invading Heavenly Gate to force the surrender or destruction of the two Hegemony starships, we are forced to reluctantly conclude that it was legal," the Kockoo said. Her voice was sweet, trickling honey, but there was something about it that grated on Shan's mind. "However, we refuse to accept that violence was in fact the answer. There were legal avenues for the human race to seek redress before resorting to war. In choosing to refrain from following those angles, it is clear that the human race is nothing more than a grievously savage half-barbarian race using technology obtained from the most advanced race in the universe."

She half-bowed towards the Speaker, the sole Cat in the chamber, and then continued speaking. "The laws of war, laid down by our great founders, insist that combatants must issue a declaration of war prior to launching any offences against enemy-held territory," she continued. Shan wondered absently what sort of deal the Hegemony had made to get the Kockoo to intervene, before deciding that it was unlikely that they'd made any kind of deal. They were arrogant enough to believe that they needed to intervene without being bribed. "In choosing to launch a sneak attack on the Hegemony, the human race violated that rule. I propose the creation of an independent committee that will investigate all breaches of galactic law and recommend action on the part of this great Commune."

Shan was careful to keep her face impassive as the Kockoo sat down. She couldn't tell if the threat was serious or just a political power play. It would be just like the Kockoo to fiddle while Center burned down around them. Their sanctimonious attitude made them few friends and far too many enemies, but there were quite a few Galactics who had been disturbed by the weapons humanity had used in the war. They wanted time to consider how to duplicate them for themselves. It was a pity that the Federation had embargoed weapons technology from Earth, or she could have made a thousand deals for support from other Galactics. But that technology was Earth's ace in the hole and it could not be surrendered.

Another Ambassador, the masked and gowned representative from the Shimmering Harmony, rose to bow to the Speaker. No one knew what the Shimmering Harmony looked like, for they always concealed their bodies from other intelligent races. Their homeworld was situated in the midst of a powerful and semi-permanent energy storm within quantum space, making it tricky for anyone to approach without a very skilful navigator. The other races had legends about them, but no one actually knew anything beyond the fact that their Ambassador was clearly humanoid. Exactly why they'd decided to join the Association was another mystery.

There was no shortage of legends about them, tales of explorers who had visited their homeworld and seen wonders beyond imagination, but none of them had ever been verified. A number of Galactics believed that the Shimmering Harmony was really nothing more than another humanoid race, concealing itself out of fear that the more active races would overwhelm them if their true nature was discovered. Others suspected that the Shimmering Harmony were much more than they seemed. They didn't participate in cultural exchanges, they didn't make war upon their neighbours... for one of them to speak publicly was very rare. Just seeing their Ambassador speak would make the other Galactics interested in the war.

"It is clear that the Hegemony was slowly preparing the human race for eventual servitude," the Ambassador said. Even the voice was flat, atonal, as if it had been produced by a primitive computer. "They were given little choice, but to fight."

He – if the Ambassador *was* a he – sat down, saying nothing else.

There was a long pause before the Hegemony Ambassador, Great Lady Vanla, rose to her feet. "It is true that we have been attempting to obtain settlement rights for Sector 666, which includes the human homeworld," she said. "However, it was never our intention to enslave them. Why, the client races within the Hegemony have the same rights and duties as other client races across the Association. We would never stoop to *enslaving* any race."

"And yet refugees from your client races frequently seek asylum in our space," another Ambassador put in. It was a serious breach of protocol to speak before the last speaker had finished. "You use them as expendable labour, in violation of the rights granted to all client races by the Association Charter. We can hardly fault the humans for wanting to escape the fate of your other *slave* races."

He smiled, savagely. "Indeed, is it not accurate that you were censured by the Commune on no less than three occasions for mistreatment of your clients? Your protests ring hollow when much testimony was produced by the refugees."

"Who were paid to lie before the Commune," Great Lady Vanla snapped. She didn't bother to rise, an equally unsubtle insult. "You brought them after preparing them with lies to blacken our name."

Shan watched with some amusement as the Ambassadors shouted at each other. The Cats had designed the building so that the merest whisper could be heard at the other side of the chamber. In one sense, the Ambassador was quite right; the Funks *had* been censured for the mistreatment of their client races. But the Galactics hadn't done anything beyond issuing a reprimand, allowing the

Funks to just carry on without needing to worry further about Galactic opinion. Even the Hegemony would have backed down if it had faced the entire galaxy, but there had been no prospect of such an alliance against them. How very... *human*.

The debate could last for hours, or even days. Many of the Ambassadors had spent years at Center, some of them under instructions not to bother coming home. They had far more experience with navigating the complex web of favours, obligations and outright bribery that steered the Commune from one issue to the next. Shan had never been sure if the Galactics realised just how badly they'd emasculated the Commune, and hence the Association, but it worked in their favour. No single power could bring them to heel.

Shaking her head, she settled down to wait. It would all be over sooner or later, and then she could get back to some real politicking.

* * *

The Tarn had always reminded Shan of hamsters, albeit hamsters that walked like humans and had hands that were surprisingly dexterous. Earth's hamsters were harmless, but the Tarn had been at the top of their food chain for centuries before they'd started to climb into space and discovered the Association. They'd been lucky enough to expand into a fairly undeveloped region of space, allowing them to claim almost a hundred stars before they'd bumped into the Hegemony. The Hegemony could probably have taken them if they'd had secure borders, but diverting enough of their navy to invade the Tarn would weaken them significantly against two other races. Even so, brushfire wars were common and the Tarn had a vested interest in anything that made the Hegemony weaker. Some of them had been quite willing to trade with humanity ever since Mentor had offered humanity the stars.

Shan hadn't been too surprised when Warf – it was as close as humans could come to pronouncing the Ambassador's name – had invited her for a private meeting

182

in the Commune Chambers. The Hegemony had been watching Earth's Embassy since the declaration of war and no doubt taking careful note of who visited Shan. Shan had her own people watching the Hegemony Embassy as well. But inside the Commune Chambers it was much harder to spy on the others, although that didn't stop people from trying. Humanity's counter-surveillance equipment was staying ahead, so far. Shan reminded herself firmly that there was no real proof they were that advanced. Some of the Galactics kept their technology to themselves.

Warf's meeting room looked rather more informal than anything a human would have considered acceptable. There were cushions, a small pile of foodstuffs positioned on the floor between them and several jugs of water. The Tarn sealed agreements through sexual intercourse, at least among themselves, although they'd changed that policy since discovering the existence of other intelligent life. It didn't stop some humans speculating on just what human traders did to win favour from the Tarn. Some people, in Shan's opinion, had too much time on their hands.

"It should be noted that Warf is speaking off the record," Warf said. His voice was surprisingly human. "Those who rule the nest will disown Warf if necessary."

"I understand," Shan said. The Tarn always referred to themselves in the third person, but they didn't seem to mind when other races spoke in first person. Just one of the many racial traits that the Association had cataloged thousands of years ago. "You may speak freely."

"Warf is very impressed by the scale of your victory and the recovery of your lost colony," Warf said. "But Warf is worried that you will be unable to continue fighting and winning the war. Warf thinks that the Hegemony is still powerful and that you have barely dented it. Is Warf wrong?"

"Warf is not wrong," Shan said. She always got confused when she tried to speak like a Tarn, but Warf seemed to appreciate it. "But we have many other tricks to show the Hegemony in the coming weeks and months. We will be victorious."

"Warf is gratified to hear that you have so much confidence," Warf said, "but Warf fears that the Hegemony will prove too much for you. Warf wishes to deal on behalf of his people."

Shan leaned forward, scenting the deal. "Warf's people are inferior to the Hegemony in numbers of ships," Warf said. "A war would be destructive for Warf's people. Warf wishes access to your weapons for his people's navy. You may name your price."

It was tempting to string Warf alone, but the Tarn had long memories. "Our weapons are not for sale," she said, finally. "However, we have much else to offer you."

"Warf feels that this is a matter of survival," Warf said. "Should you lose to the Hegemony, your people will be enslaved or exterminated. Your technological progress will be added to the Hegemony's fleet, making it deadly enough to defeat Warf's people before others can intervene. The Hegemony will make itself master of the galaxy. This is intolerable to Warf's people."

"Then join the war," Shan suggested. "Invade their space from your borders as we push on towards their homeworld. We could crush them between two angles of attack."

"Warf feels that your people cannot sustain such a long offensive," Warf said. "The Hegemony has not yet started to redeploy units towards the war front. Warf believes that your forces will rapidly run into much heavier defences as you press onwards. Should you fail to cripple their industrial base, they will out-build you and crush your tiny fleet by sheer weight of numbers. Warf feels that you cannot afford to bargain."

"I have no room to negotiate over selling our weapons," Shan admitted, even though she agreed with Warf. The real question would be how quickly the Tarn could copy humanity's weapons and outfit their ships with them. And if the Hegemony realised what was happening, they might launch a pre-emptive attack on the Tarn. "I would have to communicate with my superiors."

"Warf is prepared to offer an alternate bargain," Warf said. "Warf's people will move reinforcements to the border between Warf's people and the Hegemony. In exchange,

Warf's people will require an undertaking to ship both technical data and samples of Earth's weaponry to Warf's people if Earth falls to the Hegemony. Warf's people will also offer human refugees a place to settle, ensuring that your race will not be exterminated when the Hegemony ranges in on your homeworld."

"If," Shan said, quietly. "We do not intend to lose."

She tossed the idea over and over in her head. On one hand, the Hegemony would have to worry that the Tarn planned to jump them and keep forces deployed along at least one other border. That would limit the forces they could redeploy to meet the human offensive. On the other hand, the Hegemony might decide to call the Tarn's bluff and pull ships away from the border anyway, trading space for time. They'd certainly realise that if Earth's weapons got into the hands of their enemies, the Hegemony was doomed. Whatever it took to prevent that was worth the cost.

And yet... there was another possibility. What if the Tarn attacked the Hegemony and then demanded Earth's weapons? Earth would be in a difficult position; they'd need the Tarn, and yet sharing Earth's weapons would be the quickest way to ensure that they'd be duplicated. And it was possible that some of the Tarn were working for the Hegemony. There were certainly Funks working for Earth.

"There are other possibilities," Warf added. "Warf's people have a considerable number of older starships produced by the Association that are unsuitable for their use. Warf's people would offer them to Earth, should you accept our bargain. There are also weapons and supplies that we could give you, along with intelligence from recon flights along the borders. You would not lose out if you bargained with Warf's people."

"I would have to check with Earth, but I believe that they would definitely accept the second offer," Shan said. It was a shame that the Tarn weren't one of the races that specialised in offering loans to developing planets, but maybe they had influence Shan could borrow. Earth needed loans to finance the war effort. A single defeat could pull the purse strings tight. "I would certainly recommend to the Federation Council that your bargain be accepted."

"Warf is gratified to hear it," Warf informed her. "Perhaps you could inform Warf of their decision soonest? Warf has much to do and so little time."

"I will contact you as soon as we have a definite answer," Shan said. She had a lot to pass on to the Federation Council, starting with the fact they'd effectively gotten away with attacking the Hegemony ships at Heavenly Gate. "I thank you for your time."

"Warf is unworthy of your thanks," Warf said. "Warf is honoured to offer you the comfort of Warf's humble home."

Shan exchanged bows and walked out of the chamber, heading down towards the walkways that led back to the Embassies. It wouldn't take long to walk back to Earth's Embassy, where she could have a drink and contact Earth. Despite the stimulants she'd taken, she still felt tired. Some of the Galactics somehow managed to spend *weeks* in the Commune when the more significant proposals were debated. She had no idea how they managed it.

A handful of reporters were waiting outside, holding up scanners to record her image. She managed a confident smile as she passed them and met up with her bodyguards. It was important to stay on the right side of the press. God knew that they would help shape Galactic opinion.

And who knew? Perhaps humanity's plucky little underdog performance would win it friends and allies. And maybe the horse would learn to sing.

Chapter Twenty-One

"The entire city is supposed to be in lockdown," Barbie said, "but we just don't have the manpower to even begin to police it."

Adrienne barely heard her. The alien city was strange to her eyes, yet there was something about it that was almost appealing. The Funks might have refused to change their building style since they'd been introduced to space by the Hegemony, if only because they had been determined to remember their past, but they'd had to co-exist with a number of other races on Garston. Their city was a strange blend of styles and proportions, large enough for humanity and almost every other humanoid race. The market street was a melting pot of cultures from all over the galaxy.

Most of the civilians were in their homes, keeping off the streets, but Adrienne had heard reports that a great many scores were being paid off by races that had had to live under the Funks. The alien ghettos had become hostile territory for the Funks, while raiding parties had set out to burn Funk neighbourhoods when the human occupiers weren't looking. There were even rumours that the Funks planned an insurgency, knowing that they had little other choice, but to fight. Even if humanity didn't intend to extract revenge for how they'd treated Terra Nova, their neighbours wanted to ensure that the Funks could never grind them down again.

Armed and armored Marines patrolled the streets in groups of five, watching for trouble and trying to dampen it down when it broke out. According to one of the Marines she'd taken care to cultivate as a source, the humans were caught in the middle – and under attack from all sides. The detention camps outside the city, established for the Funk leadership, had had to be expanded rapidly to hold rioters and insurgents...and were already reaching capacity. No one really grasped how large a planet was until they had to provide ground troops to keep it under control – and there were only seven thousand Marines with the fleet. It was barely enough to keep Garston City under limited control; the remainder of the planet had to fend for itself, once the Marines had secured the planetary defence centers. Some of the reports from outside the city were horrifying.

She looked over at a small group of aliens and smiled inwardly. They were very far from human, but she fancied that she would have recognised them as reporters, if only because of the questions they kept throwing at their human minders. Some of them were clearly hostile to the human race, others seemed more inclined to be friendly – or simply didn't like the Hegemony. Adrienne chafed under the restrictions imposed by the military on what she could and could not report, but at least she had some access. The Galactic reporters received almost none, which didn't stop them sending stories back home that bore only a vague resemblance to the facts. One reporter had filed a story claiming that humanity had over a thousand invincible superdreadnoughts in orbit. Another had seen the plans for the Death Star and reported it as if humanity had actually built it. Adrienne was fairly sure that most of the Galactics wouldn't believe the more exaggerated reports, but rumour seemed to spread rapidly across the Association. The Funks would have some trouble sorting out truth from human disinformation – or stories the reporters had made up out of whole cloth.

The reporters were doing interviews with a handful of community leaders who had emerged out of the shadows to plead their case to the galaxy. Some of them had been appointed by the Funks, others had formed a shadow government, hoping they'd have a chance to declare independence and make their own bids for galactic power. Most of them were expressing their gratitude to the human race, although some of them were complaining that humanity wasn't sharing any of the tolls from Garston's quantum gate. Adrienne suspected that that issue would be sorted out after the war; for the moment, the tolls gave humanity a nifty additional source of currency. There was no way that Earth would let go of Garston until the end of the war.

Others were worried about the consequences of human starships leaving Garston behind, unoccupied. The Hegemony hadn't been beaten; all things considered, it had barely been scratched. They might come back and reoccupy the planet, or the Funks on the ground might launch their own pogrom against everyone else. Some of them were appealing to their own races to send peacekeeping forces to Garston, even though others were nervous about inviting other powers to intervene. Their ancestors had left their homeworlds to escape their governments centuries ago. It was strange to realise that Garston had been settled longer than the human race had known how to work metal for tools. Garston was effectively a world with its own culture, even under the Funks. Humanity's occupation wouldn't change that in a hurry.

"We had to put guards on the Funk neighbourhoods," Barbie said, quietly. "The others wanted a little payback for decades of mistreatment. It feels strange to help Funks, but we can't afford a massacre – or a civil war in our rear."

Adrienne smiled, although there was little humour in the expression. The Marines had expressed their own doubts about the mission, pointing out that the Funks had been humanity's tormentors for the last ten years and attempting to save them from the consequences of their own misbehaviour went against the grain. God knew that not all of the Funks were disarmed, or grateful for humanity's protection. The Marines patrolling the Funk neighbourhoods were exposed to fire from both sides.

The first national contingents had already arrived at Terra Nova, freeing up a couple of thousand Marines to rejoin the fleet, but it would be weeks – if not months – before national contingents could arrive on Garston, assuming they were even sent. Ward, her editor back home, had mentioned that resistance against sending any troops outside the Nine Stars was growing stronger. Politicians were hearing from their constituents, who were adamantly opposed to sending soldiers to keep the Funks on Garston from being slaughtered. Even if they did...

She ran through a brief calculation in her head. Ever since First Contact, when humanity had realised that there *were* hostile races out there, most Americans had bought guns and had some form of paramilitary training. A handful of promising political careers had been destroyed when some politicians hadn't realised that trying to deny citizens firearms when there was a very real threat of invasion was a sure way to lose votes. And yet... even assuming that every single American was a trained soldier, which they weren't, there wouldn't be enough manpower to hold down an entire planet. She doubted that the other powers could provide enough men to make up the difference.

And if it's bad here, she asked herself, *what happens when we take a world occupied solely by Funks?*

Once the briefing was over – the Galactic reporters had insisted on asking all kinds of questions, ranging from the sensible to the near-insane – the reporters were taken on a brief tour of the city. The cityscape seemed to vary wildly from neighbourhood to neighbourhood, even if most of the buildings followed the Funk sense of aesthetics. One building was identified as a Temple of Ra, belonging to a cult that had managed to win a multiracial congregation. Maybe it wasn't surprising that the temple was located in the most peaceful part of the city, even during the occupation. Some humans had also converted to the Temple of Ra, while others had set out to convert the alien infidels to human religions. They hadn't had great success. The Galactics were unlikely to be seriously interested in upstart humanity's native religions.

There were more people on the streets, despite the lockdown. The sight reminded her of Jeddah in the early years of the multinational occupation, with different tribes and religious factions keeping their distance from one another while pouring scorn and hatred on the occupation force that was trying to keep them from killing each other. Religious genocide wasn't unique to humanity, but that hadn't stopped some of the Galactics from accusing humanity of being a dangerously savage child-race. Some of the Hegemony's counter-propaganda asserted that humanity intended to exterminate all of the Galactics once they were in a position of power. The thought of one world

190

setting out to destroy the entire galaxy was laughable, but the Battle of Terra Nova, where five superdreadnoughts had been taken down by lighter ships at minimal loss, had concentrated a few minds.

Most of the aliens were humanoid, surprisingly close to humanity. One of her sources had suggested that Garston City was renowned for interracial sex, even though the Funks reacted harshly against the very concept. While cross-species fertilisation was impossible, all kinds of options opened up for the broadminded. Other aliens were so alien that it was hard to believe that they had anything in common with humanity. She caught sight of a floating orb, studded with eyestalks, and shook her head in disbelief. Beauty was quite definitely in the eyes of the beholder.

The reporters insisted on stopping often to interview more people, but many simply refused to talk and hurried onwards. One friendly alien was happy to lecture the reporters on why they should convert to the one true faith, yet despite some of the reporters listening patiently he refused to be drawn on current affairs. Adrienne rolled her eyes as the Galactics stalked off in frustration. How could anyone claim to have the one true faith when Earth alone had produced hundreds of different religions? The Cats had never developed a religion of their own – some of them regarded that as a sign they were superior to the younger races, who needed the comfort of belief in something greater than themselves – but they'd cataloged literally millions of religions as they'd shaped interstellar society. Some human researchers claimed that religions that shared similar messages actually worshipped the same god, if known by different names, and that comparing the different messages would allow them to build a picture of their true faith. So far, as far as Adrienne knew, their research had been inconclusive. Some religions were incomprehensible to human minds. Others had more in common with polytheistic religions than the monotheistic religions that dominated Earth.

They reached one of the Funk neighbourhoods and street activity dropped away to almost nothing. The handful of Funks in the street slipped away from the reporters, hiding in the shadows before they could be seen and interviewed. Adrienne was aware of unblinking red eyes watching them from windows, even though when she looked around she could see nothing. A patrol of Marines were walking down the middle of the street, looking hugely intimidating in their combat armor. Their suits had been set to display images, rather than automatically camouflaging themselves to match the local environment. One Marine looked alarmingly like a creature from Greek mythology. Others looked as if they were tribal warriors marching out to war.

"Most of them are hiding," Barbie whispered. Even she seemed subdued by their surroundings. "They don't think that we will protect them if the entire city rises up and comes baying for their blood. I'm not even sure that we have the manpower to protect them if the shit hits the fan."

Adrienne shivered. Humanity had gotten some good press from saving the Funks from being lynched, but the Hegemony had been spreading stories of human-organised massacres and outright terror strikes mounted against helpless civilians. There was little truth in the stories – and few of them were placed in context – yet some of the Galactics believed them, either because they trusted the Hegemony or because they disliked the upstart humans. A race rebelling against the division of their space by the Commune set an unfortunate precedent for the Galactics. Some of them were likely to hope that the Hegemony won rapidly, cheaply and totally.

The latter, at least, wasn't going to happen. Adrienne had heard rumours that covert operations teams were already preparing humanity's revenge if Earth should happen to be destroyed. Taking a well-defended planet wasn't easy, but destroying one was simplicity itself. The Galactics would be horrified if humanity destroyed a life-bearing world, yet if humanity lost the war it was likely that the human race would be beyond caring.

The damage caused by the fighting drew the attention of the reporters, who bombarded their minders with questions. One large city block had been destroyed by a KEW after the Funks had turned it into a firing position to launch HVMs at the oncoming shuttle, killing the missile crews and a number of civilians. Some of the Funks had promptly claimed that over a thousand civilians had been killed in the attack, although few of the reporters believed their statements. Even the dumbest reporter could look at the damage and wonder how a thousand people could have fit into the city block. The bodies had been removed and buried by the Marines, once they'd filmed and cataloged the entire site for future inspection. No one had attempted to claim the bodies for proper treatment, in line with the Funk customs.

Other buildings had been attacked by angry mobs, some of them composed of lesser Funks angry at their superiors. The Funks seemed to jump on any sign of weakness, perhaps driven by their belief that only the toughest deserved to lead. Their Empress, if some of the reports were accurate, had little compunction about ordering mass punishment if she felt that her position was threatened. The Funks did seem to lack the sadism that had infected many human despots, but the ruthlessness of their leaders would have made Stalin blanch. But it was the only way to keep in power.

"And so the tour goes on," Barbie muttered. "Do you still want to visit another city?"

Ward had insisted that she did, but Adrienne wasn't so sure. Many of the other cities were dangerous, perhaps more dangerous than human cities in the middle of a war zone. Some of the Galactic reporters were trusting in their media credentials to protect them, others – more careful – were demanding Marine escorts as they roamed the streets. So far, the Marines were stalling. They didn't want to expose Marines to insurgent attack and yet they knew that they had to keep on the right side of the Galactic media. If there was a right side...

"Only if escorted," she said, finally. The Federation had a policy against paying ransom to recover its people. Instead, its considerable resources were deployed to extract revenge. It had worked on Earth – the Federation had crushed piracy with savage force – but it might be harder on Garston. "I'm very attached to my life."

Barbie smiled. "So am I," she said. "I wouldn't want to go anywhere on this planet without an armed escort."

* * *

"So we're not going to be able to move onwards for at least a week," Tobias said, slowly. Ideally, he would have preferred to move onwards at once, but they had to attend to Garston and ensure that the fleet train had resupplied his fleet. At least they had been joined by a new cruiser, *Cochrane*, bringing his fleet up to its full complement of cruisers. In theory, each of humanity's cruisers was equal to a superdreadnought, although Tobias suspected that the real picture wasn't that rosy. "And then we press onwards to Hammerfall."

"It is their sector capital for this region," Commander Sooraya Qadir agreed. "ONI claims that they have at least one squadron of superdreadnoughts based there, along with a hundred smaller ships. We could attempt to outflank it, but as long as those ships are in our rear..."

"They'd be a clear threat," Tobias said. After the terrifying risk of sending the gunboats to Heavenly Gate, hitting Hammerfall seemed comparatively mild. They were already at war with the Hegemony, after all. "We couldn't afford to risk them heading to Earth."

He studied the star chart for a long moment. ONI had been trying to monitor the progress of Hegemony reinforcements ever since the war had begun, but it was difficult to track starships by monitoring their transmissions. Human intelligence specialists were among the best in the universe, capable of decrypting Hegemony transmissions at astonishing speed, yet it was often surprisingly difficult to pull useful intelligence out of them. The Hegemony hadn't managed to get organised in the wake of the Battle of Terra Nova – they were still worried about their flanks – but it wouldn't be long before Hammerfall was heavily reinforced. If he waited too long, their position might be impregnable.

And the last thing he needed was heavy losses.

"Order the recon ships to start monitoring the system," he ordered. Humanity had been using civilian ships, right up until the moment that the Hegemony had ordered all civilian ships out of their military-dominated systems. Maybe they'd realised that the humans were using some of them to spy, or maybe they were trying to convince the other Galactics to intervene. The reports from Center claimed that the Hegemony wasn't seriously looking for help – they still believed they could take humanity on their own – but they might have changed their minds. It wouldn't be the first time ONI had managed to get something wrong.

He looked back at the display. By any standard, Hammerfall was heavily defended, yet he'd been considering possible ways to take it long before the war had begun. There *was* an Achilles heel in their defences. All they had to do was survive long enough to use it.

"And then contact *Formidable*," he added. Pulling her in was a risk, but it was necessary. "I want her to rendezvous with us at Point Alpha. We're going to need the gunboats for this operation."

Chapter Twenty-Two

Kauirik had been a mistake, one of the rare worlds where the terraforming process had gone badly wrong. The atmosphere was still breathable, but the planet was hot and covered in vegetation that had adapted itself to the new environment. After attempting to fix the problem, the original terraforming team had given up and abandoned the settlement rights to the first race that wanted to claim it. The Hegemony had annexed the world two hundred years ago, after realising that it could support a colony. Most of the Hegemony's dissidents had been expelled to Kauirik if they'd been too important or well-connected to be simply executed.

There were few defences and no starships in orbit around Kauirik, which rendered it impotent in the war, hardly worth the attention of the human fleet. Lady Dalsha had gambled on that, after hiring a civilian ship to take her from Garston before the human commander thought better of simply letting her go. It would have taken too long to reach the homeworld to report in person, at least before the humans struck Hammerfall or bypassed it in their drive towards the Empress. And besides, it might be safer for her personally not to be near the Empress when she read her report.

The Association had never been able to perfect the tachyon-burst transmissions that made up the backbone of the interstellar communications network. It was difficult, and extremely power-intensive, to hold a two-way conversation over several light-years, leaving most races and corporations dependent upon recorded and compressed messages. The Great Lady overseeing the planet had agreed to let her use the communications node for a two-way message, even if it would drain her planet's power reserves. Lady Dalsha had told her enough to make her certain that the last thing she wanted was to get involved with the war – or the process of breaking the news to the Empress. She was unlikely to prove forgiving to the person who had lost five superdreadnoughts.

Even with her clan roots, calling the Empress directly was never easy and she had to wade through a series of functionaries who wanted to know why she was calling. Information was power in court, and entire careers had been made or broken because someone had gotten a crucial piece of intelligence before their rivals. Lady Dalsha patiently insisted that she had to talk to the Empress personally, ploughing her way through functionary after functionary. At least none of them quite had the nerve to cut her off. The Empress would have heard about Terra Nova by now, even if the Hegemony didn't have any sensor records from the battle. No one wanted the blame for preventing the sole known survivor access to the Empress.

Eventually, the Empress's face materialised in front of her. The image was unstable, flickering apart into bursts of static before reforming, but the voice channel was stable and the line should be fairly secure. Nothing was guaranteed in a universe where most of the Galactics waged subtle war against one another, and yet there was no other choice. She *had* to make her report to the Empress.

Protocol dictated a full prostration before the Empress, but the Empress held up one clawed hand before she could even begin the ritual. The protocols were a part of society, a reminder that the Empress – as supreme mistress of the Hegemony – held the power of life and death over her subjects, but this Empress was known for disdaining them. Lady Dalsha privately admired her willingness to avoid protocol, if only because an Empress who started to believe that she really *was* all-powerful would likely be assassinated sooner rather than later.

"We have heard disturbing reports," the Empress said. "The humans have declared war upon our Hegemony. They have claimed that they have smashed your squadron. We charge you now to speak truly. What happened at the human colony world?"

Lady Dalsha took a breath and started to explain, running through the entire battle from the first arrival of the impossible starships to her decision to surrender. The

197

Empress's red eyes watched Lady Dalsha, showing no sign of visible emotion as the entire story spilled out, followed finally by the human occupation of Garston and her release to catch a starship to the nearest colony world. Her brief description of the human weapons attracted the Empress's attention, even though the Empress didn't quite seem to believe her. But who would have thought that the human race could advance so far, so fast?

But maybe it did make sense, Lady Dalsha considered. The Cats had served as the source of most technology for the Galactics, but they'd been stagnating for thousands of years, content with what they'd had. Most of the other Galactics had concentrated on building up their own numbers rather than their research and development institutions, particularly those who believed that the Cats had taken technology as far as it could go. No genuinely new breakthrough had appeared in the Association for longer than the Hegemony had been in space. Unless, of course, the Cats had something they hadn't shared with anyone else.

That was a common belief among those Galactics who still had faith in the founding race, who felt that the Cats would act if the galactic balance of power was seriously threatened. There was no disputing the fact that the Cats had been in space longer than anyone else and that they understood their own technology; it was *possible* that they had some super-weapons they'd held in reserve for the day the younger races rose up against their vision of order. But Lady Dalsha doubted it. No race with the ability to strangle the Hegemony in its cradle would have allowed them to grow so powerful. Even now, the Cats could have stopped the Hegemony in its tracks, if they had been able to summon the will to accept the casualties.

And yet... maybe that was what Mentor had had in mind, when he'd equipped the humans with modern technology. Earth wouldn't have been any more than a footnote if Mentor hadn't contacted the planet, nothing more than a slight pause while the Hegemony crushed all resistance and established a loyal government. His gamble had worked out perfectly, from that point of view. The

Hegemony would have to crush humanity, or be crushed in turn, leaving whoever won the war badly weakened. It might have been exactly what he'd had in mind.

"This is most disquieting," the Empress said, finally. "Weapons that can shoot *through* shields, super-charged antimatter weapons, rotating shields... do you have any sensor records to support your statements?"

"No," Lady Dalsha admitted. The humans had been cooperative, but not *that* cooperative. "My ships were captured by the humans and their sensor records were wiped."

It was an open question how long it would take for the humans to repair the superdreadnoughts and press them into service. A Hegemony repair crew would take months, at least, to get the two ships ready to travel to a shipyard, and years to complete repairs. How long would the humans take? But then they might not even bother trying to repair the two ships. A contest between superdreadnoughts was one that the human race would lose.

She watched the Empress mulling over possible thoughts. One thing was clear; there could be no peace, not until the human race was crushed. The Empress could not afford to show weakness, not if the tale of the battle had grown in the telling. By now, the Galactics were probably muttering that a single human destroyer took on an entire *fleet* of superdreadnoughts and wiped them all out. It didn't matter than anyone with a gram of sense would realise that story was an exaggeration. All that mattered was that it would weaken the Hegemony.

And yet... the Hegemony's position was not good as it was. Three powers, two of them as expansionist as the Hegemony, bordered its space. Even the third, the Tarn, were too powerful to be crushed in a quick and brutal campaign. Pulling ships away from the borders would be asking for trouble, while not redeploying their forces would mean that the humans would keep chopping away at the Hegemony until the entire state collapsed into civil war. It could not be allowed, but how could it be prevented. They'd badly underestimated the human race and the entire Hegemony was going to pay the price.

"I cannot afford to lose you, not now," the Empress said finally. Lady Dalsha almost sagged with relief. Death didn't bother her, not when compared to the possible punishments for losing an entire squadron of superdreadnoughts. "The new human weapons can be countered, one assumes. Or they would have flown a fleet of invincible starships to Homeworld and demanded surrender."

"There is no such thing as an invincible starship," Lady Dalsha said, grimly. The Galactics had believed that the only thing that could stop a superdreadnought was another superdreadnought, at least until the human race had proved them wrong. "We can take out the human ships, if we refuse to panic. They can be beaten."

"I am ordering you to Hammerfall," the Empress said. "I cannot give you command of the fleet there – too many scales will start to itch – but I can instruct the Great Lady in command to listen to your suggestions. The humans must deal with Hammerfall before they head further into the Hegemony, so we will meet them there."

One pair of clawed hands clicked together. "Unfortunately, raiders along the borders have been growing more active over the last two standard weeks," she added. "Pulling small units away from the borderlands will only encourage them to continue their attacks. However, I have issued orders for the border fleets to release two squadrons of superdreadnoughts, which will be dispatched forward to reinforce Hammerfall. A number of other ships will be dispatched as they become available."

The Empress's mouth lolled open in a long smile. "Do you have any recommendations for further operations?"

Lady Dalsha considered. Reinforcing Hammerfall was sensible – and if the humans took the planet before the reinforcements arrived, the forces rushing towards it should be sufficient to retake the planet before the human fleet moved onwards. If they weren't... they might have to start pulling ships away from the borders anyway, no matter what happened with the other powers. The Hegemony would lose badly if the humans actually managed to win their war...

...But the Hegemony was far larger than the mere nine stars belonging to humanity.

"The humans cannot have built a colossal fleet," she said. Hegemony intelligence had clearly made the mistake of believing everything the humans had told them – in fact, the human turncoats had probably been telling the spymasters what the humans wanted them to know, or to believe. It wasn't so easy to operate on Earth, where aliens would be noticed by the general population, leaving them dependent upon human traitors. And if those traitors had actually been double agents...

She scratched the side of her face as she spoke. "We can afford to trade space for time; they cannot," she said. "If we can force them onto the defensive, we win. I propose that we send a fleet from Hammerfall directly to Earth. The humans will be forced to fight for their own homeworld, the world that holds most of their population. Given overwhelming force, we could crush them and take their planet for our own."

The Empress considered. "But assaulting a defended world isn't easy," she pointed out, finally. "The humans might have built *really* formidable defences around Earth."

"I don't think they would have had the resources," Lady Dalsha said. "Earth has had access to modern technology, but they would have needed years just to build up any kind of space-based industry. Mentor didn't provide them with more than a little help from the Association – they certainly never received any of the development packages the Association used to offer to newly-discovered races. They would have had to choose between building starships and planetary defences, and we know they built starships. And even if they have built something new, I don't think that it will make Earth impregnable.

"We mass our forces at Hammerfall and then advance directly on Earth," she added. "Three squadrons of superdreadnoughts – more, if we can pull them from the borders – and as many smaller ships as we can scrape up. The humans may take another couple of worlds, but they will lose their homeworld while taking worlds that mean little to us. And then we can wipe out their remaining colonies and leave their fleet paralysed, without the supplies it will need to keep functioning."

She spoke on before the Empress could say anything. "We know that it is a general rule that for every week on active service, a starship needs at least a day in a shipyard. The human ships can't be so advanced that they can afford to operate for years without maintenance. We can wear them down and eventually force them to surrender – or destroy them. And that will be the end of the human threat."

"It sounds possible," the Empress mused. "I will have to run it past my naval staff..."

"It must remain a secret," Lady Dalsha insisted. "The humans had very good intelligence on Terra Nova – and I assume they must have their own spies within the Hegemony." She would have been more surprised if the humans hadn't, if only because of the constant infighting between the clans struggling for power. Someone would be happy to slip information to humanity on the grounds that more human victories would weaken the Empress. "If they know what's coming, they might be able to prepare for it."

"And blunt the force of our blow," the Empress agreed. "Very well. It will be as you say."

There was a pause. "You will report to Hammerfall," she added. "I will communicate with you there, once the preliminary planning is underway. And if your advice helps to defend the planet, you will command the fleet that goes to Earth."

"Thank you, Your Majesty," Lady Dalsha said. "I..."

The Empress's image fizzled out and disappeared, a sure sign of dismissal. Lady Dalsha bowed her head to the screen and then headed for the hatch. The freighter that had transported her to Kauirik was still in orbit, ready to take her onwards. And at least Hammerfall wasn't the homeworld. She might be able to redeem herself...

...Assuming, of course, that the humans didn't have more tricks up their sleeves.

* * *

Blackbird coasted in towards the system primary, all drives and active sensors stepped down to the bare minimum. No one, not even human starships with the most capable sensors in the galaxy, would have been able to detect her except at very close range. She would never be able to stand in the line of battle – a single destroyer could have obliterated her with a lucky shot – but she hadn't been designed as a blunt instrument. Her mission was reconnaissance alone.

Compared to a regular starship, she was tiny, an invisible ghost crossing the stars. A cloaking device would have produced turbulence, a distortion that might be tracked by a good or lucky sensor officer, but *Blackbird* produced nothing. Her hull was crammed with passive sensors, leaving little room for the two intelligence operatives who served as her crew. They worked, ate and slept in a cabin barely large enough to swing a cat.

"I have at least five superdreadnoughts," Commander Connie Craig said. The power emissions of superdreadnoughts stood out, even among a swarm of smaller starships patrolling orbital space above Hammerfall. "Maybe another two – or maybe they're ECM drones."

"We should get a better look as we get closer," Lieutenant Bruno Lombardi agreed. Like Connie, he was an intelligence officer rather than a line officer, although the distinction between them blurred where *Blackbird* and her sisters were concerned. "But they've established a tachyon net around the planet itself. I think they must be worried about spies like us."

Connie nodded. A starship that passed through the net would be instantly detectable, allowing System Command to vector destroyers and assault shuttles to intercept the intruder. System Command itself was a colossal fortress, a space station large enough to daunt even the human imagination, bristling with weapons, sensor blisters and repair yards for the Hegemony Navy. It said something about the Hegemony's resources that they could build something out of what was, effectively, pocket change. But then, Hammerfall was their major naval base in the sector.

There were no pesky civilian ships to get in the way of defending the base.

The hours ticked by slowly as *Blackbird* made her closest approach to the planet. They'd be well clear of the tachyon net, Connie noted with some relief; *Blackbird* wouldn't have had a hope in hell of escape if she'd been detected. A larger ship might have escaped, but *Blackbird's* drives were too weak to give her a fighting chance. And her crews were under orders to destroy the ship – and themselves – if the Hegemony caught them. They couldn't risk her falling into enemy hands.

"Definitely five superdreadnoughts," Lombardi said. He hesitated. "I count roughly seventy lighter vessels, mainly destroyers. They're probably consolidating the other units in this sector at Hammerfall. They're going to outgun Admiral Sampson when he arrives."

"Hell, that's always been true," Connie pointed out. But human quality had provided a counter to Galactic quantity, at least so far. "I think the Admiral will be pleased to know what we have found. We've verified the location of a squadron of superdreadnoughts."

ONI did its best to track the Hegemony's ships, but it was difficult, particularly for the smaller vessels. Most of the Hegemony's superdreadnoughts were along their borders, or pinned down defending their homeworld, leaving only a small force to block humanity's advance. But then, five more superdreadnoughts would be quite sufficient to block a similar fleet from any other spacefaring power.

"And then we can get out of here," she added. "Maybe the Admiral will send us back for ringside seats when the fleet hits Hammerfall."

Chapter Twenty-Three

"So," Karla said, "how does it feel to be a pirate king?"

Joshua snorted. One rule that was a constant in both the business world and the pirate world – which were closer related than most people would have preferred to believe – was that success bred success. The loose network of pirates, fences, rebels and rogue colonies had fallen in love with the Clunkers, a love affair that would continue precisely as long as the stolen goods and money kept rolling in. Joshua had used their growing reputation to convince dozens of other pirates to join them, using the newcomers to crew ships he'd captured or bought on the black market. He'd known long before he'd been summoned home that there *was* a black market, but he'd never realised its extent. There was a whole secret economy operating out beyond explored space.

"Strange," he said. He'd spent years worrying about his crews, travelling through regions where piracy was epidemic. Now he was planning and organising pirate attacks against Hegemony shipping, with enough ships to ensure that even escorting vessels were badly outgunned. A few more weeks and the Hegemony would be forced to start assigning heavier escort squadrons or abandon some of their most profitable shipping lanes. Not that they were going to have much profit in the very near future; regional insurance rates were rising sharply. "If only I was sure that they would obey orders."

He had no doubt about the Clunkers, even if he *had* taken most of their personnel out of a penal colony. They knew the score as well as he did. But the other pirates wanted profit first, rather than waging war against the Hegemony, and even the rebels needed funds. The desire for loot drove them and they had a nasty habit of abandoning the chase to capture disabled freighters and take their cargo.

In one sense, it didn't really matter – and it was sure to confuse the Hegemony. But in another sense, it risked expanding the war or convincing other powers to start sending their own escort units through Hegemony-controlled space. The Hegemony wouldn't like it, but if they had a shortage of their own lighter units, they might accept it without more than token protests. And *that* risked expanding the war. As far as Joshua knew, no one had realised that the Clunkers were exclusively human – and the pirates they had recruited certainly weren't – but sooner or later someone would put all the pieces together. Who benefited from the Hegemony's woes? Humanity wasn't the only suspect, but they were the only ones who had gone to war.

Karla snorted. "You don't trust them?"

"I trust them about as far as I can pick up this ship and throw it," Joshua countered. The Hegemony had its own agents in the black market. Chances were that they were already trying to locate Joshua's base. He'd pulled a fast one by using a freighter converted into a mobile shipyard as his prime base, which should be effectively impossible to detect, but there were limits to how long they could operate without proper refitting. "But if the worst should occur, they are expendable."

And so are we, he thought silently.

The Clunker Fleet had made an impact, largely through coordinating its operations and careful planning, neither of which were hallmarks of pirate society. But the Hegemony wouldn't simply give up. They'd set traps, hoping to snare his ships in an ambush, using overwhelming power to destroy the small squadron. And when that happened, the alliance of pirates he'd pulled together would melt away like snow under summer sun. He'd done his best to prepare fallback positions, but he had no illusions about their effectiveness. They couldn't risk a major defeat.

"*But many a king on a first class throne, if he wants to call his crown his own,*

Must manage somehow to get through, more dirty work than ever I do."

Karla smiled. "What was that?"

"Gilbert and Sullivan," Joshua said. "They wrote an opera about pirates…"

206

The console chimed as the enemy ships came into view, slipping through quantum space under heavy escort. Joshua had taken up a position that should allow his ships to observe the newcomers without being seen themselves, just in case the Hegemony had prepared some unpleasant surprises for his men. Sensors rapidly picked up a pair of light cruisers, flanked by four destroyers, escorting five heavy freighters and one ship of unknown configuration. It reassembled a freighter in basic design, but it didn't match anything in ONI's records.

"It might be a Q-ship," Karla said, after a moment. The Galactics generally disdained Q-ships, pointing out that a warship convincingly pretending to be a freighter would have all of the disadvantages of being a freighter and none of the advantages of actually *being* a freighter. But if there was one area where they made sense, it was in hunting pirates. Most pirates didn't want to blow away cargos they could sell on the black market. "Or maybe it's just a kind of freighter we haven't seen before. They do have more than one design."

"Maybe," Joshua agreed. They *could* back off and let the convoy go on its way, but the pirates would complain – loudly – that they hadn't been paid for their services. Given that their job was to steal from the rich and keep for themselves, it would be a little hypocritical, yet somehow he doubted that that would stop them. And disgruntled pirates might sell them out to the Hegemony. "Signal the fleet. We advance in a body on my mark."

Standard tactics for evading interception in quantum space were to scatter, every starship heading away on a different vector. Against the average pirate ship, which operated on her own or in pairs, it wasn't a bad tactic. The storms of quantum space would cover the freighters that got away while the pirates were hunting down and disabling their comrades. But that was why Joshua had worked so hard to build a coalition, no matter the disadvantages involved in working with such untrustworthy allies. Not a single freighter would escape his fleet.

"Mark," he ordered. "Take us in, now."

Blackbeard lanced forward, weapons at the ready. The Hegemony ships altered course, the escorts forming a line to face the pirates while the freighters headed away from the battle. That too wasn't bad tactics, but it suggested that the mystery ship was merely another freighter...unless the Funks were trying to be subtle. They weren't known for being anything, but brutally direct – and yet some of them were crafty enough to match the best humanity could offer. It might still be a trap.

Any pirate force would be a hodgepodge of technology, drives and weapons systems from all over the galaxy. Few rogue colonies had the industrial base to produce their own starships – and they would be careful about selling their wares to pirates, knowing that the Hegemony or another of the Galactics might send a superdreadnought squadron to extract revenge. The Hegemony ships would have good reason to believe that they had the advantage over the pirate fleet, even though they were badly outnumbered. Under normal circumstances, Joshua knew, their confidence would be fully justified. But these weren't normal circumstances.

"Fire," he ordered.

Blackbird launched a spread of antimatter torpedoes towards her target, the first of the light cruisers. The other ships opened fire seconds later, presenting the Funks with an impossible tactical problem, even as they started to return fire. Joshua half-expected them to make an emergency transit back into normal space, which would have allowed them to evade the torpedoes, but it was already too late. Both light cruisers were blown apart, their death throes exciting quantum space and threatening the creation of new energy storms. One of the destroyers staggered out of position, spinning helplessly through space. The other two kept firing, concentrating on the pirate ships. It represented their best chance to damage the fleet before they were destroyed.

"*Serial Peacemaker* took four hits and is seriously damaged," Karla reported. "Her captain is requesting permission to break off the engagement."

"Granted," Joshua said, tightly. Their second salvo was already away. The galactic news service had been raving about new weapons from Earth over the last few weeks, but none of the Clunkers had anything that could be traced directly back to Earth. It hardly mattered, not in this engagement. The last two escorts died, leaving the path to the convoy open. "Detail ships to hunt down the freighters and remind them that we need prisoners."

"Of course," Karla agreed. "Do you think they'll listen?"

Joshua shrugged. He'd been very clear that all booty was to be shared equally between pirate ships, hopefully dissuading the pirates from breaking off and chasing prizes they considered to be more important than maintaining formation. But the pirates were a suspicious and distrusting lot. Some of them probably thought that Joshua intended to abandon them, sooner or later, and take all the loot for himself. But that wasn't a bad thing. They wouldn't suspect his real motives.

Blackbeard slowly overhauled the mystery vessel, watching suspiciously for any sign that the freighter was a disguised warship. Nothing suggested itself, apart from the fact that the crew were trying to evade Joshua rather than surrendering in the hopes that they would be well-treated. Maybe it was a rational thing to do – the pirates didn't have a good reputation for treating prisoners – but all they were doing was annoying him. It took nearly thirty minutes to chase them down enough to launch the assault shuttles, which locked onto the freighter hull without incident. Joshua was still watching carefully when Kang reported in from the captured vessel.

"Boss, I think you're going to need to see this," he said. "It's a prison ship."

* * *

It was nearly an hour after the engagement when Joshua boarded the captured freighter, after he'd seen to the *Serial Peacemaker* and reassured the pirates that they would receive their fair share of any booty from the mystery craft. The other freighters hadn't been great prizes, but there would be enough loot to pay their operating costs and reward their allies. They'd spend most of what they'd earned on a hidden asteroid and then set out again to earn more money, once the whores, gamblers and hustlers had cleaned them out. Some things were universal among humanoid races.

The Galactics generally didn't bother with prison ships. Attitudes to crime and punishment varied from race to race, with some races having strict laws and others taking a milder view of rape and murder than a human would have found comprehensible. No one knew how the Cats punished their offenders – if there *were* Cat offenders – but the younger races tended to establish penal colonies on lifeless balls of rock and leave the offenders there to rot, if they weren't simply executed out of hand. A handful of races used personality reconstruction techniques to prevent further offending, while the Hegemony tended towards inventive punishments for female offenders. Males were assumed to be naturally rogue without female supervision, an attitude that many human females would have understood.

He boarded the ship through a secured airlock and stepped into the bridge. It looked remarkably small for such a large ship, but a glance at the status panel revealed that it was completely separate from the rest of the ship. Layers of hull metal, tough enough to require phase cannon or molecular disintegrators to penetrate, protected the crew from the prisoners, who were expected to fend for themselves while they were being transported from world to world. They didn't need to worry about restraints. There was no way the prisoners could do more than kill each other.

"Odd," he said. "Why were they being transported in the first place? They can't be that short of trained labour, can they?"

Kang nodded towards one of the screens. "That's the live feed from the hold," he said. "Those aren't Funks, boss."

Joshua narrowed his eyes. He hadn't seen even a fraction of the hundreds of races in the Association, or hidden out beyond the borderlands, but he'd studied extensively and he recognised the race. The Gobbles – the closest any human could come to pronouncing their name – had been even more primitive than Earth when they'd been discovered by the Association, and then they'd been unlucky enough to be overrun by the Hegemony before they even knew that there was an entire civilization living among the stars. Their resistance had been pitiful – Alexander the Great wouldn't have had a prayer against modern technology, no matter his military genius – and the Funks had rapidly turned them into a slave race.

Aliens were rarely 'cute,' but the Gobbles came surprisingly close. They reassembled teddy bears as much as anything else, although teddy bears with sharp teeth and humanoid hands that gave them a remarkable talent for industrial machinery. Primitive didn't equal stupid and the Gobbles had managed to carve out a niche for themselves among the Funks, although never as anything other than slaves. Their treatment was a chilling reminder of the *best* that humanity could hope for if they lost the war.

"Curious," Joshua said, slowly. "Why would they bother to transport them anywhere?"

One of the other former criminals – a computer tech with a habit of exploring outside permitted areas of military datanets – looked up from one of the consoles. "Security on this thing is rubbish," he said, by way of explanation. "Those teddies have been convicted of treason against the Hegemony and were being taken to the Empress. I don't think that she's going to give them a big hug."

"Assuming any of them survive the trip," Kang put in. "They've been left to rot in their own filth. I'd bet good money that they were intended to die along the way."

"But if they wanted them to die," the computer tech said, "why didn't they simply shoot them?"

"Plausible deniability," Kang said. He leered. "When I was in the teams, there were all sorts of silly tricks meant to give political weaklings the ability to swear blind that they never gave explicit orders to the operatives. Need answers out of a suspect quickly? Give a verbal order to torture him and then send a memo – too late – forbidding torture. Want to blow up a village where you know a terrorist leader is hiding? Use the wrong equipment to create the impression that the village is empty and there are no civilians to be hurt..."

211

"I don't think the Funks have that much subtlety in them," Joshua said. He shrugged. "Find the most senior of the prisoners, give him a chance to clean up, and then bring him to me on *Blackbeard*. I'll talk to him in the secure hold, so he doesn't see the rest of the ship until we have decided what to do with him."

He shrugged. "You never know," he added. "We might just have met our first ally."

* * *

In person, there was little that was *cute* about the Gobble. The sharp teeth, more intimidating in person than in the video feed, and the burn marks on his fur created the impression of a battered teddy bear, but there was an iron look in his eye that suggested that it wouldn't go down without a fight. Joshua was wearing full powered armor, concealing his face, and yet it was impossible not to feel his skin crawling when he looked at the Gobble's teeth. Part of his racial memory remembered the days when humans had had to fear bears.

"I thank you for the rescue," the Gobble said. He spoke Galactic Three, without a trace of the hiss the Funks produced from their oddly-shaped mouths. "I fear that the" – he spoke a word that didn't translate, even though the suit's database – "will be very unhappy to lose me."

"I'm glad to hear it," Joshua said. Poking a stick in bright red eyes was why they were out here, so far from Earth. "Would you like to tell me why they were transporting you to their world?"

"My people have sought our freedom for countless years," the Gobble said. "I, Xinchub, was the leader of the Tausennigan Ob'enn, the resistance to those who have occupied our world. They left us our religion and so we used it as the only tool we had to build a resistance network, but they stumbled across us and arrested and executed many. I was scheduled to be executed in front of the Empress herself."

Joshua smiled. "And the rest of the prisoners?"

212

"Some known to me, who tried to fight," Xinchub said. "Others picked up at random, or through false information. Many will now fight if given the chance to return to our homeworld. Tauscher will be liberated if we have to all lay down our lives in the struggle."

"I see," Joshua said, slowly. Inside, he was thinking rapidly. No revolt could succeed as long as the Funks maintained their control over the planet's orbitals. They could simply bombard any rebel-held territory into submission, no matter how discontented the Gobbles were with their lot. And yet... intelligence on Tauscher was limited, but it did suggest that a major nexus of manufacturing had grown around the planet. The Gobbles did have talents and the Funks were happy to exploit them. "Do you wish to carry on the fight?"

"Of course," Xinchub said. "We swore solemn oaths before our gods that we would be victorious or die. I will not betray those oaths."

"Then I think we can help each other," Joshua said. "We're going to somewhere safe, where we can think and plan. And then we may be able to save your world."

Afterwards, he found himself considering just what he had done. Raiding Funk shipping was one thing, but actually moving in on one of their worlds? His orders hadn't covered that eventuality. But then, no one knew he was out here apart from his crews and the Admiral.

And the Gobbles, if necessary, were expendable.

Chapter Twenty-Four

No one knew much about the race that had originally lived on Hammerfall. That there *had* been a race was beyond dispute, for the Cats had noted the remains of cities created by a race that had barely learned to use steam power before it died out. They'd had the supreme ill-luck to evolve in a binary system that was teeming with debris, where the gravitational surges between the twin stars routinely tipped asteroids in and out of the system. Eventually, their luck had run out and an asteroid had slammed directly into their world. They'd been extinct for hundreds of years when the Cats had stumbled across their world.

Hammerfall itself still wasn't particularly well developed, but the Hegemony had seen value in turning it into a major naval base. At first, it had seemed like a pointless exercise in pleasing some of the clans, but now it would be worth its weight in whatever precious substance one cared to name. The human advance would *have* to go through Hammerfall or risk leaving a major fleet in their rear. And this time they would confront a Hegemony force that understood their tricks and was ready for them. Their advance would come to a halt and then the counteroffensive could begin.

"And so they let you go," Great Lady Marsha said. Her clan and Lady Dalsha's had been enemies for hundreds of years, even though no one remembered whatever dispute had originally caused the vendetta. "They must have known that you were no threat. How wise they were."

Lady Dalsha managed to contain her temper. A failure had no friends or family, for fear that it might rub off. Her clan had already disowned her, leaving her isolated from the complex network of alliances and enmities that made up the heart of the Hegemony. In some ways, it gave her a freedom others would envy; in others, it made her supremely vulnerable, unprotected against assassins or slavers – or anyone who wanted private revenge. Marsha hadn't even agreed to see her in person, exiling her to a fortress on the other side of Hammerfall. It was a very blunt gesture of contempt.

"Had I faced the entire known human fleet," she said, patiently, "I would have crushed them all with minimal losses…"

"But you didn't," Marsha sneered. "You allowed yourself to be defeated by a puny force with nothing heavier than a cruiser. Three superdreadnoughts destroyed – and two surrendered. No wonder they let you go. You are so much more valuable to them with us than you would be as a prisoner. Did they hope you might be placed in command of the next fleet they encountered?"

Lady Dalsha cursed inwardly. *That* wasn't going to happen. Technically, she still had her rank, but every female with an ear for the political realities would know that she had no practical authority. Her rank was worthless in anything more than name. She'd certainly never be allowed to command a starship, let alone an entire fleet. Besides, she'd been disowned. Why would anyone give her a starship when there were hundreds of well-connected females awaiting their chance?

"A few new tricks and you panicked," Marsha added. "They should have released your sensor crews instead. The males could at least have told us something useful."

"I did what I could," Lady Dalsha replied, tiring of the endless stream of insults from Marsha. Like her, before Terra Nova, Marsha had every confidence in her fleet – and not without reason. The Hegemony was still straining every sinew to reinforce Hammerfall, but Marsha commanded over a hundred starships, enough to destroy an entire sector if necessary. But just as the First Empress had been badly outmatched by the weapons possessed by the Cats, Hammerfall might be facing human weapons a quantum leap ahead of the superdreadnoughts in orbit. "And you would be well advised to listen to me."

She'd seen what the human weapons had done to her squadron, but they'd been careful to deny her any sensor data that would back up her claims. The Hegemony had always been weak in basic research, a weakness that had seemed insignificant when the entire galaxy had restricted itself to weapons developed by the Cats thousands of years ago. But now... the Hegemony's long list of enemies would be hearing reports of human super-weapons and pushing their own research programmes forward as fast as they could. How long would it be before the Tarn developed their own version of human weapons, giving them a colossal advantage over the Hegemony? Or any one of a dozen races – or all of them? The Hegemony might find itself in the same position as the mounted warriors who had tried to fight the Cats, only to be scythed down by plasma cannon.

And she knew, all too well, that none of the Hegemony's neighbours liked them.

The Empress was firmly in control, for the moment, but no one could stop rumours flying through the Hegemony faster than any quantum drive. Some of the lesser clans were seeing their chance to unseat the Empress and reshape the balance of power, while the client races were considering the odds of their own drive for freedom – or revenge. And there were already rumblings of discontent among the masses.

"You are a failure," Marsha informed her. "My fleet will not suffer the same defeat as your own. I will crush the humans, obtain samples of their weapons, and then launch an offensive of my own, directed at Garston and Terra Nova. And you will watch as the better officer wins her war."

Lady Dalsha raised one clawed hand in a gesture of submission. There was no point in continuing the argument, not when Marsha was clearly already determined to carry out her plan. At least the Empress's orders bound her firmly to Hammerfall until the human fleet had been defeated. Their worst nightmare had been the humans slipping in and devastating the base while the fleet was trying to recover Garston. Losing that world had been bad enough, but losing Hammerfall would put the war effort back by at least two years.

She just hoped that Marsha was right and that she did have enough firepower – and forewarning – to defeat the human fleet. But who knew what other tricks the humans had developed, holding them in reserve until they were needed? She couldn't even begin to imagine what they might have produced...

...And it was that weakness, more than anything else, that would cripple the Hegemony.

* * *

"Seems like a strange set of orders," Markus commented, as the gunboats raced through quantum space. Ahead of them, a single bulk freighter struggled to escape. "I thought we were meant to be linking up with the others and raiding enemy planets."

"Orders are orders," Carola reminded him. Gunboats *could* operate in quantum space, but their inability to jump in and out of the dimension was a serious weakness. Energy discharges that might cripple a starship would utterly vaporise a gunboat. "The brass was pretty damn clear that they wanted this done by their best pilots."

Markus nodded, sourly. Humanity possessed no more than three gunboat carriers, three more than anyone else, but a deeply limited force when compared to the vast fleets deployed by the Galactics. The other two had been deployed on raiding missions, hammering away at the other worlds in the sector, hoping to create an impression of human invincibility. Apart from Hammerfall itself, most of the other worlds had limited defences, none of which could stand up to a flight of gunboats. The attacks were pinpricks compared to the sheer size of the Hegemony, but it should make the Funks a little concerned about the security of their people – and the territories of clans whose political support the Empress depended upon.

But Grumble Squadron had been given a set of orders that didn't quite make sense. They were to intercept a bulk freighter and harass her all the way to Hammerfall, but *not* to press the offensive and destroy her. *Formidable* was just behind them, ready to pick up the gunboats when the bulk freighter finally escaped, yet he was aware that they were flying right into the teeth of the most heavily defended planet in the sector. *Formidable* was almost defenceless compared to a heavy cruiser, let alone the superdreadnoughts that were supposed to be guarding Hammerfall. None of the gunboats had challenged a superdreadnought yet and, despite simulations suggesting that they would be just as effective against the biggest ships in the galaxy, the pilots were nervous. The Hegemony had already started adapting its tactics against them.

An alert sounded as quantum space twisted in front of them. Markus felt his stomach twist – as if he was on a roller coaster – before the blackness of normal space rose up and swallowed them. The gunboat seemed to slide down a long funnel before spinning out into normal space, tossed around by gravimetric fluctuations that barely hindered a modern starship. Behind them, the quantum gate started to shut down. *Formidable* would have to enter normal space using her own drives.

"I think they've seen us," Carola said. "I make five light cruisers rushing us – and a goodly swarm of assault shuttles."

"Clever," Markus admitted, grudgingly. The Hegemony, by the most pessimistic estimate, would take at least a year to produce its own gunboats, but pressing assault shuttles into service gave them a chance to even the odds. Assault shuttles weren't designed solely for space – they landed Marines on planetary surfaces – yet they were more manoeuvrable than anything else in the Hegemony Navy. They'd take heavy losses as they tried to dogfight the gunboats, but they'd inflict losses in return. "And the freighter?"

"Running towards the fortresses as fast as its little legs can carry it, screaming for help," Carola reported. "I think the Funks are desperate to save her."

Markus nodded and threw the gunboat into a tight turn, followed by the rest of the squadron. To the Funks, it would look like an attack vector determined to obliterate the freighter before it could reach safety – and as he watched, the Funks did the one thing they could to salvage the situation. Their assault shuttles went to full power and raced ahead of the light cruisers, roaring towards the human gunboats. Markus fired a stream of implosion bolts towards the freighter, taking care to look as if he was panicking, and then led the gunboats right toward the assault shuttles. He'd expected the Funks to have outfitted them with something more dangerous than laser packs or plasma cannon, but it didn't look as if they'd had time to rig up phase cannon or their own implosion bolt launchers. Or maybe they simply hadn't thought of it. Assault shuttles were armed to support Marines on the ground, not dogfight with enemy craft.

"Open fire," he ordered, tightly. Brilliant bursts of plasma shot ahead of his gunboat, firing with a rapidity that the Hegemony couldn't match. Admittedly, the plasma containment fields had to be completely replaced after every mission – and there was a small chance they could explode, destroying the gunboat – but it made it much harder for the assault shuttles to close to effective range. Their pilots kept evading frantically, yet it was clear that they hadn't been given much time to practice operating in vacuum. Several assault shuttles were picked off before they even started to fire back. "All Grumbles, prepare for charge."

He swung the gunboat around and gunned the drives. The gunboats leapt forward, charging right at the assault shuttles – and the light cruisers beyond. No human mind could take advantage of the brief opportunities to fire on the assault shuttles, but the computers had authority to take the shots as they opened and a dozen shuttles died as they scattered. There was normally no such thing as a collision risk in open space, yet they'd be passing so close to the shuttles that they'd be able to see them with the naked eye. Markus caught sight of a flash of light as another assault shuttle died, before the gunboats closed in rapidly on the light cruisers.

Their point defence had improved, he noted, as they swung into attack formation, shifting randomly to confuse their sensors. A gunboat died just before it could open fire on the enemy ship. The remainder started to bombard the cruiser with implosion bolts as the assault shuttles reversed course and came screaming back towards their heavier consorts. It was too late to save the targeted cruiser. An implosion bolt sliced through her power plant and it blew, taking the entire ship with it. There was no sign of any lifepods.

"I think we've done enough here," he said, as the shuttles closed in. "On my mark, enter panic formation... mark!"

The gunboats swung away, as if they were fleeing in terror. Markus doubted that the Funks would be fooled, if only because the tales they told one another of war on their dry world had included plenty of feigned retreats to lure the enemy into a trap, but they would keep watching the gunboats until they linked up with *Formidable* and escaped into quantum space. The Funks had to know that they wouldn't be able to overrun the gunboats, so why would they bother trying? Anything that looked like a trap would raise their hackles.

He glanced back at Hammerfall. It was nowhere near as industrialised as Heavenly Gate, but his sensors could pick up hundreds of starships and orbital fortresses orbiting the world. And the freighter they'd chased into normal space was heading right toward the largest fortress, without a care in the world. Markus watched her for a long moment, wondering exactly what their superiors hadn't bothered to tell them, before returning his attention to the escape. A handful of assault shuttles were giving chase, but the remainder were hanging back. They definitely suspected something, all right. He felt a moment of pity for the crews who had been ordered to advance, and then shook his head. They would kill him and the rest of the squadron, if they were given the chance.

* * *

"They seem to have believed our lies," Abdul Raman commented. There were only two crewmen on the entire freighter, both volunteers. "They think we're escaping from a far more formidable foe."

He smiled. Ever since his brother and his family had been murdered on Terra Nova by the Funks, he'd wanted revenge. His native Iran hadn't been able to pay its way onto the Federation Council, but it had been able to supply a handful of Revolutionary Guardsmen who were determined to seek martyrdom in the name of God. It seemed likely that the Iranian Government had sent them in the hope that they wouldn't come back, yet Abdul found it hard to care. Whatever guilt he had felt in preparing to kill his fellow humans faded when he was facing an alien foe, an enemy of the entire human race. The Funks would crush Iran with the same uncompromising brutality they would use against the rest of the planet, if they were given half a chance. It was up to the Federation Navy to ensure that the Funks could never range in on Earth.

It felt strange to be working with the Americans, and the British, and the Russians, all of whom had been declared enemies of Iran at one time or another, but there was no choice. God had created the human race and ordered his believers to do whatever it took to defend it – and the Galactics posed a deadly threat. Even the ones that weren't openly hostile might have disastrous effects on Earth. What was humanity if alien ideas subverted everything that God had given the human race? And what could one make of aliens who had never been sent their own prophets?

He felt calm, and perfectly in control, as the target came into view. The alien fortress was massive, larger than anything humanity had ever produced, a blocky cubical mass of structures right out of an American science-fiction program. It was surrounded by some of the most powerful shields in the galaxy, capable of standing off a squadron of superdreadnoughts long enough for reinforcements to arrive, and defended with hundreds of emplaced weapons. Abdul checked that the liar – the computer-generated representation of an aristocratic Funk – was still talking, convincing the Funks that the freighter was too important to be destroyed. He would have been surprised if the lie had been believed right up until the end of the mission, but it hardly mattered. They were already close enough to the fortress to do some damage.

He smiled as the Funks started broadcasting orders to the freighter, ordering them to deactivate their drives and hold position. They suspected something, all right. He ignored the orders as weapons started to lock onto the freighter's hull; instead, he tapped a particular command sequence into the ship's computers. The freighter drive powered up and sent them lunging forward, while all remaining power was routed to the shield generators. No one could miss the freighter – it was nowhere near as nimble as a gunboat – but if the Funks still believed the lies...

They opened fire, but it was already too late. The freighter slammed right into the fortress's shields, destroying the containment fields separating the antimatter in her holds from the matter surrounding them. Abdul had a fraction of a moment to realise that they'd succeeded, a microsecond before the freighter and the fortress were wiped from existence in a brilliant white flash.

Chapter Twenty-Five

"*Recon* has transited from Hammerfall, Admiral," Commander Sooraya Qadir reported. "The enemy command and control center has been destroyed."

Tobias nodded, keeping his thoughts to himself. The whole idea of using suicide attacks didn't sit well with him, even if there had been no other way to cripple the enemy before the battle began. If Mentor hadn't come to Earth, it was quite possible that he and the men he'd sent to launch the suicide attack would have been trying to kill each other in another now-pointless human scrabble. At least alien contact had brought some semblance of peace to Earth along humans, if only because there were greater threats out there than their fellow humans.

"Good," he said. "And *Formidable*?"

"She has returned to quantum space and reports that she is rearming the gunboats and will be ready to support the offensive in ten minutes," Sooraya said. "Do we delay long enough for her to join us?"

"No," Tobias said. The Funks were believed to have their own chain of command, with a designated replacement for any commander killed or rendered incommunicado. "Order the fleet to advance into the Hammerfall system."

Space twisted around *Nimitz* as the First Strike Fleet made transit, emerging into the Hammerfall system. Quantum space was oddly distorted around Hammerfall, although no one had been able to come up with a theory that explained it to anyone's satisfaction. Their best guess from humanity's scientists was that the gravimetric distortion caused by the presence of two stars in such close proximity had somehow created a permanent impression on quantum space, perhaps an impression that extruded back naturally into normal space and accounted for the periodic gravity surges that tipped debris in toward the stars. If the

Cats knew why it happened, they'd kept the knowledge to themselves.

"Launch recon probes," he ordered. They hadn't been able to risk coming in close to Hammerfall, certainly nowhere near as close as they'd come to Terra Nova. "Can you confirm the destruction of their command and control center?"

"Destruction confirmed," Sooraya reported, after a moment. "The entire station seems to have been vaporised."

And if there had been a major population on Hammerfall, we wouldn't have dared use such a tactic, Sampson thought, coldly. The *Trojan Horse* had carried enough compressed antimatter to render a planet completely uninhabitable, if it had detonated on the surface. When the containment fields failed, the blast would have been powerful enough to bathe the planet in radiation – as well as disabling or destroying many of the Hegemony's automated defences. But much of their fleet had clearly survived...

"I'm reading at least five superdreadnoughts and fifty-seven cruisers of varying types," Sooraya reported as the probes started to send their reports back to the fleet. Recon probes were designed to be expendable; after all, the enemy wouldn't have much difficulty detecting them and vectoring light cruisers or destroyers in to pick them off. "They do not appear to be significantly damaged, but there their formation appears to be very confused. We may have killed the second-in-command as well as the supreme commander."

"Perhaps," Tobias agreed. It would be nice to believe that that was true, but he doubted it. Standard doctrine – and there had been no sign that the Funks disagreed – called for placing the second-in-command on a different fortress, preferably one well clear of the command and control center. But the Funks had just lost their acknowledged commander. It was quite possible that the various squadron commanders were arguing over who should take supreme command, yet even Funks had to be aware that there was an enemy fleet bearing down on them. Surely that took priority. "Or maybe they're trying to lure us in closer."

He shrugged. This time, the Funks had a powerful network of fortresses to support their fleet. It was quite possible that whoever was in command – if someone had managed to establish their superiority – was intent on holding the ships back where they could be covered by the fortresses. They would have to concede the rest of the system, allowing Tobias to raid their asteroid and gas giant mining facilities at will, but as long as the fleet remained in his rear, Hammerfall was dangerous. The fortresses were a headache, yet he could leave them to wither on the vine; the starships were a deadly threat to the entire Federation. They had to be destroyed.

And he had another trick up his sleeve.

"Order Task Force 1.4 to enter the system," he said. "I want them to be ready to deploy on my command."

* * *

Lady Dalsha had watched in disbelief as Great Lady Marsha and her entire command fortresses vanished in a sheet of white light. She'd scented trouble as soon as the human gunboats had broken off the attack, for she'd seen the sensor feeds from their attack on Garston. They'd killed an entire battlecruiser for minimal losses; why had they been unable to kill a freighter, even one that claimed to have been part of a convoy that had been intercepted and destroyed. And even though it had had the correct codes to approach, it shouldn't have been allowed to approach the command fortress until it had been checked by a security team. If Marsha had listened…

But Marsha *hadn't* listened and Marsha was dead. The humans might not have realised it, but the blast had completely scrambled the datanets that held the fleet together. If they'd been able to press the offensive at once, they might have cut the fleet to ribbons as each ship suddenly found itself fighting alone. Even as the command and control network was re-established, Lady Marsha's former subordinates were arguing over who should take command. None of them had been marked as a clear successor, if only to prevent them from attempting to assassinate their superior. A tactic for dividing one's subordinates – and therefore preventing them from uniting against their superior – had made perfect sense on the homeworld, or even in peacetime since the Hegemony had been founded. But in wartime, it was likely to be devastating.

The appearance of the human fleet was no surprise, not after they'd killed Marsha and destroyed the defenders' unity. They had to know that their fleet was badly outgunned, even though it had weapons that were individually superior to Hammerfall's defenders. Their best chance at a victory would come by pressing the offensive before the defenders managed to rally behind a new supreme commander, yet they seemed oddly hesitant. It was an article of faith among the Hegemony that no other race was as brave and determined as themselves – certainly, no other race had managed to build something like the Hegemony – but Lady Dalsha had to admit that the humans were just as determined as any of the Hegemony's warriors. Even starting the war on their own terms, despite the imbalance of power between them and their enemies, suggested a ruthless determination to succeed. So why, she asked herself, weren't they advancing on Hammerfall?

She watched the arguments between the different commanders, wishing that she could take command herself. But none of them would have followed her; they'd probably have executed her if they'd been face to face. Arguments over command back before the Cats had discovered their homeworld tended to result in blood on the sand; here, it was just possible that the different fortresses and starships would start *shooting* at each other. Only the certainty that the Empress would punish them harshly for starting a civil war kept the commanders under some kind of control.

Angrily, she pushed caution to the winds. If there was one advantage to her outcast status, it was that she could speak the truth without fear of repercussions for her clan. "This is no time to bicker over who's in command," she said, sharply. "The humans have come to destroy the fleet. We can scrabble over who is rewarded for the victory *after* we win."

The human fleet was growing stronger as new ships arrived from quantum space. Many of the long-range sensors had been crippled by the antimatter blast, but enough had remained to allow her to deduce that the newcomers appeared to be nothing more dangerous than freighters – although if they were all crammed with antimatter, the concept of freighters being harmless would need to be revised. The humans were led by males, she recalled; no wonder they were willing to resort to suicide tactics, as long as they destroyed their enemies in the process. Males had no sense of self-preservation.

But it would be better to think of their males as females, she told herself. The Hegemony had been blinded by the discovery that human females had been treated as second-class citizens for much of human history. If the females were so weak as to allow the males to treat them like that, surely the males must be weaker than the Hegemony Queens. But if the balance of power between the sexes was reversed for humanity...

They'd underestimated their foe all along. In the Hegemony, males were competitive, to the point where winning the overall campaign didn't matter as long as they won the battle. The Hegemony had found it hard to focus male energies on long-term projects. Males just charged at their targets, without bothering to wonder if a flanking offensive might have worked better than hitting the enemy at their strongest point. But if the humans had succeeded in directing male energies into research and development, it might have explained their sudden development of new and dangerous weapons.

Blasphemy! It was hard to grasp the concept without feeling the revulsion that would be felt by any right-thinking being, but her automatic faith in the Hegemony's superiority had been destroyed by the defeat at Terra Nova. What if... the humans *were* naturally superior to the Hegemony? Mere possession of advanced technology didn't grant superiority – the Cats had been weak, decaying from within long before they'd encountered the First Empress – but the traits that *did* grant superiority existed within humanity. Determination, ruthlessness and a clear thrust towards domination...

She could never share the insight with anyone else. They wouldn't believe her, even if the Battle of Hammerfall turned into a disaster. Or they *would* believe her and society would crumble. What was the Hegemony if it wasn't superior, destined to replace the Cats as the master race of the galaxy?

The humans might not have known it, she thought, but they'd started a process that could easily tear the Hegemony apart.

* * *

Task Force 1.4 slipped out of quantum space and advanced on Hammerfall. On the bridge of *Lightning Lass*, Captain Ivan Ankundinov watched as his squadron started to spread out, while their escorts headed towards Admiral Sampson's fleet. None of the modified freighters were designed to enter the line of battle, even though they were armed to the teeth. As long as the Funks stayed in orbit around their planet, Ivan had little compunction about drawing closer to their targets than their orders specified. The closer they were when they sprang their surprise, the better.

"Admiral Sampson has authorized us to proceed," his communications officer reported. "The gunboats are advancing to cover us."

Ivan grunted. The Hegemony starships might have been cowering near the fortresses, but their assault shuttles had other ideas. ONI hadn't been able to provide even a rough estimate of how many assault shuttles had been stockpiled on Hammerfall, or how quickly the Funks could press them into service; looking at the displays, Ivan counted over two hundred closing in on his ships. Freighters were simply too lumbering to be warships, even if their hulls were crammed with weapons and defences. The assault shuttles would tear them apart if they ever got into range.

The gunboats lanced into the advancing force and started to rip it apart. It was clear that Funk males rather than females were flying the ships, for they allowed themselves to be lured into dogfights rather than charging towards the freighters and forcing the gunboats to pick them all off one by one. Fighter jocks had been hotshots even while they'd been flying the first aircraft humanity had produced; gunboats might not have precisely been starfighters from *Star Wars*, but they were close enough to allow their pilots to show off. Only a handful of shuttles managed to make attack runs on the freighters and they were picked off by point defence. The sensor readings suggested that the assault shuttles were not as manoeuvrable as the gunboats, as if they'd been weighed down by their new weapons mix. Ivan's worst nightmare – that the shuttles had been crammed with antimatter – failed to materialise. He wondered, absently, how long it would take the Funks to think of it. It was certainly well within their capabilities to produce vast amounts of antimatter on demand.

"We are entering optimal firing range," the weapons officer reported. He was Chinese, barely old enough to remember the days when Russia and China had hated and feared one another, even though they had both been forced to work together against America and her allies. If someone had told Ivan, before First Contact, that he'd have a Chinese officer on his bridge, he would have laughed at them. "I request permission to proceed."

"Granted," Ivan said, as the helmsman brought the ship to a halt, relative to the planet. They were outside weapons range from Hammerfall, thankfully, but it wouldn't be long before the Funks realised what they were doing. And then they'd send in more gunboats or even capital ships. "Begin rolling pods."

Bulk freighters had been designed by the Cats as little more than massive holds with drives, the bridge and crew quarters added as something of an afterthought. Unlike some of the freighters Mentor had brought with him to Earth, they were incapable of landing on a planetary surface, requiring an orbital station and a small fleet of shuttles to unload their cargo. *Lightning Lass* had had her cargo space crammed with missile pods, a concept that the Galactics had abandoned as unworkable. Point defence could take out torpedoes unless they were fired in vast quantities or at very close range; what did they have to fear from missiles that were launched so far out that there was plenty of time to track and destroy the missiles before they entered attack range?

Each of the missile pods carried ten missiles, each one several times the size of a standard Galactic torpedo. Ivan had watched as the concept was tested several light years from Earth and he'd noted that the missiles were actually easier to detect than torpedoes. The Funks, once they'd realised what was happening, would have good reason to be overconfident, at least until the second surprise was unveiled. Their ships didn't have to fear missiles so large that tracking them was easy. The only danger they'd see lay in the sheer volume of missiles that were about to be launched at them.

It had been an open question if the Funks would realise what was happening before the missile pods were fully deployed. They showed no response, not even directing an additional flight of shuttles to attempt to take out the pods. But then they had good reason to feel unthreatened. Galactic torpedo drives provided an immense burst of speed, yet they didn't last long before burning out, limiting their range. Targets flying a ballistic trajectory would be even easier to track than oversized missiles.

"All pods deployed," the weapons officer reported.

"*Bart Simpson* reports that a couple of pods got snarled in the chutes," the communications officer reported. "They've isolated the pods from the command network; the remainder are ready to fire at your command."

They'd rehearsed the whole operation time and time again, but there had always been problems in deploying so many pods so quickly. The engineers claimed that the problems would eventually be ironed out, yet it would come too late to help his crewmen. They'd just have to hope that the absence of two missile pods out of hundreds wouldn't be decisive.

"Fire," he ordered.

* * *

It had taken several minutes for the battered sensor network to confirm that the humans were deploying missile pods. Lady Dalsha had watched without being quite certain of what the humans were doing, although she was sure that there was a nasty surprise waiting for the defenders. The human tactics made no sense when considered conventionally, which suggested that there was an unconventional tactic about to be deployed.

The missile launch had been detected at once, the sensors reporting over ten *thousand* missiles being deployed from the pods. Each of the missiles was an obvious sensor target, to the point where she wondered if the humans had deliberately made them rather more detectable than they should have been. Unless they'd made a colossal improvement in drive technology, and they'd seen nothing to suggest it, the missiles would burn out long before they reached their targets. The whole tactic made no sense.

At least a new commanding officer had finally been able to assert her authority. Her orders echoed through the remains of the command network, organising the fortresses and starships to prepare to destroy the enemy missiles once they went ballistic and raced through their formation. It was possible that the humans were trying to bombard the planet – it wasn't as if there was a population that could be exterminated – but it would have been a pointless exercise in mass destruction. Even the Empress wouldn't engage in mass destruction for the sheer hell of it.

As predicted, the human missiles started to flare out, their drives dying into nothingness. There were no longer any active missile drives to track, but they couldn't change course – and their trajectories would be easily predicable. They'd be wiped out long before they reached attack range, even if they were crammed full of antimatter...

And then new icons flickered into life on the display.

No!

Chapter Twenty-Six

Tobias watched the missiles deploy with heavy satisfaction. He'd had his doubts about the whole concept – rumour had it that the design team had borrowed it from a science-fiction book written in the days before humanity had discovered real aliens – and it had been impossible to test it under anything like realistic conditions, but they appeared to be performing perfectly. Each of the oversized missiles had been carrying no less than five standard missiles, ready to be fired directly at the enemy. The Funks would see *fifty thousand* missiles bearing down on their positions, almost all of them targeted on the starships. A handful had been detailed to attack the industrial nodes and shipyards in orbit around Hammerfall, although Tobias knew that destroying them was very much a secondary objective. The starships were the main target.

But antimatter missiles weren't the only things that had been fired towards the enemy. Some of them had had their warheads removed and replaced with ECM nodes that disrupted the enemy's best efforts to lock onto the missiles. They'd *know* that most of the missiles coming towards them were nothing more than sensor ghosts, but it would be incredibly difficult for them to isolate the real missiles from the illusions. Their defences would have to try and engage *all* of their sensor returns, both illusions and real missiles. Even the most advanced datanet in the galaxy would be swamped.

The Funks opened fire desperately as the missiles closed into attack range and went to full power, zeroing in on their targets. It looked as if someone had ordered the assault shuttles to try to intercept the missiles, but they didn't have the time to get into position before the missiles blew past them. Their only real hope was to pick off enough of the ECM missiles so the illusionary missiles would just vanish, yet even locating them would be difficult. The designers had spent years building in enough countermeasures to make it almost impossible to isolate the real missiles. A tachyon net might be able to separate out the real missiles from the illusions, but the tachyon net had been shattered by the antimatter blast. They'd never be able to get another one online in time to save themselves.

Hundreds of missiles vanished as the Funks picked them off, but thousands survived to strike home. There hadn't been enough space onboard the missiles to stock them with significant amounts of compressed antimatter, yet the warheads carried enough to unsettle even a superdreadnought – and the superdreadnoughts were the prime targets. Even when the Funks hit the command and control missiles, the remainder – suddenly finding themselves on their own – homed in on the closest available enemy target. The designers had warned that it was possible that some of the missiles would fling themselves on other missiles, but it hardly mattered. Task Force 1.4 had fired enough missiles to swamp the defenders, even if a number were destroyed by their fellows.

No starship in the universe could survive hundreds of missiles striking home in quick succession. Four superdreadnoughts lost their shields, wallowed out of formation and were destroyed in quick succession. The fifth was only saved by a battlecruiser that physically imposed itself between the superdreadnought and certain destruction, vanishing in a blast of superhot plasma. Dozens of other ships died as missile after missile slammed home, tearing the formation apart. The sole superdreadnought survivor was accompanied by nothing heavier than a light cruiser. All of the battlecruisers and heavy cruisers had been wiped from existence.

Other missiles, deprived of their original targets, slammed against the fortresses. They were tougher targets, but even they weren't designed to take such a hammering. One fortress was destroyed outright, another nudged towards the planetary gravity well...and several more were badly damaged, if still trying to fight. They'd been so intent on saving the fleet that the missiles aimed at the shipyards managed to home in and destroy their targets. One way or another, it would be years before the Funks managed to rebuild the installations the missiles had destroyed. Hammerfall had only had one purpose – a purpose it could no longer carry out.

"Shame we can't do that again," he commented. One secret that had been very closely held was just how many multi-missile missiles the human race had produced. He'd fired around 90% of the human race's entire stockpile at Hammerfall and it would be months before the freighters could be reloaded. But the Hegemony wouldn't know that. They'd be forced to deploy hundreds of remote platforms to defend their starships and orbital fortresses, cursing the day they'd accepted the Cats military doctrine without question. It was true that hiding in a planet's gravity well, supported by one's fortresses, would force the enemy to come into range – until the human race had changed the rules. "Task Force 1.4 is to return to quantum space and inform Task Force 1.5 to deploy into the system when ready."

He smiled as he settled back in his command chair. If the Funks had been shocked by the Battle of Terra Nova, they'd be terrified when they heard about the Battle of Hammerfall. It had been probably the most one-sided victory in galactic history, superseding the Battle of Terra Nova. Who knew? Maybe they would back down and offer humanity acceptable peace terms if they believed that they were totally outmatched. And if humanity no longer looked weak, the other Galactics might come out in support. A Tarn offensive would destabilise the Hegemony still further.

It was tempting to consider entering engagement range and taking out the remaining starships, but that would bring them into range of the fortresses. Besides, there was little need to risk his ships. Task Force 1.5 had its own surprise for the Funks. They were about to get another lesson in what human ingenuity could do when mixed with Galactic technology.

"Broadcast a demand for surrender," he ordered. It would be a bluff, but the Hegemony might not know that. "And then order Task Force 1.5 to move to attack position."

* * *

The fleet had been crippled.

No, Lady Dalsha told herself firmly; it had been destroyed. The sole surviving superdreadnought was badly damaged, to the point where it would be cheaper to replace it than to make the necessary repairs. Most of the other starships had been badly damaged, with destroyers and frigates being the only undamaged ships. The human missile cloud – she could think of no other term – had devastated a fleet that had considered itself safe. It was only through the surprisingly *limited* destruction that she realised that most of the missiles had been illusionary. If there really *had* been fifty thousand missiles, the defenders would have been completely obliterated.

The command network, already badly damaged, had been destroyed. Most of the officers who had claimed supreme command were dead. Some of the datanets were being re-established – the Cats had designed them to be resilient – but there was so much confusion that it was difficult to say how many senior officers remained alive and in control. The entire defence force had been badly shocked. They'd never run into anyone who could give the Hegemony such a bloody nose, ever. Even the Cats, if they'd worked up the nerve to intervene, would have found it costly.

"Send a general signal to the entire fleet," she ordered. "I am assuming command."

It was a sign of how badly shocked they were that no one tried to argue, or to point out that a failure and an outcast had no place in command of an entire defence force. Outcasts couldn't be trusted, even if they *did* sometimes serve a valuable role in society. Females thought to the long term, but an outcast had *no* long term. Maybe someone would brush her scales with poison or slice her throat with the traditional knife, yet she found it hard to care. The important issue now was saving what she could.

The sensor network had been badly crippled, but it still managed to detect a new force of human freighters manoeuvring themselves into position around the planet's gravity well. They would have seemed laughable if another squadron of human freighters hadn't just crushed an entire fleet. Now...what did *they* intend to unleash upon Hammerfall? Some of her subordinates were suggesting retreat, that the remaining starships should attempt to escape, leaving the rest of the planet's defences to their fate. The energy storms that pervaded this part of quantum space might have seemed a safer alternative to facing the next human surprise.

Ignoring them, she ran through some calculations in her head. The humans had launched ten thousand of their missile-carrier missiles at Hammerfall. That much was fairly certain. Assuming that their pods were no bigger than the ones the Cats had experimented with, they could only stuff no more than fifteen missiles into each pod, probably fewer. And that meant...she wasn't sure, but quantifying the threat seemed to calm her mind. The human tactic had been devastating, yet it hadn't been devastating *enough*. If they had had more freighters stuffed with missile pods, they would have deployed them. And *that* suggested that they didn't have any more missile pods in their fleet.

Unless they thought that the first attack would be enough to destroy us, she thought. *They might have held some pods in reserve.*

She would never have been so unsure of herself before Terra Nova, but now she found herself questioning everything. The Hegemony had studied Galactic doctrine, yet it had never seriously *questioned* the tactical knowledge it had learned from the Cats. But it had all seemed to work perfectly, the best tactics to use in every possible scenario worked out centuries before her people had known that the lights in the night sky were other suns. And yet when the rules changed, so did the rule book. They'd never considered the possibility of someone developing new technology before it had been far too late.

Because we would lose if someone did develop new surprises, she admitted, to herself. *We told ourselves that it was unthinkable. We wanted to believe it.*

"The human freighters are holding position," the sensor officer reported. "It is difficult to generate a sensor focus on their ships. They may be deploying missile pods."

Unsurprising, she thought. It needed an intact sensor network to generate a sensor focus and the defence force's sensors had been shot to pieces. But missile pods would have shown up, wouldn't they? Unless the humans had some new surprise.

"Watch and wait," she ordered. There was too much to do, starting with sorting out the command network and reforming battlegroups. "And pass a signal to the destroyers. If the humans start flushing missile pods at us, they are to advance and engage the missile-carriers before they can deploy their parasite missiles."

It was a sound tactic, she told herself firmly. She just hoped that it would be enough to deal with whatever else the humans had waiting for her.

* * *

"We're ready," the military officer said. Captain Verity Lambert snorted inwardly at his spit and polish attitude. She might have been part of the Federation Naval Reserve – a formality that had allowed her to apply for a loan to purchase a starship – but she'd never considered herself part of the military. Even though she detested the Funks with as much feeling as the rest of the human race, she didn't want to be anywhere near armed starships. *Trade Hard* was unarmed, save for a pair of popguns that might – *might* – discourage pirates. "You may start deploying the dupes."

"Of course," Verity agreed, sweetly. She was in command of her ship and God help anyone who tried to take her ship from her. It gave her a life less ordinary, even if her ship was several hundred years old and originally designed for a race of aliens that were smaller than the average teenager. "Mr. Thompson, begin deploying the dupes."

The Cats had been in space for so long that they'd forgotten some of the technology they'd originally developed to challenge the high frontier, while the Funks had never had to go through the long process of developing steam, oil, nuclear and eventually antimatter power, let alone build rockets and focused drive fields. They'd been given their Galactic technology, just like the human race, but they'd been far less well equipped to start understanding the technology, let alone considering whole new applications that even the Cats hadn't considered. Or so the briefers had confidently claimed. Verity would have been happier if the briefers had accompanied the ramshackle squadron on its mission, preferably fixed to the hull with duct tape. They might just provide enough armor to save the ship for another few nanoseconds.

Human researchers had been working on railguns long before Mentor had arrived at Earth and instantly made much of their research outdated, but they hadn't given up. Human technology might not be able to produce starships, yet it *could* produce items that were so heavily stealthed that the Galactics would have had trouble detecting them, and railguns that could impart enough velocity to direct them towards Hammerfall. With enough care, the mines would enter stable orbits around the planet until they hit something. And each of them carried enough antimatter to seriously disconcert a starship. It had certainly discomfited her when she'd heard what her ship was going to be carrying. Mines were cheap, easy to produce, and extremely difficult to detect except at very close range.

"Launch sequence underway, Captain," Thompson reported. They might have been long-term lovers – people on small ships either got close or started hating each other – but on the bridge he was already professional. "We should have them all out within twenty minutes."

"Twenty minutes too late," Verity said. If the Funks rushed the freighters, they were likely to wipe them out before the Navy could cover their escape. "Speed the process up if you can."

* * *

"They're just waiting, doing nothing," the sensor officer reported. "I cannot understand it."

Lady Dalsha nodded, slowly. No one, not even the humans, would simply position freighters above the gravity well and wait. It was possible that they hoped to lure the remainder of the fleet away from the forts, but if that was the case she had no intention of taking the bait. Her fleet was still too badly damaged to risk a fight with other starships, even if they'd been technological equals. Some of her ships couldn't even generate shields. The humans would cut them apart with ease.

The human freighters started to slip back, heading for the quantum gate. It was proof that they hadn't built a quantum drive into their hulls, which at least suggested that the humans would have logistics problems in deploying further forward from their bases. But there was still no explanation of their actions. Why had they just waited? What had they done? Hours passed slowly and there was still no answer.

It was possible, she knew, to produce a phase cannon that fired invisible bursts of energy, but they'd still be detectable by active sensors. Maybe the humans had been trying to lure them out, or...

"I have something," the sensor officer snapped. "It just appeared..."

* * *

"Active-1 has been triggered," Sooraya reported. "They'll see her for sure now."

Tobias nodded. A handful of the mines had been directed right at the fortresses, instead of being pushed into relatively stable orbits around the planet. Active-1 had even carried a beacon that would allow the Funks to get a good look at it, just before the antimatter containment field collapsed and the mine vaporised. The Funks would now know that countless stealth mines were floating in high orbit around Hammerfall, mines that would render the entire planet virtually useless until they were swept and removed. And yet...they'd never be able to be *sure* that they'd destroyed them all. It was quite possible that any starship that tried to leave the planet's orbit would hit a mine and be crippled. Hammerfall had effectively been neutralised.

And how long would it be, he asked himself silently, before the Funks found themselves forced to sweep *every* star system, just to be sure that there were no mines waiting for unwary ships? Mining quantum space was technically illegal – it would certainly interfere with free navigation – but there was no law against mining normal space. But then, the logistics of mining open space were daunting. The only way to make it work was to mine orbital space above a planet.

"Send a signal to the fleet," he ordered. "We've done what we came here to do. It's time to leave."

A handful of ships had been dispatched to obliterate the Funk mining and industrial complexes outside Hammerfall itself. Destroying a cloudscoop would not win Galactic approval, but the Marines had rigged the scoop to blow unless the correct codes were entered, denying it to the Funks. They'd been careful to advertise what they'd done, ensuring that the Funks wouldn't be able to blame the scoop's destruction on Earth...

"All ships have reported in, Admiral," Sooraya confirmed. "They're ready to depart."

Tobias smiled. Hammerfall had been crippled, effectively put out of action for years, and all it had cost him was a handful of gunboats and thousands of missiles. They wouldn't be able to do it again in a hurry, at least not until missile stockpiles had been replenished, but the Funks wouldn't know that. The disinformation they'd receive from Earth would suggest that there were millions of missiles, just waiting to be deployed. Maybe they wouldn't believe it, but would they be able to take the chance that humanity was bluffing?

"Take us out of here," he ordered. There was no point in pressing against the enemy starships, even though they would continue to pose a threat. Without shipyards and industrial nodes, their ability to pose a long-term threat would be limited. "It's time to take our leave."

Chapter Twenty-Seven

"Why me?"

Barbie smiled, a smile that didn't quite touch her eyes. "The Admiral feels that your reports have been most impressive," she said. Adrienne suspected that that wasn't quite truthful. Ever since wars had started being fought with PR as well as guns, the military had had to develop its own PR departments – and a blacklist of journalists who simply couldn't be trusted to respect military security. "And besides, GNN has acquired quite a following on Earth – and among the Galactics."

Adrienne had to smile. The Galactics had their own news networks, most of which operated on similar lines to GNN. Some of them had simply copied reports sent home by human reporters and rebroadcast them across the Association, while others hadn't hesitated to exaggerate the news from the war front. Adrienne hadn't heard that a thousand Hegemony superdreadnoughts had been destroyed until she'd seen it in a Galactic news report. The Hegemony didn't even *have* a thousand superdreadnoughts. A lie made up out of whole cloth, or a simple translation error? Even the Cats hadn't been able to establish perfect communications between alien races.

"Thank you," she said. "I understand that recordings are not permitted?"

"I'm afraid not," Barbie confirmed. "There are security issues involved, you see. You never know what might prove useful to enemy intelligence officers."

"Oh," Adrienne said, dryly. "Those bastards are always one step ahead."

Barbie did have a point, even though she would have preferred to believe otherwise. She'd travelled on a dozen starships, including three military warships from Earth, yet she didn't really understand how they worked. The tours she'd been given on *Wellington* had been sanitized, enough to let her gain a sense of her surroundings, but no direct access to anything remotely sensitive. Some of the other reporters had been too ignorant to realise it, others had demanded access, as if the military was keeping them from the classified equipment out of spite. They didn't realise that humanity's only edge was its tech superiority and if that happened to be defeated, the Hegemony would simply roll over human space.

The interior of *Nimitz* didn't look much different to *Wellington*, but there was a sense that the cruiser was far less *solid* than the assault carrier. She didn't have anything like the same number of crewmen or Marines as *Wellington*; indeed, the Federation Navy had built a high degree of automaton into their ships, pushing the Association's limits on developing AI right to the line. From what she'd picked up from a few of her sources on Terra Nova, the small crews were sometimes a handicap for the cruisers. They couldn't put together boarding parties without running their manpower dangerously thin. War was teaching lessons that no amount of exercises could teach. No one could simply declare victory and expect it to be taken seriously.

Barbie paused outside a hatch and pressed her hand against a scanner. There was a brief pause, followed by the hatch slowly opening to reveal a cabin not much bigger than the one Adrienne had been assigned onboard *Wellington*. The holographic display covering the rear bulkhead was deactivated, leaving the compartment appearing small enough to be claustrophobic. Admiral Sampson was seated behind a small desk, reading through a set of documents on his datapad. He rose to his feet and held out a hand, which Adrienne took and shook firmly. For someone who had become Earth's darling, with near-global approval, he looked reassuringly unconcerned about publicity. Adrienne had heard – from Ward – that some political parties back on Earth were already considering drafting Sampson to run for President. Did he even *have* ambitions to sit in the White House? Running a country was not the same as running a military.

"Admiral," she said, as she took the other seat. Some of the other reporters had complained about their tiny cabins, but Adrienne knew better. Space was at a premium on starships and even admirals didn't get very much more than anyone else. On *Wellington*, ten junior officers – or crewmen – shared the same bunking space. "Thank you for agreeing to meet with me."

"You're welcome," Sampson said, gruffly. He didn't seem intimidated by her reputation, or inclined to be more talkative than necessary. "Recent events have provoked much speculation on Earth, among the armchair generals."

Adrienne nodded. Hammerfall might have been a crushing victory, certainly compared to any of the brushfire wars between the Galactics, but in the end the human fleet had retreated from the system, leaving it in the Hegemony's claws. No matter how much tonnage had been destroyed, or how badly crippled the Hegemony's installations on the planet, there had been some alarm on Earth. The public had expected the conquest of another Funk world and found it difficult to understand why the Federation Navy had retreated. There were already political leaders who were turning it into a major issue, asking questions their governments found difficult to answer.

"Which leads to the first question," she said. "Why did we retreat from Hammerfall?"

Sampson smiled, rather dryly. "The battle was won," he said. "We didn't need to occupy the planet to render it useless to the Hegemony. I chose not to push the offensive against fortresses that could no longer help our foes."

"But the system remains in their hands," Adrienne protested. "Their propaganda has been claiming that they beat us, that they forced us away from Hammerfall."

"All the propaganda in the universe cannot disguise the fact that we smashed their fleet," Sampson said, firmly. "Fortresses cannot leave planetary orbit, let alone start raiding our space. Hammerfall is largely useless to the Hegemony now – it would take them years to repair or replace all the installations we destroyed, even if we gave them the time. And by crushing their fleet, we have made it impossible for them to launch a counteroffensive against Garston, or even Terra Nova. It gives us time to prepare for the next offensive."

Adrienne nodded. "And where is the next target?"

"I'm afraid that would be telling," Sampson said. His face suddenly twisted into a grin. "But you'll be among the first to hear of it."

"Thank you," Adrienne said. Armchair generals had been speculating on the course of the war ever since they'd first realised that the Federation Navy had attacked Terra Nova. Some of them believed that humanity's tech advantage was enough to allow the Federation Navy to carve its way to the Funk homeworld, others – more pessimistic – suspected that the Funks were already adapting their tactics to counter humanity's tricks. "Do you feel that you can continue to press the offensive until the war comes to an end?"

"I feel certain that we can carry on the war as long as necessary," Sampson said, blandly. "It is my deepest wish that the Hegemony will understand that we have no intention of destroying them, that our goal is merely to convince them to treat us as equals. We do not wish to occupy all of their territory."

"Which leads neatly to the next question," Adrienne said. "What are the long-term plans for Garston?"

Sampson shrugged. "Such matters are political issues," he said. "You would be better off directing that question to the Federation Council."

"But the Council is itself divided," Adrienne said. "Where do *you* stand on the issue?"

There was a long pause. Even though humanity had lowered the taxes and tithes collected by the Hegemony on Garston – and the fees for using the quantum gate – Garston still represented a net gain to the Federation's economy. The Galactics still used the world as a transhipping point along a dozen shipping lines, which meant that humanity's limited stockpile of Galactic credits was slowly rising, allowing the Federation to purchase weapons, starships and production nodes on the Galactic market. Hammerfall was much less economically important, but that simple fact seemed to have been missed by the armchair generals, who seemed to believe that the more planets humanity held, the more currency they could obtain and use to purchase weapons.

And yet, Garston's surface was a seething mass of Funks and other aliens, with humanity's forces caught in the middle. The first national contingents had arrived – Chinese and Russian soldiers, mainly – but there weren't enough of them to pacify more than a handful of alien cities. They'd been forced to start separating the Funks from the rest of the population, which had started the Funks screaming about how they were being punished for the sins of their former superiors. Outright civil war threatened to break out at any moment, with a constant stream of assassinations, bombings and sniper attacks pouring fuel on the fire. Humanity, as the occupying power, was supposed to protect the settlers, but how? Anything they did that supported one side hurt the other.

"If giving up Garston would get us a peace we could live with, a recognition that the Hegemony wasn't going to crush us when it felt that it could, I would recommend surrendering the planet," he said, carefully. "Unfortunately, the Hegemony deliberately created an environment where they could play different factions off against one another to maintain their control of the planet, a balancing act that collapsed when we took Garston from the Hegemony. All of those issues are bursting out now, forcing us to try to keep the peace when no one actually *wants* peace."

"But some of those alien factions have offered to work with us," Adrienne pointed out. "Wouldn't it be a betrayal to hand them back to the Funks?"

"I wouldn't dispute that for a second," Sampson agreed. "In the long term, I could see definite advantages to keeping Garston, if only because of its location. But the Federation was never devised as a government, certainly not one that could occupy an alien planet permanently. Ideally, we'd want the planet to govern itself while we provided security, but I doubt that any faction on Garston would be willing to trust its neighbours enough to relax its defences.

"One distant possibility is to separate *all* of the factions, but that would require massive upheaval and certainly provoke an insurgency directed at us. It may happen with or without our encouragement anyway, given just how deeply the hatreds have sunk into the planet's population.

245

An alternative is to ask some of the Galactics to contribute peacekeeping troops, but that would certainly come with a political price."

"A share in the profits from the system," Adrienne said. Sampson nodded. "Do *you* feel that the planet is worth the hassle?"

Sampson paused to consider his answer. "The Hegemony didn't have time to destroy most of the industrial stations in orbit around the planet, or butcher the workforce," he said. "We can use their facilities to produce weapons for the campaign, even if they are primitive compared to our own, and we need a much larger orbital-trained workforce than we have. But using non-humans raises security issues, even if we are not building anything advanced on Garston."

He shrugged, expressively. "There are plusses and minuses to everything we do," he added. "Nothing is ever perfect, or certain – even death and taxes."

Adrienne smiled at the weak joke. Some of the Galactics were governed – if governed was the right word – by political systems that made human anarchists look like fascists. There were no taxes, or any form of government control. Some humans held them up as the perfect governing system, although humans were probably less suited to such governments than the aliens. And the Cats were biologically immortal. They might have been very cagey about their biology, which was odd given that they'd once collected and distributed information on every other alien race in the galaxy, but their immortality was a proven fact. Some of the Galactics, who'd been in space for thousands of years, had been dealing with the same Cat for all that time.

The other Galactics used nanites to extend their lifespans, as did humanity, but none of them had ever managed to create their own version of immortality. Adrienne had heard rumours that wealthy humans were funding massive research projects into life-extension – if the Cats could do it, humanity could surely do it too – and yet they'd produced nothing. Or perhaps they *had* developed something and kept it to themselves. It was easy to be cynical where the super-rich were concerned. Some of them probably had ties to the Galactics.

"There are only a handful of other questions," she said. "The first one is simple; how do you feel that the Federation Navy has performed in its first real combat test?"

Sampson smiled. "I feel that the Navy has performed magnificently," he said. "Ever since we obtained our first warships, fifth-hand from a used starship trader, we have concentrated on training and drilling to the point where our crews can carry out their duties in their sleep. Each new weapon has been tested, integrated into our fleet and then put through its paces until we know exactly how it works and what it can do. The Hegemony didn't have a clue what was going to hit them until it was too late."

Adrienne nodded. "And crew morale?"

"Very high," Sampson said. "We knew that we were going to be badly outnumbered by our enemies, but the success of the new weapons and the recovery of Terra Nova sent morale skyrocketing through the fleet. I have every confidence in the men and women under my command and their ability to meet every challenge the Funks throw at them."

"So I hear," Adrienne said. "And when do you feel that the Funks will mount a counteroffensive?"

"I hesitate to speculate," Sampson said. "After Hammerfall, they will certainly be careful about coming into weapons range of our starships and fortifications. But they *must* launch a counterattack sooner or later, or they have to surrender when we finally hack our way to their homeworld. We expect that they will attempt to attack us as soon as they feel confident they can produce a victory."

"Yes," Adrienne said. "Can we touch on a delicate subject?"

Sampson lifted an eyebrow. "On or off the record?"

"It depends," Adrienne admitted. "I've heard a rumour" – it had leaked from the French Government and Ward had forwarded it to her, although Sampson didn't need to know that – "that you made the decision to release the enemy commander and return her to the Hegemony. That seems like an...odd decision when you've been so determined to keep the secrets of humanity's weaponry..."

"Unfortunately, secrets have a habit of getting out," Sampson said. Flying the gunboats to Garston or Heavenly Gate would have allowed the Galactics to get a good look at the new ships. "I needed the Hegemony to understand just how badly they were outmatched by our weaponry. They would certainly have picked up rumours from Terra Nova even if we did manage to prevent them from escaping, and kept all of the captured POWs in detention camps. And besides, we used some of the new weapons when we took Garston. The secret is out."

"But she was the enemy *commander*," Adrienne protested. "Surely she knew too much. I couldn't find any incident in recent history where such an officer has simply been returned to their people, at least not without making a trade of equal value."

"It *has* happened in human history," Sampson said. "One particularly interesting example was the decision by Julius Caesar to return Ptolemy of Egypt to his loyalists during his campaign in Egypt. The irony was that a eunuch without any military experience was doing an excellent job of prosecuting the siege when the boy was returned to his own lines. Some historians have claimed that Caesar was a fool, but it seems evident that returning Ptolemy divided the enemy command and made it easier for the Romans to win."

"But that was... *old* history," Adrienne pointed out. Hardly anyone talked about *Ancient* history these days, not when the Association had been around for longer than all human civilization. "Surely it doesn't apply now?"

"It has also been practiced among the Hegemony as a gesture of contempt," Sampson said, seriously. "They don't really have a tradition of total war as we understand the term. And besides, they're not very kind to failures. It's quite possible that they executed the unfortunate officer as soon as she returned home."

"Or that she might have deserted in the direction of the Galactics," Adrienne said. "I don't think I would return home if I knew I was likely to be killed."

"Moral courage isn't just a human trait," Sampson admitted. "We consider the Funks to be barbarians because they didn't develop their technology, merely obtained it from the Cats, and because they treat their client races like shit, but that doesn't mean that they can't be as brave, loyal and determined as ourselves. They're individuals, just like us. I dare say that some Funks might even be good people."

"Not an attitude that will win you many friends on Earth," Adrienne said. "Or Terra Nova, for that matter. What do you think of the trials?"

"I think the settlers want revenge," Sampson said. "Trying the collaborators for lesser crimes than treason may not be the ideal way to handle the situation, but no one could suggest a better way. The alternative was a long and complex legal struggle."

Adrienne stood up. "Thank you for the interview, Admiral," she said. "Can I ask a question, completely off the record?"

Sampson nodded, slowly. "The Federation's limitations have been exposed by the campaign," she said. "Do you feel that it needs to move towards becoming a proper world government?"

"That's another political issue," Sampson said. "Practically speaking, none of the Federation's member states will want to give up more independence to the Federation – and the nations that aren't members certainly won't want to join unless they get a say in how the Federation operates. I don't think that a world government is practical, at least not for a very long time."

He smiled. "But that's just my opinion," he added. "If we survive this war, who knows what might become possible?"

Chapter Twenty-Eight

"No sign they've detected us, boss," Karla reported. "There's so much activity in this system that they probably wouldn't notice if we charged in transmitting a list of Captain Haddock's favourite curses."

"Don't get overconfident," Joshua warned. "We're just here to have a look at the system, nothing else. If they realise that we're watching the system, they might suspect what we have in mind."

The Tauscher System had been utterly undeveloped when the Funks had arrived, established their supremacy over the natives and then started to put them to work on behalf of the Hegemony. Over several hundred years, they'd built up a respectable orbital industry and a set of cloudscoops to provide fuel. Oddly, the system wasn't operated by a single clan, but several clans – and it was clear that they didn't get along, even though the natives were restless. Unlike Earth, or most of the Hegemony's worlds, there was no unified command authority in the system, even in orbit around Tauscher. Hundreds of STL asteroid miners swarmed through the belt, while FTL freighters docked at the orbital installations or the cloudscoops. The Funks had been careful about just what technology was imported onto the planet, but the Gobbles had admitted that they had much more than their masters realised. It hadn't taken Joshua long to understand why. They served in thousands of minor roles in the system, doing the work the Funks considered beneath them. It was easy to evade most of their security, as long as they were careful.

Joshua had to smile as *Blackbeard* drifted closer to the planet, all passive sensors online and pulling in data from all over the system. Officially, they were nothing more than a trading ship built on a light cruiser hull, an adaption that had proven popular with freighter commanders who had to fly through regions of space infested with pirates. Most pirates wouldn't be able to separate out the freighter variant from the light cruiser elements, and would rather let the ship go than chance attacking a warship.

"They look paranoid," Karla added. "Look at that formation."

Joshua studied the display, puzzled. Normally, there was little order to interstellar shipping, even among the races that made the Funks look like anarchists. Starships came and went almost at random. But now... hundreds of freighters waited well away from the planet, while Funk shuttles moved from freighter to freighter, inspecting them before they could slip into orbit. It made little sense to him, until he remembered the reports from Hammerfall. There was no way to be sure about their accuracy, but if the Federation really had used a freighter to ram a control fortress and take it out, the Funks had to be worried about the same thing happening elsewhere. They had so much interstellar shipping that inspecting it all would take days, delaying travel by weeks or months. It was hard to be sure, but that was bound to have an adverse effect on the Funk economy.

He smiled, coldly. But they couldn't assume that only human or Funk freighters would be used in suicide attacks. They would have to search *every* freighter that entered orbit, something that would have a knock-on effect far outside the Hegemony. Freighter crews often lived on the margin – he'd been luckier than most, and even he had had to struggle – and a number were sure to go bankrupt, creating political trouble for their homeports. It was even possible that a number of the big combines would be adversely affected, perhaps even withdraw their freighters from the Hegemony. And *that* would have an unfortunate effect on the Hegemony's economy.

The Clunker Fleet and the pirates allied to it had taken out or captured over seventy freighters and warships in the Hegemony's rear. Joshua had been careful to target only Hegemony ships – the pirates had been less restrained, which might give humanity some political cover if the shit hit the fan – and he'd confirmed that shipping insurance rates were going through the roof. The Hegemony might have a fine fleet – it *did* have a fine fleet – but how long could it operate the starships if the logistics behind them were falling apart?

For want of a nail, a shoe was lost; for want of a shoe, a horse was lost...

Joshua knew more about the economics of interstellar shipping than most and it was easy to understand just how much damage the attacks were doing. Starships needed a secure supply line just to keep operating, with freighters bringing everything from HE3 to replacement torpedoes to food. Military-grade components were tough, but action wore them down quickly to where they needed to be replaced. The Funks would have to make tough decisions fairly soon; abandon the shipping lanes and lose the revenue they brought in, or divert freighters and escort ships from the war front. One way or another, the human race would benefit.

All the more so if we keep profiting, he thought, coldly. Nothing succeeded like success; each of the freighters and cargos they captured bought in enough credits to fund the entire fleet. He'd even started buying up warships from shifty dealers, warships that could be crewed by the Gobble resistance or other rebels from the hidden colonies. The Funks could probably have destroyed them all if they'd managed to intercept them with a superdreadnought squadron, but the odds were massively against a successful interception. It was a shame one couldn't buy superdreadnoughts on the black market, although even if he had he wouldn't have been able to crew them.

But each successive purchase risked the danger that they would be betrayed...

"Some of the ships are bugging out," Karla said, breaking into his thoughts. "The Funks are screaming at them, but they're not stopping."

Joshua nodded. Independent freighter commanders weren't inclined to listen to anyone else, even military starships with weapons locked on their hulls. If the Funks were forcing them to waste time – and credits – they'd take their ships elsewhere, heading onwards to their next port of call. The Funks didn't have the numbers to chase them all down before they reached the quantum gate – and some of them even had quantum drives. Their departure from Tauscher was a neat way of giving the Funks the finger as they left.

"We may as well bug out ourselves," he said. "There's no point in letting them have a good look at our hull."

Karla nodded and tapped commands into her console, bringing the drives online. "Do you think we have enough intelligence to proceed?"

"Maybe," Joshua said. The Gobbles wanted their homeworld liberated and were prepared to pay any price, readily supporting humanity's war against the Funks. But even if they did manage to take the system intact, the Funks would certainly react harshly – and there were no less than three superdreadnought squadrons within five days of the system. They were supposed to be watching the Tarn – the Tarn had reinforced their borders, something that had forced the Funks to keep a sharp eye on them even as they waged war on humanity – but they'd certainly react to a rebellion that took the entire planet. Joshua had yet to think of a way to defeat those ships when they arrived at Tauscher, with blood in their eyes.

The quantum gate opened up around them and they slid into the safety of quantum space. "Take us back to Shadow," he ordered. By now, most of his operations were masterminded well away from the concealed colony, but it was still a good place to pick up intelligence and offload their stolen goods. "I need to think, carefully."

"Of course, Your Majesty," Karla said. "Your loyal subjects will be more than willing to help you think. Just remember that there's no such thing as a garment that can only be seen by clever men."

Joshua snorted. "And since when did that stop anyone falling for something that looked too good to be true?"

* * *

Joshua would have preferred not to have to go onto Shadow in person – there was too great a chance of someone realising that he and his crew were human – but the fences refused to meet with an electronic personality. Shadow's location was probably known to the Hegemony's intelligence agents by now, if only by tracing back the smuggling routes. Every time Joshua entered the system, he half-worried that he would encounter a Hegemony fleet intent on revenge. Whatever benefit they gained from monitoring the smugglers had to be outweighed by the losses they were taking to the Clunkers.

"Your crews have amassed much wealth," the crab said. As always, the alien was within its water tank, beady eyes peering at Joshua through the gloom. "I am happy to help you dispose of it."

That was presumably a joke, although with some of the Galactics it was hard to tell. "And I am happy to accept your help," Joshua said. The crab sat at the center of a spider's web of contacts who passed on goods or gathered intelligence for the pirates. Not all of the intelligence dealers were trustworthy, but the crab had a good reputation for verifying everything before it passed the data on to people who could use it. "How might you assist me?"

There was a rustling sound from the tank. "Intelligence has come my way about planned counter-piracy operations by the Hegemony's rulers," the crab said. Its voice, as always, was completely atonal, yet Joshua fancied that he could hear a note of amusement within the electronic voice. "You may find the information useful."

"Maybe," Joshua agreed. The Hegemony was perfectly capable of inventing false data and passing it on to the pirate intelligence network. Hell, they might even have kept their own crews in the dark until they were in quantum space and could open their sealed orders. It never creased to astonish him that so many Funks were on the take. But then, the ones assigned to this part of the Hegemony were the ones without the connections that would assure them a glittering career. "I will certainly consider the offer."

He smiled at the crab, fighting down the urge to run. Joshua was no xenophobe, no racist who feared aliens simply because they were alien, yet the crab was truly alien, utterly inhuman. Even *looking* at its body provoked the arachnid reaction, the sense that something was deeply wrong. Intelligence could only go so far in countering feelings that lay deeply buried in the human mind.

"I asked you to keep looking for other warships," he said, changing the subject. "Have you located any more since we last spoke?"

"Five," the crab said. "Unfortunately, some have been worked hard by their previous owners, or have been largely disarmed. They may not be worth the money you will have to pay for them."

"Send me the details," Joshua said. He'd made deals with a handful of hidden colonies, ones with space-based industries. They'd help repair damaged ships in exchange for vast sums of money and first call on supplies they desperately needed. "I'll consider them and then get back to you."

"I have also verified the credentials of the Gobbles you liberated," the crab added. "They are definitely listed as wanted terrorists by the Hegemony. The puppet government on Tauscher has sentenced them to death. If the Funks hadn't wanted to kill them in front of the Empress, they would be dead by now. As it is, they may not have realised that they were intercepted in transit."

"Let us hope not," Joshua said. It should have taken weeks for the convoy to reach its destination, but it was quite likely that they'd intended to pause somewhere along the way. The Funks might well have realised that something had gone wrong by now, although they couldn't do much about it. Would they assume the worst, or would they conclude that the prison barge had been blown away on the grounds that it *might* be a disguised warship? "And the weapons I asked you to find?"

"Have been located," the crab said. "You should be well on your way to outfitting a small army."

"Good," Joshua said. "Have them shipped to the RV point. We'll meet them there and take them onwards to their final destination."

* * *

In one sense, almost everything owned and operated by the Galactics was standardised, built using comparable technology developed by the Cats. Practically, there were differences in almost everything, particularly weapons. A plasma rifle designed for human hands couldn't be used by a Funk, or a Gobble, without considerable problems. They had to be refitted to suit alien hands, or whatever they had that passed for manipulating digits. Obtaining weapons suitable for Gobbles wasn't particularly easy. The Funks had never designed them and forbidden the Gobbles from designing their own. It hadn't stopped them for long.

"Suitable," Xinchub said, after testing the rifle. It had been redesigned on one of the hidden colonies, once they'd tested the Gobbles to find out what they needed. "How many of these can you produce?"

"Thousands," Joshua said, shortly. Arming a resistance movement was technically outside the letter of his orders, but it was a chance they couldn't allow to slip past. He hadn't hidden the scope of the problem from Xinchub, or the fact that the Funks would certainly respond with overwhelming firepower when the shit hit the fan. "And plenty of other weapons as well. The problem lies in getting them to the surface."

The Gobble looked up at him, his mouth twisting into a smile that showed sharp teeth. "That will not be a problem," he said, firmly. "There are plenty of shipping lines between the asteroids and the planet, ones we have used before to smuggle weapons and technology to the surface. Even with the new regulations, we can run rings around the Hegemony's inspection teams, if we have not already managed to subvert them. They will suspect nothing until it is too late."

"I hope you're right," Joshua said. He'd picked up enough intelligence to suggest that the inspections were cursory, looking for nothing more dangerous than hulls crammed with antimatter. They had little choice – the time it would take to search each ship thoroughly would cause massive additional delays – but relying on it didn't seem particularly safe. One nosy inspector and the whole secret would be blown open. "I will not commit myself to assisting you unless I am fairly confident of success."

"A wise attitude," the Gobble agreed. "But we have been their slaves for far too long. If we are to fight and die, at least we will deny them our service for the rest of time."

"There are billions of you, scattered over the Hegemony and outside," Joshua said, quietly. Such an attitude appalled him. "They might all be slaughtered by the Funks, if they realise that you have risen up in rebellion. Your people might be completely destroyed."

"We know the dangers," Xinchub said. "But we cannot go on like this. Whatever the risk, we will be free."

It still bothered Joshua hours later, when they made the agreement to have thousands of modified weapons prepared for the resistance. He'd known the risks when he'd allowed Admiral Sampson to talk him into leading the operation, including the simple fact that they were all expendable. Earth would never know what had been done for her. But risking an entire planet of harmless aliens...? He couldn't accept that they might trigger off a genocide unmatched in galactic history; alien races had died out before, but never on such a scale. How could *anyone* be comfortable with it?

He looked up at the star chart, searching for options. They could take Tauscher, if not easily. Most of the pirates wouldn't want to join an attack on a fortified world, but the Clunker fleet and the warships crewed by rebels could destroy the defenders on their own. But what would happen when the superdreadnoughts arrived to take revenge? The entire fleet he'd assembled couldn't stand up to one superdreadnought, let alone three entire squadrons of superdreadnoughts. It wasn't as if they had the weapons the Federation Navy had used at Terra Nova.

A dozen schemes for crippling or destroying the superdreadnoughts crossed his mind, only to flounder on cold hard facts. The Hegemony would be on their guard. They wouldn't allow a ship crammed with antimatter close to their superdreadnoughts, not after what had happened at Hammerfall. And no aliens served on their ships. They might be able to bribe one of the superdreadnoughts into

257

taking an antimatter mine onboard, but not all of them. And there was little hope that the Federation Navy would be able to intervene. They wouldn't even know what had happened at Tauscher until it was already over.

Unless...

Flicking through the star chart, he brought up a strategic display of the local sector. The Hegemony bordered three other powers nearby, one of the reasons why there was so much shipping – and pirate activity – running through the sector. He doubted that any of the powers would risk intervening to protect the Gobbles, but maybe...

It would be a gamble, but they had little choice.

"Karla," he ordered, "start digging through the shipping manifests. I think we took a handful of recon drones from the Funks. Can you let me know what happened to them?"

There was a long pause as Karla brought up the captured manifests. "We stockpiled them at Base Seven," she reported. "No one wanted to buy them unless we knocked down the price to a handful of credits, so we didn't sell."

"Lucky for us," Joshua said. It wasn't too surprising that none of the pirates would want them – they weren't that useful without a space navy capable of standing up to other navies – but they'd come in handy. Maybe they could take Tauscher after all. "Have them brought to the support fleet. I've got a cunning plan."

Chapter Twenty-Nine

"The Traders Alliance formally protests the Hegemony's decision to impose new security measures on independent trading ships," the Ambassador from the Alliance said. Shan listened with interest, concealing her amusement behind a carefully-controlled expression. It had surprised her when she'd discovered that Westerners considered her people inscrutable – she'd never had any difficulty reading her fellow Chinese – but the aliens probably found all humans inscrutable. Reading body language wasn't easy when a nod could mean something different to a dozen different races. "The penalties imposed have already cost a number of commanders their ships."

There was a long pause. The Traders Alliance wasn't exactly a galactic power, but they were entitled to a seat on the Commune for reasons that no human had ever been quite able to figure out. Shan privately suspected that the traders had managed to bribe one of the independent planets to allow the traders to claim their seat. If it had happened a few thousand years ago, it had probably become tradition by now. The traders hadn't been particularly interested in the war – they preferred a long tradition of neutrality – yet the Hegemony had started hurting them indirectly. It would have to provoke some kind of reaction.

"We do not expect that the Hegemony will understand the problems faced by the Alliance," the Ambassador continued. "The Alliance has therefore resolved that if the matter is not resolved to our satisfaction, the Alliance will withdraw all trading ships from Hegemony space and – furthermore – embargo any other galactic power that continues to trade with the Hegemony."

For the first time in decades, the entire Commune stared at the speaker. Shan certainly hadn't expected it to go so far. Humanity must have had more friends than she'd thought, for the Traders Alliance held an economic stranglehold over parts of the Association. The Hegemony's ability to trade with the rest of the Galactics was about to take a body-blow. They did have their own trading fleet, even if it was smaller than most, but they'd find it impossible to trade openly if the Traders Alliance stood ready to crush anyone who traded with them. They'd still be able to use the black market smuggling networks, yet they couldn't guarantee deliveries. And some of the smugglers had their own ties to the Alliance.

"This is not a step we take lightly," the Ambassador concluded, "but we feel that it is necessary to prevent the Hegemony from doing more damage to our interests."

He sat down and waited. Formal protocol demanded that the Hegemony had a chance to reply, although Shan suspected that nothing their Ambassador could say would have any effect on the disaster unfolding in front of her red eyes. If the embargo went into action, the Hegemony's economy would start to collapse. The factions on their homeworld who wanted to replace the Empress would see it as a gift from the gods. And if their great clans lost enough money to cause them to fold, they'd almost *have* to end the war on human terms.

Great Lady Vanla rose to her feet, red eyes flashing around the chamber. "So," she said. "So we are faced with an impossible situation. The humans have used freighters to attack us, to raid our systems and wreak havoc on our worlds. And yet we are to be denied the right to ensure that such a successful attack is not to be repeated? We are fighting for our lives and yet you see fit to infect our scales?"

A human would have spoken of stabbing a knife in someone's back. "We are the ones fighting to prevent the humans from overrunning the galaxy," she added. It was an astonishing change from her earlier attitude, but Hammerfall had shocked the Galactics – and the Funks. "We are the ones who have been attacked, without provocation, by a race intent on establishing itself as a new interstellar power. You say that your crews have suffered? How many of them have died in treacherous attacks? You say that your ships are being raided? It is the humans who

260

are raiding your ships! And yet you blame us for taking reasonable measures to protect ourselves!

"The Hegemony cannot give in to blackmail by those who feel that they have the right to dictate to us. Your cowardly attack on our interests when we are fighting for our lives will not go unavenged. It is the *humans* who have attacked us, it is the *humans* who are raiding our shipping, it is the *humans* who must be defeated before the very shape of our society is reformed. You think you can force us to accept a dishonourable peace? We will go onwards to win this war and then we shall see."

Shan listened as Ambassador after Ambassador rose to have their say. It was difficult to know just how much of their speeches should be taken seriously, if only because making statements of principle was easy, but it was far harder to actually back up their words. The powers nearer to the Hegemony seemed less inclined to confront it directly, while the powers with thousands of light years between them and the Funks were more than willing to condemn the Funks openly. But what if the Traders actually *did* carry out their threat? How many galactic powers would have no choice but to stop trading with the Funks?

She made a mental note to have her staff look into it, while starting to prepare her own speech. Whatever the Traders thought of the human race, they'd created a very dangerous situation for her people. It was quite possible that some of the other Galactics would try to impose a peace, one that might be unfavourable to humanity. They'd certainly want access to humanity's weapons and other technological developments. Finally, after many other ambassadors had had their say, it was her turn to speak.

"The Federation was forced into war by constant pressure from the Hegemony," she reminded them, again. It was easy to see how many Galactics had forgotten that in the wake of humanity's unexpected victories. "We do not seek conquest, we do not seek economic damage to the entire galaxy; our only goal is to prevent the Hegemony from eventually crushing us and turning Earth into yet another slave world. If that could be guaranteed, we would be happy to end the war right now. No one else on either side would have to die."

Great Lady Vanla rose to her feet before she could be officially recognised. "But you have committed atrocities on Garston," she thundered. The Funks had started broadcasting propaganda as soon as they realised that Earth wasn't going to be a pushover. Garston's multiracial stew had, unfortunately, provided more than enough grist for their mill. "You clearly have no intention of returning that world, to which you have no claim..."

"But we now know that you have been committing atrocities against other races on Garston," another ambassador said. The floating orb of flesh glared with all three eyes towards the Funk. "You have mistreated other races who have settled on the planet. I propose that the Commune dispatch a fact-finding mission to establish the truth and then place Garston under neutral control."

Shan sat back in her chair as the Galactics argued. The Hegemony would oppose the measure, of course, and be regarded as a pariah because of it. Earth would make a show of reluctance, but eventually accept, provided that the forces sent were enough to prevent the Hegemony from snatching it back. Assuming, of course, that the Commune managed to agree. There were so many factions involved that it was unlikely that anyone would agree on anything in a hurry. By the time they did, the war would probably be over.

* * *

She was back in the Embassy, reading through reports from Earth and Garston, when her aide interrupted her musings. "Ambassador," he said, "you have a visitor."

Shan looked up, crossly. "I do?"

"You do," her aide confirmed. "It's Great Lady Vanla herself."

Shan felt her eyes widen as she stood up. "Have her sent into the meeting room at once," she ordered. "I'll be through directly."

The meeting room had been designed to be suitable for representatives of every known race, at least the ones that could operate in a standard atmosphere. It still felt weird, almost discomforting, to her, but at least the Funk probably felt the same way. The chairs, formed from a substance that altered itself to match the contours of the visitor, had been provided by the Cats. Her intelligence team still suspected that the material concealed bugs beyond their ability to detect, even if the Cats had stagnated over thousands of years. They'd certainly want to keep an eye on what the younger races were doing as they withdrew from galactic affairs.

Great Lady Vanla looked... almost furtive as she sat down, giving Shan precious moments to compose herself. She'd expected visitors from the Tarn, or the Traders, or any one of a dozen races that might be friendly to humanity, but she'd never expected the Hegemony to send a representative. Her security staff had noted that Great Lady Vanla had come alone, without even her aide or a bodyguard, which suggested... what? The meeting was clearly intended to be completely off the record.

"Great Lady," she said, by way of welcome. "I thank you for visiting my home."

The Funk didn't smile. "In her infinite wisdom," she said, "Her Majesty the Empress of the Hegemony, the Heir to the First Empress, has ordered me to raise the issue of peace terms with you and your people."

Shan blinked in surprise. The Hegemony had taken blows, but they were very far from defeated. Earth's ability to keep fighting was limited, even with the loans they'd secured from the various banking combines among the Galactics. Whatever the Traders did, it was quite possible for the Hegemony to win the war if they kept fighting. Or... could it be that they'd decided that continuing the fight was not worth the effort?

"I have always stated that we are willing to discuss peace terms," Shan said, carefully. "Does your Empress wish to listen to ours, or does she have terms of her own?"

"The Empress believes that continuing the war would be disastrous for both of our races," Great Lady Vanla said. It was hard to tell, but Shan suspected that anything less than dictating peace terms at gunpoint wouldn't have sat well with her. The Hegemony's superiority complex was astonishingly powerful. "She is willing to propose terms for an end to the war."

Shan listened, carefully. "The Empress is prepared to accept your independence from the Hegemony, now and forever," Great Lady Vanla said. Shan, who knew that 'forever' really meant for as long as it suited the Hegemony, said nothing. "If you return to your pre-war borders, we will recognise them as inviolate."

It was hard not to laugh. "So you want us to surrender everything we've taken from you and in exchange you will graciously agree to recognise our right to exist?" Shan asked. "Do you really think that those terms would be acceptable to the Federation?"

"When the alternative is total obliteration," the Funk pointed out, "you would find those terms very acceptable."

She did have a point, Shan had to admit, but the situation wasn't that dire. "I strongly doubt that the Federation Council would agree that your claim on Terra Nova is valid," she said, instead. "You not only held a human population in bondage, but you oppressed that population savagely. The Federation will not return that planet to you."

It didn't feel right to her to impose such a strict rule on discussions, but Ambassadors had been sacked before for regarding inalienable rights and solid positions as things that could be negotiated and given away. Diplomats liked to keep talking, and to keep the lines of communication open, but some things couldn't be surrendered or the results would be disastrous. At bottom, the Federation wanted – needed – the Hegemony's formal recognition of Earth's independence. Giving the Funks a sign of weakness would be disastrous.

"And you will lose it when we finally recapture the world," Great Lady Vanla said, coldly. "You clearly have no intention of negotiating openly."

"Neither do you," Shan said. "You came to see me in private. I assume that you don't want word of this discussion getting back to your own people."

"They would not believe you if you chose to tell them," the Funk hissed. "I shall go."

"I have terms that the Federation would regard as acceptable," Shan said. "Don't you want to hear them before you slither out of here?"

If the Funk noticed the subtle insult, she said nothing. "We cannot accept terms imposed at gunpoint," she said, flatly. Shan barely managed to refrain from pointing out that the Funks expected *humanity* to accept being dictated to. "But we will consider them."

"You recognise our independence, including that of Terra Nova," Shan said. "Garston becomes independent, governed by the settlers on the planet; Earth continues to administer the high orbitals, but agrees not to turn the system into a naval base. You refrain from rebuilding Hammerfall or basing naval units within twenty light years of the border. And neither side will seek any reparations from the other."

The Funk hissed in amusement. "You must think us insane," she said. "Why would we accept such unpleasant terms?"

"Because the longer this war continues, the greater the chance that your Empress will lose her head," Shan said. She smiled in cold amusement. "It will take years for you to repair the damage we've inflicted upon you, assuming that your neighbours give you the chance. What happens when they decide they have a chance to take you down forever?"

"The Hegemony will not go quietly," Great Lady Vanla said. She rose to her feet. "I will report your words to the Empress, but I do not believe that she will accept."

Shan watched her go, and then walked back into her office. Whatever else could be said of her, the Great Lady would not have come on such a mission without permission from her superiors. Maybe, just maybe, there was a chance to end the war before it was too late. Or maybe the Hegemony had been hurt badly enough that they couldn't settle for anything less than total victory. There was no way to know. She'd report it to Earth and hope that wiser minds than herself might be able to decide what to do next.

* * *

Hammerfall had once been a proud system, the linchpin of a defensive line intended to keep any aggressor away from the core worlds. Now... it had been crippled. After a frigate had struck a mine and had been almost destroyed, most of the remaining starships had had to withdraw to higher orbits where they would be reasonably safe. Or so Lady Dalsha hoped. It was impossible to say just how many mines the humans had laid, or precisely where they'd all gone as they drifted into orbit around Hammerfall. Some of them even seemed to have been rigged to explode when they picked up an active sensor sweep at close range. None of the fortresses could even risk dropping their shields, for fear that a mine would get through the shield boundary and detonate against their hulls. It was all a fearful mess.

The propaganda claimed that the Battle of Hammerfall had been a victory for the Hegemony, but the long list of destroyed or crippled starships told their own story. One way or another, the plans for a mighty counterattack would have to be put back weeks, perhaps months – and what if Earth was defended by similar missiles? The entire Hegemony Navy might be unable to break through the defences and range in on the planet. It was no help that most of the independent freighters travelling through the Hegemony had decided to go elsewhere, at the command of the Traders. If they couldn't find a way to crack through humanity's network of mines, they might have to completely abandon the planet. And *that* would be difficult to justify to an increasingly angry population.

At least no one had questioned her command. The smarter ones probably reasoned that they didn't want to get the blame for the disaster; the stupider ones were probably too frightened to see the opportunity for advancement. But she needed to do *something* before the morale problem got out of hand. How long would it be before starship commanders started refusing to go up against human starships? Millions of rumours were spreading through the fleet, each one crazier than the last. The humans had built weapons that could take out a superdreadnought with a single shot, the humans had created a planet-killer that could eat an entire world and use the debris as fuel, the humans had created a form of rogue nanotech that could destroy an entire fleet in seconds. Each of the rumours had very little connection to the truth, but that didn't help. How could it?

The last update had stated that heavy reinforcements were still two weeks away from Hammerfall, if they didn't get diverted to inner defence lines. Apart from the homeworld itself, many of the inner worlds hadn't received updated defences before the war had begun, if only because fortifying the border had seemed more important. None of the planners had taken the humans seriously.

She stared down at the latest report and cursed under her breath. Sending a handful of smaller ships to raid Garston was – technically – exceeding her orders, but it might just win her some time. And if it didn't... at least the humans would be responding to her for a change. Anything that could slow down their offensive would be worth it.

And if the Empress disagreed, she'd lose her head.

Someone still had to take the blame, after all.

Chapter Thirty

"The new guys are shaping up nicely."

"Looks that way," Markus agreed. He grinned over at his wife. "But how will we know until we actually see them in action?"

If there was one advantage of the pause at Garston, it was that Grumble Squadron had had a chance to get some downtime and integrate the new pilots and gunboats from Earth. Their mothership might have gone off to raid a Hegemony world with the other squadrons, but Grumble had been left behind at Garston. Part of Markus resented the fact that he'd been left behind to babysit the newcomers, yet he had to admit that the reformed squadron needed time to train. They'd never exercised with the newcomers before the war had begun.

Garston was slowly coming back to life, even if it *was* in the middle of a war. The various Galactic trading combines were still calling in and drawing HE3 from the gas giants, as well as making use of the facilities in orbit around the planet. Several of the freighters, Markus had heard, were almost certainly intelligence ships belonging to other interstellar powers, powers that had a keen interest in learning about the human weapons that had done so much to shatter entire Funk fleets. He'd asked if they should be training so publicly, but ONI had insisted – and ordered that the gunboats alter their IFF signatures on every flight, creating an impression of hundreds of gunboats ready to zoom into action. Privately Markus doubted that many of the Galactics would be fooled, yet the Hegemony could hardly take the chance of discovering the hard way that so many gunboats existed. They'd certainly be deterred from launching a counterattack until they worked out new tactics to deal with the gunboats.

"You were young once," Carola gently reproved him. "You weren't born an ace pilot."

"Of course I was," Markus said mischievously. "My mother always said that I came out of the womb sporting a handlebar moustache."

He shrugged. There had also been time for the Federation Council to approve the medals and promotions recommended by the post-battle assessment teams. The Federation didn't have its own medals for its crews, but both of them had been awarded the highest decorations of their homelands, as had a number of other pilots. And they'd given extensive interviews to the reporters, interviews that would encourage young cadets to try out for the gunboat training programs. The military hadn't been so popular since the end of World War Two. Whatever doubts had fermented in the minds of civilians since the murky dawn of the War on Terror, they'd been blown away by the occupation of Terra Nova and the Hegemony's ruthless pressure campaign against Earth. Now that Terra Nova had been liberated, humanity's stock was rising high...

There was a chime from the console. "And now the drones are coming online," he said. Four Funk ECM drones, captured when Garston fell to the Federation Navy, had been deployed to simulate Hegemony superdreadnoughts. They weren't quite up to the standards of human technology, but they'd serve as targets for gunboat exercises. The pilots who got picked off by the – simulated – point defences would be buying the beer in Pilot Country afterwards.

"All Grumbles, form up on Grumble Five," he ordered. He should have led the attack – and he would have, if it had been real – but all of the pilots needed to practice leading the charge. His luck would run out, sooner or later, as it had for Eagle's CO, who'd died at Heavenly Gate. "Grumble Five...take us in as soon as you please."

Grumble Five altered course and swooped down upon the simulated superdreadnoughts. Markus watched the chaotic formation with approval, even as the superdreadnoughts came to life and started to spit bursts of brilliant light towards the incoming gunboats. Their weapons systems had been upgraded by the simulation planners, who'd pointed out that – sooner or later – the

Hegemony would find ways to improve its technology. Besides, if the gunboats practiced against tougher targets than they expected to encounter, it would make their operations much easier.

"Fire at will," Grumble Fire ordered. "I say again; fire at will."

Implosion bolts rained down on the lead superdreadnought, tearing into its hull. Unlike the ships the gunboats had targeted so far, superdreadnoughts were so heavily armored that it was difficult for the gunboats to inflict enough damage to destroy them quickly. But picking off their weapons and sensor blisters would cripple them, leaving their commanders forced to choose between withdrawing or becoming little more than sitting ducks for the human cruisers. Markus diverted part of his attention to check the overall exercise feed. The simulated superdreadnoughts were suffering, but not enough, not yet.

Their point defence was doing well too. A pair of gunboats had been blasted out of space in a moment of carelessness – one pilot was going to get chewed out when they got back to base – and another had narrowly avoided a burst of plasma fire that would have scorched the hull, if it had been real. Markus twisted his gunboat into an evasive pattern as they slashed closer to the lead superdreadnought, before pulling up and slipping into a new formation. The Hegemony had, so far, been content to ignore gunboats that were heading *away* from their targets, but it wouldn't be long before they realised that gunboat pilots had a tendency to fly predicable vectors while they were leaving and started programming their point defence to pick them off. Another gunboat died in a burst of simulated energy and Markus made a mental note to remind his pilots not to get cocky. A superdreadnought could soak up one hell of a lot of damage before exploding, but a gunboat could be wiped from existence by a single shot.

Still, the superdreadnoughts were starting to stagger under the weight of the gunboat attack. The rear superdreadnoughts started to drift closer to the lead ships, linking their point defence through the datanet into one entity. After what had happened at Hammerfall, the

Hegemony would have plenty of incentive to tighten up their datanets and coordinate their fire against incoming ships. The point defence fire thickened until it seemed impossible that anything could survive, even something as small and nimble as a gunboat. Grumble Squadron pressed the attack, closing in to point blank range...

Markus cursed as his gunboat's consoles flashed up a mocking message. He was dead. It rankled, even in a simulation. But it was preferable to being picked off in a real battle. In theory, gunboats were expendable compared to the heavier cruisers, yet the human race didn't have enough gunboats to swarm the entire Hegemony Navy. They'd have to hope that the new weapons and tactics that were already being rushed into development would even the odds. One gunboat – just one – survived the final assault.

"Well," Markus said, as the exercise came to an end. "I hope we've all learned something from this..."

His radio buzzed. "Grumble Lead, this is System Command," an unfamiliar voice said. "Long-range sensor platforms are picking up cloaking turbulence near your location. Request that you go active and ID the bandits."

"Understood, System Command," Markus said. The first order of business, once Garston's high orbitals had been secure, had been to seed the system with stealthed sensor platforms, ones that were capable of picking up a quantum gate several light-days from the planet. Their passive sensors were remarkably capable – and they were almost undetectable unless someone happened to literally stumble across one of them. "We're on our way."

He switched back to the gunboat command channel. "All Grumbles, go active; I say again, go active. The exercise is terminated."

Carola looked up from her console. "It's a very minor contact," she said. "It might be nothing more than a frigate trying to spy on us."

"Or the sensor platform might just have picked up the tailing edge of an entire assault fleet," Markus added. The Galactics had produced an impressive cloaking system for their starships, one that – as far as he knew – humanity hadn't managed to surpass. But a moving starship produced very faint turbulence that could be detected by a watching sensor platform, allowing the cloaked ships to be tracked to some degree. One way or another, they had to find out before the unknown ships got any closer to the planet. An attack fleet that managed to get into firing range was going to do a great deal of damage before it was destroyed. "Are you picking up anything on our own sensors?"

"No," Carola admitted. The gunboat sensors were nowhere near as capable as the systems on the sensor platform. "But they have to know that we've seen them."

Markus nodded. A squadron of gunboats flying directly towards the oncoming ship - or ships - would be hard to miss. He tossed possibilities around in his head as the distance closed, wondering just what was out there, trying to sneak in on Garston. A scout, or an attack fleet? They could be flying right into an ambush if the enemy commander had the nerve to wait until the gunboats entered attack range. Or... there were just too many possibilities, none of them good. There were only twelve gunboats in the system, after all - and the Hegemony would know it the moment the other gunboats failed to materialise. Maybe they'd be lucky and the unknown ship would be a simple destroyer.

"Picking up turbulence," Carola snapped. "Datanet calls them targeting systems."

"Evasive action," Markus snapped. The icons for a dozen starships appeared in front of him, the heaviest a battlecruiser. Five battlecruisers and seven destroyers, enough to overwhelm many star systems - and there might be more waiting under cloak. A moment passed, and then the starships opened fire, trying to pick off the gunboats before they got too close. Their targeting systems had been improved, Markus noted; they'd had a chance to reprogram their computers after the first encounters at Garston and Heavenly Gate. "Prepare to attack."

* * *

Tobias had been catching up on his sleep when the alarm rang, bringing *Nimitz* to general quarters. He threw himself out of his bunk, pulled on his trousers frantically and raced for the CIC, yanking his jacket off the hook and carrying it with him. It felt faintly absurd to be going into battle without any shoes on, but that would be the least of his worries if *Nimitz* was badly hit. Regulations stated that all crewmen were supposed to wear protective clothing if the ship was going into battle, yet Tobias had cancelled those orders. The protective shipsuits were simply too hot to wear for more than a few minutes.

"Report," he barked, as he stepped into the CIC. The starship was coming to life around him, her systems flash-waking as she prepared for battle. Even human-designed technology couldn't be run at full power indefinitely, or wear and tear would grind the equipment down and eventually force the ship to return home for a full refitting. "What do we have?"

Commander Jake Lucas looked up from where he was filling in for Commander Sooraya Qadir, who'd been granted shore leave on Garston. Tobias had been allowing a handful of officers and men to take shore leave every day, giving them a chance to relax and explore an alien world. Now that some of the cities were reasonably peaceful, it had seemed safe enough.

"An inbound enemy attack fleet," Lucas reported. "At least twelve starships, including five battlecruisers. The gunboat CAP is preparing to engage."

"Call them back," Tobias said, studying the display. The Hegemony ships had to have arrived several light-days from the star and made the rest of the transit in normal space. No one, not even the Cats or humanity, could open a quantum gate any closer to the star without being detected. And that suggested a degree of pre-planning that indicated that the Hegemony had finally recovered its balance. Hammerfall might have shocked some of them to the point where they were beginning to consider peace terms, at least according to Ambassador Li, but the Empress really needed a victory before she could end the war. "Twelve gunboats won't make much of an impression on them."

"No, sir," Lucas agreed. "Admiral, all ships are reporting ready for action."

"Good," Tobias said. He'd been the attacker in every other battle fought by the Federation Navy; now he was the defender – and he didn't like it. Ideally, he would take his ships away from Garston and fight it out in open space – the Hegemony force *was* inferior to the First Strike Fleet – but that would mean leaving the planet's orbital facilities open to attack. They had made some progress in pressing captured Hegemony automated weapons platforms into service, yet they wouldn't be enough to stand off an assault on Garston. And the uneasy peace on the planet below depended on the Federation Navy retaining control of the high orbitals.

In theory, the 1st Cruiser Squadron alone could handle the incoming fleet, but it would be tricky. Their shields might be more capable than the Hegemony shields, yet they'd be taking fire from several starships simultaneously, including torpedo fire. And every ship he lost hurt the Federation Navy more than every lost superdreadnought hurt the Hegemony...

And he couldn't afford to lose. "The 1st and 2nd Cruiser Squadrons are to form up on the flag and prepare to engage the enemy," he ordered. "The 3rd Cruiser Squadron is to remain in orbit as a reserve."

"Understood, Admiral," Lucas said. His hands danced across his console. "Orders sent."

"Take us out," Tobias ordered. The Funks would see them coming, of course. One possibility was that they would simply jump back into quantum space and escape, without attempting to engage the human ships. The Funks might have been barbaric, but they were hardly stupid...and they'd know that Tobias's fleet had smashed *superdreadnoughts*. "All units are to prepare to engage the enemy."

He settled back into his command chair, worrying. Something didn't quite add up. He could have understood the Funks raiding the asteroid mining complexes or the cloudscoops, even though that would have irritated the other Galactics, but why would they send a demonstrably inferior force into a battle that could only have one outcome? Maybe the Empress wanted to get rid of the commanding officer... no, surely the Funks wouldn't throw away so many ships just to assassinate someone who had displeased their Empress. Unless there were more ships hiding in cloak...

..But it would have required omniscience to *know* when they would be detected by the human defenders. One tactical lesson the humans – and the Funks, he assumed – had taken directly from the Galactics was that military operations should always follow the KISS principle. Keep It Simple, Stupid. The more complex a military plan, the greater the potential for a screw-up that would cost lives and equipment. Unless the Funks had their own secret stockpile of advanced technology, they couldn't have detected the sensor platforms... maybe they'd hoped to get closer to the planet before being detected. And yet even *that* didn't make sense.

"Admiral, the Funks are altering course," Lucas reported. "They're heading in right towards us."

It *had* to be a trick, Tobias told himself. The Funks weren't *insane*. They had to know that their force was about to get chopped into mush, even though they'd damage the human fleet before they were destroyed. Were they so reluctant to go home and admit failure that they would prefer to be destroyed instead? There had certainly been some human commanders who would have understood that feeling, even shared it. Better death than dishonour...and yet, the outcome of a battle was never as important as the outcome of a war.

"Order the fleet to spread out," Tobias ordered, finally. Maybe the Funks had come up with their own version of the missile cloud and arsenal ship. They might not have anything specially designed for the role, but they could cram extra torpedo launchers into their hulls or outfit a freighter as an additional torpedo platform. It would be surprisingly inventive, yet the Funks weren't idiots. They'd seen the missile cloud in action and had plenty of incentive to duplicate it for themselves. Not that it would be *that* helpful against human technology, but it would certainly threaten the other Galactics. "Launch recon probes towards the enemy force."

He watched as the probes slid away from his ships, heading out past the Funk formation. Recon probes were the most sensitive platforms in the fleet, although they weren't as stealthy as the satellites they'd positioned around the system. If there were additional cloaked units hiding behind the ships they'd spotted, they'd be detected before the human fleet flew right into their waiting jaws. But what if the Funks were trying something else...?

"Two minutes to engagement range," Lucas reported. The human cruisers would pick up speed and manoeuvre around the enemy ships, rather than the battering match that the Hegemony commander seemed to be trying to entice them to accept. Phase cannon would tear through their shields and obliterate the enemy ships. "Admiral... one of the enemy ships just transited out."

"Odd," Tobias said. Something was nagging at the back of his mind. Why hadn't they *all* fled? "Why would they send one destroyer away...?"

He broke off as an alarm sounded. "Admiral, a new quantum gate is forming, right on top of us," Lucas snapped. Tobias swore out loud as the shape of the enemy trap became clear. "I'm reading another nine battlecruisers and seventeen destroyers, closing rapidly on attack vector. They're broadcasting a demand for surrender."

"Alert all ships," Tobias ordered, ignoring the surrender demand. They'd been suckered, all right. The Hegemony had kept the other half of the assault fleet in quantum space until the human ships were in the right position. And he'd flown right into the trap! "Prepare to engage the enemy."

Chapter Thirty-One

"Force Two closing to engagement range," Lucas said. "Enemy ships are locking targeting sensors on us."

"Deploy ECM countermeasures," Tobias ordered. He would have preferred to keep those surprises for the next attack on a Hegemony system, but there was no other choice. Even if they wiped out the entire attack force, they'd still take heavy losses. "And then bring the fleet around. Take us right at Force Two."

The Funks had planned their trap well, even though there were some aspects they'd have had to leave to chance. Hide a fleet in quantum space, dangle bait in front of the human defenders...and wait until the humans walked right into the trap. They'd even had the unexpected bonus that Tobias had left a third of his fleet in orbit, rather than bringing it all out to challenge the cloaked ships. There was no way they could have counted on that, which suggested that they felt that they had enough firepower to defeat all three cruiser squadrons. The only alternative to an engagement was to run – and that would mean leaving Garston undefended, ready for the Funks to move back in and launch reprisals against the non-Funk population.

Humanity's ECM drones spread out ahead of the fleet. Each one was capable of creating a dozen sensor ghosts, a variant on the tactic that had made the missile cloud so effective. The Funks would be unable to tell the difference between real or ghost ships at long range, but they presumably had locked their sensors on the real ships. Using countermeasures, the locks broke, rendering it far harder for them to work out which ships were real. It still wouldn't be enough, if only because the ghost ships couldn't engage the enemy. The Funks would just fire on any ship that fired on their formation.

The distance between the two forces closed rapidly. Behind the Federation Navy, Force One abandoned its casual approach to Garston and brought its drives to full power, intent on helping Force Two to crush the human fleet. Once they combined their ships, they would presumably advance on Garston and force Tobias to engage them or surrender the planet. The gunboats twisted around, ready to slash down into Force Two. There would be so many targets that the point defences would have problems tracking the gunboats. But there were still only twelve of them...

"Force Two entering phase cannon range," Lucas reported. Humanity's slight range advantage might just even the odds. "All ships report ready to engage the enemy."

"Fire at will," Tobias ordered.

Nimitz opened fire, brilliant beams of energy lancing out towards the enemy ships and striking their shields, just before the rotating modulation hit on the right frequency and slashed directly into the target's hull. The enemy ship twisted at once, rotating its own shield frequency in hopes of avoiding serious damage, but it was too late to stop the phase cannon from digging deep into her hull. She rolled out of the enemy formation, trailing plasma as her crew fought to save their ship. An antimatter torpedo from one of *Nimitz's* consorts finished her off before her crew could escape.

The enemy fleet opened fire seconds later, bombarding the entire human fleet with phase cannon fire. They seemed to be scattering their fire, something that made no sense until Tobias realised that it was a way to separate the sensor ghosts out from the real ships. *Nimitz* rocked as a phase cannon burst stuck her hull, just before she unleashed a spread of torpedoes towards an enemy battlecruiser. Compressed antimatter flared out in the darkness of space and the enemy ship lost her shields. A moment later, she vaporised as a torpedo exploded against her unprotected hull.

Tobias smiled darkly as the range continued to narrow. The Funks had largely separated out the sensor ghosts now, but they were still drawing fire as skilled ECM crews projected the ghosts forward, ahead of the advancing ships. Several human ships had taken damage, yet they were all still moving, their weapons digging into enemy hulls. The Funks opened fire with antimatter torpedoes of their own, only to discover that humanity had learned how to deploy their phase cannon as point defence weapons. Only a handful of torpedoes survived to strike home.

"*John Paul Jones* is taking heavy fire," Lucas reported. "Her captain is requesting permission to disengage..."

"Granted," Tobias snapped. It was too late. The cruiser had been broadsided by a pair of enemy battlecruisers, her shields failing before she could escape. A brace of antimatter torpedoes finished her off and she vanished in a ball of fire. "Order *Farragut* and *Cochrane* to watch for survivors as they blaze through that part of the enemy formation."

Nimitz rotated in space, spinning alongside the hull of one of the enemy battlecruisers. They were far too close to risk unleashing antimatter torpedoes, but her phase cannon dug deeply into the enemy hull. A direct hit blew through one of the battlecruiser's fusion plants and a chain reaction of explosions tore her apart. Two of her consorts attempted to use her death agonies as cover to bring their own weapons to bear on the imprudent human ship, but *Nimitz* turned and showed them her heels, launching a spread of torpedoes to cover her retreat. Open space beckoned in front of the human ships and they raced for it, two cruisers trailing plasma as they escaped Force Two's wrath.

"Order the 3rd Cruiser Squadron to leave orbit and reinforce us," Tobias ordered. Between reinforcements and the damage they'd inflicted on Force Two, the odds would be a great deal more even. If he'd been in the enemy's shoes, he would have seriously considered taking advantage of the brief pause to open a quantum gate and escape, knowing that he'd already dented the myth of human invincibility. "*Togo* and *Surcouf* are to break contact and jump out to Point Shiloh."

"Aye, sir," Lucas said. Point Shiloh, one light year away from Garston, was where the fleet train was waiting, a handful of ships loaded with supplies and repair workers. The mobile shipyard and fabricator wasn't exactly a new idea, but the Federation Navy had taken the risk of constructing mobile units rather than a handful of heavily-defended shipyards like most of the Galactics. Earth had only had fifteen years to produce a space-capable industry and a number of corners had had to be cut. "Force One and Force Two are uniting now."

Tobias nodded. He'd expected as much, but unless the enemy chose to withdraw he would have to engage them again. There were hundreds of thousands of human soldiers on the planet, mostly national rather than Federation units. Abandoning them could bring down the entire edifice. In hindsight, they'd badly underestimated the Funks – and their ability to bounce back from losing more tonnage than the entire Federation Navy.

And a single defeat could mean the end of the war.

"General Chekov is attempting to raise you, sir," Lucas said. Chekov was the overall commander on the ground, now that the Federation Marines had been relieved by national units. "The message is marked urgent."

Tobias scowled. The Funks were sorting out their formation, slipping Force One's ships forward to replace the losses inflicted on Force Two. Their datanets were presumably as capable as those belonging to the other Galactics; slotting the other ships into their holes wouldn't take longer than a few minutes. If they'd attacked then... but they couldn't, not until his fleet was concentrated.

"Pass him to me," he said, picking up his earpiece. "And order the fleet to prepare to move on my command."

"Admiral," Chekov's voice said. Like most officers cleared to work with the Federation, his English was perfect, although with a faint Russian accent. "I understand that we have visitors."

"Yes," Sampson said, tightly. Multinational operations had always been a headache even before Mentor had arrived and turned Earth upside down. At least Chekov had a reputation for being competent, commanding the Russian forces that had assisted in disarming and occupying North Korea after the Second Korean War. Some of the horror stories about multinational forces from before First Contact had been chilling. "I suppose you could put it that way."

"I have ordered my forces to go dark," Chekov said. "If you have to withdraw from the system, we'll give the bastards a welcome they'll never forget."

"It's not over yet," Sampson said. He understood what Chekov was trying to say – and he was grateful – but the Funks would simply bombard the planet into submission from high orbit, once they drove away the Federation Navy. Chekov would be forced into surrender once his forces were targeted from well outside their own range. It was possible that the Galactics would respond harshly, particularly after so many horror stories about how the Funks had treated the other races had been transmitted onto the news networks, but Tobias knew that they couldn't take it for granted. "If we have to leave…"

He shook his head. "Thank you," he said. "Earth will not forget."

* * *

"Here they come," Markus said. "On my mark...engage!"

The gunboats slipped out of their holding formation and raced towards the enemy rear. Unsurprisingly, the Funks had continued their drive on Garston, knowing that the humans would have to either engage them or surrender the planet when they got into orbit. Markus had positioned Grumble Squadron outside the Funk engagement range and waited. Now all twelve gunboats, supported by the most advanced ECM systems in the galaxy, closed in on their targets from the rear. It was the closest thing they had to a weak spot that could be exploited.

A handful of Funk destroyers turned to intercept them as the gunboats closed in on their targets, spitting point defence fire towards the human ships. It wasn't a bad tactic, Markus had to admit, but it didn't quite take account of gunboat speed and manoeuvrability. The gunboats lanced through the destroyers, holding their fire, and left them behind in their wake. Markus would have preferred to remain behind and engage them, wiping them out one by one, but there was no time to clear the way properly. Their targets were the big battlecruisers before they could engage the human cruisers.

The Funks refused to be distracted by the gunboats, either because they knew there were fewer gunboats in the attacking force than it seemed, or because they intended to absorb the damage inflicted by the gunboats and keep going. Without either gunboats or assault shuttles of their own, there was really little other choice. Markus braced himself as they slid into engagement range, and then led his squadron mates towards the enemy battlecruiser. He touched the trigger and sprayed a handful of implosion bolts towards the big drive structure at the rear of the ship. There were fewer point defence blisters surrounding their target, making it easier to hit.

There was an explosion and the Funk starship fell out of formation as her drives failed. Markus wanted to finish her off, but there was no time; instead, they had to cripple as many of the other battlecruisers as possible. The destroyers had caught up with them and were attempting to shield their larger companions, knowing that even if they served as targets for the gunboats they could still distract them from their mission. Markus cursed aloud as one of the maggots – the new pilots – slammed right into a destroyer's shields, vanishing in a ball of flame that barely scratched the ship's defences. A mistake at the wrong time could cost a pilot everything.

Another Funk battlecruiser loomed up in front of him and he led his gunboats towards her, firing implosion bolts that dug deep into the ship's hull. The sheer volume of point defence fire was impressive, suggesting that the Funks had outfitted their ships with extra weapons from Hammerfall. There had certainly been enough cripples from the last battle to serve as a convenient source of spare parts.

Tiny explosions blossomed along the target's hull as the gunboats raced towards her drives. A destroyer appeared out of nowhere, targeting the gunboats and picking off two of them before they could evade. Markus swallowed a curse as the remaining gunboats flipped over and drove away from the new threat, their weapons automatically tracking and picking away at their target. The battlecruiser would have time to engage before the remains of Grumble Squadron could reform and fall on her again. At least the maggots had more than proven themselves, those who had survived. Only six Grumbles remained to take the offensive once more.

They have to know we were bluffing now, he thought. *We'd have launched every gunboat we had at them, if we'd had the gunboats to launch.*

* * *

Tobias braced himself as *Nimitz* lanced towards the enemy formation, ready to open fire as soon as she came into range. This time, he intended to try a variant on an old Galactic tactic, one he wouldn't have dared try against superdreadnoughts. The fleet advanced and came to a halt, relative to the enemy fleet, as soon as it entered weapons range. Humanity's phase cannon could harm the enemy ships from outside their own range, at least in theory. It was time to find out if that was actually true.

"Open fire," he ordered. Deadly beams lanced towards their target, splashing away from enemy shields. The rotating modulation trick wasn't so effective at long range, if only because the phase cannon beams tended to fade as the range opened. Rotating shields randomly wasn't supposed to be possible for the Galactics, but once they realised what the humans could do it was certain that they'd attempt to discover a countermeasure to the human weapons. "Damage report?"

"Minimal," Lucas admitted. "We're hurting their shields, but beam diffusion is too great to damage their hulls. We need to engage at closer range."

Tobias nodded. "Take us in," he ordered. "Open fire with antimatter torpedoes as soon as we enter range."

Space became a boiling mass of energy as antimatter torpedoes slammed into their targets. Five more Hegemony battlecruisers vanished in the blaze, along with a pair of destroyers, but they didn't die alone. *Perry* died before any of her crew could escape, while *Jellicoe* staggered away, too badly damaged to even open a quantum gate and escape the battle. If the Hegemony had targeted her, they would have blown her apart before it was too late; instead, the battlecruisers started to angle away from the planet. Tobias watched in disbelief as the Funks turned and retreated, leaving their puzzled opponents in command of the battlefield. Moments later, they opened a quantum gate and vanished. The battle seemed to be over.

"Maybe it's a trap," Lucas said, as puzzled as his superior. "Maybe they expect us to chase them into quantum space and run right into another formation of ships."

Tobias shook his head. The Galactics were reluctant to fight battles in quantum space, for fear that the disruptive storms would give the weaker side an advantage. It was a known fact that quantum space responded to weapons fire, although no-one had managed to come up with an explanation as to why. The Funks would hardly have risked a battle in quantum space if there was any alternative.

"Curious," he said. "I wonder..."

"Sir, I'm picking up transmissions from Convoy-46," Lucas said, suddenly. "They just entered the system. Her CO didn't even realise that there was a battle underway until they picked it up on their sensors."

Tobias started to laugh, despite himself. The Funks had detected the convoy too and had assumed that the freighters were more arsenal ships. It wasn't as if the missile cloud would be so useful against targets in clear space, where they could jump into quantum space and escape, but they couldn't have risked the total obliteration of their force without inflicting equal or greater losses on their foe.

"Welcome her CO to the system and thank him for his timely arrival," he said. "And then get the repair crews to work. I want all of the damaged ships repaired before we return to Hammerfall."

He settled down in his command chair. "And pass a message to all ships," he added. "Well done."

* * *

An hour later, he found himself studying a report that didn't please him in the slightest. Two of the damaged ships could be returned to service within five days, but the remainder would require several weeks at the very least. Whatever they'd had in mind – retaking Garston or reconnaissance in force – they'd accomplished at least one of their goals. The Federation Navy would be unable to take the offensive and return to Hammerfall, unless he called up reinforcements from Earth. And doing that risked leaving humanity's homeworld uncovered.

The Hegemony could lose a dozen worlds like Hammerfall and keep going. Humanity couldn't afford to lose Earth and the industry that had been painstakingly built up in the solar system over the last fifteen years. Presumably, the Funks knew that as well as he did. He was mildly surprised that they hadn't already tried to raid the system, even if they *were* spooked by the thought of what kind of defences humanity might have emplaced around Earth. Tobias was one of the very few who knew that humanity's fixed defences were minimal, almost non-existent. There had been no time to construct fortresses when the Federation Navy needed starships.

He shook his head. But there was no real choice. They had to call up the reserves and continue the advance, hammering away at the Hegemony. It couldn't be long before someone overthrew the Empress. Even if the war ended tomorrow, the clans would need years to rebuild all they'd lost. If the Hegemony recovered first, humanity was screwed, without lube.

They'd just have to see what they could do to keep the Hegemony off-balance until they were ready to win the war.

Chapter Thirty-Two

"What do we have today?"

"One bulk freighter, two general freighters and a pair of destroyers," Karla said. "Traffic has been really slowing down lately."

Joshua nodded. The Traders Alliance wasn't the only organisation that claimed to supervise interstellar trade, but it represented hundreds of thousands of independent shippers and small trading companies. Joshua was a member himself. Even their rivals, as much as they would appreciate the chance to sneak business from under the Alliance's nose, wouldn't be inclined to break the embargo on the Hegemony. The Funks were making it harder for independent freighter commanders to make an honest living.

Ironically, it was also making it harder for the pirates. With fewer ships travelling through the threatened sectors, the Funks had a chance to escort more of them with escorts heavy enough to daunt even the Clunker fleet. The rebels were still committed but some of the pirates were edging away, perhaps to the point of considering selling Joshua out to the Funks. They'd find it harder to make a living if the Funks kept escorting their ships – and they were less inclined to pick fights with any warship. Getting rid of Joshua had to seem like a bargain to them. He'd responded by moving most of his activities away from the known asteroid colonies and keeping as much as he could firmly out of sight. Even if they did manage to sell him out to the Funks, the rebellion would go on.

"It can't be a very important cargo," Joshua said, thoughtfully. The last convoy they'd seen had been escorted by four heavy cruisers, far too much to tangle with for his little fleet. What intelligence they'd picked up had suggested that the Funks had been moving heavy industrial equipment. Unlike most Galactics, the Funks weren't too keen on the idea of developing colonies building their own industries, even though it would save them a great deal of money in shipping costs. "But if we could take out those destroyers..."

He smiled, coldly. The Hegemony had been losing a great many escorts lately, thanks to Joshua and his men. Even a force the size of the Hegemony Navy had to be feeling the pain; light units were needed to escort their superdreadnoughts as well as everything else and they couldn't replenish their losses quickly enough. It was hard to tell if his tactics were having a major effect on the Hegemony, but with the trade embargo and the pirate raids, the Hegemony had to be in trouble. Their currency had been falling compared to the Galactic Credit for the last two weeks. It wouldn't be long before they had to dip into their own stockpile of credits to purchase almost anything they wanted from outside the Hegemony. The knock-on effects would certainly destroy the economy...

...On the other hand, plenty of human governments had gritted their teeth and kept fighting even in the face of economic disaster. Why couldn't the Funks show the same resilience?

"Take us in on attack vector," he ordered. There were enough ships in the raiding force to hunt down all of the freighters if they tried to scatter. "Prepare to engage the enemy."

The standard Hegemony tactic for dealing with pirates was to mount a resolute defence and hope that that deterred the pirates from pressing the offensive. Joshua had planned for that, but instead the Hegemony seemed to be playing it very cagily. The destroyers were hanging back, guarding the freighters, a tactic that suggested that they weren't eager to fight. And that made little sense.

"Maybe one of their Great Ladies is onboard the freighter," Karla suggested. "Someone worth a few million credits to them."

Joshua shrugged. It was possible, but Great Ladies normally didn't travel on anything smaller than a battlecruiser. On the other hand, it was also possible that the Hegemony had recalled most of its good crews and starships to the war front and left behind the dregs of the service, Funks who were less inclined to die for the Hegemony. But if they wanted to live, they should have scattered and hoped to lose themselves within quantum space. What was going on...?

"The bulk freighter is coming apart," Karla said, puzzled. "The hull appears to be crumbling into its component pieces."

"Odd," Joshua said. The Cats had developed hulls that were held together by a combination of prehensile materials and the ship's structural integrity field. They could be damaged, but it was rare for one to simply wear out, certainly on a starship belonging to a reasonably capable galactic power. It made no sense at all, unless...

"Break off," he snapped. "It's a trap!"

The power signature of a Hegemony battlecruiser appeared, rising up out of the remains of the bulk freighter. Someone on the other side had heard of Q-ships and decided to go one better, hiding a battlecruiser within a bulk freighter until the enemy ships entered attack range. The battlecruiser couldn't have used its own targeting sensors without giving the game away too soon, but there was no reason why it couldn't draw targeting solutions from the destroyers falling in behind it. Joshua and his ships were already within range.

"Order all ships to scatter," he said, grimly. The pirates were going to hate him for leading them into a trap. Some of the rebels might even have second thoughts about facing the Hegemony. They might be able to defeat the battlecruiser, but the cost would be far too high. "We'll regroup at Point Delta."

"They've locked onto our hull," Karla snapped. "The battlecruiser is opening fire."

"Evasive action," Joshua ordered. "Configure the torpedoes for proximity detonation and return fire."

Blackbeard lurched as she launched a spread of antimatter torpedoes, just before the first enemy torpedo slammed into her shields. If the battlecruiser had concentrated her fire, they would have been vaporised. As it was, *Blackbeard* spun like a top, hopefully convincing the Hegemony ship that she'd been badly damaged. Eddies of quantum space energy shimmered around her as the fleet scattered, leaving the battlecruiser and her two escorts to pick targets and go after them. Joshua wondered, grimly, if someone had managed to sell them out already, before deciding that it was unlikely. The Hegemony had simply gotten lucky – and he'd got sloppy. He should have sensed the trap before they committed themselves.

"They're coming after us," Karla reported. "Damn – those sensors are powerful."

"Crash transition," Joshua snapped. They might be able to hide in quantum space's energy storms, but not if the battlecruiser had a clear lock on their hull. "Get us into normal space."

Blackbeard shuddered, as if the hull was about to break apart, before finally crashing back down into normal space. "Go dark," Joshua ordered. They'd already taken down most of the systems that would have released betraying emissions, but even a pirate ship had active sensors and targeting systems. There was no point in trying to run if the battlecruiser came after them. "Shut down everything we can without compromising ourselves."

Karla snorted. "Worse than we are already?"

An alarm from the tactical console cut off the retort that rose to Joshua's lips. "The bastard just made transit," he said. "Maybe they *did* know who we are after all."

The enemy battlecruiser wasn't trying to hide. Her active sensors swept space, projecting an image of iron determination to track down her prey. Joshua watched her through passive sensors, wondering just what kind of reward would be offered to the enemy commander if she managed to take the infamous pirate king alive. After all the chaos he'd caused, the Funks had probably put millions of credits on his head. But then, how would they know they'd caught the *real* pirate king?

Karla looked over at him. "If she paints us, we're dead," she said. Her voice was very quiet. "Now what?"

"We wait," Joshua said. He keyed the intercom. "All hands, an enemy battlecruiser is hunting us. Do *not* activate anything that might betray our location."

"Everyone is going to be whispering," Karla said, softly. They shared a grin. "We don't dare even risk a VR simulation."

"I always thought those were bad for kids," Joshua said. "I guess we'll have to have our pleasures the old-fashioned way."

He shook his head slowly. Hollywood had been slow to understand the potential in Galactic-designed VR simulation packages, which had left the big-name film producers struggling to catch up when the bell finally rang. Who wanted to watch the latest actor playing Spiderman when a VR simulation could put a watcher directly *into* Spiderman's outfit? Joshua had made millions of dollars selling systems imported from nearby Galactic worlds by the time Earth had finally produced its own version. Unsurprisingly, the pornography industry had been among the first to capitalize on the market. VR sex was clean, private and almost any kind of fantasy could be played out inside a person's head.

A long hour passed as the enemy ship hunted them, her sensors probing every last piece of space dust. Luckily, her transition had come several minutes after *Blackbeard's*, leaving her some distance from the point where Joshua had returned to normal space. A few kilometres in quantum space could mean light-minutes in the mundane universe. It was also quite possible that *Blackbeard* had broken apart through the stress of the transition and had been vaporised. But the Funks wouldn't want to assume that if they knew who they were chasing.

"They might go dark themselves," Karla said, slowly. "It might trick us into believing that they've departed."

"We'll just have to be careful," Joshua said. He'd evaded pirates in quantum space, but normal space was a whole different problem. Even the slightest transmission might betray their location, let alone powering up the drives and trying to flee. He worked it out, piece by piece, in his mind. By the time they managed to power up enough to jump back into quantum space, the enemy battlecruiser would be right on top of them. "Unless..."

He looked over at her. "Do we have any of the static bombs left onboard?"

"Only a couple," Karla said. She stared at him. "We'll never be able to use them to destroy that ship."

"I don't intend to destroy that ship," Joshua assured her. "I have something sneakier in mind."

* * *

Almost every Galactic-designed starship carried a Worker Bee, a tiny self-contained spacecraft intended to allow the crew to do outside the ship and carry out routine maintenance work on the hull. Only one human could fit inside the Bee at any one time, which limited its use as far as starship maintenance was concerned, but Joshua had other plans. It took nearly twenty minutes to pack both of the static bombs inside the Worker Bee, during which time Karla reported that the enemy battlecruiser was slowly, but surely drawing nearer. Their search pattern would have been admirable if they hadn't been chasing *Blackbeard*, Joshua had to admit; they'd be able to give any suspicious sensor reading a thorough examination before deciding that it was nothing more than a stray atom.

"We're ready, sir," the Chief Engineer said. "Seems a bit of a waste, man, but better it than us."

"Yep," Joshua agreed. Losing the entire Bee would be a fine trade if it saved their lives. "You may fire the gas cylinders when ready."

The Funks would have detected a drive field the moment it powered up, but they wouldn't be able to detect a stream of gas shielded by *Blackbeard's* hull. It would take several minutes for the Bee to reach the best position for stage two of Joshua's plan, giving him time to prepare his crew for action when the time came. They'd have to move swiftly. Even if the plan succeeded perfectly, the Funks wouldn't be surprised for long. Guided by a pinpoint communications laser, the Worker Bee moved steadily away from the hull. Unless they got very lucky, the Funks would be unable to detect her.

"She's nearing Point Fred," Karla said. She'd mocked his choice of name mercilessly, but now she was all professional. "Do you want me to take her active?"

Joshua sat down in his command chair, and then nodded. "You may fire when ready, Gridley."

The Worker Bee's active sensors came online. With a little careful tweaking, they looked like a damaged starship's sensors trying to work out just what had happened to their opponent, risking detection in the process. The Funks certainly picked her up at once; their battlecruiser wheeled around and raced towards the Worker Bee, her sensors locking onto the new threat. It wouldn't be more than a few seconds before they realised that they'd been tricked, but there would be just enough time for them to get too close to the Worker Bee. The static bombs detonated together, destroying the Bee and flooding space with brilliant radiation. Static bombs were useless in fleet actions – they blinded both sides indiscriminately and their effects didn't take long to shake off - but they worked very well as part of a sabotage mission. For as long as it took the Funks to reboot their computers and replace blinded sensor blisters, the battlecruiser was blind.

"Bring up the drive," Joshua ordered. *Blackbeard* hummed to life, alarmingly close to the battlecruiser's last reported position. Her passive sensors had been damaged too, even though she'd been further away from the Bee than the battlecruiser. "Take us out of here, now!"

It took several minutes for the battlecruiser to repair its sensor systems. By the time it started sweeping space again, *Blackbird* was already opening up a quantum gate and vanishing. The battlecruiser gave chase, but it was far too late. Joshua and his crew had made a clean break and lost themselves within the storms of quantum space.

"Thank God," he said, as they realised that they were safe. A single error in the timing could have cost them their lives. "That could have ended badly."

Karla chuckled. "I suppose it could have done, sir," she agreed. She seemed to hesitate, and then winked at him. "Want to join me in my cabin to celebrate?"

Joshua blinked at her, and then pushed his doubts aside. "Why not?" He asked. A hundred possible answers arose in his mind, but he pushed them down. It would be two days until they could return to Shadow, whatever else happened. "I don't think we'll have much more to celebrate for a while."

* * *

Joshua had been feeling paranoid when they returned to Shadow and had taken care to bring *Blackbeard* out of quantum space some distance from the asteroid. Even so, it was easy to see the expanding shell of debris where the asteroid had once been, torn apart by antimatter torpedoes launched by Hegemony starships. Some of the drifting clouds of debris looked to have come from starships, hunted down and destroyed by the invaders while trying to escape. The Funks had hit the system, blown apart the asteroid, and left again, leaving the debris as a silent warning to anyone who had thought that the secret colony was a safe place to hide from their wrath.

Few of the people on Shadow had been morally uptight citizens, even of societies where anarchy was the general rule. They'd been criminals, hunted by their own governments and every other government in the galaxy, or rebels from the Hegemony and a dozen other repressive powers. But one man's terrorist was another's freedom fighter. The Funks would have obliterated rebels from any other power with the same lack of compassion they would show to the Gobbles, or insurgents on Terra Nova. They'd probably sent the other governments a bill.

"They've mined local space," Karla said. She was quietly professional, betraying nothing of the passion she had shared with him over two long nights. Joshua found it easier to grasp than most; freighter crews got very close or they ended the voyage hating each other. He'd always found it easier to assign ships to married couples than singletons. "Nothing particularly subtle – they *wanted* the mines to be detected."

"Their version of sowing the ground with salt," Joshua muttered. "They wanted to make sure that the message was rubbed home. Thou shall not conspire against the Funky bastards."

He shook his head. Someone had definitely betrayed him, probably one of the pirates he'd pulled into his growing fleet. Or maybe one of the rebels was actually a long-term sleeper agent from the Hegemony. Some of the tricks the Galactics had developed had horrifying implications. It was possible to program someone to be an unwitting spy, leaving them unaware of their actions – and if tested under a lie detector, swearing that they were innocent because they *believed* that they were innocent.

But unless they'd had access to more information than was possible, they wouldn't have been able to wipe out the other bases, or even the rest of the Clunker fleet. The tiny fleet of freighters carrying his supplies wouldn't have been touched. And that left him with options, including some the Funks would never suspect. They might believe that they'd killed the pirate king, or at the very least scattered and unnerved his followers, but they were in for a surprise. Joshua smiled to himself, remembering the strange civilization that had existed inside the asteroid, and then looked over at Karla.

"Take us out of here," he ordered.

"Aye, sir," Karla said. She looked down at her console, before looking up at him again. "And where exactly are we going?"

"Point Pooh," Joshua said. They'd meet up with the remainder of the fleet, at least those who had stayed loyal, on the way. Some of the pirates probably wouldn't stop running until they reached a whole different sector, but the rebels had nowhere else to go. "And then we're going to Tauscher. It's time to give the Hegemony a very unpleasant surprise."

Chapter Thirty-Three

"I must say that Earth was not impressed with Third Garston," Admiral Sun said. "I spent far too much time soothing the nerves of old women of both genders."

"Neither was I," Tobias said. Garston had been settled long enough to have a first-class interstellar communications array. Right now, part of him was wishing that it had been accidentally destroyed during the invasion of the system. "It was just a reminder that our enemy is more inventive than we would prefer."

"The incident certainly disturbed our political masters," Sun confirmed. "It took hours of arguing to convince them to sign off on the transfer of the 4th Cruiser Squadron to the war front. That will have consequences back on Earth."

He wasn't explicit – for fear of interception, even with the best encryption programs in the galaxy – but Tobias knew what he meant. Earth's defences would rest in the hands of a single squadron of modern cruisers, a number of refitted seventh-hand starships purchased from the Galactics and a handful of gunboats that were meant to be working up for their own transfer to the war front. It was just possible that the two captured superdreadnoughts could also be pressed into service, but the last report had suggested that it would be at least six months before they were ready for even local defence. Besides, if Earth started building superdreadnoughts rather than cruisers, they'd be massively outgunned by the Hegemony.

But there would be little difference, he reminded himself, dryly. *We are massively outgunned by the Hegemony.*

"There have also been political consequences on Center," Sun added. "Some of the negotiations for loans and starship purchases have stalled. The Hegemony is still proclaiming its faith in total victory and you can bet your life that they won't pick up our tab if they win. Not all of the Galactics are badly spooked, but even the ones who are still willing to deal want collateral for any loans. And we don't have much to offer them. A couple of the bastards want us to sign *Garston* over to them. The Federation Council is divided on the question – if we accept, we lose all revenue from the system, but if the Hegemony takes it back..."

"We lose it anyway," Tobias agreed. "And simply denying it to the Hegemony doesn't really impact upon their ability to fund the war."

"Not so much as the Traders Alliance has," Sun said. "I've had teams of sociologists studying the question ever since they laid down the embargo on the Hegemony. Some believe that the Traders Alliance can afford to keep up the embargo for several years, others think that a few months would be enough to convince it to rethink its policy. It's really just a gigantic trade union and a union that conspicuously fails to look after the interests of its members is doomed. There are really too many factors for them to make a precise estimate."

"There always are," Tobias said. He had limited faith in sociologists, let alone the headshrinkers that infested the personnel departments of the Federation Navy. Most of them were purely civilian and never had any real understanding of the military mindset, doing more harm than good. "As always, perception is *so* much more important than reality."

He shrugged. "I believe that it is time to move ahead with Operation Doolittle," he said. "It carries risks of its own, but we need to re-establish the myth of human invincibility as quickly as possible. I'd also like to take First Strike Fleet forwards and deal with the remaining starships at Hammerfall. Recon missions have confirmed that the enemy ships came from that system."

"Despite the mines we laid in orbit," Sun said. "I understood that you opposed invading and occupying Hammerfall."

"Taking it would be pointless, once we reduced the defences and its ability to support a fleet," Tobias said. "Unlike Garston, there are no interstellar shipping lanes that rely on the planet as a base. The Funks would simply destroy everything in orbit before they left, leaving us without any gains to show for our losses. But if we take out the starships, we should throw them back on the defensive."

"And hope it's enough to unseat their Empress," Sun agreed. "We *have* been picking up reports of... social unrest on a dozen Hegemony worlds. The Empress appears to be firmly in control, but discontent is spreading. I think that our policy of raiding worlds connected to the major clans is starting to pay dividends."

"Let's hope that it pays off in a big way soon," Tobias said. "It was clear from their attempt to negotiate with Ambassador Li that they weren't serious about talking peace."

"Some of the diplomats wanted to accept the offer," Sun said, dryly. "The US State Department was very vocal on the subject. You'd think they'd have learned a few lessons from pretty much their entire existence, but..." He shrugged. "The President is made of sterner stuff, luckily for us. America was one of the major investors in Terra Nova, after all, and lost thousands of colonists to the Funks. But in the long term, public opinion may swing against the war. The Hegemony has been crowing to everyone who will listen about Third Garston."

"And elections are coming up in Britain and France," Tobias said. "At least the Hegemony didn't make their offer publicly."

"Some of the details leaked out," Sun admitted. "Probably from the State Department. The Funks would probably be forced to deny that they'd ever considered talking peace if challenged – the Empress's position would become untenable. I've been pressing for strong action to be taken against the leakers, but you know how hard it is to punish anyone for leaking information to the press in Washington. It may even have cost us our chance to end this war while we're ahead and the bastard reporters don't give a damn."

He shook his head. "I'll keep you informed of developments," he said. "There is a more serious matter that needs to be addressed. The Hegemony has filed a formal complaint against Earth in the Commune."

Tobias blinked. "Another one?"

"This one may be far more serious," Sun said. "According to the case they've filed, they have evidence to prove that human agents were behind the massive upsurge in piracy in their rear areas over the last few months."

"Unfortunately, there have been human pirates ever since we entered the interstellar community," Tobias said. He kept his voice under firm control. "And there are the Funk raiders who raid pretty much everyone they can, even the Cats. Are the Funks blamed for their actions?"

"You know that they are not," Sun said. It had been a sore point for years. The raiders were officially independent agents, but they had links to some of the Hegemony clans. Some of their operations had weakened local governments to the point where they'd been forced to accept an offer of 'protection' from the Hegemony. "But the Funks have managed to identify one of the humans. It's Captain Joshua Wachter, the CEO of Stellar Trading. That's a little more serious than a handful of ex-mercenaries who will be arrested the moment they return to human space."

Tobias nodded slowly, his mind racing. In truth, he'd expected a security leak the moment he'd heard that Wachter was recruiting pirates and rebels to his cause. But only Wachter – and Tobias himself – knew that Earth had provided the first starships and seed money to the pirates. Tobias had been careful, very careful. No one else had enough of the pieces to draw a link between their work for the CNO and the pirate raiders. Even the endless paperwork was deliberately misleading. The starships he'd given to the pirates had been listed as destroyed in gunboat training exercises. There should be nothing to *prove* that Earth was directly involved with the pirates.

"Wachter is not exactly Earth's favourite son," he said, mildly. There were still people in the Federation Navy who wanted to try him for treason, or kill him without bothering with a trial. It wasn't a particularly rational response, but rationality rarely overcame cold logic – or the fact that Wachter's refusal to be bound to Earth had come in handy over the last decade. The money and intelligence he'd sent home had been very helpful. "I hardly think that we can be held accountable for his actions."

"The Funks don't see it that way," Sun said, "and this time they may manage to sway some of the uncommitted Galactics onto their side. You know how they feel about pirates, even ones who only raid the shipping belonging to evil bastards. God forbid that anything should disturb their precious status quo. The Federation Council feels that we need to make a statement disowning Wachter – and putting a price on his head."

Tobias had known that it might come to that. He'd picked Wachter, rather than a random agent from SpecOps, because there *was* a strong case for Wachter being independent of Earth. After he'd formed his own company, he'd been careful to incorporate on a galactic tax haven rather than on Earth, evading the heavy taxes levelled on all businesses that drew in Galactic Credits. He'd certainly paid more than he would have owed, over the years, but various governments didn't see it that way. It was *their* job to determine how much their people should pay in tax.

Still, it pained him to cross that line. He'd known it might happen, he'd even warned Wachter of the danger, but still... it pained him. Betraying someone who had put their life on the line for Earth – at his personal request – didn't sit well with him. It happened, more often than anyone would care to admit, yet there were always consequences. Perhaps Wachter would tell all from a safe distance... no, Tobias knew better than that. Wachter had known the dangers from the first day he'd embarked on his career as a pirate king.

And Earth couldn't afford the full weight of Galactic opinion swinging against her.

"I have to agree," he said, feeling each word taste like ashes in his mouth. "We can disown him at once. Putting a price on his head might even encourage some of his associates to turn him in to Earth."

"The Hegemony can probably outbid us," Sun said, crossly. "But we have to try."

Tobias nodded. At least Stellar Trading wouldn't be immediately affected. The Canaries weren't threatened by pirates and were unlikely to allow the other Galactics to push them around; they'd probably stall on seizing

Wachter's assets for a few months, depending on who was doing the pushing. But in the long term... he hoped that Wachter had taken the chance to convert his holdings into untraceable currency and made provisions for his crews. The Hegemony wasn't likely to believe that Stellar Trading wasn't involved – an interstellar company would make an excellent front for a pirate operation – and they'd come down like a hammer on anyone who fell into their hands.

"Keep me informed," Tobias ordered. "Now, if you'll excuse me, I have an operation to plan."

"Of course, sir," Sun said. "Good luck."

His image vanished from the display, leaving Tobias shaking his head sadly. As a young recruit, he'd long believed that military service was primarily about honour, about fighting beside your fellows and never letting them down. A proper team of sailors – or soldier – would discover new reserves of courage rather than panicking and fleeing for their lives, leaving their comrades in the lurch. But as he'd grown older, and risen to ranks where playing the political game was more important than military competence, even genius, he'd become more cynical. He sent men and women out to fight and die on Earth's behest – and he'd known many of the dead personally – yet he'd never had to betray someone who trusted him.

Years ago, Jackson Sampson – nine years older than his brother – had become a Navy SEAL and served in Afghanistan. He'd died in combat fighting the Taliban, fighting to the finish; it hadn't been until much later that Tobias had discovered that the only reason the SEALs had been ambushed and forced to fight their way out was that a uniformed politician, fearful of the bad press that came from deploying the promised air support so close to so-called civilian populations, had ordered the pilots to remain firmly on the ground. Four SEALs had died and two more had been badly wounded, just so that an officer could feel good about himself. He should have been shot for gross incompetence. Instead, he was firmly positioned working for a firm that produced military hardware for the Pentagon. Tobias had taken a small measure of revenge by ensuring that everything they provided for the Federation

Navy was checked and rechecked, but it wasn't enough. He had wanted the man dead.

And now, older and wiser, he understood how the officer had felt.

He tapped his console, pushing the issue aside. "Commander Qadir, report to my office," he ordered. "We have an operation to plan."

* * *

"Are you sure that this is such a good idea?"

The Russian general looked at Adrienne as if she were something he'd scraped off his shoes. It had taken every bit of Adrienne's formidable persuasive abilities to convince the man to agree to be interviewed, and yet as soon as she'd arrived at the base he'd insisted on showing her the troops exercising on the training field. None of them were human. A dozen races were represented in their ranks, with a single glaring exception. There were no Funks at all.

"Your nation found it extremely difficult to hold down a small country with only a handful of ethnic and racial divisions," General Chekov said, finally. Adrienne had met dangerous men before, but the General was the first she'd met who might have been an outright sociopath. "I have been tasked to keep an entire *planet* under control and Earth has refused to forward me more troops. There is no choice, but to recruit local supporters, people who do not wish the Funks to return."

Adrienne couldn't disagree with his assessment. Earth had undergone a major panic attack as soon as the news of Third Garston had reached home. Judging from some of the reports, large parts of the human race expected a massive fleet of invincible superdreadnoughts to jump into orbit and bombard Earth into radioactive debris. The fact that the assault had been beaten off didn't seem to matter too much. Pundits had been pointing out gleefully that the Hegemony's total losses were tiny, compared to its entire navy. They'd been forced to keep silent about humanity's losses, but it didn't take an expert to realise that every human loss had a greater effect than every Hegemony loss.

"But the Funks themselves are not represented in your army," she said. "How do you expect them to react to us arming and training the others?"

"I do not expect them to react well to anything we will do," Chekov said, slowly. "Their districts have become armed camps. Gangs of every race have been practicing ethnic cleansing on their neighbours, whenever they think they can get away with it. We simply do not have the manpower to stop them from paying off every petty dispute over the last hundred years."

Adrienne snorted. "But your army might turn on the Funks," she pointed out. "Won't that just make us look bad before the Galactics?"

Chekov placed a hand on her shoulder, swinging her around to face him. "Let me put it as simply as I can," he said. "When the Funks occupied Terra Nova and enslaved thousands of humans, the Galactics did nothing. The Funks claimed a fig leaf of legality and the Commune used it as an excuse to avoid confronting the Hegemony. When the Funks started to slowly increase the pressure on Earth, what did the Commune do? Nothing. The Association's glory days are long over. Galactic opinion doesn't care what happens to us, so why should we care about what they think of us?"

He snorted. "You Americans always expect war to be clean," he added. "It should be a nice tidy affair, with only a few enemy killed and none of your own lost in combat. But war doesn't work out that way, does it? The Federation Council has ordered this world to be pacified. I do not have the manpower to convince everyone on this goddamned world to play nicely, so I am doing the only thing I can do to actually carry out my orders. And if the Funks don't like it...

"Tell me; when was the last time the Funks liked anything we did?"

"I see your point," Adrienne said. She could too, although she wasn't so inclined to dismiss Galactic opinion. It might have been difficult to restrain the Funks, but intervening against Earth would have to look a great deal easier. All the Galactics would have to do was threaten to

302

call in their markers and demand immediate repayment of their loans. "But do you feel that the locals can be trusted?"

"I have faith that none of them want the Funks to return and reassert control over this planet," Chekov informed her. "That should keep them motivated to work with us – or to put up a fight, should the Funks return to Garston. The recent battle concentrated a few minds on the prospect of hanging."

Adrienne grinned. "And on the fact they were going to be hanged?"

"But enough of this matter," Chekov added, thawing a little. "I'm not at liberty to talk about our current deployments, but I would be happy to discuss the early stages of the occupation. We've actually managed to pacify a few additional cities. We may have to start moving the Funks and isolating them from everyone else..."

"Maybe," Adrienne said. "But how do you intend to do it fairly?"

"We can't," Chekov admitted. "But since when were the Funks fair to everyone else?"

Chapter Thirty-Four

"Congratulations on your victory, Your Majesty."

"And thank you for your contribution," the Empress said. She'd claimed personal credit for the plan that had bled the humans at Garston. "Your position has been secured, for the moment."

Lady Dalsha nodded, careful not to betray her relief. The Empress would need a scapegoat for the defeats the Hegemony had suffered so far and she knew that she was the prime candidate. Ironically, having been disowned by her clan gave her a freedom shared by few others among the Hegemony. There was something to be said for living an independent life.

"We have also crippled the human raiding operation," the Empress added. Lady Dalsha wasn't so sure – the humans understood basic security far better than most Galactics – but there was no point in contradicting the Empress directly. "One hopes that we will shortly be able to reassert our position against the human invaders and evict them from our space."

"Yes, Your Majesty," Lady Dalsha said. Personally, she was less confident. The Empress might have proclaimed Third Garston a glorious victory, but it had cost – badly. At least the force's commander had had the sense to break off from Garston when human reinforcements had arrived. Intelligence hadn't been able to provide any definite figures for how many long-range missile pods the humans possessed, but no one wanted to find out the hard way that the humans had more than expected. Given enough time, someone would duplicate the human system, yet would it come in time to reshape the course of the war? "I have proposed two more plans for raiding human space."

"So I have seen," the Empress said. "My advisors inform me that cutting loose so many squadrons will weaken Hammerfall and allow the humans to claim the system. To lose another world would be a grave defeat...?"

She waited, inviting Lady Dalsha to have her say. The Empress's position was not enviable, not now that the humans were raiding other worlds along the borders, worlds that belonged to powerful clans whose interests were threatened. They might all be publicly allying themselves with the Empress, but in private they would be considering other options. What was their loyalty to the Hegemony when they faced – at the very least – massive expenditures in rebuilding the installations the humans had destroyed? An unfavourable peace could only be tolerated if it happened over the Empress' dead body.

In some ways, that would be the ideal solution. Few of the human weapons were really *new*, at least according to the Hegemony's contacts among the Galactics. They were really applications that the Association had either never considered or never put into practice, something that made a certain kind of sense. The Cats had been the unquestioned masters of the universe for thousands of years. They wouldn't want a new weapons system coming online that threatened their dominance. What if someone *did* develop a weapon that could blow apart a superdreadnought with a single shot? Every navy in the galaxy would be instantly rendered obsolete.

The study of human history hadn't found favour among the Hegemony, not when it was an article of faith that no other race had anything to teach the heirs to the galaxy. Human history was very short compared to the Cats, but a surprising amount had leaked out into the galaxy after the Galactics had realised that a rogue Cat had invited the humans to join the interstellar community. It was difficult to be sure – humans just didn't think like her people – yet it seemed that much of human history was based around developing new weapons that altered the balance of power. The steam-powered ironclad, the tank, the aircraft, the machine gun, the dreadnought, the aircraft carrier, the precision-guided missile… and even the atomic bomb. Even the human superpowers had been forced to press ahead with weapons development, if only because their competitors would certainly do the same, seeking something that would alter the balance of power in their favour.

And the Hegemony clans had completely skipped that part of history. They'd never had to advance beyond mounted riders and spears; even basic metalworking had been limited before the Cats arrived. And like most of the Galactics, the Hegemony had accepted the myth that the Association had taken technology as far as it could go. But...what if the Cats, with the long-term perspective granted by immortality, had seeded that myth throughout the galaxy? They would never have to worry about being overthrown if everyone believed that they could never be matched, let alone surpassed.

But what if the other Galactics *didn't* buy into the myth? The galaxy was a big place and even the Cats couldn't hope to watch it all. What if the other Galactics had been running their own research and development programs into surpassing the technology they'd received from the Cats? The thought was terrifying, for the Hegemony's supremacy rested upon brute force and a willingness to do whatever it took to maintain their power. And yet, of all the major powers, the Hegemony was the *least* capable of operating its own independent research and development programs. It was quite possible that the other Galactic powers had already built their own advanced weapons long before humanity exploded onto the galactic stage.

It didn't seem likely, viewed through bright red eyes. Given superiority over an outsider, the Hegemony's first step would be to make sure that that outsider understood that the Hegemony *was* superior, that their mere survival would be only on the Hegemony's terms. And yet it was true that other races didn't think like her own people. What if one of the Galactics had developed superior weapons and merely decided to keep them to themselves? The long-term plan to replace the Cats as masters of the universe might be doomed from the start...

She outlined her thoughts to the Empress, who didn't seem amused. Humanity simply didn't have the numbers to crush the Hegemony; they had a quantitative answer to qualitative superiority. But the Tarn, or the Melkot, or even the Yel-Throd... *they* could combine advanced technology with the numbers required to win a decisive victory. None of the brushfire wars had grown out of control because the combatants had known that victory would come at a staggeringly high cost, but with advanced weapons...that might change.

And even if the Galactics *hadn't* developed advanced weapons, there was no reason why the humans couldn't start selling their wares on the arms market.

"There is little we can do about that at the moment," the Empress said. "Our priority remains the defeat of the human race before some of the other Galactics decide to join the war on their side. Your planned operations are approved, but you will not be commanding them."

Lady Dalsha felt cold ice trickling down the back of her neck. The Empress might have decided that she needed a scapegoat immediately. Her position wasn't very strong, even if there *had* been a victory at Garston. Lady Dalsha had hoped that commanding the operations would give her a degree of protection, assuming that the humans didn't manage to kill her when they struck back. But there was one definite advantage for the Hegemony in humanity's limited number of ships. Technologically superior they might be, but they couldn't be in two places at once.

"I have given orders to withdraw three squadrons of superdreadnoughts and escorts from the Tarn border," the Empress said. "They will travel to a position near Hammerfall, where you will assume command of the ships and take them directly to Earth. Once in orbit, you will force the humans to surrender or systematically destroy every last piece of military hardware and industry in the system. The humans do not have a secondary shipyard complex – destroying their industry will certainly cripple their war effort. They will be forced to surrender or we will force them into a war of attrition."

Lady Dalsha had devised that original plan, but now she hesitated. "The Tarn have been fortifying their border," she warned. "They may take advantage of our weakness."

"Which is why we will not broadcast anything about this operation," the Empress said. "Officially, the superdreadnoughts are on routine patrol. The remaining ships in the sector will switch their IFF signals routinely, disguising their absence until it is far too late. And the Tarn do not appear to have developed any new weapons. They will be bogged down if they try to invade our space, giving us time to beat the humans and then turn on the Tarn."

"It should work," Lady Dalsha said, finally. "But what if it fails?"

"Neither of us will see the end of the war," the Empress said. She would throw Lady Dalsha to the wolves, but they wouldn't be satisfied with a mere outcast, not if three entire squadrons had been lost. It took two years to build a superdreadnought from scratch and the war had already destroyed or crippled twenty of the most powerful ships in the galaxy. Replacing what they'd lost would take decades. "I suggest you bear that in mind."

* * *

Markus painted a smile on his face as he stopped in front of the armed Marines guarding the Admiral's office. The summons to *Nimitz* had come during his rest period, after spending hours trying to put Grumble Squadron back together again and deflecting 'suggestions' from superior officers that perhaps it was time to disband the remains of Grumble and have her pilots and gunboats distributed to other squadrons. At least Admiral Sampson hadn't weighed in so far, but perhaps that was about to change. He could imagine no other reason for the Admiral to order him to report in person. Electronic communications worked perfectly for most discussions.

The Marines nodded and stepped aside, allowing him to pass through the hatch and into the office. It was smaller than Markus had expected, even though he'd known that human-built starships simply didn't have the colossal interior space of Association-designed superdreadnoughts. Some of the reports from the post-battle assessment teams crawling over the captured ships had made entertaining reading; Hegemony superior officers, it seemed, had huge quarters, including what appeared to be private mud baths.

It was hard to think of any human officer who would want the mud baths, but they'd probably take everything else if they could. The quarters for junior officers and enlisted crewmen were, as expected, tiny. Some things were universal.

Admiral Sampson looked up at Markus as he saluted, returning the salute before waving him to a chair. They'd met several times before, but Markus couldn't have said that he knew the Admiral socially. He'd had to report on the progress of the gunboat program, receive one of the medals a grateful Earth had granted to her pilots, and commend a handful of the maggots who'd fought at Third Garston. The survivors would never be called maggots again.

"Commander," Admiral Sampson said. "Captain Walsh is dead."

Markus looked up, sharply. He'd worked closely with Captain Walsh on *Formidable*; he'd been one of the few officers who had believed in the gunboats from the start. The program had now been amply justified, but losing him was still a blow. And if he was dead...

"*Formidable*," he said. He'd had friends on the ship. "Is she..."

"Intact," Sampson said. "The Funks managed to score a lucky hit that took out the main bridge. Commander Rogers took command and managed to pull the carrier out before we lost her, but he's too inexperienced with the gunboats to retain command. I'd like you to take Captain Walsh's position."

Markus stared at the Admiral. One rule he'd learned as a cadet was that if you declined promotion when it was offered to you, it was never offered to you again. An officer who considered himself unfit for higher position was likely to find his superiors agreeing with him. But command of *Formidable* would mean that he couldn't fly a gunboat any longer. The Captain had no business abandoning his ship to fight the enemy directly, not when his ship was the only way out of the target system for the gunboats. He would have to watch helplessly from a safe distance as the three squadrons went up against the enemy.

But it hadn't been a safe distance for Captain Walsh, had it?

"Grumble Squadron needs me," he said, finally. "Surely Commander Rogers could remain in command."

"I've ordered him transferred to *Pinafore*," Sampson said. "She needs a CO and Rogers has had considerable experience on destroyers. I think he'll do fine as her commander, but whoever commands *Formidable* has to have experience with gunboats, experience that tells him what they can and cannot do. And *Formidable* has been placed to one side for a special operation. She needs you in command."

It wasn't really a choice, Markus realised. Take command... or see his naval career stagnate and eventually decline. "I will take command," he said, finally. "But you do realise that my own command experience is limited to gunboats?"

"I have to balance the options," Sampson admitted. "Lieutenant-Commander Spinner is also being promoted and will take up the post of XO. He was earmarked for the position when Walsh or Rogers went to *Lexington*, once she finishes her trials and is declared ready to join the fleet. I think you'll get along."

His voice hardened. "And if you have problems with each other, I expect you to button them up and do your duty," he added. "This is war. I don't have time for officers who let their personal issues get in the way of serving the navy."

"No, sir," Markus said. He had no real problem with Spinner, although the young man had come up through a tactical career path rather than as a gunboat pilot. That would probably change when there were enough gunboats and carriers to allow officers to be selected with the ideal mix of experience. "You mentioned an operation for us?"

Sampson nodded and tapped a key. "This remains in confidence," he said. "You'll be given sealed orders before you depart, but you are not to discuss this with anyone – including your wife – until you are safely in quantum space. If we can free up a handful of other ships to serve as an escort, I'll brief their commanders personally." He lifted one hand and pointed at a single red star floating in the midst of the star chart. "Your target: Hegemony Prime."

"Their homeworld?" Markus asked. "But they must have it heavily defended."

"They do," Sampson said. "Most of our data comes from before we hit Terra Nova, so it is quite possible that some of it will be outdated, but they have at least forty orbital fortresses and a sizable fleet stationed in the system. Intelligence thinks that they will have scraped up every assault shuttle within fifty light years to give them some counter-gunboat capabilities. They could also have pulled in starships from their inner worlds..."

He shrugged. "You'll have to carry out reconnaissance before you launch the attack," he added. "We'll give you the latest recon drones we've produce, including some that haven't been risked in action before now. Your overall objective is to destroy their primary industrial complex here" – an icon on the display started blinking – "and embarrass the Empress. It's always difficult to untangle their politics, but we have good reason to believe that several clans would be financially destroyed if the complex went up in smoke. Added to the chaos caused by the Trader Alliance placing an embargo on the Hegemony and it's quite possible that their entire economy would collapse and a civil war break out.

"I won't lie to you, Captain. It's also quite possible that this is a suicide mission. Even if they haven't reinforced the defences since the war began, you'll still be facing their most complex network of sensor stations, backed up by their most formidable fleet. That's one of the other reasons for hitting their homeworld; if they decide they can free up some of their defending starships and send them against us, it would tip the odds in their favour. The entire navy is counting on you."

"I understand," Markus said, feeling a little dazed. Command of a starship was one thing, but a suicide mission right into the heart of enemy territory...? "I won't let you down."

"I'm going to give you complete freedom in planning your operation," Sampson said. "You will have access to the latest intelligence we possess, although they've been very good at sealing off their system since the war began. Don't take anything for granted. What happened in the recent battle should remind us all that our enemy isn't stupid."

"Yes, sir," Markus agreed. A thought had already crossed his mind. "With your permission, sir, I'd like to request a company of Marines. I've had an idea."

"I'll cut them orders at once," Sampson assured him. He smiled, as if he'd thought of something more pleasant than suicide missions. "And as for the matter of Grumble Squadron..."

Markus hesitated. "Sir?"

"I feel that the name has earned a chance to live on," Sampson said. He smiled as Markus relaxed in obvious relief. "Some of the reporters have been telling tales about your heroism and kids back home are pretending to fly gunboats in mock battles. New pilots and gunboats are already on their way, but you'll have to draw pilots from the other squadrons to replenish your losses. I need you on your way as soon as possible."

"Yes, sir," Markus said. He'd have to check up on *Formidable*, but the ships had been designed for easy repair. It was possible that the carrier was already ready to return to active service. Any longer than a week and the Admiral would probably have assigned another carrier to the mission. "I'll make sure we leave quickly."

He left the office, shaking his head. How was he going to explain it to Carola?

Chapter Thirty-Five

Nimitz exploded out of quantum space in a blaze of light, heading right towards Hammerfall and the remaining Hegemony starships near the planet. Her consorts followed, not even trying to hide, as they spread out and slipped into formation. Behind the main body of the fleet, three carriers and a dozen freighters emerged through the quantum gate, which faded away after the final ships returned to normal space. Every Funk outpost in the system would have picked up their arrival and know that the Federation Navy had returned to Hammerfall.

"Report," Tobias ordered, as the fleet shook down. He'd considered coming out of quantum space closer to the planet, but the strange disruptions in quantum space near the system had dissuaded him. They'd just have to rely on their technology and skill to defeat their enemies. "What do we have?"

"Two of the enemy squadrons appear to be missing," Commander Sooraya Qadir reported. "The remainder are coming to life now."

Tobias nodded, unsurprised. They'd given the enemy plenty of warning before the two fleets entered engagement range. Even a half-crewed ship would have time to get ready to repel attack. Curiously, the sole remaining enemy superdreadnought in the system looked to have been completely powered down, even though she was on the front lines. Maybe the enemy had believed that she was beyond repair, or perhaps they intended to tow her through quantum space to a repair yard. Tobias's last visit to the system had wrecked all of the shipyards and industrial nodes that would have normally supported the fleet. Judging from the state of the fixed defences, the mines he'd left behind had taken their toll on enemy installations.

"They're sweeping drones through low orbit," Sooraya added. "I'm not entirely sure why."

"Probably trying to trigger the mines," Tobias commented. It wasn't a bad idea, if someone on the other side had figured out that some of the mines were triggered by active sensor pulses at very close range. Losing a drone, no matter how expensive, had to be a bargain compared to losing an entire ship. But not *all* of the drones were programmed to expend themselves on enemy sensors. It was quite possible that the Hegemony would declare victory, only to discover that they'd only accounted for a third of the mines. "Mark the drones down for attention once we've dealt with the rest of the ships."

He studied the display as the two fleets converged. The Hegemony ships, some badly damaged after the Battle of Hammerfall or Third Garston, were forming into a simple defensive formation, linking their point defences together into a single coherent unit. Tobias had half-expected them to retreat into quantum space after taking stock of the fleet bearing down on them, but they probably had orders to fight to the death. After giving the Federation Navy a bloody nose at Third Garston, the Hegemony was pumping the victory for all it was worth. The last thing they wanted was another defeat, particularly of a seemingly superior force by an inferior.

Tobias smiled. He was determined to deny them another victory, even if it meant occupying Hammerfall for a short period. The world was still largely useless to the Federation Navy and that wouldn't change, not when the Funks would destroy anything left in the system before pulling out or surrendering. Perhaps they would simply surrender, rather than trying to force him to bleed his fleet white. There was nothing left on Hammerfall worth the loss of so many personnel in a futile defence.

"Time to engagement, seven minutes," Sooraya reported. "Enemy ships are turning and attempting to close on attack vector."

Tobias frowned. That was odd, odd enough to puzzle and worry him after Third Garston. The smartest thing the Funks could do was cut their losses and retreat from the system, leaving the remaining defenders to blow the installations and surrender. Some Funk propaganda claimed that humans had slaughtered prisoners out of hand, but the Galactic reporters had countered it by running extensive interviews with POWs who reported good treatment. It was certainly better treatment than they'd received from their own leaders; ONI had picked up on reports that several Funks had been shot for losing battles. How long would it be, Tobias asked himself, until the Funk commanders became more terrified of their own Empress than of the human invaders?

"Maybe they don't dare retreat without trying to bleed us," he said, slowly. "Or maybe they have a trick up their sleeve."

He shrugged. There was no need to worry about defending a planet this time. If the odds grew too unfavourable, he'd pull the fleet out and leave the Funks in possession of a ruined system. But those missing ships worried him. There weren't enough of them to pull off another surprise like Third Garston – unless the Funks had additional reinforcements the recon ships had missed – yet they could cause havoc if they slashed into humanity's lines. Earth itself should be able to stand them off, but no other colony world had serious defences. They only had a handful of ships from various Galactics working up before they were added to the battle line.

The thought made him scowl. They'd been able to purchase hundreds of ships from the Galactics – mainly using revenue from Garston, or taking out loans from the bigger powers – but none of the second-hand ships had been armed with the latest weaponry. The Funks would face them on even terms until they were refitted, giving them a decisive advantage if they managed to get back on their feet and come blazing for Earth. It didn't help that some of the Galactic used-starship dealers had played down the age or condition of their ships until it was too late to refuse to pay. One day, he promised himself, there would be a reckoning.

"Alert all ships," he ordered, calmly. "They are to open fire the moment they enter weapons range."

"Aye, sir," Sooraya said. "Weapons range in two minutes."

The Funks were still picking up speed, the healthier ships setting their speed to match their damaged consorts. It was surprising behaviour from the Funks, even though Tobias had witnessed some of them sacrificing themselves to save others in the past. Just another reminder, he told himself, that some of the Funks were capable of more than humanity would prefer to admit. They weren't completely alien, not like some of the weirder beings in the Association. Some of them were so alien that it was impossible to hold a rational conversation with them about anything. Even the Cats had problems talking to them.

"Weapons locked on target," the Captain said. "Firing...now."

Tobias watched in disbelief. The human phase cannon were still rotating through the various modulations, but it seemed as if the Funks had *no* vulnerable frequency any longer. They still weren't firing themselves, even when the human ships closed into their range and started launching antimatter torpedoes at them. And yet their shield seemed to be almost impenetrable. It was impossible...

"Sir, I have a report from battle analysis," Sooraya said. "They confirm that the Funks have established inner and outer shield layers. The best guess is that they've cannibalized the shield generators from wrecked craft to produce a second deflector bubble around their ships."

Tobias cursed. A simple counter, provided one didn't mind not being able to fire back at the targets. Each starship configured its shield generators to provide a path for the phase cannon to shoot through without hammering their own shields, but two different shields on two different frequencies made it impossible to open fire. Getting two shield generators to work together was tricky – the human researchers hadn't even tried, having found their own way to generate improved shields – yet the Funks had apparently solved the problem.

He hastily thought back to the briefings when they'd discussed Funk countermeasures to new and advanced human weapons. There were other problems than simply making it impossible to fire back when two shield generators were paired. If he recalled correctly, there would be weak spots where the two shields actually interfered with each other, although a starship with enough power to generate two different shields might be able to compensate for such weaknesses. Or maybe not. Some of the ships hit by antimatter torpedoes were already showing power fluctuations, suggesting that they were running their shield generators over the limits. It was a dangerous risk; if the generators overloaded, the shields might vanish without having to be battered down.

"Continue firing with antimatter torpedoes," he ordered. "Scan for weak points and attempt to target them with phase cannon."

The human fleet passed through the Funk formation, just as several Funk ships dropped their inner shields and opened fire. Their phase cannon lashed out at human cruisers, forcing them to slip into evasive patterns even as their own phase cannon dug deep into enemy hulls. Warning lights flared up on the display as the Funks unloaded hundreds of antimatter torpedoes towards the human ships, driving them away from their targets. Their targeting had improved too, Tobias noted absently, although it was rare to risk using torpedoes at such close range. Human torpedoes had already smashed a number of Funk ships.

One of the cruisers, *Sydney*, twisted in an attempt to avoid a spread of torpedoes, but it was too late. Nearly thirty torpedoes slammed into her shields, battering them down through sheer weight of numbers and destroying the entire ship in a blinding flash. There was no hope of survivors. Tobias snapped orders and the fleet reformed, firing a spread of antimatter torpedoes back to distract the enemy as they prepared for another run. Some of the Funk ships had lost their dual shield generators, either through overloads or direct hits, leaving them vulnerable. Human tactical officers started marking them down for engagement as the fleets started to close again, even though the Funks were heading away from the planet. Tactically, they'd already won the battle, Sampson had to admit. The Funks inflicted another loss on the already overstretched Federation Navy.

317

"Take us back towards them and engage as soon as we enter weapons range," he ordered. Human starships still had a high tactical speed advantage, enough to let him pick and choose the best attack vector. The Funks couldn't outrun them unless they retreated into quantum space and abandoned the planet. "Order the freighters to advance on attack vector" – he designated a course on his console – "and attempt to bluff them."

He hesitated. "And transmit a demand for surrender," he added. "Maybe they'll decide to surrender instead of continuing the fight."

There was a pause as the Hegemony ships altered course again. "No response, sir," Sooraya reported. "They're still under tight control."

The Hegemony ships opened fire as soon as the human fleet came into range, forsaking their reinforced shields for firepower. Tobias braced himself as an antimatter torpedo struck *Nimitz's* forward shields, only to be deflected away as the starship lashed out at the nearest Hegemony battlecruiser. The enemy ship staggered out of line and fell astern of the fleet, spinning helplessly in space. Tobias designated a pair of Marine assault shuttles to be dispatched to receive surrender, if the enemy was interested in doing so. It was possible that the crew would wait until the shuttles were close to the hull and blow their fusion plants, taking the shuttles with them to a fiery grave.

"Enemy ships altering course and attempting to evade," Sooraya said. "I think...correction; enemy ships attempting to open a quantum gate."

"Take us away from their formation," Tobias snapped. It was theoretically possible to overload a quantum gate and create an explosion with the force of a small supernova. No one had actually done it in recorded Galactic history – unless the Cats had done it during their first explorations and covered it up from their clients – but if the Hegemony intended to try, they would wipe out First Strike Fleet in the blast. "Prepare to make an emergency jump into quantum space."

The two fleets separated at terrifying speed as the quantum gate blossomed open in front of the enemy ships.

One by one they retreated into quantum space and vanished, leaving humanity in possession of the system. The quantum gate closed behind them and vanished. Tobias let out a sigh of relief. They weren't going to die today. There was a theoretical proposal for disrupting quantum space, making it impossible for a fleet to escape an enemy trap, but it had never been tested. He'd ordered it held in reserve, just in case Earth herself was threatened by the enemy.

"Broadcast a signal to the planet," he ordered. "Assure them that we will treat them well if they surrender – and if they refuse, we will simply leave them here to die on the vine."

The recon ships had deduced that the Funks had attempted to evacuate most of the remaining fortresses, an exercise fraught with peril in a mined orbit. There would be a skeleton crew left onboard to ensure that the Funks maintained their claim to Hammerfall, although under the circumstances Tobias wasn't sure why they'd bothered. The installations around Hammerfall had already been destroyed, leaving only the cloudscoops and a handful of asteroid miners. Destroying them might have irritated the other Galactics, though Hammerfall rarely supplied fuel to anyone else. It was nowhere near as connected to the galactic trade lanes as Garston.

"I'm picking up a response," Sooraya said. "The current commander of the fortresses is prepared to surrender if his personnel are repatriated to the Hegemony."

Tobias blinked. "*His?*"

"Apparently so," Sooraya said. "Intelligence doesn't have a file on him, but there are a number of male senior officers in the Hegemony Navy – just not very many of them."

"Interesting," Tobias mused. And also dangerous, he admitted, privately. The Hegemony females were worse than the human patriarchs who thought that women should be left barefoot and pregnant while slaving over a kitchen stove. Even now, there were parts of Earth where women were very much second-class citizens. Their men claimed that women were supposed to be under men, unsuited for the rough and tumble of political life, or even controlling their own destinies. The Hegemony females actually had some measure of *proof* for their claims. Any Funk male who rose to become a senior officer had to be far *better* at his job than a female officer. At least the Funks didn't have any tradition of officers sleeping their ways to important posts.

He shrugged. "Tell him that we will return his personnel to the Hegemony once the war is over," he said. "Until then, they will be well-treated in a POW camp on Terra Nova or Earth – any of them who wish to defect will be welcome to do so."

"Yes, sir," Sooraya said. "Should we add a warning against murdering their own crewmen?"

Tobias nodded. Some high-ranking Funk POWs had murdered subordinate officers, for no reason that made sense to the human mind. Tobias was inclined to wonder if they'd been fearful that their subordinates would pay off a few private scores now that they had been reduced to equality, but at least two of the murders hadn't even made that much sense. The sociologists had finally suggested that the Funks had wanted to kill the weak. Tobias had privately given orders that all such murders were to be prevented. One way or another, they would make the human race look bad.

A long moment passed as messages raced to and from the planet. "He's accepted your terms," Sooraya said. "They don't want to lower their shields, however, until they receive assurances that we've disarmed the mines."

"Unsurprising," Tobias said. "We'll get around to them once we've finished securing the system. They can keep their shields up until then."

He tapped his console, assigning a handful of starships to take up defensive positions. The Funks had used the defence of Hammerfall for propaganda, even though the system had been rendered effectively useless. Now that humanity had taken the system, the Empress would be under immense pressure to launch a counterattack as soon as possible. ONI had been tracking enemy transmissions and noted that several more squadrons were being deployed to face the human advance, forming a defensive line that would combine with the fixed defences to stall the human fleet well before it reached Hegemony Prime. It was a pity that the deep-strike concept remained a concept for the moment, but there was little hope for developing it until thousands of additional missiles were produced. The last report had warned of delays in missile production facilities.

Still, Hammerfall's capture would look good, at least on paper. The Funks themselves would probably know better, but the Galactics – and human public opinion – was unlikely to see anything other than another world falling to the human advance. Once again, a fleet numerically superior to its opponents had been defeated, even if it hadn't been as crushing a victory as the Battle of Terra Nova. They'd even captured another half-wrecked superdreadnought. Given enough time, the raw material of the hull would be broken down and turned into new weapons and starships for the Federation Navy.

"Organise the reporters so that they can inspect the captured fortresses," he ordered. PR reared its ugly head once again. At least most of the reporters from Earth were sensible – and those that weren't had their reports heavily censored before they were transmitted home. The Galactics were less sensible, but they didn't have the sources human reporters could develop. One particularly enterprising reporter had apparently seduced both a missile tech and a Russian soldier on Garston. "And then see if we've captured a tachyon beam array. If so, I'll use it to report to Earth."

He allowed himself a grim smile as the fleet stood down from battlestations. They'd won – and the Hegemony had taken another blow – but how long could they go on? What had an ancient king, back before the Roman Empire, said about a costly victory?

One more victory like Hammerfall and Earth might be ruined...

Chapter Thirty-Six

"That's interesting," Joshua said. "Are you sure about this?"

The rodent-like alien nodded. Plenty of pirates had been scared by the destruction of Shadow and the – presumed – capture and interrogation of the habitat's population, but the intelligence networks that attempted to track potential targets were still active. The pirates, Joshua had discovered, beat even the Association hands down when it came to building multiracial coalitions. They'd managed to seduce or corrupt a vast range of bureaucrats from a dozen different races.

"There is little room for error," the alien assured him. Like the crab, he was an information broker first and foremost, although he had a less stellar reputation. "I actually had their drive signatures monitored. Three squadrons of superdreadnoughts have departed the sector; the remaining two squadrons are attempting to convince observers that all five superdreadnought squadrons are still in the sector."

Joshua frowned, looking down at the raw data. Every starship had a unique drive signature, but it was possible to distort it to the point where it was difficult to positively identify the starship at long range – and few would dare to slip close to a superdreadnought just to get a more accurate read of its drive fields. And yet the report had the ring of truth. The only reason he could think of for the Funks attempting to convince observers that they were still at full strength was that they were no longer at full strength – and *that* meant that three squadrons of superdreadnoughts had gone somewhere else. But where?

There was no logical reason for the superdreadnoughts to be deployed against the pirates, even if the Hegemony believed that Joshua and his men were still a threat. Superdreadnoughts were designed for destroying enemy fleets and invading hostile planets, not for routine anti-piracy operations. They would have no trouble swatting any pirate ship that came into range, but any pirate ship worthy of the name would smell a rat and start running long before the superdreadnought had a chance to blow them away. Fifteen superdreadnoughts were massive overkill against pretty much anything short of another interstellar power... and the last thing the Funks would want was to tempt the Tarn into crossing their border and snatching a number of undefended worlds. In fact, the performance – the attempt to convince everyone that fifteen superdreadnoughts were still there – might be aimed at the Tarn. They weren't the most powerful of the Galactics, but with the Hegemony on the verge of collapse and fighting one war against Earth, the Tarn might be able to topple the Funks and destroy the Hegemony.

And yet...where had the superdreadnoughts gone?

A human might have been tempted to lay a trap for the Tarn – and the Funks were more imaginative than anyone would have preferred, a lesson Joshua had learned when they'd attempted to trap and destroy his fleet. But they wouldn't want to risk playing games when the Hegemony was in a dangerous situation, not when the game could spill out of control. And besides, assuming that they'd intended to lure the Tarn into a trap, why wouldn't they put up a show of weakness instead of strength? It made little sense. Applying human logic to aliens was often nothing more than a way to be wrong with confidence, but even the most cunning Funk wouldn't want to risk expanding the war. The Hegemony had too many enemies.

"I'll want the hard data, of course," he said. "I assume you'll want the regular payment?"

"Yes, My Lord," the alien said. His race had been spread throughout the Association by the Cats, although they had never developed spaceflight on their own or built an empire like the Funks – or humanity. There were enclaves in a hundred different Galactic powers, giving them unprecedented access to information and technology. Some of them had made common cause with humanity right from the start, even though they preferred to work indirectly.

The Funks didn't treat the enclaves on their worlds particularly well. "And I wouldn't object to information on your operations either."

Joshua snorted. There were limits to how far he trusted any information broker. One of them had probably sold Shadow out for a large infusion of cash. Why would the Funks bother with torture when a few thousand credits would loosen lips? Even in the midst of a growing economic crisis, the Funks could easily scrape up enough galactic currency to make someone rich for life.

"Maybe later," he said. The encounter suit he wore concealed everything human about him, but someone with access to information from Shadow could probably guess at his race. This asteroid was even less civilised than the previous asteroid, if such a thing were possible. If they realised just who and what he was, they'd sell him out to the Funks before a Funk battlecruiser turned up with orders to blow the asteroid into a cloud of debris. "Here."

He passed a loaded credit chip over to the information broker and retreated out of the doorway, into the asteroid's massive cavern. It was a crude piece of work, generating gravity by rotation rather than using a standard gravity generator, inhabited by criminals, drifters and rebels with nowhere else to go. He'd been careful to bring along a small army of bodyguards just to ensure his own safety, although no one could be relied upon completely. The Funks had put a massive price on his head...

...And so had Earth. Joshua had known that that would happen, sooner or later, but it still hurt. He knew that the Federation Council had had little choice. One thing that annoyed all of the major galactic powers was piracy – and Joshua had become the greatest pirate in the galaxy's recent history. It didn't matter to them that it had been a military tactic aimed at keeping the Hegemony off-balance, at crippling the Hegemony's economy, not when the effects of Joshua's activities had spread far beyond the Hegemony's stars. Admiral Sampson had told him, right at the start, that he might be declared rogue, that Earth would disown him and put a price on his head. It was funny how much it still hurt, when the bad feeling he'd created by going to the stars and building his own commercial empire had washed off him like water off a duck's back.

He smiled, rather bitterly. *Who had it been who'd said that patriotism was the last refuge of the scoundrel?*

The asteroid was poorer than Shadow had been – and almost certainly known to the Funks, even if they hadn't destroyed it – but it had been able to supply some of the weapons and equipment he needed. He'd worried about the risk of exposing himself to detection – someone with a brain might put together his different purchases and realise that he was supporting an entire fleet, not to mention a rebel army – yet there had been little choice. His plans had been too far advanced when Shadow had been destroyed and pulling back now might have been disastrous for the rebels. Some of the Gobble cells wouldn't get the word in time and launch their uprisings without support from his fleet. It would be a nasty shock for the Funks, but they'd still control the orbitals and they'd be able to bombard the rebels into submission.

Shaking his head, he allowed the bodyguards to lead him back to *Blackbeard*. It was only a few hours to the nearest interstellar communications array, and then they would be free to advance on Tauscher. One way or another, the Hegemony's supreme self-confidence wouldn't survive the war. Who knew? Maybe it would shock them into becoming a civilised race.

* * *

"You do realise that they disowned us?"

"Of course," Joshua said. He'd been the only person mentioned by name, but then he was one of the few humans – at least prior to the war – with a reputation that had spread beyond the Nine Stars. The remainder of his human personnel would probably be able to return home and slip back into civilian life – or go to the Federation Navy, if they chose to remain in service – but he'd never be able to go home. At least the people who worked for him would be safe. He'd passed ownership of the company to one of his subordinates, creating the impression that she'd managed to launch a coup and take over against his will. It would probably serve as a plausible motive for turning pirate. "But does that really mean that we don't have any obligations to Earth?"

"They sent us out here to do their dirty work," Kang grunted. He'd spent most of the last month working with the Gobble rebels, helping them learn how to use their new weapons. "And if they catch us, they'll put us in front of a wall and shoot us out of hand."

"We knew the risks when we took the job," Joshua said, flatly. He had his own doubts, but he'd never had much sympathy for people who signed contracts without reading the small print first. At least Admiral Sampson hadn't lied to him. "Those superdreadnoughts have to be going to the war front."

Tracking Hegemony starships wasn't easy – the only way to locate them without maintaining a permanent recon post in a system was to track their transmissions – but it was clear that a number of starships were moving toward the war front. The Hegemony had clearly decided that taking the risk of thinning the defences on their other borders was preferable to admitting defeat and asking for reasonable terms from the human race. From a human point of view, the incredibly wealthy and greedy Hegemony wouldn't be giving up anything more than a couple of rebellious planets by conceding human independence, but it would be a colossal loss of face for the Empress. The kind of mindset that would take the risk of the war suddenly turning into a four-against-one conflict rather than merely accepting reasonable terms was alien to him, although some humans had shown a similar desire to keep fighting against all logic and reason. Hitler and Napoleon, for example, had both kept fighting even when they could have won a liveable peace.

Karla snorted. "Don't you think that ONI will already know about them?"

"I don't know," Joshua said. He'd often shared information with ONI before he'd become a pirate, but he didn't know just how widespread humanity's intelligence network in the Hegemony actually was. Certainly ONI had concentrated on spreading the net as widely as possible, yet... just how many assets could they have hundreds of light years from Earth? And besides, he'd never been particularly impressed with human intelligence services even before First Contact. It was too easy for analysts back home to assume they knew everything when they were only looking at a small part of the puzzle. "I do know that if they *don't* know about the newcomers the Federation Navy is going to be in for a nasty surprise."

"Assuming that they challenge the Federation Navy," Kang said. He grinned, unpleasantly. "First rule of combat; fight where your opponent is weak, not where he is strong. Why send fifteen superdreadnoughts against a force that has already destroyed or captured ten of them when there are nine vulnerable targets behind the lines?"

Joshua blanched. "You mean *Earth?*"

"But Earth has to be heavily defended," Karla countered. "Surely the Federation Navy has reserves there..."

"Maybe," Joshua said. He wasn't so sure. The Federation Navy kept its exact strength secret, but Joshua had had plenty of experience with constructing, purchasing and maintaining starships. Mentor had brought some mobile fabricators to Earth to assist in human development and expansion, but those – and the additional ones Earth had acquired since – had limits. Building the fleet that had retaken Terra Nova and given the Funks a bloody nose might have only been possible by skimping on planetary defences. Earth's population might have been much more armed than it had been before First Contact, yet no amount of weapons in private hands could defeat a force holding the high orbitals. "But we have to warn them. Even if they already know..."

"But that would allow them to locate us," Kang said. "And they would know that you were alive."

Joshua shrugged. "I doubt anyone believes that I died on Shadow," he said. The Funks had proclaimed his death, but they hadn't managed to produce a body. Deep-space combat rarely produced bodies, so the Funk claims wouldn't be disbelieved on that ground, but Joshua had been quick to contact the rebels. They'd know better – and so would any skilled information broker. "Besides, we'll use one of the spammer hack workarounds we took from Earth. They won't be able to locate us in time."

He stood up. "Take the helm," he ordered. "We have work to do."

"Yes, boss," Kang said. "Do you intend to let Earth know about Tauscher?"

"It would only upset them," Joshua replied. "Besides, someone might intercept the signal and let the cat out of the bag too early. We'll just warn them about the superdreadnoughts and nothing else."

Admiral Sampson had given him a copy of a limited edition dictionary to serve as the base for a simple substitution cipher. It had amused hell out of Joshua when he'd discovered that even the most advanced Galactics hadn't been able to eliminate spam email, despite having far more control over the tachyon-burst network than any of Earth's pre-Contact computer authorities. No one would think twice about a message that tried to sell Admiral Sampson pornography, but Sampson would know what it meant. Fifteen superdreadnoughts were heading for humanity's lines, perhaps even heading for Earth. He would have time to prepare a reception committee.

The asteroid had no quantum gate to use as a transmitter, so *Blackbeard* made the flight through quantum space to the nearest gate in the sector. It had originally been built by the Cats, unlike most of the later gates in the Hegemony, and was over five thousand years old, far older than anything built by humanity. The gates built by the younger races didn't have the same elegance as the Cat-built gates – and they wore out far quicker than the original gates. It was quite possible to imagine the slow decay of the network until the association finally collapsed into rubble, leaving countless stranded civilizations in its wake. How long would it be until someone rebuilt a galaxy-spanning power?

"No sign of any unfriendly patrols," Karla reported, as they emerged through the gate. For some reason of their own, the Cats had installed it at the very edge of the system, rather than close enough to the planet to make commercial shipping economical. It was almost as if they'd been trying to hide the gate, but any race with even the faintest awareness of tachyons could have detected its presence unless they shut it down completely and allowed it to drift off the network. According to the data they'd downloaded from the Association Almanac, the system was completely uninhabited. It was a mystery that Joshua would have liked to solve, one day. But that would have to wait until the end of the war. "You can spam the network at will."

Joshua chuckled. He'd prepared the message in flight. All he needed to do was upload it to the quantum gate, pay the small fee for transmission, and then depart long before the message reached Earth. The access code he'd added to the message would get it through most of Earth's spam filters completely undetected.

"Spamming now," he said, tapping his console. There was a slight pause while the message uploaded and was then scanned for viruses by the automated gate security protocols. It was harder to transmit viruses through the network than spam messages, but that didn't stop some of the Galactics from trying. There were tales of entire civilizations brought to a sudden halt by a single carefully designed computer virus. Joshua had never placed much credence in them, but it *was* theoretically possible. It was a pity no one had worked out how to do it to the Hegemony, at least not without humanity getting clear blame. "Message away."

He smiled as Karla brought *Blackbeard* around and reopened the quantum gate, taking them back through the vortex into quantum space. Even if the Funks *were* patrolling the unnamed system, they wouldn't have a hope of intercepting them in time. The cruiser raced away from the system, using the energy storms to hide her trail. It wouldn't be long until they met up with the rebel fleet and then headed to Tauscher. Joshua had never planned on a direct confrontation with the Hegemony until he'd realised that he had an opportunity, and yet... now he was committed, he had doubts. A failure could destroy his entire fleet.

But if he succeeded...at least one world would accept him after he'd been declared rogue.

"Rebel fleet coming into view now," Karla said. Joshua stood up and crossed over to the main display screen. The rebel fleet, five hundred starships from a hundred different worlds, was waiting for him. Some were crewed by pirates who expected loot, unaware of Joshua's real plans; others were crewed by rebels willing to fight and die for liberation from the Hegemony. It was an impressive sight, larger – in numbers – than the entire Federation Navy. But a single superdreadnought could trash them without working up a sweat. They'd have problems dealing with a squadron of heavy cruisers. There was a *lot* of room for the entire plan to go horribly wrong.

"Inform them that it's time to move," Joshua said. The pirates hadn't been told the objective either, just that they'd have an excellent chance to loot if they joined up and followed orders. There was plenty of wealth in the Tauscher System, enough to satisfy the survivors. And some of them would probably run when they discovered just where they were going. They wouldn't get anything from the mission. "Our target is waiting for us. Let's go."

Chapter Thirty-Seven

"Transition in three... two... one... zero!"

Joshua braced himself as *Blackbeard* exploded out of the quantum gate, weapons primed and ready. The Funks had only stationed a handful of automated weapons platforms near the gate – they were functionally illegal, after all – and they were picked off before they had a chance to open fire. A small customs station floating next to the massive gate was eliminated rapidly with its occupants still screaming for help from the ships guarding the planet. Behind *Blackbeard*, the remainder of the fleet rapidly followed her into normal space.

"All targets destroyed," Karla said, as the fleet started to shake down into something resembling a formation. "Picking up seventeen Type-5 orbital weapons platforms and twenty-two starships, led by a light cruiser squadron. Other ships in the system appear to be freighters, but some results are inconclusive."

"Keep an eye on them," Joshua ordered. Now that they were in action, he felt his doubts drain away. Some of the ships picked up moving to and from the asteroid belts might be warships, but they were too far away to be immediately dangerous. "Hack the gate – take out their interstellar communications node."

"Done," Karla said. The Funks could still transmit messages begging for help, but it would take weeks for them to reach anywhere with a Hegemony Navy Base. They'd never bothered to give the system a communications array that could bypass the quantum gate if necessary, something that was going to cost them dearly. "Enemy fleet is forming up into a defensive formation."

Joshua smiled, even though he knew that the coming battle was going to hurt. The Hegemony had seen fit to take advantage of the Gobbles, using them to create a space-based infrastructure that was superior to what Earth had built in fifteen years. But they hadn't realised, perhaps because of their own inability to understand everything they'd inherited from the Cats, just how much the Gobbles would learn from their servitude. The defences of the Gobble homeworld looked tough until one considered how much of it was built and maintained by the teddybear-like aliens.

"Inform our friend that he can begin transmitting," he ordered. Some of the captured freighters had been pressed into service as troop transports, housing rebels from across the Hegemony. They'd form the first elements of an army that would seek to bring down the Funks and replace them with something a little more friendly. "And prepare to engage the Funks."

The two fleets closed with remarkable speed as the first signs of rebellion broke out on the orbital stations. Some of the defences lost power, or became bloody slaughterhouses as the Gobbles turned on their former masters; others began to fire on enemy-controlled installations on the planetary surface. The Hegemony would have real problems sorting out friendly from rebel stations, assuming they even tried. If they'd allowed the Gobbles on their starships, the entire battle might have ended there and then. Joshua half-suspected that the Funks would pull out of the system before the defences started firing on them, but instead they picked up speed and aimed right for the rebel fleet. Some of the pirate ships turned and ran when they realised what they were facing, despite the chaos breaking out in high orbit. Others stayed loyal, despite the risk. Looting an entire planet would be worth the possibility of death or capture.

"Enemy ships are locking on," Karla reported. They had one advantage over their enemies, even though they were badly outnumbered. The Funks were presumably much more experienced in operating as a formation. "They are preparing to fire."

"Fire at will," Joshua ordered. Phase cannon opened fire, followed by volleys of antimatter torpedoes. They weren't as powerful as the improved versions devised by human engineers, but there were enough of them to make up for any deficiencies. The Funks returned fire savagely, switching their targeting over a dozen starships as they pumped out their own antimatter torpedoes. *Blackbeard* lurched violently as a torpedo exploded on her forward shield, followed by a tearing scream as phase cannon burned into her hull. Joshua cursed as the entire ship shuddered, just before their tormentor was blown away by two of the other ships. "Damage report!"

"Major damage to forward hull," the engineer reported. "They've taken out a couple of our drive nodes and all of our forward weapons. We're looking at around two weeks to replace them and repair the hull."

"Keep firing," Joshua ordered. The Funks were passing right through his formation, trying to take out as many ships as they could before they had to retreat. Joshua would have preferred a clean kill, wiping the entire enemy force out, but the Funks didn't want to oblige him. Why should they throw themselves away for no return? It might have been different if they'd had ships nearby that could retake the planet quickly... but if the information broker was right, the closest reinforcements were several weeks away. "See if you can get a link to the rebels in orbit."

The last of the Funk starships escaped the formation, fired a final volley of torpedoes and then opened a quantum gate and vanished. They probably hadn't gone far – the Funks would need someone to remain in the system and watch the rebels – but for the moment they were no longer an issue. Joshua barked orders as *Blackbeard* caught up with the remainder of the formation and headed right towards Tauscher. The planet's orbital space seemed to have dissolved into chaos. Automated platforms were firing on most of the manned platforms, while some of the other platforms had shut down completely. Joshua whispered a prayer for the unfortunate souls on the dead platforms, even if they were Funks. No spacer wanted to die slowly as the atmosphere turned to poison, rendering the platforms completely uninhabitable.

"Nineteen ships destroyed outright, twenty-seven damaged," Karla reported. "And seven fled for fear of losing their lives, the cowardly fuckers. You want to shoot them if they show their faces around here again?"

"If they do," Joshua said. The range to the planet's orbital space was dropping sharply. They had to know who was friendly by the time they reached orbit. "Can you raise someone – anyone?"

"Nothing," Karla said. "The orbital datanets appear to have been completely scrambled. It's possible that they've uploaded subversion software to disable platforms that weren't likely to fall to the rebels. Even if they can still fight, they won't be doing so cohesively."

Joshua winced. "Hold our position outside their effective range," he ordered. "If anyone tries to fire on us, assume that they're hostile and mark them down for later attention."

He tapped his console, opening a link to Xinchub. Whatever cuteness the alien had once had was lost in the sheer number of weapons he carried as he prepared to head down to the planet. The Funks had never bothered to design battlesuits for their clients and even the hidden colonies hadn't been able to produce a workable version in time, leaving the Gobbles at a disadvantage when facing their masters. It didn't seem to bother them.

"We need to sort out the friendly platforms from the hostiles," he said. "Can you get through to your allies?"

"I'm trying," Xinchub said. "The Funks are trying to jam radio transmissions from the planetary surface. What little I'm picking up suggests that all-out war has broken out and both sides are being slaughtered."

Joshua shuddered. Even humanity couldn't match the Gobbles when it came to sheer unthinking hatred for the Funks. And the Funks had a major population down on the surface, treating the natives in ways that would have made the worst of South Africa's apartheid racists blanch. Black men had been human too, however reluctant their enemies were to acknowledge it, but there was no such tie between the Gobbles and the Funks. Even without weapons, the Gobbles were likely to slaughter their masters and bathe in their blood.

"Keep trying to get through to them," he said. He'd warned Xinchub that he didn't want a slaughter, let alone effective genocide, but it didn't look as if he was in control of the situation any longer. "I'll..."

"I've got a laser link from one of the stations," Karla interrupted. "They're asking to speak to Xinchub."

"Put them through to him," Joshua ordered. There was a long pause as the two Gobbles chattered together in their high-pitched language, defeating the translation program he'd bought from Shadow. From what he'd picked up from the rebels, the Gobbles actually had a simpler version of their language they used to talk to the Galactics. They called it, roughly translated, the Stupid Speech. "What's happening down there?"

"We have control of most of the platforms," Xinchub said. "Tactical data is being uploaded now. The ground is still horrifically confused. We have to get down there as soon as possible."

Joshua glanced at the data from the captured platforms. "It should be possible to get you and your men down to the surface without being intercepted by the remaining platforms," he said. "I assume you wish to launch immediately?"

"Of course," Xinchub said. "I'm going home!"

The fleet slowly advanced on the planet, targeting and picking off the remaining enemy-controlled platforms. Joshua watched dispassionately as they died, one by one, even though they claimed victims before they were finally destroyed. Some of the planet's defences would have to be rebuilt quickly before the Funks gathered the forces to return and reclaim the planet, although he had been informed that the Funks had used their client world as a base for manufacturing missiles and other military equipment.

It had seemed a curious oversight on their part to put valuable production nodes near a rebellious planet until Joshua had looked into the history of the occupation. The Hegemony clans that had claimed the planet – and its inhabitants – hadn't had much of a presence anywhere outside the system, for internal political reasons that Joshua hadn't been able to follow. They'd regarded the Gobbles as their last chance to regain prominence – under the Empress, of course – and their lust for power had overridden their common sense. But then, the Gobbles *had* been under control until Joshua had destroyed or driven away the starships guarding their planet. Resistance would have been pointless.

Xinchub launched his shuttles as soon as he came into range, hurling thousands of heavily-armed rebels into the teeth of enemy positions. The Funks fought with a savagery born of desperation, pressing every last craft into military service and forcing civilians to join their defenders. Joshua watched helplessly as the captured orbital platforms turned on the planet they were supposed to defend, wiping out Funk fortifications and settlements with a ruthlessness that shocked him. In no more than two hours, hundreds of thousands – perhaps more – of Funks had been slaughtered. There was nowhere to hide for the former masters of the planet. The only survivors were the ones who lived far from any Gobble settlements.

Joshua redeployed his fleet and sent small detachments to claim the various colonies and industrial nodes scattered throughout the system. Most of them were run by Gobbles and they were quite willing to join the rebels; the remainder, mostly operated by Funks, refused to surrender until Joshua promised not to hand them over to the Gobbles. The penal ship he'd captured months ago would come in handy as a place to hold them until they could be returned to the Hegemony. None of them were any use as hostages. Finally, an uneasy peace covered the entire system. Joshua didn't want to *think* about how many Funks had died when their slaves had turned on them. The final death toll would probably be in the *millions*.

"It was necessary," Xinchub said, when he returned to *Blackbeard* a day later. The Gobbles seemed to be firmly in control of most of the system's infrastructure and they'd already started offering their services to repair the damaged ships. Others were starting work on restoring the disabled platforms, after Joshua had sent shuttles to pick up the Funks. "They needed to understand just how badly we hate them."

Joshua found himself at a loss for words. Three Hegemony clans – relatively minor ones, true – had been almost exterminated by the uprising. Whatever their exact relationship with the rest of the clans, or the Empress, the Hegemony could hardly let that go past without retaliating. Even if they didn't blame humanity for the whole affair – and they probably would – they'd still want to punish the Gobbles. A single antimatter torpedo would render the entire planet uninhabitable. The debris falling into the planet's atmosphere probably wouldn't help. God knew that the Funks had left large parts of the surface an ecological disaster area.

"I think they got the message," he said, finally. He'd seen the images from the ground, the pictures of burning cities and slaughtered Funks, their bodies piled high so they could be cremated by orbital lasers. No Funk who remained alive on the planet's surface could ever feel safe when their family had been brutally murdered. "How do you intend to explain it to the Galactics?"

"The Galactics have never done anything for us," Xinchub snarled. "Why should we care about their opinion?"

It wasn't an attitude Joshua found hard to share. The Association *had* done nothing to protect humanity from the ravages of powerful neighbours, any more than they'd done anything to force the Hegemony to let the Gobbles develop in peace. There was something to be said for rubbing their noses in the trauma inflicted on slave races, and what happened when that trauma finally found an outlet, yet it would make it harder for the Gobbles to win allies from outside the Hegemony. And they would *need* those allies to stave off the Hegemony when the Funks came back, bent on extracting revenge.

"Because you might need their help," he said, tiredly. If Earth hadn't already disowned him, it would have done so once news of the slaughter reached home. "They might be willing to help you now that you have freed yourself."

"I wouldn't have bet money on that," Xinchub said. "The Galactics simply don't care. There is no justice in the universe, or even any agreement on shared ethics and morals. How long will it be until everyone realises that there is no common law?"

"Not long," Joshua said. The brushfire wars had started the process, but humanity's war against the Hegemony had probably accelerated it. Laws had no power unless they were enforced and no-one was interested in serving as the enforcer. The Cats didn't have the will and no one else had the power. Anyone who tried would probably force several other powers to unite against them. "I don't think it will be very long at all."

* * *

"*Blackbeard* will be a week in the yard," Karla said, an hour later. "The Gobbles seem pretty sure that they can rebuild her faster than we estimated."

"We'll see," Joshua said, slowly. He felt tired; not physically tired, but mentally tired. The war had turned savage and it was partly his fault. "And the orbital fortifications?"

"Repaired," Karla said. "They've improvised a number of systems that will give them a few unexpected surprises when the Funks return. The defences are maybe not as deep as we would like, but the Funks will definitely know that they've been kissed."

She smiled. "I'm afraid a number of pirates want their loot and then out of here before the Funks come back," she added. "The rebels are more interested in turning this system into a permanent base. They have families who need somewhere to live where the Funks can't threaten them."

"Maybe they can find a home here," Joshua said. "God knows there's plenty of room for them now."

Karla reached over and shook him, firmly. "What exactly do you think the Funks expected?" She demanded. "You know how they treated anyone who even dared to question their orders. They might be able to integrate their own race into society after a few generations of slavery, but how could they do that when they couldn't even breed with the non-Funk slaves? The Gobbles were doomed to permanent servitude until we came along and helped them to be free."

338

She snorted, loudly. "The Hegemony wasn't *innocent* before they encountered us," she reminded him. "You should know exactly how they treat their own people – and what happens when the masters lose control. How much worse is it on a planet populated by aliens who cannot even claim to own their world?"

"And it *will* solve the problem of what to do with the Funk population," Kang added. "They would have been a major issue if they'd been left alive…"

"And now millions of them are dead," Joshua snapped. "Try as I might, I cannot see that as a victory. The blood on our hands will never wash off."

"You don't need to be dramatic about it," Kang said, dryly. "Look; the Funks treated everyone on the planet below like shit. They got exactly what they deserved when they lost control. It wasn't your fault that the Funks built up such a reservoir of hatred and anger among the locals. You couldn't be blamed for not realising that the teddy bears would turn on their masters as soon as their masters lost the ability to keep them under control."

He stood up and headed to the hatch. "I think that we have more important problems," he added. "You need to prepare this system for the inevitable counterattack."

"He's right," Karla said, as the hatch closed behind him. "Hey, do you want to go to bed and celebrate again?"

"I don't feel like celebrating," Joshua said. The thought of the dead chilled him to the bone, even though part of his anatomy was insisting that he take her up on her offer. "We won today – but I feel as if I lost. What does that say about me?"

Karla didn't try to answer.

Chapter Thirty-Eight

"Come and take a look at this."

Trader captain William O'Hare smiled to himself as his youngest son looked up from the sensor console. A warship would have had a trained and experienced officer, but *Mother's Milk* was no warship. She was a freighter that was officially older than five hundred years, purchased on the open market by human investors and leased out to William and his family as long as they brought in the goods. His son had yet to lose the certainty that each voyage would bring in a new and remarkable discovery, even though all he'd discovered was a handful of comets and an asteroid that would have been worth something if there hadn't been millions more like it in the asteroid belt. Clarke was not a particularly well-travelled system, yet anything really interesting would have been noted long before the human race learned about the community that existed across the stars.

He looked down at the sensor console and frowned. There should have been nothing between them and the quantum gate, their only way of entering quantum space. But there was something… it looked almost like turbulence from a cloaked ship. Space wasn't as empty as the average civilian thought, and there were frequent energy discharges that could be mistaken for a cloaked starship, yet this pattern looked too regular to be natural. Someone seemed to be trying to sneak up on Clarke…

"Send an emergency signal to the planet," he snapped. "Cloaked ship – or ships – operating near the quantum gate!"

He hoped – prayed – that the unknown ship wasn't intent on wiping out the human presence within the system. The freighter couldn't run or hide if the enemy wanted to kill them; there was no way she could even get into the quantum gate before being obliterated if the enemy ship opened fire. His action might have doomed them all, but he knew his duty. Humanity had to be warned, even if it cost him his ship and family...

"I'm picking up a change in energy readings," his son said. "I think they're decloaking..."

William had wondered, briefly, if the ship was a Federation Navy starship running through its final trials. But the decloaking ship was clearly not of human design. The battlecruiser that wobbled into view was Galactic, almost certainly belonging to the Hegemony. William cursed their ill-luck as the battlecruiser locked weapons on their hull, ripping their ship apart with a single burst of phase cannon fire.

He barely had time to hug his son before the ship exploded around them and they fell into darkness.

* * *

Calling Clarke a habitable world required stretching the definition of 'habitable' about as far as it would go. Clarke possessed a breathable atmosphere for humans – and most other humanoid races – but its surface was completely infested by foliage that might actually be a sentient life form in its own right. The first settlements on the planetary surface had been destroyed by the local plant life, which had moved with stunning speed to repel the invaders. Later research had discovered that the plant life actually hunted fish and seemed to have domesticated several species of animal. There were even reports that a handful of human survivors had been domesticated and allowed to live in harmony with the plants.

The main human settlements on the planet had been established on small islands, the largest barely the size of Nantucket. They'd had to use firebombs to sweep the islands clean of native life and replant with seeds from Earth before they could support a growing population, something that couldn't really be applied to the larger continents. It said something about how useless the system was that the Hegemony had never attempted to claim it, which might have been a mistake on their part. Clarke had plenty of surprises on its surface and some of them were potentially very profitable.

Governor Mountbatten had been in office for two years when researchers had discovered that the strange plant life could be harvested to produce a surprising number of vaccines and pleasure drugs. Some of them were useless – even poisonous – for humans, but they promised to be a gold mine when they were sold to the Galactics, assuming that the Hegemony didn't simply grab the planet as soon as they realised that it was turning a profit. Mountbatten had been devising a cunning plan to prevent the Funks from discovering the truth when the war began. Since then, he'd prayed for victory. If Clarke became a gold mine, the world he'd come to love might grow into a proper human community – and his career would be boosted into the stratosphere.

He looked up as the door opened and his aide ran in without knocking. "Governor," he said, "we're picking up a very disturbing report from the deep-space tracking network. I think you'd better come see this at once."

Mountbatten nodded and followed his aide through the corridors of Government House to System Control. Clarke just didn't have the room for massive sprawling mansions, or separate installations; everything was jammed together in Government House. The Marines had a small training base nearby, shared with the local militia and national contingents from Earth, but apart from them Clarke was almost defenceless. A handful of third-hand automated weapons platforms weren't going to slow any serious attacker down for long.

A single red icon glowed on the display as it came closer to the planet. "One battlecruiser, almost certainly Hegemony," the operator reported. Mountbatten felt his chest turn to ice. "It destroyed a freighter near the quantum gate before advancing on us..."

"Send out the alert," Mountbatten ordered. The local militia would muster, for all the good it would do. There weren't any Federation Marines on Clarke apart from the training cadre. A battalion from the French Foreign Legion, part of the 10th Mountain Division and a handful of SAS soldiers were running exercises on the mainland, but they'd never be able to get back to the settlements before it was too late. "And then we'd better put the evacuation plan into operation. Now."

Clarke had never expected to be attacked, not when the world was generally believed to be almost worthless. Mountbatten had developed a plan to defend the settlement, but no one knew better than him that any determined attacker could take the planet or exterminate the human population without much trouble. The only drill they'd held had been a disaster, which had at least concentrated a few minds. By now, the schools would be ordering their children to head to the shelters while the entire planet went dark. Most of the fishing boats didn't normally bother with radio transmissions, thankfully. They might be missed if the enemy didn't look closely.

"Enemy ship entering firing range of the platforms," the operator said. "Am I authorized to open fire?"

"For God's sake, *yes*," Mountbatten snapped at him. The enemy ship was already firing on the platforms. Two of them were gone before they even managed to fire back. "See if you can hurt the bastard!"

He took one last look around the command center, and then led the way to the door and out into the small town. Government House would surely be targeted first if the enemy intended to invade and occupy the planet and he could do no more good by remaining in the mansion. Once outside, he could put on his militia hat and take command of his forces, such as they were. The Federation had encouraged the development of a militia and even supplied weapons, but the population was too low to put up a real fight. And their enemy could bombard them from orbit anyway.

* * *

"All right, listen up," Sergeant Tommy Hawkins bellowed. He'd been in 3 Para before First Contact, a line on his resume that had ensured his current rank in the militia when he retired and emigrated to Clarke. "We have

343

incoming assault shuttles and they're going to be coming in hot."

He glared at his troop until they stopped looking so nervous. A handful had had military experience on Earth, but most of them were youngsters who had been raised on Clarke by their parents and had never seen anything more dangerous than hunting expeditions and rescue missions. Some had declared their intention to join the Federation Marines, but in Tommy's rather less than humble opinion few of them had the dedication to join and remain in service for the ten year period. It might not matter in the long run. Many of his men were going to die today.

"You've trained on the Super-Stinger," he continued. The Super-Stinger was an antiaircraft HVM built using Galactic technology, capable of shooting down anything that flew within range. And yet they'd never been tested in combat. "You know how to handle it. Anything that comes close is a target, understand?"

He caught sight of a nervous-looking blonde farm girl holding a rifle and rolled his eyes. She didn't look particularly dangerous at all. Rumour had it that her father had ordered her into the militia for political reasons, rather than any desire on her part to serve. But she did her part, which was more than could be said for some of the others with political ambitions. Some of them seemed to think that all they needed to do was be on the rolls, without training and exercising with the others. Tommy had worked hard to expel those layabouts from the militia, but he hadn't been completely successful.

The training had been makeshift compared to what pre-Contact soldiers had been offered, but at least they'd been able to hammer proper rifle skills into their heads. Some of the youngsters had picked up bad habits from hunting rifles they kept on their farms. The riflemen would provide limited protection to the missile crews, or so Tommy had explained. They didn't need to worry about the enemy bombing them from high overhead, if only because there was nothing they could do if the Funks simply decided to kill everybody.

"Once we run out of missiles, we get back to the RV point as we practiced," he concluded. "And I will personally kick any slowcoach up the ass, you got me?"

He could hear the sound of shuttles in the distance as the team scattered, the missile crews picking up their weapons while the riflemen took up guard positions. Tommy had picked their firing location with malice aforethought. The enemy should have problems locating them under the small forest of trees, at least until they landed ground troops to flush out the resistance. At least the Funks weren't likely to be as unpleasant as certain human forces, although they wouldn't hesitate to kill insurgents.

There were nine large settled islands on Clarke and a hundred smaller ones, some housing no more than a dock and a few fishermen's shacks. Logically, the enemy would land on Colchester Island first and take the spaceport, using it as a place to land their forces and deploy out to seize Wells City. His position should give them a clear shot at a handful of enemy shuttles before they had to cut and run, unless the enemy had their own plans for landing. It was just possible that the Funks might drop into the sea and attempt an amphibious landing, if they really wanted to outflank the defenders.

"Here they come," he said. "Take aim and...fire!"

The HVM blasted out of his launcher and roared for the sky, tracking its target at terrifying speed. They were too close for most countermeasures, although the Funks did what they could by throwing their shuttles into evasive patterns. Two missiles had tracked the same target, part of Tommy's mind noted, blowing the Funk shuttle into a pile of falling debris. The remaining shuttles followed, save one which rocketed away over the ocean. Tommy tried to form a mental picture of it trailing smoke and crashing into the water, but he had to admit that it was unlikely. Besides, the native seawater life would eat the Funks for dinner and probably get even more hostile to land-dwelling life forms.

"Grab your weapons and run," he barked. The Funks knew where they were now; active HVM launchers would show up on every orbital sensor. "Run, now!"

The militiamen turned and ran for their lives. They'd practiced often enough, once Tommy and his fellow trainers had managed to convince them that retreat wasn't always a cowardly act. He heard the scream seconds before the missile plunged down and detonated where they'd been, blowing a colossal fireball into the air. The shockwave picked him up and threw him forward, sending him crashing down into a prickly bush.

He'd been one of the lucky ones. The blonde militiawoman was less lucky. She'd been blown right into a tree and her head had almost been severed from her body. One glance was all it took to confirm that there was no point in calling for a medic. Tommy dropped a small grenade beside her body, booby-trapping it to surprise any Funk troopers who found her, and then led the remains of the platoon into the untamed wilderness. They could hide out there until the Funks retreated or the Federation Navy organised a relief mission.

He shook his head tiredly as they headed further onwards. At least they'd hurt the bastards, even if they hadn't hurt them badly enough to make them think twice about invading Clarke. Raid or occupation, a lot of people were about to die – and all he could do was hide and await the opportunity to strike back. There was nothing else he could do.

* * *

Jeanette saw the shuttle fall out of the sky and hit the ground, sending up a massive fireball that could be seen for miles around. She hadn't bothered to go to the shelters, even though she knew that she should; her general store was about to be destroyed by the Funks and without it, what would become of her? She'd seen the indentured workers on the mainland, the men and women who hadn't been able to repay their settlement loans and ended up working as virtual slaves for the development corporation, and she had no intention of ending up like them.

She'd ordered her two sons to the shelters and taken up a position just outside Wells City, along the road leading to the spaceport. The last update she'd had from the Government had warned that shuttles were landing there, brushing aside the militia units that attempted to delay them. Her worthless ex-husband was probably among the dead; oddly, despite her feelings for the man who had given her children and little else, she found herself hoping that he'd died well. The radio had gone silent soon afterwards, suggesting that the Funks had taken out the transmitter. A handful of plumes of smoke in the distance suggested the worst.

The faint sound of vehicles caught her attention, coming down the long road to the spaceport. No-one drove on Colchester Island, except the police and the emergency services. Fuel was incredibly expensive on Clarke, limiting the kind of vehicles they could use. Besides, Colchester was a relatively small island. Anywhere she wanted to go was within walking or bicycle distance. No, the oncoming vehicles had to belong to the Funks. She peered down the scope on her rifle as they came into view, heavy vehicles without any of the elegance that some of the Galactics insisted on working into everything they produced. They bristled with weapons and lizard-like troopers, who looked around nervously with flickering red eyes. Some of them wore combat armor; others wore nothing more than protective breastplates and helmets. They seemed ready for anything.

Jeanette took aim at the nearest unarmored Funk and pulled the trigger. The hunting rifle jerked in her arms, but she had the satisfaction of seeing the Funk staggering backwards and stumbling into two of his comrades. She was already moving as the vehicle's turret moved with stunning speed, bringing a pair of heavy machine guns to bear on her position. Jeanette dived into the stream as a fusillade of shots tore through where she'd been hiding, leaving a dusty mess hovering in the air. She started to crawl down the stream, praying that they wouldn't dismount and check to be sure they'd caught her; a second later, she heard a shot and felt something crack into her left leg. The pain was so agonising that she couldn't help screaming, even as she realised dimly that she'd been shot.

Her leg seemed to refuse to work properly and she found herself twisting over and over again, only to see a pair of green legs appear beside her. She looked up into the bright red eyes of a Funk, pointing a gun at her head. Jeanette tried to reach for her rifle, but it was gone. She couldn't even think of where it might be.

The Funk pulled the trigger – and her entire world went black.

* * *

Carolyn Jonson had been hiding in the shelters, with a number of other refugees, when the doors were flung open and they came face-to-face with the Funks. Carolyn had never considered herself a xenophobe – her settlement application would probably have been rejected if she'd disliked aliens – but the Funks looked horrific in the bright sunlight. Their hissing voices, speaking barely intelligible Galactic Three, ordered the humans out of the shelter. Those who tried to move slowly found themselves being helped along by rifle butts and heavy shoving. The Funks were stronger than they looked.

Wells had never been a pretty city, but now it looked like a war zone. Buildings had been shattered, casually destroyed as if they had been struck by an angry god. A handful of vehicles were nothing more than burning wrecks. And there were a dozen dead bodies within easy view of the children. Carolyn felt tears welling up behind her eyes and started to sob. She wasn't alone.

The Funk leaned forward. "Your world is ours now," the alien hissed. "Resistance is futile."

Chapter Thirty-Nine

"It's confirmed, then?"

"I'm afraid so," Admiral Sun said. "Clarke has definitely fallen to the Hegemony."

Tobias cursed. The Funks had finally managed to start launching counterattacks – and he couldn't hope to stop them all. Apart from Earth itself, the defences of humanity's worlds were minimal; Hammerfall alone had had more defences than all of the Nine Stars combined. It was a reminder of humanity's greatest weakness; the Hegemony could afford to lose hundreds of smaller ships without making a serious dent in its combat power, while each lost human ship weakened the Federation Navy.

"I took the decision to send one of the scouts to Clarke," Sun continued. "The Hegemony landed at least two divisions of ground troops and remains in possession of the high orbitals. We were unable to make contact with our forces on the ground, which could mean that they were observing radio silence..."

"Or that they've been destroyed," Tobias said, tightly. "Did they capture any data on Clarke itself?"

"We don't know," Sun admitted. "The Governor and his staff were under strict orders to destroy all of the data in the files if the planet was invaded, but too many people knew something about the planet's actual value for us to be completely certain that the Funks don't know anything. Someone might try to bargain with the bastards if they feel that the Federation can't liberate them."

"And they'd have something to bargain with," Tobias mused. The Funks enslaved those they captured, but slaves who had something to bargain with could press for better treatment or even a fast track to citizenship. And if the Funks suspected Clarke's true value... they'd definitely be willing to deal. "I assume that the Council had something to say about it?"

"They met in emergency session only an hour ago," Sun confirmed. "So far, the news hasn't leaked out on Earth, but it won't be long before the Funks start crowing about their great victory to anyone who will listen. The general public will realise that there's a Funk battlecruiser only nine light years from Earth and start to panic."

"Even though a single battlecruiser would be cut to pieces if it tried to break through Earth's defences," Tobias said. But there was no proof that it *was* just a lone battlecruiser. The Funks were devious and it would have been easy for them to hide an entire fleet in quantum space, or simply under cloak a few parsecs from the planet. They'd be well beyond any risk of detection as long as they were careful. It was possible that Clarke was nothing more than the bait in a trap.

"The Federation Council wishes you to dispatch a cruiser squadron to liberate Clarke," Sun informed him. "We cannot allow the Funks to remain in control of human territory for any longer than strictly necessary."

Tobias winced. "I understand their point," he said, "but do they understand that Clarke is meaningless in a strategic sense?"

"I think they understand that losing Clarke and forty thousand human colonists is a PR disaster," Sun said, dryly. "Even if Clarke was hardly a net gain to us, it still makes us look weak; we have to push back as hard as we can. They're quite insistent on that point, Admiral. I've never seen the Federation Council so united."

"Fear is a great motivator," Tobias agreed, dryly. The Russian and Chinese permanent members didn't have to worry about public opinion, but the remainder of the permanent members definitely did. Even after the great victories at Terra Nova, Garston and Hammerfall, there had been a sizable minority that wanted peace at any price. That minority would be taking the opportunity to press its case upon ears that were suddenly willing to listen. "I'll have to consider our options carefully."

"I think that this isn't a time to resist our political masters," Sun warned him. "They're united, Admiral. The absolute last thing we need right now is your relief and a power struggle over who gets to nominate the next CNO."

Tobias nodded sourly. Sun would have made an ideal replacement for himself, when his term as CNO expired, but the political leaders wouldn't see it that way. The Chinese would want him because he was Chinese; the Russians would oppose him on the same grounds. America wouldn't be too keen on the idea; the Japanese would be utterly opposed. Given the weighted voting system, it was a hell of a lot easier to veto candidates than have one selected and confirmed by the full council. Tobias had had to fight hard over the years to prevent his political lords and masters putting forward candidates for high positions purely based on nationality and political connections. He hadn't won all of the battles. The best he'd been able to do was make sure that some of the less reliable or competent officers were shunted off to meaningless posts and makeshift work. And he still worried about the recent crop of potential commanding officers.

But strategically, Clarke was meaningless – unless the Hegemony *did* know that the planet wasn't as worthless as everyone thought. And yet that didn't make sense. Tobias knew just how extensively the Hegemony had tried to penetrate Earth – and how ONI and Federation Intelligence had worked to counter them – and if they'd realised that Clarke might be a valuable possession, they would surely have bullied humanity into surrendering the world before the Federation Navy was ready to start the war. Why wait until now to move in? No, that made no sense. The Funks had gotten lucky and were in a stronger position than they knew.

"And if we offered to trade Garston for Clarke, they'd be bound to smell a rat," he commented. "I don't suppose there's been any word from Ambassador Li?"

"Nothing new," Sun confirmed. "They keep going over and over the same issues in the secret peace talks. She thinks that they're stalling, hoping that we'll surrender our gains and let the Empress claim a victory of sorts. The sociologists agree with her, although I wouldn't trust those bastards to guess my weight." He smiled. "And the news from the Gobbles doesn't help one little bit."

Tobias smiled. Humanity knew little about the Gobbles, one of the Hegemony's two client races, but all of a sudden they'd become very important. Their homeworld had risen up against the Hegemony...and, according to some reports, they'd been aided by the dreaded human pirate king. In the short run, the plan to send a completely deniable agent to the sector to wreak havoc had succeeded beyond his wildest dreams; in the long term, everything would depend on how well the Gobbles could defend themselves when the Hegemony returned to their system.

But according to ONI – and some of humanity's alien allies – the Hegemony had suffered a colossal political earthquake. Two clans had collapsed, leaving their people at the mercy of their enemies. Their creditors were already moving in and enslaving lesser clansmen to ensure that they got at least some of their money back. The projections varied from analyst to analyst, but they all agreed that the shockwaves had only just begun. How long would it be until the Hegemony collapsed into civil war? Some reports claimed that martial law had already been declared on Hegemony Prime. It might not bode well for *Formidable* and her mission.

"I'll ensure that starships are sent to deal with the enemy force on Clarke," he reluctantly said. At best, they'd mop up the enemy ground troops quickly, assuming the enemy battlecruiser was alone or pulled out before the cruisers arrived. The alternative was that an isolated human force would fly right into a trap. "I suppose they're not going to release any of the ships covering Earth?"

"Not a one," Sun agreed. "They won't even release the damaged ships we purchased from shady used-starship dealers. God knows that most of them aren't fit for combat anyway. We need more cruisers, Admiral."

"Tell me about it," Tobias agreed, tiredly. Humanity had strained every muscle to build the Federation Navy, yet there had only been twenty-five cruisers at the start of the war. Ten more were under construction in the Luna Yard, but the most optimistic estimate said that they wouldn't be completed and worked up for battle for another six months. By then, Earth's economy would probably have collapsed even if the Hegemony was still hanging on. God alone knew what would happen to the market once the news of Clarke's fall got out to the media. "I'll update you once I decide which ships to send."

He closed the channel and tapped his console, bringing up the fleet's order of battle. The new squadron of cruisers from Earth – which had arrived just prior to news of Clarke – made up the holes in his force, but their crews weren't anything like as experienced as the veterans from the original squadrons. Tobias had ordered extensive training and exercises while the repair crews worked on the damaged ships and salvaged what they could from the remains of Hammerfall's once-proud facilities. The irony would have been funny if it hadn't been so irritating; the Galactics used standardized equipment, but some human technology was incompatible with items that any other race could plug into their own ships and expect to work perfectly.

A message blipped up on his screen and he frowned. His galactic mail account was known to only a handful of people, which didn't stop him from receiving his fair share of spam messages from across the galaxy. Quite why a spammer would think that he would be interested in sexual treatments devised for a race that had five different sexes was beyond him; it made less sense than sending him messages that offered to improve the size of his breasts. At least they went to the right race, if not the right sex. Some of the messages were clearly useless, but one of them was from an address he recognised.

He opened it and read it, and then reached for the dictionary. The code was a simple one, but almost unbreakable without an understanding of English and a copy of the book used to encode the message. Earth's vast spectrum of languages had puzzled the Cats when they'd first discovered Earth; they'd unified their languages into Galactic One by the time they'd left their solar system and started poking through quantum space. The insurgents on Terra Nova had used languages as code at first, but the

Funks had eventually started programming their translators to decrypt them automatically. They had had their own multiple language problem, although in their case a unified language had been forced on them by the First Empress.

Joshua Wachter had learned something, something so important that he'd decided to take the risk of communicating with the Federation Navy. Tobias had no intention of actually enforcing the Federation Council's orders regarding the pirate king, but it would cause a great deal of political embarrassment if the media realised that Wachter had had a direct line to the CNO. It wouldn't take a conspiracy theorist to realise that the CNO might have been quietly backing him ever since he'd left Earth. Tobias read through the message twice, feeling ice congealing within his chest. There were fifteen enemy superdreadnoughts that had left their sector and were – presumably – on their way to the war.

Tobias calmed his mind with as much mental discipline as he could muster and tapped a key, bringing up the star chart. Every spacer knew how to estimate transit times – and every spacer knew that the estimates were rarely completely accurate. The enemy ships might have been in transit for up to a week prior to Wachter discovering that they were gone; hell, the discovery might have been what tempted him to liberate the Gobbles in the first place. And that meant...

Where were they going? Hammerfall made little sense any longer, not now the system had been rendered totally worthless. The Funks could plan on crushing the Federation Navy, but they had to know that Tobias wouldn't fight for Hammerfall against superior forces, no matter how important the media claimed the planet to be. They couldn't hope to catch Tobias if he chose to avoid engagement...

...Unless they went to Earth. He wanted to avoid even considering the possibility, but the Federation Navy had extensively gamed Earth-Hegemony scenarios ever since the occupation of Terra Nova. They'd *known* that the Hegemony was far larger than Earth's paltry Nine Stars. The best option for the Funks to win outright was to fight a delaying action, concentrate their naval forces and then attack Earth directly. If they were lucky, the main body of the Federation Navy would be light-years from the planet when they attacked – and even if they weren't lucky, they would have a chance to force the Federation Navy to fight on unfavourable terms. Speed meant nothing when the enemy was advancing on a target the Federation Navy *had* to defend.

And if the Funks took that objective... game over.

There was Bolthole, of course, but no one knew better than Tobias that Bolthole was a gamble with no guarantee of success. Past the Rim, past the space explored by the Association, it was far harder to navigate in quantum space. The Bolthole ship might find a habitable world several thousand light years from Earth and establish a colony that would become a new homeworld for the human race, or it might run into hostile aliens and be destroyed. ONI had collected all the information it could on the space beyond the Rim, but most of it boiled down to 'here there be dragons.' Anyone who knew anything concrete wasn't talking.

The Funks were certainly watching Hammerfall. Their ships had been detected making brief transmissions to their superiors before they vanished back into cloak. A star system was an immense place to hide, particularly if they were only monitoring drive signatures with passive sensors; there was little hope that the Federation Navy would track them down and destroy the spies. And that meant that the Funks would know if the Federation Navy withdrew from the system. Or would they?

A plan slowly started to take shape in his mind. The Funks were gambling, drawing down their forces on the Tarn border to dangerously low levels. It *had* to be their final attempt at winning the war outright. Another failure would topple the Empress and trigger a civil war. If Tobias could get First Strike Fleet back to Earth in time to intercept the enemy superdreadnoughts, Earth might be saved. And if the Hegemony believed that First Strike Fleet remained at Hammerfall, their estimates of how powerful the Federation Navy was would become distorted. ECM drones could pose as the cruisers for a few weeks. If worst came to worst,

Hammerfall would be recaptured – but keeping Hammerfall wasn't worth losing Earth. Without Earth, their only option would be surrender.

He keyed his console and opened a channel. "Command conference, right now," he ordered. He'd have to share his thoughts with his officers, make the deployments – and then order a complete media blackout. At least he didn't need anyone's approval for fleet deployments. Even sending a message back to Earth might be risky. Who knew who might be listening? "And then authorize Blackout. I say again, authorize Blackout."

* * *

The newspaper had been in decline before first contact, challenged by television and then by the internet, the most remarkable medium for spreading lies and half-truths ever invented. But First Contact had given them a new chance at life. Streaming video over light years was incredibly expensive, making it far cheaper to simply send compressed text. Adrienne was halfway through writing a report on Hammerfall when her cabin's hatch chimed. When she opened it, she saw a grim-faced Marine carrying a sidearm.

"Excuse me," he said, in a tone that was both polite and firm, "but I'm afraid I have to secure all of your electronic devices."

Adrienne gaped at him. "I beg your pardon?"

"I have been ordered to secure all of your electronic devices," the Marine said. There was no give in his voice at all. "All of them, including your watch. I must warn you that attempting to conceal electronic devices until the lockdown is lifted will result in brig time and charges of attempted espionage when we return to Earth. If you would prefer brig time, please let me know."

"No, thank you," Adrienne said, stiffly. The Marine was only doing his job, even if it did impinge on her ability to do hers. It was about as pointless as ordering passengers on a jumbo jet to turn off their cell phones, but pointing that out would be equally pointless. "I have a tablet, a laptop and a secure storage hard drive. And a watch."

356

The Marine picked them up and scribbled out a receipt for her. "I have to search your cabin as well," he added, more apologetically now that she was cooperating. "Blackout has been declared."

Adrienne lifted an eyebrow. Blackout? Hadn't there been something in the papers she'd signed when she'd embedded about Blackout? She thought back, remembering that the military had the right to completely forbid transmissions from its ships if it believed that making transmissions would violate operational security. Taking her laptop seemed like pointless paranoia, but some reporters had managed to hack starship communications systems before and use them to get messages out.

"I forgot to bring my lacy underwear," she said. "It's all strictly functional, I'm afraid."

She'd hoped to get a rise out of the Marine, but he ignored her and searched her cabin with rigorous efficiency. Adrienne rolled her eyes behind him as he removed the sex toy she'd brought along and dropped it into his bag. Did he think she'd hidden a transmitter in a vibrator?

"Thank you for your cooperation," the Marine said, gravely. "The items will be returned as soon as possible."

He left, leaving a puzzled Adrienne sitting in her cabin.

Something was up, but what?

Chapter Forty

"Miserable looking world, isn't it?"

"I couldn't say, sir," Commander Spinner said. "I grew up in Nevada. We were used to deserts."

Markus shrugged. The Funk homeworld – called Squeak Hiss Squeak by the Funks and Hegemony Prime by everyone else – was as dry as dust. Most of the planet's water existed below the surface, with only a couple of Australia-sized seas. It wasn't a pure desert, but it was easy to see how it had evolved a race determined to reach out and take every resource it could. The Funks had yet to evolve past the patterns they'd developed for survival on their world and they might never manage to do so. It wasn't as if anyone had stood up to them before humanity had given them a bloody nose.

The Funks might have copied Galactic technology without developing more for themselves, but they'd used what they'd copied ruthlessly. A massive shipyard hung near Hegemony Prime, protected by a network of fortifications and patrolled by destroyers and frigates. The Funk Home Fleet orbited the planet itself, watching endlessly for signs of a possible attack – and, according to the transmissions, providing a very visible reminder of the Empress's power. It sounded as if parts of the planet were under martial law.

"I don't think we'll get much closer," Spinner added. "They're checking every freighter before it even enters orbit."

"Clever of them," Markus said. The Funks didn't want another freighter crammed with antimatter detonating anywhere in their system. It would probably render Hegemony Prime uninhabitable, which would have brought the wrath of the Galactics down on Earth, but in their place he wouldn't take it for granted either. The Traders Alliance had actually helped, in some ways, by declaring their embargo. They'd managed to limit the number of freighters visiting Hegemony Prime, which made it easier for the Funks to inspect them all without undue delay. "And the minute they get a close look at our hull, they'll realise that we're rigged up to launch gunboats."

It was unlikely in the extreme that the gunboats would be able to inflict any major damage on their own. Even if their enemy hadn't the experience and motivation to develop countermeasures, they'd have had to burn through massive defences before reaching any vital target. A swarm of gunboats – or the missiles deployed at Hammerfall – might have worked, but Earth didn't have enough gunboats to punch through the planet's defences. Markus was silently grateful that he'd hashed out a plan that might work, even though he felt guilty about asking people to take on risks he wouldn't be facing himself. But if the Hegemony managed to capture him alive, they'd ensure that his death was slow and very painful.

He tapped his console. "Sergeant McDonald," he said, "are you ready to deploy?"

"Yes, sir," the Marine said. He'd volunteered for the mission, once he'd understood what the mission actually entailed. It would be one hell of a stunt if they pulled it off and got out alive. "How long do we have before you go hot?"

"Roughly seventeen minutes," Markus said. The enemy shuttles hadn't reached *Formidable* yet, but they might decide to inspect her earlier once they realised that she was the same class as the ships humanity had turned into gunboat carriers. Or maybe they'd already had plenty of false alerts. The Galactics only had a few dozen different freighter designs. "You may deploy when ready."

"Understood, sir," McDonald said. "Good luck."

In the cockpit of his gunboat, Markus been calm and ready to face danger. On the bridge, a helpless observer, he found himself fretting about all the things that could go wrong. His wife Carola was going to be out there, fighting the Funks, while he watched from afar. He could bug out at any minute while she would have to fight her way out. They'd known that they could die together; somehow, the thought of living on without her was intolerable.

359

The minutes ticked away as the Marines deployed and the enemy shuttles came closer, sweeping nearby freighters with tactical sensors. Markus braced himself as the gunboats powered up, knowing that this was the most dangerous part of launching them. It hadn't bothered him before that an alert enemy might just be able to destroy *Formidable* before her gunboats were launched; now, he found himself unable to avoid thinking the worst. How had Captain Walsh made it look so easy to take command?

"Here they come, sir," Spinner said. "Two minutes to intercept."

"Punch the gunboats," Markus ordered. Grumble Squadron was blasted free of the carrier, followed rapidly by Eagle and Dare Squadrons. Dare had been transferred from *Illustrious* to ensure that *Formidable* had three veteran squadrons, but they'd fit in nicely with the other two. It had probably helped that Markus had chewed out anyone who wanted to pick a fight. "Tell them to fire at will."

Led by Carola, Grumble Squadron formed up and charged right at the enemy shuttles. The Funks, caught by surprise, didn't stand a chance. They were picked off and destroyed before they could even scream for help. The remaining gunboats fell on the freighters, hacking them apart before moving on to the next targets. Markus watched helplessly as the planet's defenders came to life, launching a wing of assault shuttles towards the gunboats. They didn't have the endurance of the gunboats, which was limited compared to that of a starship, but they did have guts – and numbers. Nearly a hundred assault shuttles were closing in on his wife.

"Grumble Squadron is altering course and deploying drones," Spinner reported. "Drones are going active... now!"

Markus smiled. The Hegemony had seen humanity's improved ECM drones at Hammerfall, but they had yet to devise a counter. ONI had been certain that one or more of the Galactics would be inspired to invent countermeasures – and sell them onwards to the Funks – sooner or later, but none had materialised in time to aid the defenders. They had to know that some of the sensor returns they were

360

getting were nothing more than ghosts, but it would be impossible to tell the difference unless they reached close range. And if the sensor ghosts were hiding missiles, allowing them to close could be disastrous.

There were no illusions about how long the sensor ghosts would fool the Hegemony. A smart tactical analyst could probably have sorted half of the fakes from the real gunboats by now, but the ghosts would work long enough to keep the Funks distracted. The real threat lay elsewhere.

* * *

The immensity of space could defeat even the most hardened soldier. Humans were less than sand grains on an immense desert; even the largest artificial structures built by the Association were tiny compared to stars and planets. Conrad felt... meaningless, almost insignificant, as he and his Marines drifted closer to their target. It was that very insignificance that gave them a limited immunity from detection, but he knew better than to take it for granted. The Funks would be listening for anything that might betray their presence. A second of radio chatter could get them all killed.

He watched as the Funk shipyard slowly came into view. It was immense, larger than the shipyards built in orbit around Luna by the human race, a spidery network of structures right out of a science-fiction movie. Unlike the free-floating shipyards designed by humanity, it was one vast structure, a design that provided the Funks with a number of advantages – and at least one weakness. A disaster on one part of the platform might spread to other platforms and cripple the entire complex. His blood ran cold as he saw three superdreadnoughts in varying stages of construction, being slowly assembled by the Funks. How long would it be until they were ready to join the fleet massing to attack the human-held stars? ONI hadn't ventured to even *guess* at the answer.

The tachyon web appeared in front of him and he braced himself, even though he knew it was futile. A cloaked ship couldn't have slipped through the network without being detected, simply through disrupting the tachyon field. The Marines had an ace up their sleeve, unless the Funks had anticipated their tactics and planned accordingly. Conrad smiled to himself as the tachyon generator came into view, a structure roughly about the same size as a destroyer – and copied from plans developed by the Cats. The Marines touched down on its surface and scrambled towards the access port embedded in the generator's hull. If the Funks had anticipated their arrival...

No enemy shuttles appeared to pick off the Marines while they were helpless. Two of the tech experts linked their suits into the systems and started to hack into the computers, using hand signals to keep the other Marines informed. It would have been neat if they could have shut down everything, but the Funks weren't stupid enough to link all of their systems together. They'd discovered that that was a bad idea long before film director Ron Moore had made famous the idea of using computer hacking to take down a defending fleet.

A hatch opened and he smiled, leading the Marines into the interior of the generator. There was another hatch on the other side, one that would allow them to get into the shipyard without triggering any alerts. He opened it and peered out, watching for traps. There was no sign of anything dangerous, apart from a handful of Worker Bee vehicles buzzing about the shipyard.

Probably giving tours for political leaders, he thought, as the Marines started to drift through the shipyard. He'd seen human shipyard workers giving similar tours to their political superiors, back when he'd been in training. There had always been the danger, if highly unlikely, of a collision that would leave them all dead. The shipyard grew closer and closer...and then he found himself standing on the superstructure. His head swam, despite the training, as his mind struggled to cope with the shifting perspective. Some of the skills he'd learned as a Royal Marine were actively harmful to a Federation Marine. In space, there was no need to have everything in the same orientation.

And it was quite possible that someone working on the ships would see them with the naked eye. The combat suits were designed to blend in with their surroundings, but there were limits, particularly if the person who saw them was experienced enough to know what should and shouldn't be there. Quickly, the Marines split up into four fire teams and headed towards their objectives, the mules unloading their backpack antimatter mines and beginning the arming sequence. It was a shame that they couldn't bring enough antimatter to vaporise the entire shipyard, but carefully-placed charges would wreak havoc. The first point – a worker's den, hidden *inside* the superstructure, came into view – and he cursed. There were at least five Funks in the den, wearing light shipsuits.

Probably slacking off, he thought, remembering the 'peacekeeping' missions the Royal Marines had handled on Earth. The Western troops had been professional, but the ones from Asia or Africa had been a very mixed bag. Some had been reasonably professional, others had been looters, rapists and child molesters. It had been a relief when they'd pulled out, even though it hadn't solved much for the locals.

Shaking his head, he extended the knives on his suit and opened the hatch. The Funks were caught completely by surprise, unable to react before he was among them, lashing out with augmented strength. Training accidents had crippled a number of would-be Federation Marines before they'd ever been commissioned into the force; he hit one Funk's scaly head and saw it disintegrate in a shower of disturbingly human-like red blood. The other four died before they could summon help, or even alert their security teams. Conrad positioned his mine in the right place, nodded to his comrades and then led the way back up the superstructure.

A superdreadnought hull loomed below him, her vitals exposed as Funks worked on her; absently, he wondered just how badly it would cost them when the ships were destroyed. The other teams met up with him at the RV point and exchanged brief hand signals, confirming success. Keeping a wary eye out for guards, they started to run back towards the rigged tachyon generator – and collided headlong with just a small group of workers. The Marines tore them apart in a storm of whirling knives, but not

363

quickly enough to prevent them from transmitting a distress signal. It was vaguely possible that the Funks wouldn't realise that the shipyard was being attacked by humans...

...But Conrad knew better than to rely on it. *Formidable* and her gunboats were still wreaking havoc in the system, daring the Funks to uncover their homeworld and come after them. There was no longer any point in trying to hide; the Marines leapt off the superstructure and raced for open space. Behind them, the timers on the mines started to count down the seconds to detonation. Even if the Funks killed them all, they'd be too late to save their shipyard.

"Assault shuttles inbound," one of the Marines sent. "Weapons hot?"

"Weapons hot," Conrad confirmed. The Marines hadn't brought their plasma rifles, but the internal weapons on their suits should be enough to let them give a good account of themselves. "Time to detonation; two minutes, seventeen seconds."

The shuttles came into view and the Marines opened fire, targeting vulnerable points like cockpits and portholes. A shuttle staggered out of the firing line, another exploded... but the remainder could track the Marines by their own blazing fire. Three Marines died within seconds as the Funks returned fire, followed rapidly by two more. The remaining shuttles drew back out of range, puzzling Conrad until he realised that they'd probably want to try to capture the would-be infiltrators alive. He smiled as the counter on his HUD ticked down to zero. They were in for a nasty surprise.

His suit's visor dimmed automatically as the antimatter charges detonated, sending colossal fireballs racing down the superstructure and into the half-constructed ships. They blew apart, throwing massive pieces of debris into the remaining parts of the shipyard. He found himself laughing as a Funk cruiser, caught docked to the shipyard, was destroyed before her crew could even begin to disengage and retreat. They probably hadn't realised what had hit them until it was already too late.

The devastation swallowed up the massive industry built to support the shipyard, certainly at least five to ten percent of the entire Funk space-based industry. Even *they* had to be hurt by so much destruction and the loss of a valuable investment; God alone knew how many clans had just seen their entire financial resources wiped out. The Funks weren't even familiar with the concept of insurance! If they won the war, they were still going to be weakened compared to the other Galactics. Maybe the Tarn would work up the nerve to jump them while they were still reeling from the loss of one of their major shipyards.

Piece of debris were flying everywhere, some heading down towards the planet. Conrad hoped that they would burn up in the atmosphere, if the Funk defenders didn't blow them into more manageable chunks first. If pieces of Skylab could survive the passage through Earth's atmosphere, he was sure that pieces of metal built to Galactic standards could come down hard on a planetary surface. The results might be devastating. But no one, not even the Empress, would be able to cover up what had happened.

His suit rocked suddenly as a tractor beam caught hold. With bloody-minded persistence, the Funks were *still* trying to capture the Marines, even though they might be better off recovering the remaining workforce before they all died in the vastness of space. The analysts had claimed that losing the workforce alone would cripple the Funk industries, forcing them to retrain workers from the planet and hire experienced personnel from the other Galactics. Who knew how many of them might be in the pay of humanity?

He looked up at the Funk shuttle and felt an odd calm sinking over him. There was no escape, not now. He remembered Cindy and felt a twinge of remorse, but there was no time to record a message for her. The one he'd left on *Formidable* would have to suffice.

As they pulled him into the shuttle's hatch, he calmly deactivated the suit's safety precautions and overloaded the plasma confinement chamber. The world vanished in a blinding flash.

* * *

"Gunboats have picked up two of the Marines," Spinner reported. "We haven't been able to pick up beacons from the others, but they might be lying low..."

Markus nodded. Two Hegemony battlecruisers were already playing catch with *Formidable*. He should have ordered the carrier to break off and withdraw ten minutes ago, but he wasn't going to abandon the Marines as long as there was a chance to get them out alive. And yet.... could he risk the entire ship for a handful of Marines? They'd known the risks going into the mission.

"Recall the remaining gunboats," he ordered. The guilt would haunt his dreams for the rest of his life, but there was no other choice. It wouldn't take long for the Funks to get other ships out, once they realised that there was little hope of rescuing survivors from the shipyard or salvaging enough to make recovery worthwhile. "We'll bug out as soon as they're within gate range of us."

He shook his head. By any standards, the mission had been a monumental success. The Funks hadn't just been embarrassed, they'd been humiliated. And their people would see just how badly their defenders had failed them. No amount of scapegoating could save the Empress now. Surely even the Funks would give up the war when they couldn't even guarantee the safety of their homeworld.

"And transmit the propaganda as we leave," he added. "We might as well ensure that they know what we've done."

Chapter Forty-One

Task Force Retribution was the single most powerful force assembled by the Hegemony outside of Home Fleet. Lady Dalsha was not blind to the implications of the Empress giving her the command, clearly calculating that an outcast who had been disowned by her clan wouldn't be able to seize the throne and declare herself Empress. Her trust had limits, as the presence of a number of Ghost Soldiers indicated; Ghosts were known for being completely loyal to the Empress and being ready to execute anyone at her merest whim. Lady Dalsha had orders to take her fleet to Earth and crush the human race. Any other direction would have signed her death warrant.

Fifteen superdreadnoughts made up the core of her fleet, backed by two squadrons of battlecruisers, three squadrons of heavy cruisers and seventy destroyers. It had been decided that there was no point in including a ground assault element, not when the human race had had years to prepare for an invasion. They'd either force Earth to surrender or systematically bombard the planet into radioactive debris. Even if they encountered Earth's full strength, Lady Dalsha was confident of victory. Not being confident would also have signed her death warrant.

The Task Force had another advantage that hadn't been granted to other forces that faced the human race. Lady Dalsha had trained them hard, incorporating all the lessons learned through previous battles against human technology. The humans might be ridiculously inventive, but they weren't gods, a theme she had hammered into her personnel's heads until they believed her. What the humans had done so far was shocking, yes, yet they weren't invincible. They could be beaten. And besides, most of their fleet was trying to hammer its way towards Hegemony Prime. They'd be surprised when their homeworld was captured or destroyed – and where would they go, if their worlds were lost to them? Their ships wouldn't be able to keep operating without supplies and no one would be helping them. Even the Tarn would give up the humans rather than face the Hegemony's wrath.

She looked down at the display showing her fleet and smiled, coldly. Some of the fleet's officers whispered that she'd been beaten by the humans and returned, a gesture of contempt that echoed back to the days before the First Empress. Such people could never be trusted fully, not when they'd been pushed into submission. They might have moved against her if the Empress hadn't sent the Ghosts, allowing them to watch her back while she planned her war against Earth. But the Ghosts might have orders to remove her anyway once the battle was won. The Empress wouldn't want anyone else claiming the credit for the victory.

There was a hiss from the speaker. "My Lady, you have a priority call from Hegemony Prime," the communications officer said. He was a male, oddly enough, serving as something of a mascot for the female officers on the ship. And a leman when they wanted to mate. Apparently the humans had similar problems, only reversed. "The Empress wishes to speak with you directly."

"Put her through," Lady Dalsha ordered. A direct call from the Empress could not be rejected, not if one wanted to keep one's head on one's shoulders. The Empress's face appeared in front of her, looking tired and worn, almost defeated. "My Empress..."

"The humans have attacked Hegemony Prime," the Empress said. Lady Dalsha stared at her mistress, her mind reeling. Had they been forced to surrender? "A raid, but one that inflicted staggering damage for minimal cost. The shipyards have been destroyed."

Lady Dalsha felt her mouth drop open in shock. The human pirate who had led the attack on Tauscher had taken down two entire clans, both losing everything and entering permanent servitude as the only way to pay their debts. But both of those clans had been small, hardly significant compared to the other clans. The destruction of the shipyards would have crippled over a dozen other clans, including some of the ones who had backed the slow pressure on humanity that would have led to eventual annexation. And a few who hadn't cared one way or the other would probably go down too. It didn't take much imagination to visualise the slow collapse that would eventually lead to civil war...

...And the High Clan would go down as well. By law laid down by the First Empress herself, the High Clan maintained a stake in each and every space-based industry or facility built by the Hegemony. In the case of the shipyards, the High Clan had poured vast sums of money into the facility, unwilling to trust other clans with control over one of the most vital facilities in the entire Hegemony. The High Clan was the richest in the Hegemony by a very long way, but could even its resources survive the loss?

It might have been worse than the humans had anticipated when they'd struck at Hegemony-Prime. Lady Dalsha knew that *her* former clan had accepted loans from the High Clan, loans that helped keep them firmly under control. How many others had done the same? What would happen when those clans went under because they ran out of money to pay their debts? If there was only one clan, the entire population would be enslaved and sold off to help pay for their debts, but what if most of the clans went down? Some of the most powerful aristocrats in the Hegemony wouldn't accept slavery tamely. Why not take up arms against the Empress? They might just win.

And many of them had friends, family and allies among the military. The Empress had tried hard to keep the defences of Hegemony Prime under her direct control, but some of the female officers had probably been subverted. And males didn't have the imagination to realise that they were being ordered to wage war against the Empress or the independent mindset to refuse if they did. Outright civil war would turn bloody very quickly as the remains of the shipyard burned up in the planet's atmosphere.

She found herself looking closely at the Empress. Was that *shooting* she could hear in the background? The Imperial Palace was the most heavily-defended building on the planet, but no building was invulnerable, even one that the attackers needed reasonably intact to support their claims to being the new Empress. And if the Empress fell...

The High Clan had survived because it allowed no strong rivals. That much was clear, even though many of the other clans had power enough to block the Empress if they united on a single issue. If the High Clan fell, there would be no single dominant power, no unifying leader. Without a strict dictator who could keep things in order...

...The entire Hegemony might collapse into chaos.

"My Empress," she said, slowly, "do you need me to bring my fleet to Hegemony Prime and...?"

"No," the Empress snapped. "You are ordered to depart at once for Earth, observing strict communications silence along the way. Once you arrive at their homeworld, you are to demand surrender – and if they refuse, you are to exterminate every last human within the solar system. Once you have cleansed their filthy system, you are to do the same to their other colonies. There will be no second chance to surrender."

Lady Dalsha hesitated. She could understand the need to exterminate humanity before they reached a position that would allow them to crack the Hegemony like an eggshell, but it would enrage the Galactics, particularly the ones who already hated the Hegemony. If enough Galactics agreed, they could probably put together a fleet that would crush the Hegemony – or what remained of it. It would be the end of her people's independence...

...But if the Empress lost her head, and the Hegemony had a civil war, her people were doomed anyway. At least humanity wouldn't be around to expand into a power vacuum caused by the civil war.

"I understand, My Empress," Lady Dalsha said. She wanted to say something reassuring, but the code that bound her people together admitted of no reassurance from an inferior to a superior. The Empress was likely to die long before the fleet reached Earth on its final voyage. What could she do once she had carried out her final order? The remains of the Hegemony might need her, if the Galactics didn't intervene...

"Good luck," the Empress said. She smiled, suddenly. "And thank you for carrying out your duty, even now. Not everyone is so loyal."

Her face vanished from the display. Lady Dalsha stared at the blank screen for a long moment, and then tapped her communicator, issuing orders. At least activity would keep her busy long enough to keep her from brooding. There would be time for that later, once the fleet was as ready to attack as she could make it. And she had ensured that no one could communicate with the outside world until after the battle.

One hour later, the task force jumped into quantum space and started its voyage towards Earth.

* * *

What if I'm wrong?

The question echoed through Tobias's mind as the First Strike Fleet raced back towards Earth, desperately preparing for a final confrontation. He was the Admiral in command, yet he had little to do once he'd issued his orders apart from paperwork...and brooding. What if he was wrong? History was littered with commanders who had misjudged their enemies and ended up with egg on their faces – or dead. And *they* had been guessing at enemies who at least shared a same basic humanity. The Funks were very far from human.

Human commanders had cursed the development of radio – and satellite communications networks – because they made it easy for their superiors to intervene. Tobias was old enough to hear stories about how micromanaging politicians had issued orders from the safety of Washington to the troops on the ground, orders that often bore little resemblance to reality. At least the Federation Navy spent much of its time on deployment outside of easy communications range, allowing him latitude to make his own decisions – but then, the disunity of the Federation Council made it easier to run the war. They set the objective; Tobias and his subordinates concentrated on making it happen.

But right now, he would have sold his soul for a far more capable form of interstellar communications network. In quantum space, they were blind. It was impossible to tell if *Formidable* had succeeded in her mission, or if the Funks had realised what she was and destroyed her before she could launch her gunboats. And... what if the data they'd picked up from the pirate king was inaccurate. If the Funks had left a week earlier than reported, it was possible that they'd already reached Earth while the Federation Navy remained in quantum space. They might return home to discover that their world was a charred cinder, with the defence force burning in space. What would be left for them, but revenge?

He'd passed on a coded warning to Sun, who would command the fleet defending Earth, but he hadn't gone into details about his own plans. Once they reached Earth, he intended to keep the First Strike Fleet under cloak, well away from the shipping lanes. The Funks would probably have the system under observation and would report to their commanders if a fleet of cruisers arrived from Hammerfall. He suspected that smaller ships would soon recover the wrecked system in the name of the Hegemony, but it would be a pointless victory. The loss of Garston would be more serious.

And there was another danger. If the Federation Council declared a state of emergency, warning Earth's population to get to the shelters, there would be panic – and enemy observation ships might pick up on it. The shipyards would have to be evacuated, the asteroid mining colonies would have to go dark... all precautions that were senseless, unless someone expected an attack. If the Funks realised that their arrival had been anticipated, they might change their plans. Or maybe they'd attack anyway. If *Formidable* had succeeded, the Hegemony was going to have a very rough time of it before it pulled back together. Taking out Earth would cripple the human race.

But that decision wasn't his, thankfully. He just had to assume the worst.

The Admiral had no one he could confide in, not even his aide. He was solely responsible for the First Strike Fleet, the man who ordered it into battle. No one could become close to him without violating regulations. Lower ranks might be allowed to fraternise provided they were careful about who they slept with – and gunboat pilots enjoyed a degree of freedom no other personnel could dream of – but the Admiral was alone. Some military officers in the past had enjoyed having their mistresses or even their wives with him, yet Tobias would never have been able to allow himself to fall so far. The Federation Navy *needed* a tradition where its officers didn't rub their advantages in the faces of the enlisted men.

Shaking his head, he headed for his bunk and sleep. His officers knew to wake him if there was a problem, such as an energy storm that forced them to alter course. And he needed rest before arriving at Earth, assuming they weren't too late.

And what if he was wrong?

Despite himself, he got very little sleep that night.

* * *

The President of the United States didn't care for Admiral Sun and he suspected that the feeling was mutual. It had been the United States that had blocked Sun's candidature for the Federation Navy's Chief of Naval Operations, a political deal that had been planned with the Russians to ensure that General Chekov was named Supreme Allied Commander Extra-Solar Expeditionary Force, and Sun presumably suspected it. Even an officer from a state where it was unwise to dissent too openly with one's superiors could resent his superiors; officers like that were often the best intelligence sources in the business.

But with Admiral Sampson at Hammerfall, Admiral Sun was in command of the Earth Defence Fleet.

"Assuming that the reports are accurate," Admiral Sun said, "we can expect a Hegemony battle force to reach Earth within one week to two months."

The President watched the reactions of the other world leaders. Organising the conference at such short notice had been difficult, even though the Federation Council had been conferring regularly ever since the war had kicked off. The secret of politics was that it was often more important to seem to be doing something rather than actually doing something, even if you couldn't do anything more than get in the way. He'd told himself that he'd do things differently when he became President, only to discover that there was little choice. Politics often got in the way of politicking.

"But the Hegemony has just lost a major shipyard," the Japanese Prime Minister said. He sounded worried, but then Japan had had plenty of experience with surprise attacks as a way to start a war. They always tended to be merciless. "Surely they cannot risk additional losses."

"I have a different question," the German Chancellor grunted. "How is it that we know about this?"

Sun hesitated. "Classified intelligence sources," he said, finally. "I'm afraid we have to keep them strictly compartmentalised…"

"How dare you?" The French President demanded. "The Federation Council is above suspicion!"

The President would have sniggered if he hadn't had good control of his expressions. Trying to steer the Federation Council was rather like herding cats, with each member trying to get an advantage for his own country out of the system. At least they were all grown up enough not to bring down the Federation in their power games. The same couldn't be said for some of their countrymen. Despite Terra Nova, despite the endless threats from the Hegemony, there were plenty of Americans who saw the Federation as just another prototype world government, one that would swallow up America and destroy everything that made the country great. It had amused the hell out of him to discover that every other world leader had similar problems.

Admiral Sun didn't snicker either. "The Federation Councillors are supported by small armies of aides," he said. "Are they all trustworthy? What about the secretaries? Or the interns? Or the guards? Are they all such paragons of virtue that secrets can be freely discussed in front of them?"

The President smiled. Bill Clinton should have been more careful about trusting the intern who'd given him oral sex, although he had no idea how Clinton had found the time. The President was always busy, mostly reading reports, listening to briefings and pressing the flesh. It was easy to believe that one of the people working for him reported to someone else without his permission. Information was power in the American government, particularly if you got it first.

"That isn't the issue at hand," the President said, cutting into the discussion. Perhaps Sun wasn't such a bad guy after all. "We believe that we have an attack incoming. Do we declare a state of planetary emergency or do we take the chance that the reports are false?"

He looked from face to face. "This has to be a joint decision," he said. "We cannot have one of us declaring a state of emergency and expect the media not to notice. There will be panic."

"And if we *do* declare a state of emergency," the French President pointed out, "the economy goes down the tubes. It's fragile right now, even with the loans from the Galactics."

The President scowled at him. He would have bet good money that the Frenchman's ugly wife, bratty teenage daughter and two preteen sons were already on their way to somewhere safe. The Secret Service had provided him with a dossier on their behaviour during a state visit to the White House that had made interesting reading. It was a pity that it probably couldn't be used for blackmail material.

"I don't think that any of us would want to be in office when the survivors start asking questions," he said, flatly. Maybe he could push the council in the right direction. "I'm going to declare a state of emergency. My very strong advice is that you all do the same. So far, the war has been far from our world. That may be about to change."

He stood up. "We may not meet again," he added, allowing himself a little melodrama. "But even if we lose this war, we gave them a lesson they won't forget in a hurry. Maybe we will upset the Galactic apple cart so badly that the Hegemony won't be able to keep up."

Chapter Forty-Two

"Status report?"

"*Voyager* transited back into quantum space," Sooraya said. "So far, the Funks have not arrived in the solar system. Admiral Sun has uploaded a tactical sit-rep for you."

Tobias nodded. Lurking in quantum space was an old tactic, well known to the Galactics, but assuming the Funks didn't know that he'd abandoned Hammerfall, they wouldn't be expecting it. By keeping his fleet hidden, it was just possible that he could induce the Funks to commit themselves to attacking Earth before realising that they were about to put themselves into a meatgrinder. If the Funks had realised just how many ships were waiting for them, they might have thought better of their plans.

But perhaps it wouldn't make any difference, he realised as he scrolled through the report. The strike on Hegemony Prime had succeeded beyond his wildest expectations, leaving the Funks tumbling down into civil war. None of their intelligence sources had even *seen* their Empress for the last three days. She might be dead, or in hiding, or attempting to rally her supporters for a counterattack... if she had any supporters left. Even the worst human dictators had been able to call upon considerable support when their positions were threatened, but the Funks seemed to do it differently. Some of their traditions even included the concept of honourable betrayal, abandoning a leader whose position had become untenable before civil war could devastate the entire system.

The Hegemony was going down; according to one report, units of the Hegemony Navy had even started firing at each other. They'd be too busy for the foreseeable future to worry about humanity, assuming that humanity survived the coming battle. But in its death agonies the Hegemony might just take Earth down with it. Perhaps that was why they'd launched a mighty fleet at Earth. Maybe they'd learned the concept of total war from the human race.

"Hold our position here," Tobias ordered. He'd reorganised his squadrons as best as he could, although the losses from recent fighting had forced him to combine units that had never served together before the flight to Earth. They'd been training hard ever since, yet there were limits to how well simulations could teach lessons. But there was no time for proper exercises. "Admiral Sun will update us when the enemy fleet arrives."

If it does arrive, he added, in the privacy of his own thoughts. Knowing the Funks, it was quite possible that the enemy commander, realising that she was in command of the largest surviving segment of the Hegemony Navy, might make her own bid to become Empress. Or he might have been completely wrong and the Funks merely intended to hit Garston or even Terra Nova...although three entire squadrons of superdreadnoughts were massive overkill for any target, but Earth.

He shrugged. Coordinating operations between normal space and quantum space wasn't easy, but it was easier than trying to coordinate across interstellar distances. One lesson humanity *had* learned quickly – and so had the Funks – was that the simpler the plan, the better. He'd just have to hope that he wasn't being too clever for his own good. But the opportunity to deliver a final blow to the Hegemony was too good to allow to slip by without at least trying to take advantage of it.

"Back to training," he said. There was nothing he could do now, but wait. "But tell the Alpha crews that I want them to get some rest. God knows how long it will be before the shit hits the fan."

* * *

Admiral Sun knew himself to be more of an administrator than a fighter. His career in the People's Liberation Army Navy had been devoted to building up a force that could challenge American dominance of the seas near China, a task that had forced him to concentrate on fighting paper wars with Communist Party planners rather than actually training and preparing for the actual fighting.

He'd been rather amused to discover that his American counterparts envied his budget and access to the resources of China, apparently because they believed that a Communist state could simply order whatever resources it needed devoted to the military. Anyone who believed *that* had clearly never tried to operate within a Communist economy.

The Federation Navy had faced hundreds of very real limitations in building up a fleet that could challenge the Hegemony. Earth had had a pathetic space program before Mentor had arrived and gave the human race the technology it needed to burst out into the solar system. There was a staggering shortage of trained manpower, even after fifteen years of development, and dozens of production bottlenecks. And the Federation Navy hadn't had first call on *all* of humanity's resources. Earth's growing space-based industry had needed manpower and spacecraft too.

He studied the fleet taking shape in orbit and scowled. It looked formidable, all right, but he knew its limitations. Five *Admiral*-class cruisers, the most advanced ships in the galaxy, had taken point, but they were tied to their comrades. A hundred military starships, all bought or begged from the Galactics, and fifty-seven modified freighters. He knew, better than anyone else on Earth, precisely what would happen if the older ships came to grips with Hegemony superdreadnoughts: they'd be slaughtered.

Fifty years, he thought, sourly. Americans seemed to place more faith in planners than the Chinese, an irony that would have amused him under other circumstances, but he had no doubt about those figures. Fifty years of uninterrupted development would have made Earth invincible, at least until the Galactics duplicated Earth's advances and installed them in their fleets. The Hegemony wouldn't have been able to even stay in the running. Perhaps that explained why they had brought so much pressure to bear on Earth. They'd understood, dimly, that human advancement was a deadly threat and acted to squash it before it was too late. But if they had really understood...

...They might have attacked Earth without warning.

He turned and looked at the viewscreen, which showed Earth rotating slowly under his fleet. The planet was panicking, law and order steadily breaking down; a mocking reminder of the pre-Contact days when most of human civilization had been reasonably safe and secure. Few civilians really comprehended the crushing power of the Galactics, but those who could read fleet lists would probably be able to work out that humanity was badly outnumbered. The results of the coming confrontation might be disastrous. Hundreds of thousands were fleeing for shelter; millions were scrambling to find a safe place to hide. A handful of politicians who had opposed building shelters for the population had been threatened with lynching as people sought someone to blame. The fact that the politicians had been right – antimatter weapons could crack the entire planet in half – would be meaningless to them. It was far better to spend that money on the Federation Navy.

"Admiral," Commander Gustav Wallenberg said, "I have the latest update from the OWPs."

Sun nodded, careful to keep his face immobile. "I presume that they have finished their work?"

"The engineers report that three of the five platforms are now operational," Wallenberg said, "but I'm afraid that the other two need their components switched out before they can be activated. The dealers who sold them to us didn't take very good care of them."

"Which explains why they were on the market in the first place," Sun said. Galactic technology was tough, robust in a way that few human products could match, but even it wore down. And most military suppliers among the Galactics were not entirely trustworthy. ONI had speculated that the more powerful Galactics rigged the market to ensure that the weaker powers didn't get any stronger. "Make a note of the dealer. Maybe we can hunt him up for damages later."

Back in China, the PLAN had had real problems with quality control. Sun had worried – endlessly – over state-sponsored factories that produced shoddy goods, even with everything they'd learned from the West. Even when they'd tracked down the source of the useless technology, they'd often found it difficult to punish the people responsible. Their political connections were always first-rate. But supersonic missiles intended to be fired at American aircraft carriers were more complex than AK-47s. At least the Federation Navy had had the clout to challenge defective factories. Maybe the *real* reason why he'd been denied the post of CNO was that he'd put too many noses out of joint while serving under Admiral Sampson.

"Yes, sir," his aide said. "I'm afraid that Alan Beresford has been in contact again, demanding to speak with you personally."

Sun wanted to order his aide to tell the British MP that he was busy, perhaps on a week-long EVA inspection trip, but he knew better. The politicians always wanted their hands held, even the ones who had the experience or insight to realise that it was a waste of time. Beresford had been a thorn in his flesh since Clarke had been occupied by the Hegemony, largely because he had vast investments on the planet which stood to make him very rich – assuming that the human race survived the war. He'd been demanding that the Federation Navy liberate Clarke yesterday, if possible. Sun, who agreed with his superior that Clarke was probably a feint to draw the Federation Navy away from Earth, had declined.

"I'll speak to him in my office," he said, tiredly. His body wanted sleep, but he had no time to rest. Too much needed to be done in too little time. At least Admiral Sampson was in position. They'd certainly give the Funks a bloody nose when they attacked. "Has there been any update from the IDG team?"

"Nothing since the last update," his aide said, patiently. "They merely reported that they were in position and running test cycles on the generator."

Sun nodded, slowly. He'd named the generator personally, pointing out that the Galactics probably weren't interested in the teachings of a military theorist from a society that hadn't possessed gunpowder at the time. And besides, the name was fitting.

"Inform me at once if there are any changes," he ordered.

He'd go talk to the politician. Maybe that would distract him from the endless waiting.

* * *

"Layabouts," Ward thundered. "Look at them down there, screaming for help. Why didn't they think about the dangers before it was too late?"

Betty, his secretary, shrugged. She was an elderly woman, appointed to the post at the insistence of Ward's wife, even though *he* would have preferred a young and charming girl just out of college. Not that he would have touched her, of course; he could hardly have afforded the scandal after years of making political enemies. It had been bad enough when the IRS had insisted on auditing their accounts, twice in a row.

"Young people these days have no sense of history," Ward continued. "A whole universe of opportunity awaits them and they don't even *care*."

He'd been a grown man when the human race had been contacted by Mentor. The world had seemed to be entering a decline that might have resulted in anarchy, or so he'd feared. There were no longer any hopes and dreams for the young, no clear crusades against evil and politicians who were little more than crooks. An angry man had gone into journalism, fully expecting to spend his last days reporting on another seeming constant that had just turned upside down. And instead the Galactics had arrived and offered humanity the keys to the stars.

Terra Nova had seemed a blessing when it had first been settled. A new world, one that could be shaped by its first settlers...if they ever got the chance. Every nation on Earth had insisted on contributing colonists, creating ethnic and racial tensions that might have torn the planet's fragile society apart. The Funks might have proved a blessing in disguise, at least according to some of the reporters on the ground. Uniting against a common foe had forced

381

humanity to put its own conflicts on the backburner. And it helped that the Funks had managed to convince Earth to throw all the money it could at the Federation Navy.

But now the Funks were on their way to Earth.

He looked down at the screaming mob and snorted unpleasantly. Fifteen years of warning and yet relatively few people had done the smart thing and prepared an emergency plan to leave the cities and find shelter. *Ward* had purchased a ranch in Texas with his brother and made plans to move there as soon as necessary, once the shit really hit the fan. But he'd been reluctant to leave until it was clear that there was nothing more he could do to keep reporting the news. Maybe he'd already left it too late. The roads out of every city in America were jammed with terrified civilians trying to get out of Dodge before it was too late. Constant broadcasts from the President appealing for calm were having almost no effect at all. Everyone knew that the President and *his* family were going to be in a bunker when the Funks arrived, safe from everything apart from planet-crackers. But what about *their* family?

The police – what remained of them after nearly half of the NYPD had deserted – finally moved in to try to contain the riot. Ward watched emotionlessly as some rioters scattered, while others tried to fight – or carry on looting under cover of the riot. Some of the reports from the inner cities, where the police were too overstretched to go, were horrifying. He caught sight of a young man, blood streaming from a blow to the forehead, being carted away by a pair of police officers, just before the first gas canisters started to burst. God alone knew what would happen to the poor bastard. The police were generally good at taking care of injured civilians, even would-be rioters, but Ward had heard that the hospitals were overwhelmed and short-staffed. A blow to the head that would have been easy to handle in hospital might prove fatal if he didn't receive medical treatment in time.

"They should get their heads out of their asses," he muttered, as a line of rioters charged the police. Someone had been distributing weapons, probably one of the professional troublemakers who kept getting involved with peaceful protests and turning them into violent riots. "What the hell sort of good do they think that this is going to cause?"

The building rocked, slightly. "And what the hell was that?"

Betty checked her Ipad. "Security reports that some of the rioters just slammed against our doors," she said. Ward had ordered them closed with the emergency shutters as soon as the riot had started to take shape. There was a fine line between reporting the news and becoming part of it. "They're recommending that we evacuate the building, just in case."

"Tell the crew that anyone who wants to go can go, if they use the tunnels," Ward said, shortly. He hired brave journalists, men and women ready to put themselves into danger just for a scoop, but the editors and other supporting staff weren't chosen for their bravery. "At least we moved operations to our country site."

He looked down again and shook his head. The police had counterattacked, knocking the rioters down and securing their hands with plastic cuffs, pushing male and female protestors against the walls and forcing them to wait until they could be taken away. Most of the dangerous rioters scattered, intent on taking the fighting elsewhere. The police would normally have thrown up a cordon to catch them, but Ward had no idea if they had enough manpower to do it now that the entire city was on the verge of collapse. He caught sight of a pair of bodies wearing NYPD uniforms and shuddered. The young might talk of living without rules, but Ward was old enough to know that anarchy was never a good thing.

"Who needs the blasted Funks?" He demanded. "We're perfectly capable of wrecking our own planet without them""

The television switched from a CNN update to another speech from the President. Ward rolled his eyes and changed the channel. The President wasn't the solution, not when he was part of the problem. People were scared and no amount of empty reassurance from politicians would change that. And no one had the moral stature to stand up and ask for calm, with the possible exception of Admiral Sampson. He could run for President based purely upon his war record and probably win in a landslide.

Assuming we have a next election campaign, he thought. Even if the Funks didn't destroy the world, who knew what would happen after this week of anarchy?

And all the human race could do was wait for Judgement Day.

* * *

"We are approaching Earth, My Lady."

Lady Dalsha opened her eyes and clambered out of the water bath in her quarters. Sleeping in water had once been an unimaginable luxury; even now, when they had access to the boundless resources of space, it was still regarded with awe. At one time, she would have considered it nothing more than her due. Now... she knew it was perhaps her last chance to experience luxury.

"Proceed as planned," she ordered, as a force field flicked the water off her scales. "I will be on the bridge directly."

Oddly, she found herself thinking of her hatchlings. All females were expected to contribute at least two clutches of eggs to her clan before going into danger, a tradition that dated back to the days where they'd struggled for water and resources. She'd never seen them since they'd been taken by the clan mothers, not knowingly. It was tradition. The clan came first, beyond any maternal instincts. And yet they would carry on her genes even if she lost the coming battle.

But what sort of universe would they inherit?

She put the thought aside as she donned her uniform and walked to the bridge. Everything had just become simple again. Either she would win, or she would die.

If the Hegemony had to fall, at least it would take the human race down with it.

Chapter Forty-Three

"Admiral?"

Admiral Sun looked up from his desk, fighting back the urgent desire to yawn. He'd caught a couple of brief naps in-between reading reports and monitoring training simulations, but not enough to keep him from feeling sleepy. The doctors had given him a booster, adding strict warnings that he was not to even consider using it until the enemy actually arrived.

"Yes," he said, "what is it?"

"Long-range sensors have detected quantum gates opening near Mars," Wallenberg said. "CIC calls them Hegemony superdreadnought gates."

"Understood," Sun said. He pressed the tap against his bare arm and grimaced as it pumped the booster into his bloodstream. Users got nearly a day before they had to go to bed to sleep it off. A second dose was out of the question. "I'm on my way. Alert the fleet and dispatch a courier boat to Admiral Sampson."

He glanced around his office, taking a final look at the wall he'd covered with medals and decorations from his career in both the PLAN and the Federation Navy, and then headed to the CIC. The booster was starting to work, leaving him feeling supercharged, as if he had eaten enough sugar to turn him into a hyperactive child. It was a shame that he couldn't feel so good permanently, but the doctors had made it quite clear; boosters were more addictive than even Joy Juice and breaking the addiction was almost impossible. Even an admiral couldn't order boosters without facing hard questions from the medical staff. He strode into the CIC, waving aside the Marine who was about to announce his presence, and took one look at the display. A handful of red icons clustered near Mars.

"Curious," he said, aloud. CIC's tactical staff had already started attempting to project the enemy's intentions, yet their tactics made little sense. Even if the Funks intended to slip back into quantum space and reach Earth that way, the Federation Navy had already been alerted. Standard doctrine ordered starships to emerge as close to their target as possible, to minimise the time their enemies had to prepare their defences. "Tactical analysis?"

"Maybe they intend to blow up the Marine facilities at Olympus Mons," Wallenberg suggested. "Or perhaps they intend to destroy Scarlet Base."

"Or Robinson City," Sun agreed. And yet that didn't quite make sense either. None of humanity's facilities on Mars were in any way *vital*, certainly not compared to the Luna Yards or Island One. There might have been a few million humans on Mars slowly turning the planet into a decent place to live, but why bother to target them…

…Unless the Funks aimed at total extermination. The thought made him shiver, despite what the sociologists had claimed time and time again. They pointed to Funk history and asserted that the Funks didn't destroy their enemies; they merely assimilated them into the victorious clan. But that hadn't worked out too well for the Gobbles, or anyone else unlucky enough to fall into their claws. Multiracial breeding was just as impossible for the Funks as for any other race, limiting how far outsiders could blend into the victorious Hegemony.

Not for the first time, he found himself cursing the limitations of active and passive sensors. Opening a quantum gate generated a pulse that travelled faster than light, but all other sensors were restricted to light-speed. The Funks could be bombarding Mars now and Earth wouldn't know about it for several minutes. Mars would send an update as soon as possible, yet even if Mars *was* under attack the Federation Navy couldn't move out of position to cover the red planet, not when Earth was threatened. The separatists on Mars would make vast amounts of political capital out of it.

"Earth has issued a warning," Wallenberg said, a minute later. "All emergency procedures are going into effect."

"Keep the Federation Council informed, but don't give them an open channel," Sun ordered. There was no point in the Council issuing orders, not now, but few politicians would realise that. Maybe it would cost him his career... if, of course, enough humans remained alive afterwards for him to be put in front of a court-martial board. "Inform me if anything on Earth requires my attention."

It shouldn't, he knew. All civilian aircraft would have been ordered to the nearest airport, regardless of who they were or where they were going. The shelters, such as they were, would be taking people in, while others headed for basements or homes in the countryside. Everyone had been advised to prepare for several days without food or drink, causing a rush on supermarkets and drugstores. The results were chaotic, but assuming Earth survived, they should be tolerable. He'd had plenty of time to ensure that the Federation Navy's entire complement of personnel – including reserves – were called up for duty. Down on Earth, national formations would be taking up their own defensive positions, or hiding in the countryside to launch an insurgency against alien occupiers. Sun knew he wouldn't live to see the insurgency. One way or another, he had no intention of surrendering his command to the Funks.

"Update," the sensor officer snapped. "Enemy fleet is moving towards Earth."

Sun frowned as the display updated. The Funks seemed to have chosen to ignore Mars completely, yet why had they decided to come out so far from Earth? Unless...they *wanted* the human defenders concentrated? Did they have some new superweapon? The Funks might have been very bad at basic research – ONI estimated that they had only a handful of really competent scientists – but they might have bought something from one of the other Galactics. Some societies were far better at keeping secrets from the human race than the Funks.

"Order Commodore Yu to prepare to engage," Sun ordered. The Hegemony force bearing down on Earth was too powerful for him to stop if he played by the rules, at least as the Galactics understood them. But he had other ideas. Humanity had had plenty of time to think of nasty tricks, some of them coming from science-fiction writers who had been thinking about space warfare long before Earth had started to build a fleet to defend the planet. "And send in the gunboats as soon as Yu deploys. We need to keep him covered as long as possible."

* * *

The planet the humans called Mars was worthless, at least to the Hegemony. Apart from establishing a tiny observation post on the planet hundreds of years ago, the Association had largely agreed. There were plenty of habitable worlds without intelligent races in the galaxy to settle, so why bother colonising Mars? The human terraforming project had been viewed as a sign of weakness by the Hegemony, an admission that humanity didn't have the nerve or the strength to establish itself as a galactic power. Lady Dalsha wondered, instead, if it was a sign of something else, a grasping nature that rivalled the Hegemony. How many worlds could the humans have claimed by now if the galaxy had been largely unpopulated?

She pushed the thought aside as her fleet shook down into battle formation. Two of her subordinates had revealed their nervousness by questioning her orders. Thankfully, they'd had the sense to do it privately, saving her the need to assert herself by having them both killed. The humans seemed to promote their officers based on merit rather than political connections; indeed, they seemed to *disapprove* of nepotism. Lady Dalsha found it difficult to grasp why human clans weren't expected to boost their members where possible, but she had to admit that it worked out for them. Squashing potential rivals from other clans might not have been the best strategy since the Hegemony had been invited into the stars. But that was something they hadn't been able to change.

It was tempting to send a message back to the Empress and learn what was happening on Hegemony Prime, but she'd forbidden all communications. The civil war was probably underway by now, with the Navy fragmenting along clan lines and Household troops fighting for dominance. It was quite possible that the Empress was dead. Not knowing was agony, yet if she had known... what could she do about it? Nothing, save ensuring that the human race was in no condition to take advantage of the coming power vacuum. Revenge was all they had left right now.

"Take us towards Earth," she ordered, flatly. Coming out near Mars flew in the face of tactical doctrine, but it made it harder for the humans to surprise her. And perhaps her tactics would confuse and worry them. Humans had more imagination than most of her kind, so maybe they'd imagine all kinds of superweapons she didn't possess. Another lesson from the clan wars prior to the First Empress was that care, deliberation and an unflinching refusal to allow herself to be bullied into making mistakes could keep even a weaker force from being trapped and forced into surrender. "Launch recon probes on a constant transmission loop."

No one questioned the order, even though it too flew in the face of tactical doctrine. Recon drones were stealthy, but not stealthy enough to escape sensors. Some reports suggested that human sensors were considerably better than Galactic designs, probably allowing them to track the drones easily. There was nothing to be gained by ordering the drones to remain silent if they could be detected and picked off before they could transmit.

Slowly, as the fleet crawled the distance between Mars and Earth, data started to flow into the tactical network. The human fleet didn't seem to be anything like as powerful as the fleet that had struck fear into the heart of the Hegemony, although she had to caution herself not to take anything for granted. A freighter armed with the cursed human phase cannon could probably inflict some damage on a superdreadnought before it was destroyed. Five cruisers, a design she had learned to hate, led the human fleet, but the remainder were all old model ships from the Association. The largest of them was a battlecruiser that looked to be over five hundred years old. It didn't seem as if its drive had ever been replaced, let alone updated.

"Tactical analysis suggests that the older ships are operating on minimal crews," one of the tactical officers said. He was unusually imaginative for a male, channelling the natural competitive instincts of the male mind into his struggles to understand what the humans had created. "They must not have the manpower to crew them properly."

Lady Dalsha hadn't put any faith in what Hegemony Intelligence had been reporting about human development since they'd smashed her squadron at Terra Nova, but even they had to have limits. Training up personnel for their crews took time, perhaps longer than they had had before kicking off the war. Galactic starships might be largely standardized, thanks to the Cats, yet each ship had its differences. The Hegemony had had its own problems when it had been restricted to purchasing starships from other powers.

"So it would seem," she agreed. A battlecruiser required upwards of a thousand humanoids to crew it properly. The Cats, for reasons no one understood, had placed limits on the development of automated systems for starships, even though they would have saved manpower considerably. Not that it really mattered. Fifteen superdreadnoughts could crush even the human fleet waiting for them.

"Incoming ships," the tactical officer said, suddenly. "I'm picking up... seven freighters, Type-56 medium transports."

The human squadron seemed to be racing directly towards them, which was nothing more than suicide. Or so it seemed. The humans had taken out an entire command fortress with a starship crammed with antimatter. Why wouldn't they try to repeat their feat against a fleet of superdreadnoughts? But the freighters didn't seem to mount military-grade shielding. They'd be blown to dust long before they got into ramming position. Unless the humans had invented a way to compress even more antimatter into a freighter...

"Order the destroyer screen to intercept," she ordered. Splitting her fleet was yet another tactical innovation, but nine destroyers didn't represent a significant part of her combat power. And if the freighters *were* loaded with antimatter, sacrificing the destroyers would be an acceptable trade. "And then slow the main body of the fleet. Force them to come to us."

The minutes ticked away until the display changed rapidly as the human formation separated into two groups. Thirty gunboats appeared, as if from nowhere, and lanced forwards towards the destroyers, while the freighters they were covering turned and ran back towards Earth, trying to hide from the wrath of her superdreadnoughts. They'd taken the gunboats into battle intending to launch them close to her fleet! The freighters had to be another form of gunboat carrier, just like the one that had hammered Garston and sneaked up to Hegemony Prime. Of course the humans would have more than one design suitable for carrying the accursed little craft.

But without their carriers, the gunboats would rapidly run out of life support and their pilots would expire.

"Increase speed," she ordered. The freighters didn't seem to have military-grade drives either. Her superdreadnoughts could run them down before they reached the shelter of Earth and the Federation Navy. "I want those freighters destroyed the moment we enter range."

The gunboats were savaging her destroyers, despite the best efforts of their crews. Destroyers carried plenty of point defence weapons, but their hulls couldn't take a constant bombardment from implosion bolts without being rapidly overwhelmed and destroyed. Her fleet closed into range, firing on the gunboats in the hopes of picking them off, yet the gunboats merely turned and fled back towards Earth. Hegemony Intelligence claimed that one of their best sources on Earth had said that there were over five *hundred* gunboats assigned to the defence of Earth, but she knew that they were wrong. So many gunboats could have destroyed the entire Hegemony Navy.

And the range between her and the freighters was dropping rapidly. Soon they would be able to open fire...and then they would see.

* * *

"Commodore Yu reports that Operation Squash is underway," the communications officer said, "but he feels that his squadron cannot get away from the Hegemony ships in time."

Sun nodded. He'd known the likely cost of Operation Squash almost as soon as it had been proposed. But trading a handful of freighters for a superdreadnought or two was a net gain by Galactic standards. At least losing Yu's ships wouldn't decrease his combat power any, nor would the Martyr Brigades donated by Iran. No one had been quite sure if the Iranian Government was sincere about wanting to rejoin the world's community or merely trying to get rid of a vast number of potential terrorists, but at least their deaths would achieve more than butchering harmless civilians.

He started to issue orders, and then stopped. There was no point in micromanaging Commodore Yu from the safety of his cruiser. Yu knew what he had to do to escape and no orders from his superior would change that. All they would achieve would be to irritate him.

The distance between Yu's squadron and the Hegemony fleet closed with staggering speed. Someone on the other side clearly intended to wipe Yu out before he could make it home, precisely the conclusion the tactical planners had hoped that the enemy would draw. Offering them a chance to destroy Earth's tiny carrier force was something they couldn't pass up; their very eagerness proved that they'd drawn the wrong conclusion. Gunboats didn't need to be *inside* the freighters to hitch a ride.

He settled back in his command chair and waited. It wouldn't be long now before the Funks realised that they'd been conned.

And if they kept going for another two minutes, they were about to be savaged.

* * *

The core difference between males and females from the Hegemony was that males were excitable, emotional creatures while females were cold, calculating and capable of working together with other females to keep the males under control. Or so they were taught at birth, with enough

392

discipline hammered into their scales to make sure that they rarely lost control. No female *would* lose control unless shocked beyond all recognition.

Lady Dalsha's head snapped up as one of the female tactical officers yelped in alarm. "Mines," she shouted, as new icons flashed into existence on the displays. "Mines ahead!"

"All stop," Lady Dalsha ordered, keeping a firm grip on her own emotions. There was no time for panic, whatever the tactical officer thought. "Evasive action!"

The humans had tricked her, despite all of her careful preparation. Those freighters hadn't been carriers at all, but minelayers. Everyone had *known* that mining interplanetary space wasn't cost-effect, not when a potential attacker could approach from almost any angle. The mines the humans had used at Hammerfall had floated into a relatively small area of space...

Here, they'd lured her right onto the minefield. No... they'd laid it right in front of her fleet and she hadn't even noticed. She'd been so captivated by the opportunity to take out the carriers for no loss that she hadn't considered the possibility of a trap.

The first mine detonated against a cruiser's shields, exploding with staggering force. Others targeted destroyers or superdreadnoughts, activating tiny one-use drives that sent them hurtling towards their targets before they could escape. The superdreadnoughts opened fire, sweeping the remaining mines from space, yet it wasn't enough. Three superdreadnoughts were badly damaged, including one that wasn't fit to continue the offensive. Just like that, the humans had evened the odds.

But it wouldn't be enough to save them.

"Sweep space for further minefields," she ordered.

They wouldn't catch her that way twice, she vowed. She was prepared to run the risk of burning out her active sensors in exchange for avoiding any further traps. At least these mines weren't as dangerous as the ones they'd used at Hammerfall.

"And then resume course," she added. "Take us to Earth."

Chapter Forty-Four

"Well, we didn't expect that to stop them, did we?"

The mood in the CIC had darkened as the Funks resumed their course for Earth. A handful of destroyed ships weren't enough to convince the Funks to think better of their plans, even though at least two superdreadnoughts were badly damaged. They were still in formation, however, which suggested that the damage wasn't *that* serious. It was difficult to tell at long range, but the techs who had swarmed over the captured superdreadnoughts had reported that they could take a hell of a lot of punishment before being crippled or destroyed. The Cats had designed them very well.

"This is definitely the Battle of the Line," one of the sensor operators muttered, just loud enough to be heard. "We're going to get our asses kicked."

"That will do," Sun said, mildly. "General orders to the fleet; the battle line will prepare to advance against the enemy."

The Funks were playing it carefully, very carefully. Their speed had slowed to the point where it would take them upwards of an hour to range in on Earth and – according to the stealth recon drones – they were probing every atom in space with intense suspicion. If Commodore Yu had had the time and supplies to lay more mines, they'd probably have seen them before the mines entered attack range. They'd probably learned a great deal from their attempts to sweep the skies over Hammerfall.

Sun could feel the tension rising on *Pompey's* bridge as the crew braced themselves for the coming onslaught. The Italians had insisted on naming her – they'd contributed enough money to the Federation to pay for one of the cruisers – but there had been a shortage of famous Admirals from Italy that passed through the Navy's approval process. Eventually, they'd named her after the son of Pompey the Great, the man who had bedevilled Caesar Augustus. The thought of the political strife over the naming of a handful of cruisers never failed to amuse him, and distract him from the coming battle.

The seconds ticked down relentlessly. "Admiral," a sensor tech reported, "the enemy fleet is approaching Point Custer."

"The battle line will advance," Sun said. He tapped his console. "Formation Alpha-Three; I say again, Formation Alpha-Three."

Pompey shivered as her drives pushed her out of orbit, heading right towards the enemy fleet. The cruisers could easily have outraced the other ships, but Sun had ordered them to keep pace so they could attack in a body. Most of the converted freighters were really little more than missile platforms, or suicide vessels ready to try to ram the enemy ships. The remaining warships were no more advanced than anything belonging to the Hegemony. Buying warships from the Galactics had its disadvantages.

And the Funks were almost at Point Custer.

The tactical display updated itself, displaying projected trajectories and the likely point of contact between the two fleets. Each projection varied from time to time, as the Funks altered course slightly or slowed to continue scanning for mines lying in wait for their ships. Sun had to smile, even though he knew that their efforts were wasted. There were no other mines waiting for them to make a mistake.

And if their timing failed, he'd be committed to close action against an enemy fleet that outgunned him by at least ten to one.

Sun was one of the very few people on Earth who knew about Bolthole. Admiral Sampson had ordered it done in complete secrecy, choosing not to inform the Federation Council. The Council would have debated endlessly over who should be allowed to go, wasting time the human race needed to prepare its last ditch strategy. A small crew, a few hundred colonists... and a complete genetic bank for humanity had been prepared and launched into space, along with a pair of destroyers for escort. If Earth died today, and the Nine Stars were wiped out soon afterwards, the human race would live on. And with a complete technological base at their disposal, the new colony would develop far faster than anyone would expect. By the time they encountered the Galactics again, they would be more advanced than anyone except – perhaps – the Cats.

The thought was reassuring, even though he could never have shared it with his crew. Bolthole's best defence was secrecy...and if that meant leaving the vast majority of people convinced that humanity was about to become extinct, it was a worthwhile price to pay.

He smiled as the two fleets converged. One way or another, the Battle of Earth was going to go down in the history books. And some of those books *would* be written by humans.

* * *

Lady Dalsha watched calmly as the human fleet slowly deployed in front of her. The humans were good at using their gunboats to destroy the recon probes, but she'd already managed to get a fairly complete picture of their fleet. Apart from the five cruisers, there was nothing in the fleet to concern her – even if they *were* suicide ships. They'd programmed their datanets to compensate for human tricks; any starship that came within ramming distance would instantly be targeted by every superdreadnought within range.

"Target the cruisers first," she ordered. The warships the humans had somehow obtained from the Galactics, using the funds from Garston, wouldn't be a serious problem unless they did manage to ram the superdreadnoughts. They just couldn't put out enough firepower to deter her fleet from advancing. Besides, she had a surprise of her own up in her claws. "Open fire as soon as they come into range."

She felt her mouth drop open in a cold smile of anticipation. "And launch the special missiles as soon as we engage the enemy," she added. "Your target is Earth."

* * *

"Enemy fleet is targeting us," a tactical officer said. "Request permission to bring jammers online."

"Power them up, but do not activate until they are about to open fire," Sun ordered. The jammers were supposed to work, according to the experts on Galactic technology, but they'd never been tested outside of simulations. One word of warning leaking out and the technology might become useless very quickly. At least humanity had a slight range advantage. "All ships are to open fire as soon as we come into range. The targets are the superdreadnoughts."

The Funk formation was shifting rapidly, showing a well-drilled precision that would have been admirable if they hadn't been enemies. Their smaller craft hung back, while the superdreadnoughts slipped into the lead, ready to turn their awesome firepower on his ships. Someone on the other side had more imagination than he would have liked, he realised; they knew that their smaller ships would get chopped apart by human phase cannon, so they weren't exposing them as doctrine suggested. Instead, the superdreadnoughts would hammer his ships while their smaller comrades covered their flanks and made attack runs difficult.

Coming to think of it, he thought, *they can probably enhance their point defence from those positions. Someone on that side has been thinking about what we can do and how to counter it.*

The seconds ticked down… and then…

Pompey opened fire. Her consorts followed a second later, bright beams of energy flaring from their hulls and lancing out to strike the Hegemony superdreadnoughts. The beams rotated their modulation rapidly, but to no avail; the Funks had reinforced their shields until they entered firing range of their own weapons. It was clever, Sun admitted to himself, effectively defusing the human range advantage. And their smaller ships could still target the gunboats if they lunged into the attack.

"Enemy ships are preparing to fire," the tactical officer said. "Jammers online and ready…"

"Evasive action," Sun ordered. They'd simulated the results of the jammers endlessly until they'd worked out most of the possible moves and countermoves available to the combatants once the jammers were deployed. One possible tactic for the Funks was simply firing using the last firing solution they'd worked out before the jammers were activated and praying for a direct hit. "Continue firing!"

* * *

"We've lost our targeting locks!"

Lady Dalsha swallowed a curse. Targeting locks were needed to concentrate fire against a target and the humans had somehow disrupted her systems. At least they could fire at where the humans had been, but they wouldn't remain there for long. And with the Hegemony ships opening fire, they were suddenly vulnerable to human fire. The humans had timed their latest surprise perfectly.

"Adjust targeting computers," she ordered, as her superdreadnought lurched. A human beam had sliced into her hull before the shields automatically adjusted to compensate. "Track their weapons and fire back based on the origin of their shots."

It was complicated, more complicated than the standard method, but it seemed to work. And only the human cruisers were firing. The rest of their ships seemed to be hanging back, almost as if they were trying to avoid attracting her attention. Or if they wanted her to forget about them while the fiendishly capable human cruisers tore into her fleet. But once she had forgotten about them, they probably intended to ram her ships.

But they'd underestimated the sheer level of firepower she'd brought to the battle.

"Battlecruisers are to shift fire to the Galactic ships," she said. It was unlikely in the extreme that any actual *Galactics* would be onboard. Even if there were, the Hegemony wouldn't be blamed for their deaths. "Superdreadnoughts and heavy cruisers are to continue targeting the human cruisers."

* * *

"Admiral," Wallenberg said, "some of these Funk missiles are behaving oddly."

Sun tapped his console and zoomed in on the data from the recon drones. Wallenberg was right; the Artificial Stupid in charge of flagging potentially interesting pieces of data had noted it right away. The Funks might have copied all of their technology from the Association, but they'd been good students... and the Association's technology was a byword for reliability. They shouldn't be burning out mere moments after they were launched from a squadron of heavy cruisers.

He ignored the brief lurch as *Pompey* manoeuvred violently to avoid a Funk superdreadnought's determined attempt to kill her. Some of the tactical planners had questioned the wisdom of the fleet's commanding officer flying his flag on one of the ships intended for close assaults on the enemy fleet, but Admiral Sampson had set the trend for commanding officers leading their people from the front and Sun had no intention of disgracing him. Besides, if they lost this battle, Earth wouldn't last much longer than the Federation Navy...

The wry thought connected the dots for him. "Hammerfall! They learned from Hammerfall!"

Galactics only put a single one-shot drive in their missiles, mainly because long-range missiles were easy targets for point defence. Humans had used a modified missile to attack Hammerfall; the Funks, it seemed, had copied the idea remarkably quickly. Too quickly... had someone helped them, or had they simply managed to reprogram the missile drives to allow them to reactivate instead of burning out?

And those missiles were racing toward Earth.

"General alert to the defences and the gunboats," he snapped. It was already nearly too late, but they had to try. "Those missiles are the first priority. Take them out now!"

If he was wrong... but he knew with a terrible sinking certainty that he was right. Everyone *knew* that mass planetary bombardment would bring down the wrath of the Galactics on their heads, but the Funks were fighting a civil war. They no longer had much to lose.

Earth's defences were puny compared to those surrounding Hegemony Prime. The Federation Navy had concentrated on starships, leaving only a small amount of resources for fortifying Earth. A handful of purchased fortresses, a number of automated OWPs and a squadron of gunboats were barely enough firepower to slow a battlecruiser, let alone a squadron of superdreadnoughts. But they were backed up by the best sensor network in the galaxy. Targeting priorities were assigned as the defences opened fire, reacting with a speed that was quite literally inhuman. Of the two hundred missiles fired by the Funks, seventeen survived to hit Earth.

One of them came down in Greenland, another in the Sahara Desert, but the remaining fifteen maintained their systems long enough to lock in on cities. Moscow was the first to die in a colossal explosion, but it was followed rapidly by Washington, Paris, London, Bonn, Tokyo, Delhi, Tehran, Mecca, Istanbul, Beijing and five other cities. The targeting priorities confused the defending computers – nine of the targeted cities were national capitals, but the remainder seemed to have been picked at random – but it hardly mattered. Straight fusion warheads left almost no radioactivity behind them.

For the populations of the targeted cities, it was no mercy.

* * *

Admiral Sun's family lived in Beijing. The thought tore at his mind for a cold second and then he pushed it away, firmly. At least the Funks hadn't used antimatter warheads in their strikes. They would have depopulated the entire planet if they had.

The Funk fleet was slowly wearing down his own, even though three superdreadnoughts had been destroyed outright and a further four badly damaged. They'd been quick to realise the advantage they had over the ships humanity had bought from the Galactics, targeting them before Sun could realise that they were refusing to be tempted by his cruisers. Two of the would-be suicide ships had gone up in staggering explosions; a third had managed to ram a battlecruiser, vaporising both ships in a spectacular blast. Most of the modified freighters were gone, while humanity's sole battlecruiser had been targeted and blown apart by a pair of Funk superdreadnoughts. The Earth Defence Force was slowly being worn down.

Pompey twitched as she unleashed a spread of antimatter torpedoes. The enhanced torpedoes were about the only weapon the Funks couldn't counter directly and the human cruisers were firing them without worrying about ammunition stockpiles. There would be no time to return to Earth and rearm before the Funks managed to get into weapons range of Earth, although that hadn't stopped them from bombarding the planet already. A Funk superdreadnought staggered out of line as the torpedoes impacted directly on its shields, overloading and burning out the generators. One of his surviving cruisers took the opportunity to launch its own spread and vaporise the superdreadnought before it could escape, just before its two comrades bracketed the cruiser with their phase cannon. She twisted and turned, but she was unable to escape before her shields failed and the phase cannon ripped into her hull.

"*Drake* has been destroyed," Wallenberg reported. By now, they were inured to losses. He could feel it in his crew, the cold awareness that they would not leave the battlefield alive twinned with the determination to kill as many Funks as they could before their ship was destroyed. A Funk heavy cruiser tried to intercept *Pompey*, only to be savaged by the cruiser's phase cannon and left drifting out of formation. The smaller ships couldn't take anything like the punishment of the larger ones, but there was no time to complete its destruction. All that mattered was killing the superdreadnoughts.

The Funks kept firing, ignoring their losses and forcing him to stand and fight. His fleet was being torn apart, the last of the converted ships meeting a fiery end as it tried to ram a heavy cruiser. Another human-designed cruiser crashed into a superdreadnought and both ships blew apart in a sheet of fire; it was impossible to tell if one of the ships had rammed the other intentionally or if it had merely been an accident. Two cruisers left...

And his family were dead.

"Take us in to point-blank range," he ordered, savagely. No-one demurred. "Right down their fucking throats."

* * *

She was winning.

She *had* to be winning, even though it was shaping up to be the most costly victory in the Hegemony's long history. No clan would have continued a war knowing that the only outcome was certain defeat and annihilation. Any of the lesser races would have despaired of victory and lost themselves in defeatism, but the humans kept fighting. Ships that shouldn't have had any place in the line of battle were lashing out, hacking away at her forces and weakening them piece by piece. Already, her superdreadnought losses had exceeded what she'd thought were her most pessimistic estimates. At this rate, only a handful of ships would be left when she finally managed to range in on Earth itself.

And then the human race would understand the true nature of power. Her superdreadnoughts could blow the entire planet into fragments – and they would, followed rapidly by the rest of the inhabited planets in this star system. And then they would attend to the remaining human colonies. The Tarn had started to invite humans to settle in their systems – no doubt hoping to tap human inventiveness for themselves – but they'd surrender the refugees once they realised they were facing a rogue fleet that no longer cared about the consequences of its actions. There were tales from the homeworld about warriors who had fought hopeless wars, terrifying their victims and even their own clans. They hadn't cared about the survival of their own people, only about how much damage they could do before they died.

The two remaining human ships were forming up for a final attack run. They would damage her fleet, perhaps even take two more superdreadnoughts into death with them, but that was acceptable. They'd be burned out of space before they could escape again. And Earth's defences would be unable to stop missiles hurled into a planetary gravity well...

She watched, flexing her claws, as the human ships closed in. One staggered under a fusillade of phase cannon bursts, but kept going until it finally blew into a sheet of flame. The other held out for longer, closing in on a superdreadnought that had been barely scratched by the fighting until it rammed straight into its target. No ship could survive such an impact.

But the way to Earth was clear.

"Advance," she ordered. No more human tricks would stop her. "Prepare to..."

"Quantum gates," the sensor officer snapped. "Opening up right on top of us!"

Chapter Forty-Five

They had messed up the timing.

Not disastrously, Sampson realised, as *Nimitz* blew her way into open space, but quite bad enough. Opening a quantum gate at a precise predetermined location was tricky – and First Strike Fleet had taken too long to fix its location and open the gate. Reports from the stealthed platforms deployed by Earth's defenders made the picture far too clear. Admiral Sun and the Earth Defence Force had been destroyed by the enemy.

And Earth had been bombarded. Not by antimatter weapons, thankfully, but even nuclear-tipped missiles could kill untold numbers of humans. The reports scrolled up in front of him, an endless liturgy of death and destruction caused by the Funks. Was there no end to the atrocities they were prepared to commit against those less powerful than themselves? Did they have nothing reassembling common decency? Of course they didn't, he reproved himself angrily. They were aliens. Human concepts were *human* concepts, not always shared by races that had had a very different evolutionary history.

"Take us into weapons range," he said. He barely recognised his own voice. "Prepare to engage the enemy."

The Funks had been battered, with half of their superdreadnoughts and most of their smaller ships destroyed, but they were still fighting. Tobias would have expected a rational enemy to retreat once they realised that human reinforcements had arrived, yet the Funks might well believe that they had nowhere to go. The last reports from Hegemony Prime had informed him that the civil war was well underway. Who would have time for the Empress's last loyalists if she was blamed for the destruction caused by the war?

And if a force that consisted of five advanced cruisers and a hundred outdated starships could hold the line, the

Funks were going to hate what *twenty* advanced cruisers could do.

"Weapons online," the tactical officer ordered. "Entering range in twenty seconds."

"Take us right down their throats," Tobias ordered. "All ships; target the superdreadnoughts and fire at will."

Four squadrons of gunboats launched from the carriers as the Federation Navy closed in on its foes. Tobias thought he saw a new determination among his people, a determination that far exceeded the lust for revenge after the Funks had bullied Earth into surrendering Terra Nova. It was almost as if they sensed that this was the final battle, fighting to stop the Hegemony's last desperate attempt to prevent the human race from surviving the war and taking its place on the galactic stage. There had been no official announcement of the strikes on Earth, but rumours would have probably already spread through the fleet. His people wanted revenge – and more.

Back at the start, the planners had worried that the Federation Navy would be torn apart by political infighting. Tobias had shared that fear; indeed, the semi-autonomy enjoyed by the Navy had been devised in the hopes of preventing political fragmentation. But now there was something new, a naval identity that had been forged in the heat of combat. The Federation Navy was an entity now, a service that wouldn't be broken so easily. Earth's defenders had more than proved themselves against Earth's most dangerous foe.

Nimitz opened fire, her weapons slashing out and tearing into an enemy hull. The Funks didn't seem to be able to reinforce their shield harmonics, at least not any longer. Admiral Sun had damaged almost all of their ships, according to the downloads; the tactical computers were already noting weaknesses that would normally be spotted only during the post-battle analysis phase. It was quite possible that most of the superdreadnoughts had lost some of their shield generators while facing Admiral Sun, or that their jury-rigged modifications had simply failed in the heat of battle. No-one had even thought of the need to produce two separate shields until the human race had invented weapons that could shoot through a single shield.

And when they duplicate our weapons, they'll discover that they won't shoot through our shields, he thought, wryly. Even if the Funks couldn't perform R&D themselves, one of the other Galactics would probably manage to duplicate the weapons once they knew they existed. But humanity would have an edge. Some of the weapons proposed by the Next Generation Weapons project were truly frightening. One of them held the promise of being able to dissemble a superdreadnought with a single shot, if it ever proved practical.

The starship shuddered as she unleashed a spread of antimatter torpedoes. Their target fired back, phase cannon sweeping through space as she tried to target the cruiser, the enemy crew no doubt cursing their failing sensor network. Admiral Sun had shown them that human ships could break their weapons locks, but even though there was a simple countermeasure the Funks had yet to deploy it. They'd probably needed time to reflect before working it out and Tobias hadn't given them any more time than necessary.

"Five direct hits," one of the weapons officers announced. Intercepting an antimatter torpedo before it struck home was difficult, but the Funks had managed to take out two of them. Their crews had suddenly become very motivated. "Target shields down; firing again..."

An antimatter torpedo flashed into a gaping wound on the superdreadnought's hull and detonated inside the vessel. For a long moment, Tobias could see the ship's superstructure glowing brightly as the force of the explosion tore through the weaker internal structure, just before it all came apart in a blinding flash. The metal the Cats had invented to build their starships was *strong*. No wonder everyone worried about a ship ramming a planet. It would survive the trip through the atmosphere and hit the ground with a force of an asteroid strike.

"Target destroyed," the same tactical officer reported. "Gunboats covering us against enemy escort ships."

Tobias pulled his attention away from *Nimitz* – her Captain would handle her part of the fighting – and looked at the overall picture. The Federation Navy was tearing its opponents apart, its crews fuelled by rage and hatred over what had happened to Earth. One of the Funk destroyers managed to ram a cruiser, taking out both ships, just before three more were picked off by antimatter torpedoes. He tapped his console and issued orders for the cruisers to keep their distance from the smaller enemy ships. There was no point in allowing the Funks a chance to ram more ships if it could be avoided.

Another Funk superdreadnought died, leaving six – all badly damaged. The enemy seemed to have halted completely, laagering up into a formation that might have provided some protection against another fleet of superdreadnoughts. They spat fire toward their human tormentors, covering each other from human fire, but they were being slowly worn down. And each lost superdreadnought weakened the entire fleet's defences...

"Continue firing," he ordered. It crossed his mind that he should offer the Funks a chance to surrender, but in truth he didn't want to give them a chance, not after what they had done to Earth. They might claim that humanity had started the war – and they had – yet the Federation Navy had never bombarded innocent civilians. "Designate targets for battlegroups and engage."

Nimitz wheeled in space – a manoeuvre that no other comparable starship design would have found possible – and lunged towards the enemy fleet. The Funks turned slowly to meet the human ships, another tactic that would have worked against superdreadnoughts, but worse than useless against the fast cruisers. *Nimitz* could get into firing position easily before they could even complete their turn.

Tobias smiled coldly as *Nimitz* opened fire. One way or another, it would all be over soon.

* * *

Lady Dalsha stared at the display, unable to believe how rapidly she'd gone from victory to defeat. And she had been defeated. There was no hope of even managing to destroy Earth before her fleet was overwhelmed and destroyed. The first human fleet had inflicted enough damage to ensure that the second could destroy her, damage she'd accepted because she'd believed that once she'd crushed the first fleet, Earth would be easy to destroy. How had the humans done it? Coordinating an attack across interstellar space was incredibly difficult, even with tachyon-burst communicators. Had they invented some advanced form of FTL transmitter, or had the Clarke raid – intended as a diversion – brought back their strike fleet from Hegemony territory?

Or had it all been chance?

Humans worshipped an entity they saw as a big man in the sky. The Hegemony had no such concept. Their early evolutionary history had left them focused on bare survival, rather than the fripperies that were embraced by races that had evolved on kinder planets; they *knew* that the universe didn't care about them on any level. And yet it was easy to believe that someone had orchestrated events from the shadows, planning the Hegemony's defeat for years before starting the first conflict. The Cats, perhaps. They were old, with a lifespan that allowed them to plan for centuries beyond any other race – and perhaps they weren't truly blind to the threat the Hegemony represented. And a rogue Cat had given the humans the keys to the stars. Had Mentor really been a rogue?

The superdreadnought rocked again as a spread of antimatter torpedoes impacted on her rear shields. Lady Dalsha cursed the humans and their inventiveness as alarms buzzed and damage control teams raced to the overloading shield generators. Even superdreadnoughts couldn't stand up to antimatter warheads detonating against unshielded hulls. If the shields went, her fleet – all that remained of her fleet – was doomed. And they were doomed if they stayed in the Sol System. They couldn't even inflict enough losses on their enemies to make up for losing the superdreadnoughts.

"Target missiles on Earth," she ordered. This time, the missiles *would* go ballistic and be easy to destroy, but it would win them some time. The humans wouldn't allow the missiles to hit their homeworld, not if there was anything they could do to prevent it. "And then bring up the quantum drive."

She wanted to close her eyes, to blot out the display. Her failure was unmatched, even in the days before the Hegemony had been created. An entire fleet lost in battle, without significantly weakening the enemy. The Empress was almost certainly dead by now – and if she wasn't, she would be when news of this battle reached Hegemony Prime. There was never any shortage of ambitious females who wanted to make themselves Empress.

And all she could do was run.

* * *

"Admiral," Sooraya said, "the Funks are targeting Earth."

Tobias swore as new red icons glinted to life on the display, boosting toward Earth. Some of them would have antimatter warheads – and just one hit would be enough to kill eight *billion* humans. Those lucky enough to be on the far side of the planet might just survive a few months before they ran out of food and water. The Funks had presented him with a choice, which was really no choice at all; kill the superdreadnoughts and watch Earth die, or save Earth and give the superdreadnoughts a few moments to recover.

"Intercept course," he ordered. There really was no choice. "I want all of those missiles taken out before they reach Earth."

The gunboats, the only craft capable of matching speed with the missiles, raced after them, firing as soon as they had targeting solutions. *Nimitz* and the rest of the fleet followed, trying to pick off missiles that had lost their drives and gone onto ballistic trajectories. Earth's defences, thankfully, hadn't come under direct fire from the Funks and could intercept some of the missiles for themselves. But *Nimitz* couldn't take chances. They had to intercept every missile before they lost track of them completely. An antimatter warhead floating around near Earth was System Command's greatest nightmare.

Now I know how the Funks felt when we mined Hammerfall, he thought. But those mines would never have survived a brush with the planet's atmosphere. *Poor bastards.*

"Admiral," one of the sensor officers said, "I am picking up quantum gate energies emanating from the Funk superdreadnoughts."

"They're running," Sooraya said. She looked over at Tobias. "We could use the IDG system. This *is* what we invented it to do."

Tobias hesitated. The IDG projector had been designed as a last-ditch weapon – except it wasn't actually a weapon. And yet it had its limitations. One of them was that it would force the Funks to stand and fight, alarmingly close to Earth. Underlining his concerns, the Funks chose that moment to belch another salvo of missiles towards the planet. At least this time the fleet was in position to intercept them without having to race to position themselves between the planet and the oncoming storm.

But six superdreadnoughts could cause far too much havoc throughout the galaxy if the Hegemony came apart completely...

"Activate it," he said. The projector wouldn't be too difficult for the Galactics to figure out, once they realised what it did. They'd known the basic principle for upwards of thirty thousand years. Indeed, no one had been quite sure why the Cats hadn't built one for themselves. Maybe they'd felt that it was better left in the realm of theory than risk someone who disliked them building one. "But keep targeting the missiles first."

The display updated as the quantum gate started to open, ready to take the Funks into quantum space and away from Earth. It didn't look as if the projector was working...

...And then everything went to hell.

* * *

The superdreadnought rocked violently as gravity waves struck her hull.

"My Lady," the helmsman screamed, "the quantum gate is collapsing!"

Lady Dalsha stared. A quantum gate was normally a spinning disc of light in front of a starship, a hypnotic spiral that led directly into quantum space. But this one was different, a wildly-oscillating funnel that seemed to be forcing its way through the dimensions. Merely looking at the image from her ship's sensors made her eyes hurt. The ship rocked again as the gravity field grew stronger, pulling them towards the gate. Normally, there was a smooth transit into quantum space, aided by precisely-modulated gravity waves that protected the ship as it made transit. This time...

"Pull back," she ordered, feeling gibbering panic threatening to undermine her rationality. Her crew was losing control; some screaming on the deck while others lunged at their fellow crewmen, claws extended as if they were preparing to fight for the right to mate. The scent of fear grew stronger in the air, pushing others over the edge into insanity. "Pull back!"

The humans, she realised. They'd locked her out of quantum space! Or maybe... she'd seen images of what happened to starships that tried to make transit through a collapsing quantum gate, none of them pleasant. She could feel the colossal stress being exerted against the superdreadnought's hull, almost *hear* a scream as impossible forces rent and tore at the metal holding her ship together, sense the buckling as the hull finally began to give way...

She felt dizzy, suddenly, as the internal compensator field started to fail. Gravity snatched at her a second later, throwing her and her crew across the bridge and slamming them against a bulkhead. She felt bones breaking as she hit the bulkhead, just before the force grew stronger and stronger. It felt as if a giant foot was pressing down on her, threatening to crush her skull...

...And then there was fire, and then darkness.

* * *

The researchers hadn't been entirely sure of what would happen when the IDG projector was activated. They'd known since First Contact that energy discharges in

411

quantum space excited the high-energy dimension, creating energy storms that could rip a starship apart in seconds, but deliberately creating an energy storm had seemed only a theoretical possibility. One remote danger, they'd warned, was that the energy would slash back into normal space, devastating an entire solar system. Tobias watched, white-faced, as three superdreadnoughts were torn apart when they tried to enter quantum space. The remainder managed to escape before the quantum gate finally gave up the struggle and collapsed.

In death ground, Tobias thought. Admiral Sun had coined the term, pointing out that Sun Tzu had warned that preventing the enemy from retreating forced him to fight savagely – or surrender. Unable to retreat, unable to complete their mission and destroy Earth... what would the Funks do? And what would happen in the future if the Galactics realised what the human race had invented? Interstellar commerce would be badly impeded if terrorists devised their own versions of the projector and used them to blanket vital systems with energy storms.

"Transmit a signal to the Funks," he ordered. Watching the superdreadnoughts die had changed him, somehow. There were natural forces in the universe far greater than the human race. No starship could have survived a transit into an energy storm. "Tell them... tell them that we will accept their surrender."

"Yes, sir," the communications officer said. With Earth safe, the Federation Navy could capture its opponents and then deploy to assist the planet with its relief and recovery efforts. The reports made it clear that there was already a high death rate from the missile strikes, to say nothing of governments being crippled by losing their capital cities. "Sir...I'm not getting any response. I'm not getting anything, not even internal starship transmissions. They're badly damaged enough that there should be some leakage."

Tobias frowned. Could they all be dead?

He keyed his console. "Colonel Jefferson, I want a team of Marines to inspect the Funk superdreadnoughts," he ordered. If the internal compensators had failed, the entire crew would have be dead before they knew what had hit them. "Volunteers only. This could go badly wrong."

It was nearly thirty minutes before he had his answer. "Admiral, the Funks appear to have gone mad," Jefferson said. He'd led one of the Marine teams in person. "They're fighting each other."

"Deploy capture gas," Tobias ordered. At least they had a working knock-out gas for the Funks now. "Thank you, Colonel."

He keyed his console. "Transmit a message to Earth," he ordered. "The battle is over – and the human race has won."

For now, he added, in the privacy of his own thoughts. Who knew what would happen at the peace table?

Chapter Forty-Six

"While we cannot condone the occupation of Garston," an Ambassador was saying, "we see no good reason why the human claim to the system called Terra Nova cannot be upheld."

Ambassador Li Shan smiled. Four weeks had passed since the Battle of Earth, four weeks of careful diplomacy and long-winded speeches from various members of the Association Commune. Not that there had been much doubt about the outcome, although that hadn't stopped all sorts of people from having their say – even if they didn't have much to do with the Earth-Hegemony War. The Hegemony's civil war was still underway, with queens on a dozen worlds declaring independence and setting up their own clans. It was possible that a new Empress would arise out of the ashes on Hegemony Prime and reunite the Hegemony, but it would take years, years that the human race could use to prepare for round two.

There was little hope of forcing the Funks to pay an indemnity, or to acknowledge that they were responsible for the war. Great Lady Vanla was still their Ambassador – if only because it would have taken over a year for a replacement to be nominated and reach Center – and she had been firm on that point. Negotiations had been tricky – the ruling power on Hegemony Prime seemed to change daily – but none of them seemed prepared to concede more than they absolutely had to, at least to the human race. The Tarn had declared their support of the Gobbles and moved a squadron of superdreadnoughts into the rebel system. It was quite possible that the other powers surrounding the Hegemony would take advantage of its weakness and crush it before it could grow strong again.

At least the Commune had ratified Earth's possession of Terra Nova – and of the other Nine Stars, including Earth itself. The next aggressor would have to attack without the veneer of legality sought by the Funks, launching an aggressive strike against human technology that grew more advanced by the day. Shan had heard all kinds of rumours, rumours that seemed to grow more astonishing by the day. If humanity had possessed some of the weapons they'd been credited with, the war would have lasted no less than a day and the Hegemony would have been completely destroyed. She hadn't been trying to debunk the rumours. It would probably help with the peace terms if the Galactics thought that Earth was too strong to push around.

But then, she reflected, over thirty superdreadnoughts had been captured or destroyed. That in itself was a pretty impressive display of power.

It might have other long-term consequences. The Funks had had minimal research and development capability, but that wasn't true for the other Galactics. Shan had heard that R&D programs across the Association had been kick-started into high gear, starting a project to duplicate and exceed the new human weapons. It wouldn't take them too long to duplicate most of them, Shan had been warned. Most of the weapons were simply radically new takes on existing Galactic-provided technologies.

She smiled as another Ambassador started to speak. The only sticking point was Garston, but she suspected that humanity would manage to hang on to the multiracial world. Quite apart from humanity having weapons no one could match – yet – Garston simply didn't have a working government. There was no one who could speak for their world. Humanity would have to rule a Funk population as well as the other alien races on the surface. From what she'd heard, the largely Russian and Chinese occupation forces had started the task of separating the Funks from the rest of the population. Maybe in a hundred years they'd be able to meet again without starting a war. For the moment, it would keep the peace.

And besides, Earth *needed* Garston. Humanity's reserves of Galactic currency had been drained by the war. The revenues from the shipping lanes would help refill Earth's coffers and give humanity a chance to expand without having to build everything on Earth. It was lucky that no one cared enough to turn it into a major issue. She'd already assured a hundred Ambassadors that there would be no rise in shipping fees by the human administration. That should keep them from making too great a fuss.

Or so she hoped. Humanity had shocked the Galactics. Who knew what would happen in the future?

* * *

Rain was falling as an honour guard of Federation Marines carried an empty coffin from the church to the graveyard in Southampton. Adrienne watched as they reached the appointed space and lowered the coffin into the grave, shaking her head sadly as the dead Marine's friends and relatives threw dirt onto the coffin. A girl who looked far too young to be a widow was crying, one hand on her growing chest. The child would never know his father.

Politician after politician rose to speak about the dead man, talking about how he had been a true son of England and how he had died bravely so that others might live. Adrienne suspected that the Marine would have preferred a more low-key funeral, but elections were coming up and politicians wouldn't want to appear uncaring about the dead. The waves of jingoism sweeping Earth in the wake of the war would destroy any politician who tried to stand in their way. Adrienne had heard that the Federation's member nations had already approved a vastly increased budget for the Federation Navy, while a new wave of settlers were already on their way to Terra Nova. The planet has forged an odd society in the years they had spent under Funk occupation, leaving Adrienne to wonder just how welcome the newcomers would be. Terra Nova had already elected a new planetary governor, despite the Federation Council. Adrienne saw trouble brewing in the future.

A number of people recognised her, pointing when they thought she couldn't see them. Her stories from the war had won her fame, if not fortune, although she had been offered everything from her own newspaper column to a live talk show. The former would be fun; the latter tedious beyond belief. *She* certainly didn't want to simper and show off her boobs on live TV, or play the bitch to guests who hadn't quite realised that they'd only been invited so they could be publicly humiliated. But there were other possibilities too. The first memoirs about the war were already being published and she'd been offered a book deal. It would sell very well, according to her agent.

The congregation sang one final hymn and then dispersed, the widow and her father heading off before the media could intercept them. Adrienne had been told that they'd cut a deal with the politicians, one that allowed them to leave under escort in exchange for the political figures having a chance to pontificate. It didn't seem fair to Adrienne – she definitely intended to write an article slamming the political assholes who had turned a funeral into a circus – but the media wasn't known for playing fair. The less-principled reporters, denied access to the war front, had been running background interviews on the war's heroes. Some of the questions they asked people were absurd. Others were just plain insulting.

Shaking her head, she set off to follow the politicians. Who knew? Maybe one of them would slip up and say something important.

* * *

"So it seems that I will be keeping *Formidable* for a while," Markus said. "Will you stay on as my Squadron Leader?"

Carola pretended to consider it. "I suppose so," she said finally, and laughed at his expression. "If we can face death together, we can probably conspire to violate the regulations to some degree..."

Markus shrugged. They'd married long before he'd been promoted. If the CNO didn't like the idea of them having a relationship he should never have ordered Markus into the center seat on a starship. Not that he intended to stay there for long. Perhaps he could point out that he *was* ignoring the regulations and get demoted back to gunboat pilot.

Formidable would be going back to Garston as soon as the replacement gunboats were loaded onboard. That was good news, as far as Markus was concerned; the media was hounding each and every crewman from the carrier – and the surviving Marines. One of the Marines was currently in the brig for knocking out a particularly unpleasant reporter, although Markus intended to let him off with a stern warning as soon as they were away from Earth. The reporter had deserved it.

"Never mind," he said. "Are you going to help me with the supply tables...?"

"I was thinking there was something else we could do," Carola said, as she began to unbutton her shirt. "Why don't we be the first to screw on a Captain's table?"

* * *

"I'm surprised you came," Joshua said. "Don't you have a bodyguard detail or something?"

Admiral Sampson shrugged as he sat down. The bar was a multiracial environment in the middle of Garston's largest and most cosmopolitan city. Two humans might stick out on Garston, but it was unlikely that they would actually be recognised. Or so Joshua hoped. The Federation Council hadn't done anything to attempt to arrest him, despite disowning him, yet they weren't the only ones who had put a price on his head.

"I left them behind," Sampson said. Joshua had heard that he was making a brief visit to examine the security arrangements and review the local troops recruited by General Chekov. "The fewer witnesses the better, don't you think?"

Joshua nodded. "I think we can agree that I did better than you expected," he said. "And Earth now has a whole race of allies."

"So you did," Sampson agreed. He hesitated, as if what he had to say was unpleasant. "You do realise that you can't come home again?"

"The thought had crossed my mind," Joshua said, sardonically. "Wouldn't it be embarrassing for the Federation Council if they arrested me, me being a hero and all?"

"Very embarrassing," Sampson said. Joshua's exploits had made him a hero on Earth, at least to the ordinary citizens. He'd poked the Hegemony right in its red eyes and liberated an entire planet of cuddly teddy bears. The media had built him up into a hero, despite governmental opposition. "It would be a great deal easier if you just stayed with the Gobbles and rebuilt your shipping empire with them."

Joshua smiled. "I'm afraid that won't be possible," he said. "The Gobbles intend to apply for Federation membership."

Sampson's eyes widened. "I beg your pardon?"

"The Gobbles wish to join the Federation," Joshua said. "They are prepared to contribute both cash and labour to the Federation Navy in exchange for membership."

"Interesting," Sampson said. "Do the rules actually allow alien races to join the Federation?"

"I consulted a noted constitutional lawyer," Joshua said. Normally, he would have preferred not to talk to a lawyer unless absolutely necessary, but this had been a special case. "The Federation Charter specifically states that any nation can join provided that it meets its membership obligations, specifically the contribution of at least 20% of its GNP to the Federation's budget. It doesn't exclude anyone, even alien races. In fact, there are *no* grounds for refusing Federation membership if the obligations are met."

"The politicians will scream blue murder," Sampson muttered. The Federation Charter had been a compromise, necessary to prevent outright warfare between member nations and non-member nations. No one had considered the possibility that aliens would want to join. "I think they might find a way to reject the application on a technicality."

Joshua shrugged. "Let's see," he said. "The Gobbles have literally millions of trained workers qualified to serve in microgravity environments. They have a much greater understanding of Galactic technology than the Funks ever managed – and they have a small, but growing industrial base. Right now, even without the Tarn, the Funks would need at least two squadrons of superdreadnoughts to reclaim Tauscher for the Hegemony. Give them a year and their world will become impregnable.

"Do you really think that we can *afford* to turn down their request for membership?"

"I'd say as much to the Federation Council," Sampson said, thoughtfully. "But the Council might not buy that argument."

"And what do they intend to do here?" Joshua asked. He waved a hand around, encompassing the multiracial bar. "Right now, all the communities on this planet are glad that they don't have to prostrate themselves in front of the Funks, doing whatever they are told or getting their heads kicked in. But that won't last. How long do you think it will be before Garston's population start demanding a greater say in how their world is run? Do you think that the Federation Council will try to keep the revenue distribution to itself?"

"Some politicians would like to try," Sampson said, flatly.

"It won't work," Joshua said, equally flatly. "You have to make them understand that they either have to embrace change or get steamrollered when the pressure cooker finally explodes."

"I will try to convince them otherwise," Sampson said. "And I will certainly press for accepting the Gobbles as members of the Federation."

"They have already appointed an Ambassador to Earth," Joshua said. "Guess who?"

Sampson covered his eyes. "Don't tell me..."

"Me," Joshua said. "Me, with diplomatic immunity. Don't you think that that would put the cat among the politicians?
"

* * *

The flight back to Earth was uneventful, giving Tobias a chance to catch up on the paperwork he'd been neglecting while he'd been off fighting the war. He - and Admiral Sun - had cut as much paperwork as possible out of the system, but nothing seemed to stop the relentless march of bureaucracy. There were promotions to approve, a court-martial judgment to consider, budget requests to put before the Federation Council... no shortage of things that claimed to be urgent. And there was the inquiry on why First Strike Fleet had been unable to save the Earth Defence Fleet from destruction.

And *then* there was the endless political struggle over the destroyed cities.

The Federation Council had been buffeted by the war. Earth had been delighted with the defeat of the Hegemony – and the worst case projections suggested that the Hegemony wouldn't become a threat again for at least five years – but people were asking questions of their leaders, questions that had no easy answers. Why had it taken so long to save so few people from the ruins? Why had governments failed to supply help quickly enough to save so many lives? Why had the Hegemony even succeeded in hitting Earth in the first place?

Sampson knew the answer, even though it was one that the population would hate. Any large scale disaster was difficult to handle; it took time to get organised and get emergency supplies to the disaster zone. The plans drawn up before the Battle of Earth had warned of the dangers, but there had been nothing they could do to prevent those plans falling apart as soon as missiles hit the cities. The only blessing was that it could have been far worse. They could have used antimatter warheads to destroy the entire planet.

But it wasn't the Federation Navy that was taking the fire. Tobias knew that he should be relieved, yet it worried him. The Federation Navy had matured in the war, becoming a truly global force – and it enjoyed a surprising amount of autonomy from the Federation Council, allowing it to act almost independently. Who knew *what* it might become in the future?

He shook his head. Maybe he shouldn't worry. Humanity had upset too many Galactic preconceptions about the universe to risk disunity now. Most of the galaxy wasn't just inhabited, it was *taken*. The only way for the younger powers to expand would be at the expense of their neighbours. And while Earth had a lead in technology, there was no reason why the Galactics couldn't catch up quickly. It was possible that some of them had already enjoyed more advanced technology, even if they had kept it to themselves. What would happen when the Association finally collapsed?

The future didn't bode well at all.

He grinned. But at least the human race would be taken seriously in future. Perhaps the deaths had been worth it, if the human race would survive. Only time would tell.

Epilogue

His age pressed down on him like a leaden weight.

Mentor stood in his quarters and studied the report from his agent. It was hard, so hard, to remember why he cared, but he held himself together somehow. He was over five thousand years old, older than human civilization, older than anyone from any of the younger races. And he was heir to a society that traced its recorded history back over two *million* years.

He felt as if he seen everything, done everything. The mental weariness seeping into his thoughts made it hard to think, memories of worlds and peoples long gone blurring into the present day. There were machines to store his memories, to save him the task of remembering everything, but none of them were perfect. A mind that had once been smarter than any human was decaying under the sheer weight of life experience. How long would it be, Mentor wondered, before his mind finally collapsed? Even he didn't know how many of his kind had fallen to the disease affecting his society, tearing them apart from the inside.

The disease was called immortality.

It had been a mistake. He knew that now. There were limits to flesh and blood that even genetic engineering and nanotech tinkering couldn't overcome. The birth rate had slowed, and finally stopped...and then the immortals had begun to die. They'd simply given up and allowed their minds to decay into nothing, or committed suicide, or died in stupid accidents that reflected an unconscious death wish. The entire race had stagnated so long ago that none of them could even remember the joy of discovering something new. And now...

From a population that had once numbered in the trillions, only a handful were left.

The Association his people had created didn't know what was happening to its founders, but Mentor knew that some of them were beginning to suspect that the Association was a hollow shell. How long would it be until the Commune crumbled and the Galactics realised the truth? Not long, he was sure. And then?

His people had made mistakes. Some out of pride, some out of honest intentions – and some out of a desire to keep their position as the supreme power in the galaxy. Those mistakes had shaped the Association, warping it into something its founders no longer recognised. What would happen when the last of his people were gone? Would the Association splinter into war, or would the new leaders establish their own stranglehold over the galaxy?

Mentor didn't know, but he feared for the future. It was why he had gone to Earth. Maybe, just maybe, the human race could kickstart a process that would reinvigorate the Association. Or maybe they'd just start a series of wars that would depopulate most of the galaxy. Even Mentor, with access to a science of psychohistory that was far beyond anything Earth had even imagined, couldn't say for sure. There were just too many variables.

And he didn't know if he would live long enough to see the outcome of his final gamble. He didn't know if his people's pride and arrogance – their legacy to the younger races - had doomed the galaxy. He could just be trying to stop a supernova with nothing more than his furry hands...

But he had to try.

It was all he had left.

The End

Appendix: The Hegemony

The key to understanding the Mer'fuk Hegemony is to bear in mind that the Hegemony represents an attempt to graft primitive traits from a pre-steam world onto a modern technology-using culture. Much of the Hegemony is actually governed by rules and customs that no longer really need apply, although the Funks – as humans came to call them – are reluctant to alter them without a pressing need. The ones in charge feel that it works for them, as it supports their dominance; the ones at the bottom of the heap are unable to make their feelings heard.

Hegemony Prime – the exact name for their homeworld cannot be translated into any of the Galactic languages, although humans have often referred to it as Squeak Hiss Squeak – is a hot dry world, situated roughly seven light minutes from the system primary. (Earth, by contrast, is eight light minutes from Sol.) Most of the planet's water reserves are underground, forcing plants and animals to dig deep to receive their sustenance; natural oasis-like locations are among the most desirable real estate on the planet. Unlike Earth, which has water covering three-fourths of its surface, Hegemony Prime has only two oceans, each roughly the size of Australia.

The Funks evolved, therefore, from creatures that reassembled a cross between crocodiles and lizards. Their early evolutionary history was dominated by a constant search for water and food, a process hampered by the fact that large-scale farming and herding was almost impossible on their world. Very few permanent settlements were ever founded and the vast majority of the Funk population lived and died as nomadic tribesmen. Fighting between different clans was epidemic, but limited. A fight to the death might result in mutual destruction.

Also steering their development was the imbalanced birth rate between the sexes. Male births outnumbered female births by roughly four to one, resulting in a situation that could have easily led to female enslavement. Unlike humanity, however, Funk females were quick to see the benefits of cooperation – and Funks males had considerable difficulties seeing past the very short term. Their earliest forms of government were effectively directed by the females, a trait enhanced by the simple fact that males were more expendable than females. Females did the planning; males did the fighting.

The females do not have a mating season. Like humans, they are capable of mating at almost any time and females have little difficulty finding a willing mate. When impregnated, a Funk female gestates the eggs in her womb and then lays them after six months, where they are cared for by the clan females until they hatch. Each female may lay up to five eggs at any one time, although the more eggs laid in each brood the greater the chance of losing one or more of the children. (Modern medical technology gave the Funks a population boost when it was first introduced, as they would typically breed more children than they needed on the grounds that not all of them would survive birth.) Once hatched, males and females are separated until maturity, allowing them to be raised properly by the clan elders. The Funks do not have even a *concept* of bastardry.

Physically, a mature Funk stands little taller than the average human, with green-brown scales and bright red eyes. Their eyesight is generally better than unenhanced humans, allowing them to see into the infrared; their hearing somewhat weaker. Both male and females have claws which emerge from their hands if necessary, a legacy of their harsh evolution. They can move with astonishing speed for short periods of time, if forced to fight directly, but rapidly run out of energy. Although they are physically weaker than the average human, a maddened Funk male is extremely difficult to handle in hand-to-hand combat. Provoking a Funk male into a murderous range, if done at a safe distance, is a workable tactic as the madness rapidly wears off, leaving the Funk exhausted and vulnerable. Funk females rarely lose their self-control.

Funk warfare, as evolved on their homeworld, is an endless quest for resources and dominance, rather than extermination. They have no tradition of total war. Instead, there is a long period of jostling and bullying, followed by a demonstration of supremacy that should convince the weaker side to submit. The leaders of the losing side are generally adopted into the winning side, along with their people, who start out as slaves, but biologically integrate very quickly into the winners. One tradition involves sending back captured enemy leaders to attempt to convince their fellows to surrender – and as a gesture of contempt. This does not always work out as well as it should, at least according to their rules. There is, for example, no prohibition on the captured and returned leaders returning to the war.

The clans – the largest social entity prior to their introduction to the galaxy – appear confusing to human eyes, a mixture of democracy and dictatorship. Clan leaders are females who have convinced a number of other females to work with them to secure their control, outvoting females who disagree with their policies. Sometimes these social strains become too much and clans fission into two or more smaller ones. This process partly accounts for the failure to develop a permanent civilization or super-clan prior to encountering the Galactics. The larger a clan, the greater the room for dissent and eventual fission.

Funk criminals are rare, at least partly due to their communal lives. Males are known for short-term 'crimes' that are laughed off by the females, considering them a mark of 'boys will be boys.' If more serious, males are gelded and declawed, before being thrown out into the desert to starve. Female crimes are regarded more seriously, with punishments that range from enslavement to gang-rape and death, as females are held to be more responsible.

Sexism is prevalent in Funk societies, although following Matriarchal traits rather than Patriarchal. Funk females regard males, essentially, as children, creatures who need firm and considerate guidance – and who are incapable of even considering their own good. (This is not incomparable to similar male-female trends on Earth, although reversed.) Outside the traditional roles of worker and warrior, males

427

rarely attain any position of authority and the idea of positive discrimination would be a joke. There is a certain amount of truth in the female claims, although it is not clear how much of the male condition is biological and how much is cultural.

The Funks never developed the concept of religion, at least in the sense of human polytheist or monotheist traditions. They do have a tradition of venerating water as the literal source of life on their world, although they don't pray to water as humans pray to God. It should be noted that this semi-atheism allowed them to take the concept of the Galactics in their stride when their world was first contacted, far better than humanity managed.

Originally, the Galactics regarded the Funks as a source of mercenaries for brushfire wars. The Funks were quite happen to deal, with a particular clan leader providing trained males – and females to supervise them – in exchange for Galactic technology. Using her gains, she was rapidly able to conquer and unite Hegemony Prime, in defiance of all previous traditions of warfare. Declaring herself the Empress of the Hegemony and her clan the High Clan, she reshaped the entire planet's society, but failed to challenge the social underpinnings of Funk culture. The old fault lines between clans were still there, only buried.

The Funks proved themselves quite determined to copy Galactic technology and build an interstellar power base. A handful of worlds near Hegemony Prime were rapidly settled and developed, while starships were purchased and shipyards constructed in orbit around the planet. What they didn't do – and didn't realise, at least at first – was understand the basis of Galactic technology. It was impossible for them to improve upon what they copied from the Galactics, or even to realise that they *needed* to innovate for themselves. The Funks managed to be quite imaginative when it came to *applying* the technology, but never really understood what it actually did. The research and development infrastructure was almost non-existent.

They also viewed interstellar power politics through blinkered red eyes that were used to seeing stronger clans fall apart, leaving a power vacuum that could be filled by someone else. The Cats might be masters of the galaxy, but that wouldn't last – and the Association's failure to do more than weakly protest the Funk expansion into their sector was viewed as a sign of weakness. They became skilful at exploiting weaknesses within the Association Commune while never realising that other races simply didn't think like them. Perversely, the Funks paid a backwards tribute to the Galactics by believing that they were just like the Funks themselves. Racism, at least in the sense of believing that someone was permanently inferior, was never part of their culture. Ironically, this led to the Funks underestimating their enemies, particularly the human race.

Few of their social traits were really helpful in the modern galaxy. Most dangerous, perhaps, was their habit of keeping slaves. Funk slavery had had a safety valve in that Funk slaves were able to climb to freedom (and children born to slaves were not slaves themselves), but biological integration between aliens was obviously impossible. Both of their 'client' races (a race that has roughly 90% of its numbers under the control of a more powerful race) were trapped into permanent servitude. Revolts were not uncommon, as were savage reprisals.

By 2030, as humans reckon time, the Hegemony had swallowed up nearly three hundred star systems and two client races. However, three major powers now bordered their space – and were arming frantically on the assumption that one of them would be targeted by the Funks next. Further expansion would be much more difficult...and if the pace of conquest slowed, the social strains in the Hegemony might rip it apart. With that in mind, the Funks decided to target the human race. What could such a puny race do to threaten them?

For more great books, visit
www.henchmanpress.com!

Made in the USA
Lexington, KY
12 March 2015